Hitler
Victorious

GARLAND REFERENCE LIBRARY
OF THE HUMANITIES
(Vol. 624)

Hitler
Victorious

*Eleven Stories of
the German Victory
in World War II*

Edited by GREGORY BENFORD
and MARTIN H. GREENBERG
with an introduction by NORMAN SPINRAD

GARLAND PUBLISHING, INC.
NEW YORK & LONDON

ACKNOWLEDGMENTS

"Introduction: Hitler Victorious" by Norman Spinrad: copyright © 1986 by Norman Spinrad. Used with permission.

"Two Dooms" by C.M. Kornbluth: copyright © 1958 by Mercury Press, Inc. Reprinted by permission of Richard Curtis Associates, Inc.

"The Fall of Frenchy Steiner" by Hilary Bailey: copyright © 1964 by Hilary Bailey. Reprinted by permission of Wallace & Sheil Agency, Inc.

"Through Road No Whither" by Greg Bear: copyright © 1985 by Greg Bear. Reprinted by permission of the author.

"Weihnachtsabend" by Keith Roberts: copyright © 1972 by Keith Roberts. Reprinted by permission of the author and the Carnell Literary Agency.

"Thor Meets Captain America" by David Brin: copyright © 1986 by David Brin. Used with permission.

"Moon of Ice" by Brad Linaweaver: copyright © 1982, 1986 by Brad Linaweaver. Reprinted by permission of the author.

"Reichs-Peace" by Sheila Finch: copyright © 1986 by Sheila Finch. An original story used with permission.

"Never Meet Again" by Algis Budrys: copyright © 1957 by Royal Publications, Inc. Reprinted by permission of the author, with thanks to Larry Shaw.

"Do Ye Hear the Children Weeping?" by Howard Goldsmith: copyright © 1986 by Howard Goldsmith. An original story used with permission.

"Enemy Transmissions" by Tom Shippey: copyright © 1986 by Thomas Shippey. An original story used with permission.

"Valhalla" by Gregory Benford: copyright © 1986 by Gregory Benford. Used with permission.

ISBN 0-8240-8658-9

Manufactured in the United States of America

Contents

To all who suffered
under the Third Reich

Preface:
Imagining the Abyss

Gregory Benford

W hat does it mean to think of our world as arising from a vast series of past possibilities? That is, to entertain the notion that our situation is in principle precarious—sensitive to seemingly arbitrary happenings, though now stamped by history with a seeming inevitability?

This view has intrigued writers of our century, many outside the realm of science fiction. J.C. Squire published a collection titled *If; or History Rewritten* in 1931, containing essays by such notables as Winston Churchill, G.K. Chesterton, André Maurois, and Hilaire Belloc. They examined what would have happened if, for example, certain assassinations had failed or if (a common theme in later work) the South had won the Civil War. Successful "mainstream" novels have been based on "alternative-world" possibilities—for example, Kingsley Amis's *The Alteration*, which depicts a world where the Reformation failed.

Imagining paths not taken is a method of thinking about the impact of history on the present and of people on history. Inherent in the countless possible schemes is the battle between two views of history. There are those who see grand events as inevitable, with chance happenings on the human scale finally washed away if they are against the tide of time. Others prefer a more jittery view, in which a stray bumping of an assassin's hand can save a nation. Stories and articles thus become *Gedanken* experiments to illuminate one side or the other.

The first use of alternative worlds appeared as science fiction, in Guy

Dent's novel *Emperor of the If* (1926). This was a sense-of-wonder narrative, deriving its power from the dazzle of the alternative-worlds idea itself. Later sf writers achieved far more by dealing with one concrete possibility and relying on the methods of the realistic novel. Among the major works of the genre is Keith Roberts's *Pavane* (1968), in which the first Queen Elizabeth was assassinated. Events then tumbled domino fashion: the Armada won, the Reformation failed, and England in our day is a technological backwater, prostrate under a militant Catholic church. Ward Moore's *Bring the Jubilee* (1953) stands as the most adroit treatment of a South triumphant in the Civil War. Even fantasy novels, such as John Ford's *The Dragon Waiting* (1983), have used the motif.

By far the most popular theme of all is the impact of a Nazi victory in World War II. Interestingly, the first such novel appeared *before* the war. Katherine Burdekin's *Swastika Night* depicted a defeated Britain; it was published under the pseudonym Murray Constantin by Gollancz in 1937. (For a discussion see *Women's Studies International Forum*, Vol. 1, 1984, pp. 85–95.) The war itself produced several novels that were mostly propaganda, with titles like *When Adolf Came, When the Bells Rang,* and *Loss of Eden.* The theme proved especially popular with British writers after the war, as in John W. Wall's *The Sound of His Horn* (1952), which showed Nazis hunting Britons for sport. A grim documentary-style film, *It Happened Here,* appeared in 1963. To many the idea by now seems only marginally related to science fiction, so that when Len Deighton's *SS-GB* appeared in the 1980s reviews seldom remarked on its speculative character. Indeed, there appeared at the same time a "nonfiction" portrayal of a successful German assault on England in Kenneth Macksey's *Invasion!*, directed to military-history buffs.

The two outstanding examples of this subtheme are Philip K. Dick's *The Man in the High Castle* (1962), perhaps his best novel, and Norman Spinrad's *The Iron Dream* (1972). Spinrad uses the idea with a deft, cutting edge. His Hitler immigrated to the United States and became a pulp writer of sword-and-sorcery tales. Hitler's crowning work is a thinly science-fictional vision of Nazi triumph. The text is this fascist melodrama, full of eerie parallels with our reality. Spinrad follows this with a satiric critical afterword by literary bore "Homer Whipple," who chews on the significance of Hitler-as-hack with dogged tunnel vision. The book is a tour de force.

Many of the best works of this type are short, however. Some focus on England under the Nazi heel (Keith Roberts's "Weihnachtsabend" and Hilary Bailey's "The Fall of Frenchy Steiner"). Many occur in an expanded German-centered culture covering several continents. Cyril Kornbluth's "Two Dooms," for example, depicts a United States partitioned between Germany and Japan. (It is arguably Kornbluth's best work, though he died before he could polish it into a final draft. This accounts for the occasional lapses of fact; there are, for example, no Hopi reservations near Los Alamos or even in New Mexico.)

When we began work on this collection, we sensed that the range of possibilities had not been adequately explored. We commissioned several works, suggesting alternative lines of attack. Delightfully, these stories did not simply repeat earlier themes but instead ranged from the weirdly surreal-comic (David Brin's "Thor Meets Captain America") to the horror-fantasy (Howard Goldsmith's "Do Ye Hear the Children Weeping?"). Brad Linaweaver undertook an extensive redrafting of "Moon of Ice" to heighten certain effects. Sheila Finch wrote "Reichs-Peace" after we suggested exploring a world in which some things are better than our present reality. Professor Tom Shippey wrote his first piece of fiction, "Enemy Transmissions," after we asked him to bring to bear his extensive knowledge of German literature.

The Hitler years will probably remain fascinating for many centuries. In them we see the most lurid embodiment of evil in the modern world. As Norman Spinrad points out in his introduction, the Nazis were masters of symbolism and spoke to a twisted sexuality that may be ingrained in society for a long time.

Though some may find these stories too excruciating to read, we urge you to view them as explorations that cast oblique light on modern times, on our own present, and on the countless possibilities of the human soul.

Introduction:
Hitler Victorious

Norman Spinrad

Why does the memory of Adolf Hitler refuse to be exorcised? Why, forty years after his death and the end of World War II, do we have *Hitler Victorious*, an anthology of eleven stories set in various alternative worlds in which the, uh, Iron Dream of Nazi Germany did not end in the rubble of the *Führerbunker* in Berlin?

This collection does not by any means exhaust the literature on the subject. There are at least three well-known novels exploring alternative Nazi worlds, Philip K. Dick's *The Man in the High Castle,* Sarban's *The Sound of His Horn,* and my own *The Iron Dream.* What's more, *Hitler Victorious* and this essay must limit themselves to what has been published in English, and since the Nazis directly inflicted their reality not on the English-speaking world but on the vast checkerboard of peoples and cultures between the Pyrenees and the Urals, one must assume that such literature exists in other European languages as well.

And indeed the mystique goes even deeper than that. Twenty years ago I saw a shop purveying Nazi paraphernalia in Mexico City, of all places. At about the time *The Iron Dream* was published, Ballantine Books was doing quite well with a series of lavishly illustrated trade paperbacks on such subjects as SS uniforms and Nazi warplanes of World War II. Mel Brooks can hardly make a movie that does not include a Hitler impersonation. Outlaw motorcycle gangs have long decked themselves out in Nazi regalia. Both the black leather jackets of the 1950s and many present punk styles owe their inspiration to SS chic.

Even the very face of Hitler has graven itself more deeply into the public consciousness (or unconsciousness) than that of any other human who ever lived. A blank oval, a curve of hair across either top quadrant, a Charlie Chaplin moustache, and we all know who it is, don't we?

What we don't know is how and why.

Admittedly Adolf Hitler was one of the great mass murderers of history, but Josef Stalin was no slouch either when it came to secret police, concentration camps, and mass exterminations. Nor were Torquemada, Attila the Hun, or Pol Pot lightweights in the historical-monster sweepstakes when measured by the numbers.

But Adolf Hitler, in some elusive manner, stands alone as the archetype of human evil, and perhaps even as something more, for there is a strange ambiguous quality to some of this literature, a queasy fascination with, dare I say it, certain Nazi virtues.

Nazi virtues?

During the Beirut hostage crisis a professional negotiator named Herb Cohen made a telling point: "No one is crazy to *himself*, no matter how crazy he may seem to *you.*" It does not seem likely that Hitler deliberately set out to do evil by his own lights, or that the German people followed him so fanatically because they were consumed by the self-conscious lust to be vile. Hitler came to power in a defeated and humiliated nation whose economy had collapsed into mass unemployment and runaway inflation. Within five years the currency was stabilized, the economy was booming, Germany was a world leader in technology, and national pride and self-confidence had reached the point of utter mania.

How did Hitler and the Nazis accomplish this?

Leni Riefenstahl said it best in the title of a masterful propaganda film that was part of the very process. It was indeed *The Triumph of the Will.*

Adolf Hitler, it would seem, was a man utterly without doubt and a man able to project this certainty to both his subordinates and the masses. In the mid-1930s, for example, he ordered Dr. Ferdinand Porsche to design what was to become the Volkswagen with rear-wheel drive and an air-cooled engine because, he proclaimed, he wanted a car for the masses that could handle the winter on the great autobahns he planned to build in Russia after he had conquered it. Even at the very end in the Bunker, with plots swirling around the likes of Himmler, Goering, Goebbels, & Co., none of the conspirators plotted the overthrow of *der Führer:* they were all still scheming to curry his favor.

This was the heart of the Nazi "ideology," the *Führerprincip:* total obedience and loyalty to and total trust in a heroic, indeed godlike, leader who was the mystic Will of the Nation incarnate. *"Deutschland ist Hitler, Hitler ist Deutschland."*

Given this identification of the *Führer* and the Reich, deeds that would seem to defy the bounds of the politically and economically possible can indeed be performed with utter ruthless efficiency. Inflation can be curbed by fixing an arbitrary value on the currency and enforcing it with the police power of the totalitarian state. A massive buildup of the armed forces soaks up unemployment. A scapegoat is found, the malaise of the nation is layed upon it, and then it is ritually executed in gas chambers.

We are dealing with a kind of magic here, not an ideology. Hitler self-consciously wrapped himself in the mantle of Faust, of Siegfried, of Charlemagne (aka Karl der Grosse), and did it all to the music of Wagner. In German the swastika is the *Hakenkreuz*, the "Twisted Cross," emblematic of the Antichrist not as the nemesis of the Good but as the antithesis of the degenerate Christian cult of the Holy Wimp, the ancient Germanic warrior-hero, the Messiah of the *Heldesleben* of Blood and Iron.

In private, and even obliquely in public, Hitler and the inner Nazi circle were profoundly anti-Christian, pagan barbarians who viewed mercy, forgiveness, and humility as vices that sapped the will of a people. The only earth that the meek were entitled to inherit was a mass grave.

Perhaps the anti-Semitism of the Nazis was a frustrated compromise with political realities, for not even Hitler would go so far as to attack frontally the religion of thoroughly Christian Germany, except through the surrogate of the progenitors thereof, the Jews.

But in their heart of hearts the Nazis certainly longed to extirpate this alien and unmanly non-Germanic peace cult and replace it with a Germanic version of *bushido*, the Way of the Warrior, the narcissistic self-worship of a self-created Master Race that would raise itself to godhood by the bootstraps of its iron will, of a *Herrenvolk* of Faustian supermen, destined by genes and blood not merely to rule but to transcend human evolution itself.

Who can honestly deny that there is a bit of the Nazi dream in each of us? For deep down beneath the civilized layers of our spirits is there not an ego unbound? Do we not all on some level consider ourselves the secret hero of the story? Does not our species seek to transcend natural evolution through science and technology? Indeed, having broken the bounds of the planet, gained access to the secret fires of the atom, and begun to play with the very code of life itself, are we not more than halfway there already? The superego may look down its nose at the overweening ambitions of Faust, but the ego sees him as a hero. Consider that Satan, the archetype of prideful and evil ego, is also known as Lucifer the Light Bringer, or, in an earlier avatar, Prometheus, who stole the sacred fire of the gods and placed its destiny in the hands of man.

Hitler, the profoundly anti-Christian pagan mystic, dabbler in astrology, Wagner fan, and would-be Faustian superhero, certainly knew all this on some level, if not in these terms. And Hitler, the master media manipulator of his day, certainly spent much time, energy, money, and attention crafting symbol systems, ceremonies, color schemes, architecture, and even uniforms that keyed into and captured the libidinal charge locked up in this inner Nazi of the ego.

If Christianity is essentially a cult reinforcing the superego virtues of humility, restraint, empathy, and charity, then in Christian terms Nazism certainly qualifies as a Satanic cult, celebrating such egoistic virtues (and Christian sins) as pride, power, vengeance, ruthlessness, will, and ultimately the central sin of Lucifer, the lust to transcend God-given creation and seize the godhead for one's self.

Interestingly enough, both Christianity and Nazism suppress natural expressions of sexual drive for the purpose of capturing this energy to serve their own ends. Christianity channels this bottled-up libidinal drive for orgasmic release into a focus on itself as the only path to true transcendent ecstasy. Nazism channels it into psychosexually charged fetishistic militarism and violence in the service of the expansionist state.

Thus the forthrightly phallic Nazi salute, the tight black uniforms of the SS, the silver death's heads, the twin lightning bolts, the barbarian torchlit splendor, the stirring martial music, the "SS Werewolf Division," the whole obsessive and twisted Satanism of the Nazi symbol systems, as the supermen in their chrome-and-black S&M gear thrust their right arms erect and, with assholes tight and fire gleaming in their eyes, march off to bugger the world.

Which explains why, forty years after the death of Nazism as a political force or coherent ideology, people with no historical perception of or connection to the culture or theories of the Third Reich, including even Jews, are still drawn to the Nazi symbol system, are still fascinated by its late high priest, Adolf Hitler.

But why this whole anthology of science-fiction stories exploring futures in which Hitler and his Iron Dream triumphed? Why *The Sound of His Horn* and *The Man in the High Castle* and *The Iron Dream?*

While there has certainly been a huge amount of unconsciously Nazi (in the psychic sense) sf and fantasy published since space opera and the Third Reich were born more or less simultaneously in the 1930s, none of the stories in this book, and none of the above-named novels, is un-self-conscious Nazi pornography. All of these works, in their various ways, explore the consequences of a Hitler Victorious rather than pander to the secret Nazi within. To the extent that there is still a secret Nazi within, they seek to be part of the solution rather than exacerbate the problem.

This intellectual, as opposed to psychosexual, fascination with the subject stems, I believe, from the perception that World War II was the most important nexus thus far in human history, that the Battle of Armageddon has already been fought, in the form of a total war between modern humanistic civilization and the incarnation of the deepest evil within the human spirit ever to have manifested itself on earth.

If ever it could be said that there was a just war, an unavoidable war, and a war in which the forces of Light clearly and utterly triumphed over the forces of Darkness, World War II was it. And yet . . .

And yet, forty years after Armageddon, do we find ourselves in the Millennium?

Hardly. Once more the world is polarized between two armed camps, two ideologies, two systems of morality, each of which considers itself the repository of virtue and the vanguard of human evolution, and each of which regards the other as "The Evil Empire." Ironically these two camps were allies against the Nazis, though there were those in the West who at a certain stage saw Nazi Germany as a force to wield against the Soviet Union, and though World War II essentially began with a pact between Hitler and Stalin to carve up Poland.

Further, both sides now possess that ultimate Faustian power of which Adolf Hitler could only dream, the power of life and death over civilization, the human race, indeed perhaps the biosphere of the planet itself.

World War II was a closer contest than many of us would now like to contemplate. If Hitler had invaded England in 1940, when it stood alone, instead of attacking the Soviet Union and opening an Eastern Front, if Japan had not attacked Pearl Harbor, bringing the United States into the war, if the Third Reich had just held out another two years or so until it had atomic warheads for the ICBMs that it actually was developing at the end of the war . . .

Where would we be now?

Would we be extinct as a civilization or even a species, having already precipitated a nuclear winter?

Would a Nazified Europe or even a Nazified world have devolved into neomedieval barbarism? Would it have evolved into a Pax Germanica bringing an enforced peace to the world? Would the swastika flag now be flying on the moon and Mars? Would Germany and Japan have carved up the United States along the Mississippi? Would Japan and the United States now be isolated islands in the midst of a Nazi world sea? Or, decades or centuries after a Nazi victory, would we be back to business as usual in the nation-state game?

So here you have a book of stories exploring not one but a whole series of roads not taken at that most fateful crossroads in human history, a diversity of futures radiating from a single, simple, but most puissant premise: Hitler Victorious.

He came close. It might have been. And in a psychic sense, at least, it might happen yet. For forty years after his death the shade of Adolf Hitler can hardly be said to have been exorcised from the darkest depths of the human heart.

Two Dooms

C.M. Kornbluth

It was May, not yet summer by five weeks, but the afternoon heat under the corrugated roofs of Manhattan Engineer District's Los Alamos Laboratory was daily less bearable. Young Dr. Edward Royland had lost fifteen pounds from an already meager frame during his nine-month hitch in the desert. He wondered every day while the thermometer crawled up to its 5:45 peak whether he had made a mistake he would regret the rest of his life in accepting work with the Laboratory rather than letting the local draft board have his carcass and do what they pleased with it. His University of Chicago classmates were glamorously collecting ribbons and wounds from Saipan to Brussels; one of them, a first-rate mathematician named Hatfield, would do no more first-rate mathematics. He had gone down, burning, in an Eighth Air Force Mitchell bomber ambushed over Lille.

"And what, Daddy, did you do in the war?"

"Well, kids, it's a little hard to explain. They had this stupid atomic bomb project that never came to anything, and they tied up a lot of us in a godforsaken place in New Mexico. We figured and we calculated and we fooled with uranium and some of us got radiation burns and then the war was over and they sent us home."

Royland was not amused by this prospect. He had heat rash under his arms and he was waiting, not patiently, for the Computer Section to send him his figures on Phase 56c, which was the (goddamn childish) code designated for Element Assembly Time. Phase 56c was Royland's own particular baby. He was under Rotschmidt, supervisor of WEAPON DESIGN TRACK III, and Rotschmidt was under Oppenheimer, who bossed the works. Sometimes a General Groves came through, a fine figure of a man, and once from a window Royland had seen the venerable Henry L. Stimson, Secretary of War, walking slowly down their dusty street, leaning on a cane and surrounded by young staff officers. That's what Royland was seeing of the war.

Laboratory! It had sounded inviting, cool, bustling but quiet. So every morning these days he was blasted out of his cot in a barracks cubicle at seven by "Oppie's whistle," fought for a shower and shave with thirty-seven other bachelor scientists in eight languages, bolted a bad cafeteria breakfast, and went through the barbed-wire Restricted Line to his "office"—another matchboard-walled cubicle, smaller and hotter and noisier, with talking and typing and clack of adding machines all around him.

Under the circumstances he was doing good work, he supposed. He wasn't happy about being restricted to his one tiny problem, Phase 56c, but no doubt he was happier than Hatfield had been when his Mitchell got it.

Under the circumstances . . . they included a weird haywire arrangement for computing. Instead of a decent differential analyzer machine they had a human sea of office girls with Burroughs' desk calculators; the girls screamed "Banzai!" and charged on differential equations and swamped them by sheer volume; they clicked them to death with their little adding machines. Royland thought hungrily of Conant's huge, beautiful analog differentiator up at MIT; it was probably tied up by whatever the mysterious "Radiation Laboratory" there was doing. Royland suspected that the "Radiation Laboratory" had as much to do with radiation as his own "Manhattan Engineer District" had to do with Manhattan engineering. And the world was supposed to be trembling on the edge these days of a New Dispensation of Computing that would obsolete even the MIT machine—tubes, relays, and binary arithmetic at blinding speed instead of the suavely turning cams and the smoothly extruding rods and the elegant scribed curves of Conant's masterpiece. He decided that he wouldn't like that; he would like it even less than he liked the little office girls clacking away, pushing lank hair from their dewed brows with undistracted hands.

He wiped his own brow with a sodden handkerchief and permitted himself a glance at his watch and the thermometer. Five-fifteen and 103 Fahrenheit.

He thought vaguely of getting out, of fouling up just enough to be released from the project and drafted. No; there was the postwar career to think of. But one of the big shots, Teller, had been irrepressible; he had rambled outside of his assigned mission again and again until Oppenheimer let him go; now Teller was working with Lawrence at Berkeley on something that had reputedly gone sour at a reputed quarter of a billion dollars—

A girl in khaki knocked and entered. "Your material from the Computer Section, Dr. Royland. Check them and sign here, please." He counted the dozen sheets, signed the clipboarded form she held out, and plunged into the material for thirty minutes.

When he sat back in his chair, the sweat dripped into his eyes unnoticed. His hands were shaking a little, though he did not know that either. Phase 56c of WEAPON DESIGN TRACK III was finished, over, done, successfully accomplished. The answer to the question "Can U_{235} slugs be assembled into a critical mass within a physically feasible time?" was in. The answer was "Yes."

Royland was a theory man, not a Wheatstone or a Kelvin; he liked the numbers for themselves and had no special passion to grab for wires, mica, and bits of graphite so that what the numbers said might immediately be given flesh in a wonderful new gadget. Nevertheless, he could visualize at once a workable atomic-bomb assembly within the framework of Phase 56c. You have so many microseconds to assemble your critical mass without it boiling away in vapor; you use them by blowing the subassemblies together with shaped charges; lots of microseconds to spare by that method; practically foolproof. Then comes the Big Bang.

Oppie's whistle blew; it was quitting time. Royland sat still in his cubicle. He should go, of course, to Rotschmidt and tell him; Rotschmidt would probably clap him on the back and pour him a jigger of Bols Geneva from the tall clay bottle he kept in his safe. Then Rotschmidt would go to Oppenheimer. Before sunset the project would be redesigned! TRACK I, TRACK II, TRACK IV, and TRACK V would be shut down and their people crammed into TRACK III, the one with the paydirt! New excitement would boil through the project; it had been torpid and souring for three months. Phase 56c was the first good news in at least that long; it had been one damned blind alley after another. General Groves had looked sour and dubious last time around.

Desk drawers were slamming throughout the corrugated, sunbaked building; doors were slamming shut on cubicles; down the corridor, somebody roared with laughter, strained laughter. Passing Royland's door somebody cried impatiently: *"—aber was kan Man tun?"*

Royland whispered to himself: "You damned fool, what are you thinking of?"

But he knew—he was thinking of the Big Bang, the Big Dirty Bang,
and of torture. The judicial torture of the old days, incredibly cruel by
today's lights, stretched the whole body, or crushed it, or burned it, or
shattered the fingers and legs. But even that old judicial torture carefully
avoided the most sensitive parts of the body, the generative organs,
though damage to these, or a real threat of damage to these, would have
produced quick and copious confessions. You have to be more or less crazy
to torture somebody that way; the sane man does not think of it as a
possibility.

An MP corporal tried Royland's door and looked in. "Quitting time,
professor," he said.

"OK," Royland said. Mechanically he locked his desk drawers and his
files, turned his window lock, and set out his wastepaper basket in the
corridor. Click the door; another day, another dollar.

Maybe the project *was* breaking up. They did now and then. The huge
boner at Berkeley proved that. And Royland's barracks was light two physicists now; their cubicles stood empty since they had been drafted to MIT
for some antisubmarine thing. Groves had *not* looked happy last time
around; how did a general make up his mind anyway? Give them three
months, then the ax? Maybe Stimson would run out of patience and cut
the loss, close the District down. Maybe F.D.R. would say at a Cabinet
meeting, "By the way, Henry, what ever became of—?" and that would
be the end if old Henry could say only that the scientists appear to be
optimistic of eventual success, Mr. President, but that as yet there seems
to be nothing *concrete*—

He passed through the barbed wire of the Line under scrutiny of an MP
lieutenant and walked down the barracks-edged company street of the
maintenance troops to their motor pool. He wanted a jeep and a trip
ticket; he wanted a long desert drive in the twilight; he wanted a dinner of
frijoles and eggplant with his old friend Charles Miller Nahataspe, the
medicine man of the adjoining Hopi reservation. Royland's hobby was
anthropology; he wanted to get a little drunk on it—he hoped it would
clear his mind.

Nahataspe welcomed him cheerfully to his hut; his million wrinkles all
smiled. "You want me to play informant for a while?" he grinned. He had
been to Carlisle in the 1880s and had been laughing at the white man ever
since; he admitted that physics was funny, but for a real joke give him
cultural anthropology every time. "You want some nice unsavory stuff

about our institutionalized homosexuality? Should I cook us a dog for dinner? Have a seat on the blanket, Edward."

"What happened to your chairs? And the funny picture of McKinley? And—and everything?" The hut was bare except for cooking pots that simmered on the stone-curbed central hearth.

"I gave the stuff away," Nahataspe said carelessly. "You get tired of things."

Royland thought he knew what that meant. Nahataspe believed he would die quite soon; these particular Indians did not believe in dying encumbered by possessions. Manner, of course, forbade discussing death.

The Indian watched his face and finally said: "Oh, it's all right for *you* to talk about it. Don't be embarrassed."

Royland asked nervously: "Don't you feel well?"

"I feel terrible. There's a snake eating my liver. Pitch in and eat. You feel pretty awful yourself, don't you?"

The hard-learned habit of security caused Royland to evade the question. "You don't mean that literally about the snake, do you Charles?"

"Of course I do," Miller insisted. He scooped a steaming gourd full of stew from the pot and blew on it. "What would an untutored child of nature know about bacteria, viruses, toxins, and neoplasms? What would I know about break-the-sky medicine?"

Royland looked up sharply; the Indian was blandly eating. "Do you hear any talk about break-the-sky medicine?" Royland asked.

"No talk, Edward. I've had a few dreams about it." He pointed with his chin toward the Laboratory. "You fellows over there shouldn't dream so hard; it leaks out."

Royland helped himself to stew without answering. The stew was good, far better than the cafeteria stuff, and he did not *have* to guess the source of the meat in it.

Miller said consolingly: "It's only kid stuff, Edward. Don't get so worked up about it. We have a long dull story about a horned toad who ate some loco-weed and thought he was the Sky God. He got angry and he tried to break the sky but he couldn't so he slunk into his hole ashamed to face all the other animals and died. But they never knew he tried to break the sky at all."

In spite of himself Royland demanded: "Do you have any stories about anybody who did break the sky?" His hands were shaking again and his voice almost hysterical. Oppie and the rest of them were going to break the sky, kick humanity right in the crotch, and unleash a prowling monster that would go up and down by night and day peering in all the windows of all the houses in the world, leaving no sane man ever unterrified for his life and the lives of his kin. Phase 56c, goddamn it to blackest hell, made sure of that! Well done, Royland; you earned your dollar today! Decisively the old Indian set his gourd aside. He said: "We have a saying that the only good paleface is a dead paleface, but I'll make an exception for you, Edward. I've got some strong stuff from Mexico that will make you feel better. I don't like to see my friends hurting."

"Peyote? I've tried it. Seeing a few colored lights won't make me feel better, but thanks."

"Not peyote, this stuff. It's God Food. I wouldn't take it myself without a month of preparation; otherwise the Gods would scoop me up in a net. That's because my people see clearly, and your eyes are clouded." He was busily rummaging through a clay-chinked wicker box as he spoke; he came up with a covered dish. "You people have your sight cleared just a little by the God Food, so it's safe for you."

Royland thought he knew what the old man was talking about. It was one of Nahataspe's biggest jokes that Hopi children understood Einstein's relativity as soon as they could talk—and there was some truth to it. The Hopi language—and thought—had no tenses and therefore no concept of time-as-an-entity; it had nothing like the Indo-European speech's subjects and predicates, and therefore no built-in metaphysics of cause and effect. In the Hopi language and mind all things were frozen together forever into one great relationship, a crystalline structure of space-time events that simply were because they were. So much for Nahataspe's people "seeing clearly." But Royland gave himself and any other physicist credit for seeing as clearly when they were working a four-dimensional problem in the X Y Z space variables and the T time variable.

He could have spoiled the old man's joke by pointing that out, but of course he did not. No, no; he'd get a jag and maybe a bellyache from Nahataspe's herb medicine and then go home to his cubicle with his problem unresolved: to kick or not to kick?

The old man began to mumble in Hopi and drew a tattered cloth across the door frame of his hut; it shut out the last rays of the setting sun, long and slanting on the desert, pink-red against the adobe cubes of the Indian settlement. It took a minute for Royland's eyes to accommodate to the flickering light from the hearth and the indigo square of the ceiling smoke hole. Now Nahataspe was "dancing," doing a crouched shuffle around the hut holding the covered dish before him. Out of the corner of his mouth, without interrupting the rhythm, he said to Royland: "Drink some hot water now." Royland sipped from one of the pots on the hearth; so far it was much like peyote ritual, but he felt calmer.

Nahataspe uttered a loud scream, added apologetically: "Sorry, Edward," and crouched before him whipping the cover off the dish like a headwaiter. So God Food was dried black mushrooms, miserable, wrinkled little things. "You swallow them all and chase them with hot water," Nahataspe said.

Obediently Royland choked them down and gulped from the jug; the old man resumed his dance and chanting.

A little old self-hypnosis, Royland thought bitterly. Grab some imitation sleep and forget about old 56c, as if you could. He could see the big dirty one now, a hell of a fireball, maybe over Munich, or Cologne, or Tokyo, or Nara. Cooked people, fused cathedral stone, the bronze of the big Buddha running like water, perhaps lapping around the ankles of a priest and burning his feet off so he fell prone into the stuff. He couldn't see the gamma radiation, but it would be there, invisible sleet doing the dirty unthinkable thing, coldly burning away the sex of men and women, cutting short so many fans of life at their points of origin. Phase 56c could snuff out a family of Bachs, or five generations of Bernoullis, or see to it that the great Huxley-Darwin cross did not occur.

The fireball loomed, purple and red and fringed with green—

The mushrooms were reaching him, he thought fuzzily. He could really see it. Nahataspe, crouched and treading, moved through the fireball just as he had the last time, and the time before that. Déjà vu, extraordinarily strong, stronger than ever before, gripped him. Royland knew all this had happened to him before, and remembered perfectly what would come next; it was on the very tip of his tongue, as they say—

The fireballs began to dance around him and he felt his strength drain suddenly out; he was lighter than a feather; the breeze would carry him away; he would be blown like a dust mote into the circle that the circling fireballs made. And he knew it was wrong. He croaked with the last of his energy, feeling himself slip out of the world: "Charlie! Help!"

Out of the corner of his mind as he slipped away he sensed that the old man was pulling him now under the arms, trying to tug him out of the hut, crying dimly into his ear: "You should have told me you did not see through smoke! You see clear; I never knew; I nev—"

And then he slipped through into blackness and silence.

Royland awoke sick and fuzzy; it was morning in the hut; there was no sign of Nahataspe. Well. Unless the old man had gotten to a phone and reported to the Laboratory, there were now jeeps scouring the desert in search of him and all hell was breaking loose in Security and Personnel. He would catch some of that hell on his return, and avert it with his news about assembly time.

Then he noticed that the hut had been cleaned of Nahataspe's few remaining possessions, even to the door cloth. A pang went through him; had the old man died in the night? He limped from the hut and looked around for a funeral pyre, a crowd of mourners. They were not there; the adobe cubes stood untenanted in the sunlight, and more weeds grew in the single street than he remembered. And his jeep, parked last night against the hut, was missing.

There were no wheeltracks, and uncrushed weeds grew tall where the jeep had stood.

Nahataspe's God Food had been powerful stuff. Royland's hand crept uncertainly to his face. No; no beard.

He looked about him, looked hard. He made the effort necessary to see details. He did not glance at the hut and because it was approximately the same as it had always been, concluded that it was unchanged, eternal. He looked and saw changes everywhere. Once-sharp adobe corners were rounded; protruding roof beams were bleached bone-white by how many years of desert sun? The wooden framing of the deep fortresslike windows had crumbled; the third building from him had wavering soot stains above its window boles and its beams were charred.

He went to it, numbly thinking: Phase 56c at least is settled. Not old Rip's baby now. They'll know me from fingerprints, I guess. One year? Ten? I *feel* the same.

The burned-out house was a shambles. In one corner were piled dry human bones. Royland leaned dizzily against the doorframe; its charcoal crumbled and streaked his hand. Those skulls were Indian—he was anthropologist enough to know that. Indian men, women, and children, slain and piled in a heap. Who kills Indians? There should have been some sign of clothes, burned rags, but there were none. Who strips Indians naked and kills them?

Signs of a dreadful massacre were everywhere in the house. Bullet-pocks in the walls, high and low. Savage nicks left by bayonets—and swords? Dark stains of blood; it had run two inches high and left its mark. Metal glinted in a ribcage across the room. Swaying, he walked to the boneheap and thrust his hand into it. The thing bit him like a razor blade; he did not look at it as he plucked it out and carried it to the dusty street. With his back turned to the burned house he studied his find. It was a piece of swordblade six inches long, hand-honed to a perfect edge with a couple of nicks in it. It had stiffening ribs and the usual blood gutters. It had a perceptible curve that would fit into only one shape: the samurai sword of Japan.

However long it had taken, the war was obviously over.

He went to the village well and found it choked with dust. It was while he stared into the dry hole that he first became afraid. Suddenly it all was real; he was no more an onlooker but a frightened and very thirsty man. He ransacked the dozen houses of the settlement and found nothing to his purpose—a child's skeleton here, a couple of cartridge cases there.

There was only one thing left, and that was the road, the same earth track it had always been, wide enough for one jeep or the rump-sprung station wagon of the Indian settlement that once had been. Panic invited him to run; he did not yield. He sat on the well curb, took off his shoes to meticulously smooth wrinkles out of his khaki GI socks, put the shoes on, and retied the laces loosely enough to allow for swelling, and hesitated a moment. Then he grinned, selected two pebbles carefully from the dust and popped them in his mouth. "Beaver Patrol, forward march," he said, and began to hike.

Yes, he was thirsty; soon he would be hungry and tired; what of it? The dirt road would meet state-maintained blacktop in three miles and then there would be traffic and he'd hitch a ride. Let them argue with his fingerprints if they felt like it. The Japanese had got as far as New Mexico, had they? Then God help their home islands when the counterblow had come. Americans were a ferocious people when trespassed on. Conceivably, there was not a Japanese left alive . . .

He began to construct his story as he hiked. In large parts it was a repeated "I don't know." He would tell them: "I don't expect you to believe this, so my feelings won't be hurt when you don't. Just listen to what I say and hold everything until the FBI has checked my fingerprints. My name is—" and so on.

It was midmorning then, and he would be on the highway soon. His nostrils, sharpened by hunger, picked up a dozen scents on the desert breeze: the spice of sage, a whiff of acetylene stink from a rattler dozing on the shaded side of a rock, the throat-tightening reek of tar suggested for a moment on the air. That would be the highway, perhaps a recent hotpatch on a chuckhole. Then a startling tang of sulfur dioxide drowned them out and passed on, leaving him stung and sniffling and groping for a handkerchief that was not there. What in God's name had that been, and where from? Without ceasing to trudge he studied the horizon slowly and found a smoke pall to the far west dimly smudging the sky. It looked like a small city's, or a fair-sized factory's, pollution. A city or a factory where "in his time"—he formed the thought reluctantly—there had been none.

Then he was at the highway. It had been improved; it was a two-laner still, but it was nicely graded now, built up by perhaps three inches of gravel and tar beyond its old level, and lavishly ditched on either side.

If he had a coin he would have tossed it, but you went for weeks without spending a cent at Los Alamos Laboratory; Uncle took care of everything, from cigarettes to tombstones. He turned left and began to walk westward toward that sky smudge.

I am a reasonable animal, he was telling himself, and I will accept whatever comes in a spirit of reason. I will control what I can and try to understand the rest—

A faint siren scream began behind him and built up fast. The reasonable animal jumped for the ditch and hugged it for dear life. The siren howled closer, and motors roared. At the ear-splitting climax Royland put his head up for one glimpse, then fell back into the ditch as if a grenade had exploded in his middle.

The convoy roared on, down the *center* of the two-lane highway, straddling the white line. First the three little recon cars with the twin-mount machine guns, each filled brimful with three helmeted Japanese soldiers. Then the high-profiled, armored car of state, six-wheeled, with a probably ceremonial gun turret astern—nickel-plated gunbarrels are impractical—and the Japanese admiral in the fore-and-aft hat taking his lordly ease beside a rawboned, hatchet-faced SS officer in gleaming black. Then, diminuendo, two more little recon jobs . . .

"We've lost," Royland said in his ditch meditatively. "Ceremonial tanks with glass windows—we lost a *long* time ago." Had there been a Rising Sun insignia or was he now imagining that?

He climbed out and continued to trudge westward on the improved blacktop. You couldn't say "I reject the universe," not when you were as thirsty as he was.

He didn't even turn when the put-putting of a westbound vehicle grew loud behind him and then very loud when it stopped at his side.

"Zeegail," a curious voice said. "What are you doing here?"

The vehicle was just as odd in its own way as the ceremonial tank. It was minimum motor transportation, a kid's sled on wheels, powered by a noisy little air-cooled outboard motor. The driver sat with no more comfort than a cleat to back his coccyx against, and behind him were two twenty-five-pound flour sacks that took up all the remaining room the little buckboard provided. The driver had the leathery Southwestern look; he wore a baggy blue outfit that was obviously a uniform and obviously unmilitary. He had a nametape on his breast above an incomprehensible row of dull ribbons: MARTFIELD, E., 1218824, P/7 NQOTD43. He saw Royland's eyes on the tape and said kindly: "My name is Martfield—Paymaster Seventh, but there's no need to use my rank here. Are you all right, my man?"

"Thirsty," Royland said. "What's the NQOTD43 for?"

"You can read!" Martfield said, astounded. "Those clothes—"

"Something to drink, please," Royland said. For the moment nothing else mattered in the world. He sat down on the buckboard like a puppet with cut strings.

"See here, fellow!" Martfield snapped in a curious, strangled way, forcing the words through his throat with a stagy, conventional effect of controlled anger. "You can stand until I invite you to sit!"

"Have you any water?" Royland asked dully.

With the same bark: "Who do you think you are?"

"I happen to be a theoretical physicist—" tiredly arguing with a dim seventh-carbon-copy imitation of a drill sergeant.

"Oh-*hoh!*" Martfield suddenly laughed. His stiffness vanished; he actually reached into his baggy tunic and brought out a pint canteen that gurgled. He then forgot all about the canteen in his hand, roguishly dug Royland in the ribs and said: "I should have suspected. You scientists! Somebody was supposed to pick you up—but he was another scientist, eh? Ah-hah-hah-hah!"

Royland took the canteen from his hand and sipped. So a scientist was supposed to be an idiot-savant, eh? Never mind now; drink. People said you were not supposed to fill your stomach with water after great thirst; it sounded to him like one of those puritanical rules people make up out of nothing because they sound reasonable. He finished the canteen while Martfield, Paymaster Seventh, looked alarmed, and wished only that there were three or four more of them.

"Got any food?" he demanded.

Martfield cringed briefly. "Doctor, I regret extremely that I have nothing with me. However if you would do me the honor of riding with me to my quarters—"

"Let's go," Royland said. He squatted on the flour sacks and away they chugged at a good thirty miles an hour; it was a fair little engine. The Paymaster Seventh continued deferential, apologizing over his shoulder because there was no windscreen, later dropped his cringing entirely to explain that Royland was seated on flour—"*white* flour, understand?" An over-the-shoulder wink. He had a friend in the bakery at Los Alamos. Several buckboards passed the other way as they traveled. At each encounter there was a peering examination of insignia to decide who saluted. Once they met a sketchily enclosed vehicle that furnished its driver with a low seat instead of obliging him to sit with legs straight out, and Paymaster Seventh Martfield almost dislocated his shoulder saluting first. The driver of that one was a Japanese in a kimono. A long curved sword lay across his lap.

Mile after mile the smell of sulfur and sulfides increased; finally there rose before them the towers of a Frasch Process layout. It looked like an oilfield, but instead of ground-laid pipelines and bass-drum storage tanks there were foothills of yellow sulfur. They drove between them—more salutes from baggily uniformed workers with shovels and yard-long Stilson wrenches. Off to the right were things that might have been Solvay Process towers for sulfuric acid, and a glittering horror of a neo-Roman administration-and-labs building. The Rising Sun banner fluttered from its central flagstaff.

Music surged as they drove deeper into the area; first it was a welcome counterirritant to the pop-pop of the two-cycle buckboard engine, and then a nuisance by itself. Royland looked, annoyed, for the loudspeakers, and saw them everywhere—on power poles, buildings, gateposts. Schmaltzy Strauss waltzes bathed them like smog, made thinking just a little harder, made communication just a little more blurry even after you had learned to live with the noise.

"I miss music in the wilderness," Martfield confided over his shoulder. He throttled down the buckboard until they were just rolling; they had passed some line unrecognized by Royland beyond which one did not salute everybody—just the occasional Japanese walking by in business suit with blueprint-roll and slide rule, or in kimono with sword. It was a German who nailed Royland, however: a classic jack-booted German in black broadcloth, black leather, and plenty of silver trim. He watched them roll for a moment after exchanging salutes with Martfield, made up his mind, and said: "Halt."

The Paymaster Seventh slapped on the brake, killed the engine, and popped to attention beside the buckboard. Royland more or less imitated him. The German said, stiffly but without accent: "Whom have you brought here, Paymaster?"

"A scientist, sir. I picked him up on the road returning from Los Alamos with personal supplies. He appears to be a minerals prospector who missed a rendezvous, but naturally I have not questioned the Doctor."

The German turned to Royland contemplatively. "So, Doctor. Your name and specialty."

"Dr. Edward Royland," he said. "I do nuclear-power research." If there was no bomb, he'd be damned if he'd invent it now for these people.

"So? That is very interesting, considering that there is no such thing as nuclear-power research. Which camp are you from?" The German threw an aside to the Paymaster Seventh, who was literally shaking with fear at the turn things had taken. "You may go, Paymaster. Of course you will report yourself for harboring a fugitive."

"At once, sir," Martfield said in a sick voice. He moved slowly away pushing the little buckboard before him. The Strauss waltz oom-pah'd its last chord and instantly the loudspeakers struck up a hoppity-hoppity folk dance, heavy on the brass.

"Come with me," the German said, and walked off, not even looking behind to see whether Royland was obeying. This itself demonstrated how unlikely any disobedience was to succeed. Royland followed at his heels, which of course were garnished with silver spurs. Royland had not seen a horse so far that day.

A Japanese stopped them politely inside the administration building, a rimless-glasses, office-manager type in a gray suit. "How nice to see you again, Major Kappel! Is there anything I might do to help you?"

The German stiffened. "I didn't want to bother your people, Mr. Ito. This fellow appears to be a fugitive from one of our camps; I was going to turn him over to our liaison group for examination and return."

Mr. Ito looked at Royland and slapped his face hard. Royland, by the insanity of sheer reflex, cocked his fist as a red-blooded boy should, but the German's reflexes operated also. He had a pistol in his hand and pressed against Royland's ribs before he could throw the punch.

"All right," Royland said, and put down his hand.

Mr. Ito laughed. "You are at least partly right, Major Kappel; he certainly is not from one of *our* camps! But do not let me delay you further. May I hope for a report on the outcome of this?"

"Of course, Mr. Ito," said the German. He holstered his pistol and walked on, trailed by the scientist. Royland heard him grumble something that sounded like "Damned extraterritoriality!"

They descended to a basement level where all the door signs were in German, and in an office labeled WISSENSCHAFTSLICHESICHERHEITS-LIAISON Royland finally told his story. His audience was the major, a fat officer deferentially addressed as Colonel Biederman, and a bearded old civilian, a Dr. Piqueron, called in from another office. Royland suppressed only the matter of bomb research and did it easily with the old security habit. His improvised cover story made the Los Alamos Laboratory a research center only for the generation of electricity.

The three heard him out in silence. Finally, in an amused voice, the colonel asked: "Who was this Hitler you mentioned?"

For that Royland was not prepared. His jaw dropped.

Major Kappel said: "Oddly enough, he struck on a name which does figure, somewhat infamously, in the annals of the Third Reich. One Adolf Hitler was an early Party agitator, but as I recall it he intrigued against the Leader during the War of Triumph and was executed."

"An ingenious madman," the colonel said. "Sterilized, of course?"

"Why, I don't know. I suppose so. Doctor, would you—?"

Dr. Piqueron quickly examined Royland and found him all there, which astonished them. Then they thought of looking for his camp tattoo number on the left bicep, and found none. Then, thoroughly upset, they discovered that he had no birth number above his left nipple either.

"And," Dr. Piqueron stammered, "his shoes are odd, sir—I just noticed. Sir, how long since you've seen sewn shoes and braided laces?"

"You must be hungry," the colonel suddenly said. "Doctor, have my aide get something to eat for—for the doctor."

"Major," said Royland, "I hope no harm will come to the fellow who picked me up. You told him to report himself."

"Have no fear, er, doctor," said the major. "Such humanity! You are of German blood?"

"Not that I know of; it may be."

"It *must* be!" said the colonel.

A platter of hash and a glass of beer arrived on a tray. Royland postponed everything. At last he demanded: "Now. Do you believe me? There must be fingerprints to prove my story still in existence."

"I feel like a fool," the major said. "You still could be hoaxing us. Dr. Piqueron, did not a German scientist establish that nuclear power is a theoretical and practical impossibility, that one always must put more into it than one can take out?"

Piqueron nodded and said reverently: "Heisenberg. Nineteen fifty-three, during the War of Triumph. His group was then assigned to electrical-weapons research and produced the blinding bomb. But this fact does not invalidate the doctor's story; he says only that his group was *attempting* to produce nuclear power."

"We've got to research this," said the colonel. "Dr. Piqueron, entertain this man, whatever he is, in your laboratory."

Piqueron's laboratory down the hall was a place of astounding simplicity, even crudeness. The sinks, reagents, and balance were capable only of simple qualitative and quantitative analyses; various works in progress testified that they were not even strained to their modest limits. Samples of sulfur and its compounds were analyzed here. It hardly seemed to call for a "doctor" of anything, and hardly even for a human being. Machinery should be continuously testing the products as they flowed out; variations should be scribed mechanically on a moving tape; automatic controls should at least stop the processes and signal an alarm when variation went beyond limits; at most it might correct whatever was going wrong. But here sat Piqueron every day, titrating, precipitating, and weighing, entering results by hand in a ledger and telephoning them to the works!

Piqueron looked about proudly. "As a physicist you wouldn't understand all this, of course," he said. "Shall I explain?"

"Perhaps later, doctor, if you'd be good enough. If you'd first help me orient myself—"

So Piqueron told him about the War of Triumph (1940–1955) and what came after.

In 1940 the realm of *der Führer* (Herr Goebbels, of course—that strapping blond fellow with the heroic jaw and eagle's eye whom you can see in the picture there) was simultaneously and treacherously invaded by the misguided French, the subhuman Slavs, and the perfidious British. The attack, for which the shocked Germans coined the name *Blitzkrieg,* was timed to coincide with an internal eruption of sabotage, well-poisoning, and assassination by the *Zigeunerjuden,* or Jewpsies, of whom little is now known; there seem to be none left.

By Nature's ineluctable law the Germans had necessarily to be tested to the utmost so that they might fully respond. Therefore Germany was overrun from East and West, and Holy Berlin itself was taken; but Goebbels and his court withdrew like Barbarossa into the mountain fastnesses to await their day. It came unexpectedly soon. The deluded Americans launched a million-man amphibious attack on the homeland of the Japanese in 1945. The Japanese resisted with almost Teutonic courage. Not one American in twenty reached shore alive, and not one in a hundred got a mile inland. Particularly lethal were the women and children, who lay in camouflaged pits hugging artillery shells and aircraft bombs, which they detonated when enough invaders drew near to make it worthwhile.

The second invasion attempt, a month later, was made up of second-line troops scraped up from everywhere, including occupation duty in Germany.

"Literally," Piqueron said, "the Japanese did not know how to surrender, so they did not. They could not conquer, but they could and did continue suicidal resistance, consuming manpower of the allies and their own womanpower and childpower—a shrewd bargain for the Japanese! The Russians refused to become involved in the Japanese war; they watched with apish delight while two future enemies, as they supposed, were engaged in mutual destruction.

"A third assault wave broke on Kyushu and gained the island at last.

What lay ahead? Only another assault on Honshu, the main island, home of the Emperor and the principal shrines. It was 1946; the volatile, child-like Americans were war-weary and mutinous; the best of them were gone by then. In desperation the Anglo-American leaders offered the Russians an economic sphere embracing the China coast and Japan as the price of participation."

The Russians grinned and assented; they would take that—at *least* that. They mounted a huge assault for the spring of 1947; they would take Korea and leap off from there for northern Honshu while the Anglo-American forces struck in the south. Surely this would provide at last a symbol before which the Japanese might without shame bow down and admit defeat!

And then, from the mountain fastnesses, came the radio voice: "Germans! Your Leader calls upon you again!" Followed the Hundred Days of Glory during which the German Army reconstituted itself and expelled the occupation troops—by then, children without combat experience, and leavened by not-quite-disabled veterans. Followed the seizure of the airfields; the Luftwaffe in business again. Followed the drive, almost a dress parade, to the Channel Coast, gobbling up immense munition dumps awaiting shipment to the Pacific Theater, millions of warm uniforms, good boots, mountains of rations, piles of shells and explosives that lined the French roads for scores of miles, thousands of two-and-a-half-ton trucks, and lakes of gasoline to fuel them. The shipyards of Europe, from Hamburg to Toulon, had been turning out, furiously, invasion barges for the Pacific. In April of 1947 they sailed against England in their thousands.

Halfway around the world the British Navy was pounding Tokyo, Nagasaki, Kobe, Hiroshima, Nara. Three quarters of the way across Asia the Russian Army marched stolidly on; let the decadent British pickle their own fish; the glorious motherland at last was gaining her long-sought, long-denied, warm-water seacoast. The British, tired women without their men, children fatherless these eight years, old folks deathly weary, deathly worried about their sons, were brave but they were not insane. They accepted honorable peace terms; they capitulated.

With the Western front secure for the first time in history the ancient Drive to the East was resumed; the immemorial struggle of Teuton against Slav went on.

His spectacles glittering with rapture, Dr. Piqueron said: "We were worthy in those days of the Teutonic Knights who seized Prussia from the submen! On the ever-glorious Twenty-first of May, Moscow was ours!"

Moscow and the monolithic state machinery it controlled, and all the

roads and rail lines and communication wires which led only to—and from
—Moscow. Detroit-built tanks and trucks sped along those roads in the
fine, bracing spring weather; the Red Army turned one hundred and
eighty degrees at last and countermarched halfway across the Eurasian
landmass, and at Kazan it broke exhausted against the Frederik Line.

Europe at last was One and German. Beyond Europe lay the dark and
swarming masses of Asia, mysterious and repulsive folk whom it would be
better to handle through the non-German, but chivalrous, Japanese. The
Japanese were reinforced with shipping from Birkenhead, artillery from
the Putilov Works, jet fighters from Châteauroux, steel from the Ruhr,
rice from the Po valley, herring from Norway, timber from Sweden, oil
from Romania, laborers from India. The American forces were driven
from Kyushu in the winter of 1948, and bloodily back across their chain of
island steppingstones that followed.

Surrender they would not; it was a monstrous affront that shield-shaped
North America dared to lie there between the German Atlantic and the
Japanese Pacific threatening both. The affront was wiped out in 1955.

For one hundred and fifty years now the Germans and the Japanese had
uneasily eyed each other across the banks of the Mississippi. Their orators
were fond of referring to that river as a vast frontier unblemished by a
single fortification. There was even some interpenetration; a Japanese colony fished out of Nova Scotia on the very rim of German America; a
sulfur mine that was part of the Farben system lay in New Mexico, the
very heart of Japanese America—this was where Dr. Edward Royland
found himself, being lectured to by Dr. Piqueron, Dr. Gaston Pierre Piqueron, true-blue German.

"Here, of course," Dr. Piqueron said gloomily, "we are so damned
provincial. Little ceremony and less manners. Well, it would be too much
to expect them to assign *German* Germans to this dreary outpost, so we
French Germans must endure it somehow."

"You're all French?" Royland asked, startled.

"French *Germans*," Piqueron stiffly corrected him. "Colonel Biederman happens to be a French German also; Major Kappel is—hrrmph—an
Italian German." He sniffed to show what he thought of that.

The Italian German entered at that point, not in time to shut off the
question: "And you all come from Europe?"

They looked at him in bafflement. "My grandfather did," Dr. Piqueron
said. Royland remembered; so Roman legions used to guard their empire
—Romans born and raised in Britain, or on the Danube, Romans who
would never in their lives see Italy or Rome.

Major Kappel said affably: "Well, this needn't concern us. I'm afraid, my dear fellow, that your little hoax has not succeeded." He clapped Royland merrily on the back. "I admit you've tricked us all nicely; now may we have the facts?"

Piqueron said, surprised: "His story is false? The shoes? The missing *Geburtsnummer?* And he appears to understand some chemistry!"

"Ah-h-h—but he said his specialty was *physics,* doctor! Suspicious in itself!"

"Quite so. A discrepancy. But the rest—?"

"As to his birth number, who knows? As to his shoes, who cares? I took some inconspicuous notes while he was entertaining us and have checked thoroughly. There *was* no Manhattan Engineering District. There *was* no Dr. Oppenheimer, or Fermi, or Bohr. There *is* no theory of relativity, or equivalence of mass and energy. Uranium has one use only—coloring glass a pretty orange. There is such a thing as an isotope but it has nothing to do with chemistry; it is the name used in Race Science for a permissible variation within a subrace. And what have you to say to *that,* my dear fellow?"

Royland wondered first, such was the positiveness with which Major Kappel spoke, whether he had slipped into a universe of different physical properties and history entirely, one in which Julius Caesar discovered Peru and the oxygen molecule was lighter than the hydrogen atom. He managed to speak. "How did you find all that out, major?"

"Oh, don't think I did a skimpy job," Kappel smiled. "I looked it all up in the *big* encyclopedia."

Dr. Piqueron, chemist, nodded grave approval of the major's diligence and thorough grasp of the scientific method.

"You still don't want to tell us?" Major Kappel asked coaxingly.

"I can only stand by what I said."

Kappel shrugged. "It's not my job to persuade you; I wouldn't know how to begin. But I can and will ship you off forthwith to a work camp."

"What—is a work camp?" Royland unsteadily asked.

"Good heavens, man, a camp where one works! You're obviously an *Ungleichgeschaltling* and you've got to be *gleichgeschaltet.*" He did not speak these words as if they were foreign; they were obviously part of the everyday American working vocabulary. *Gleichgeschaltet* meant to Royland something like "coordinated, brought into tune with." So he would be brought into tune—with what, and how?

The Major went on: "You'll get your clothes and your bunk and your chow, and you'll work, and eventually your irregular vagabondish habits will disappear and you'll be turned loose on the labor market. And you'll be damned glad we took the trouble with you." His face fell. "By the way, I was too late with your friend the Paymaster. I'm sorry. I sent a messenger to Disciplinary Control with a stop order. After all, if you took us in for an hour, why should you not have fooled a Pay-Seventh?"

"Too late? He's *dead?* For picking up a *hitchhiker?*"

"I don't know what that last word means," said the Major. "If it's dialect for 'vagabond,' the answer is ordinarily 'yes.' The man, after all, was a Pay-Seventh; he could read. Either you're keeping up your hoax with remarkable fidelity or you've been living in isolation. Could that be it? Is there a tribe of you somewhere? Well, the interrogators will find out; that's their job."

"The Dogpatch legend!" Dr. Piqueron burst out, thunderstruck. "He may be an Abnerite!"

"By Heaven," Major Kappel said slowly, "that might be it. What a feather in my cap to find a living Abnerite."

"*Whose* cap?" demanded Dr. Piqueron coldly.

"I think I'll look the Dogpatch legend up," said Kappel, heading for the door and probably the big encyclopedia.

"So will I," Dr. Piqueron announced firmly. The last Royland saw of them they were racing down the corridor, neck and neck.

Very funny. And they had killed simple-minded Paymaster Martfield for picking up a hitchhiker. The Nazis always had been pretty funny—fat Hermann pretending he was young Siegfried. As blond as Hitler, as slim as Goering, and as tall as Goebbels. Immature guttersnipes who hadn't been able to hang a convincing frame on Dimitrov for the Reichstag fire; the world had roared at their bungling. Huge, corny party rallies with let's-play-detectives nonsense like touching the local flags to that hallowed banner on which the martyred Horst Wessel had had a nosebleed. And they had rolled over Europe, and they killed people . . .

One thing was certain: life in the work camp would at least bore him to death. He was supposed to be an illiterate simpleton, so things were excused him which were not excused an exalted Pay-Seventh. He poked through a closet in the corner of the laboratory—he and Piqueron were the same size—

He found a natty change of uniform and what must be a civilian suit: somewhat baggy pants and a sort of tunic with the neat, sensible Russian collar. Obviously it would be all right to wear it because here it was; just as obviously it was all wrong for him to be dressed in chinos and a flannel shirt. He did not know exactly what this made him, but Martfield had been done to death for picking up a man in chinos and a flannel shirt. Royland changed into the civilian suit, stuffed his own shirt and pants far back on the top shelf of the closet; this was probably concealment enough from those murderous clowns. He walked out, and up the stairs, and through the busy lobby, and into the industrial complex. Nobody saluted him and he saluted nobody. He knew where he was going—to a good, sound Japanese laboratory where there were no Germans.

Royland had known Japanese students at the University and admired them beyond words. Their brains, frugality, doggedness, and good humor made them, as far as he was concerned, the most sensible people he had ever known. Tojo and his warlords were not, as far as Royland was concerned, essentially Japanese but just more damnfool soldiers and politicians. The real Japanese would courteously listen to him, calmly check against available facts—

He rubbed his cheek and remembered Mr. Ito and his slap in the face. Well, presumably Mr. Ito was a damnfool soldier and politician—and demonstrating for the German's benefit in a touchy border area full of jurisdictional questions.

At any rate, he would *not* go to a labor camp and bust rocks or refinish furniture until those imbeciles decided he was *gleichgeschaltet;* he would go mad in a month.

Royland walked to the Solvay towers and followed the glass pipes containing their output of sulfuric acid along the ground until he came to a bottling shed where beetle-browed men worked silently filling great wicker-basketed carboys and heaving them outside. He followed other men who levered them up onto hand trucks and rolled them in one door of a storage shed. Out the door at the other end more men loaded them onto enclosed trucks that were driven up from time to time.

Royland settled himself in a corner of the storage shed behind a barricade of carboys and listened to the truck dispatcher swear at his drivers and the carboy handlers swear at their carboys.

"Get the goddamn Frisco shipment *loaded,* stupid! I don't *care* if you gotta go, we gotta get it out by *midnight!*"

So a few hours after dark Royland was riding west, without much air, and in the dangerous company of one thousand gallons of acid. He hoped he had a careful driver.

A night, a day, and another night on the road. The truck never stopped except to gas up; the drivers took turns and ate sandwiches at the wheel and dozed off shift. It rained the second night. Royland, craftily and perhaps a little crazily, licked the drops that ran down the tarpaulin flap covering the rear. At the first crack of dawn, hunched between two wicker carcasses, he saw they were rolling through irrigated vegetable fields, and the water in the ditches was too much for him. He heard the transmission shift down to slow for a curve, swarmed over the tailgate, and dropped to the road. He was weak and limp enough to hit like a sack.

He got up, ignoring his bruises, and hobbled to one of the brimming five-foot ditches; he drank, and drank, and drank. This time puritanical folklore proved right; he lost it all immediately, or what had not been greedily absorbed by his shriveled stomach. He did not mind; it was bliss enough to *stretch.*

The field crop was tomatoes, almost dead ripe. He was starved for them; as he saw the rosy beauties he knew that tomatoes were the only thing in the world he craved. He gobbled one so that the juice ran down his chin; he ate the next two delicately, letting his teeth break the crispness of their skin and the beautiful taste ravish his tongue. There were tomatoes as far as the eye could see, on either side of the road, the green of the vines and the red dots of the ripe fruit graphed by the checkerboard of silvery ditches that caught the first light. Nevertheless, he filled his pockets with them before he walked on.

Royland was happy.

Farewell to the Germans and their sordid hash and murderous ways. *Look* at these beautiful fields! The Japanese are an innately artistic people who bring beauty to every detail of daily life. And they make damn good physicists, too. Confined in their stony home, cramped as he had been in the truck, they grew twisted and painful; why should they not have reached out for more room to grow, and what other way is there to reach but to make war? He could be very understanding about any people who had planted these beautiful tomatoes for him.

A dark blemish the size of a man attracted his attention. It lay on the margin of one of the swirling five-foot ditches out there to his right. And then it rolled slowly into the ditch with a splash, floundered a little, and proceeded to drown.

In a hobbling run Royland broke from the road and across the field. He did not know whether he was limber enough to swim. As he stood panting on the edge of the ditch, peering into the water, a head of hair surfaced near him. He flung himself down, stretched wildly, and grabbed the hair —and yet had detachment enough to feel a pang when the tomatoes in his tunic pocket smashed.

"Steady," he muttered to himself, yanked the head toward him, took hold with his other hand and lifted. A surprised face confronted him and then went blank and unconscious.

For half an hour Royland, weak as he was, struggled, cursed feebly, and sweated to get that body out of the water. At last he plunged in himself, found it only chest-deep, and shoved the carcass over the mudslick bank.

He did not know by then whether the man was alive or dead or much care. He knew only that he couldn't walk away and leave the job half finished.

The body was that of a fat, middle-aged Oriental, surely Chinese rather than Japanese, though Royland could not say why he thought so. His clothes were soaked rags except for a leather wallet the size of a cigar box that he wore on a wide cloth belt. Its sole content was a handsome blue-glazed porcelain bottle. Royland sniffed at it and reeled. Some kind of super-gin! He sniffed again, and then took a conservative gulp of the stuff. While he was still coughing, he felt the bottle being removed from his hand. When he looked he saw the Chinese, eyes still closed, accurately guiding the neck of the bottle to his mouth. The Chinese drank and drank and drank, then returned the bottle to the wallet and finally opened his eyes.

"Honorable sir," said the Chinese in flat, California American speech, "you have deigned to save my unworthy life. May I supplicate your honorable name?"

"Ah, Royland. Look, take it easy. Don't try to get up; you shouldn't even talk."

Somebody screamed behind Royland: "There has been thieving of to-matoes! There has been smasheeng and deestruction of thee vines! Children you, will bee weet-ness be-fore the Jappa-neese!"

Christ, now what?

Now a skinny black man, not a Negro, in a dirty loincloth, and beside him like a panpipes five skinny black loinclothed offspring in descending order. All were capering, pointing, and threatening. The Chinese groaned, fished in his tattered robes with one hand, and pulled out a soggy wad of bills. He peeled one off, held it out, and said: "Begone, pestilential barbarians from beyond Tian-Shang. My master and I give you alms, not tribute."

The Dravidian, or whatever he was, grabbed the bill and keened: "Een-suffee-cient for the terrible dommage! The Jappa-neese—"

The Chinese waved them away boredly. He said: "If my master will condescend to help me arise?"

Royland uncertainly helped him up. The man was wobbly, whether from the near-drowning or the terrific belt of alcohol he'd taken there was no knowing. They proceeded to the road, followed by shrieks to be careful about stepping on the vines.

On the road, the Chinese said: "My unworthy name is Li Po. Will my master deign to indicate in which direction we are to travel?"

"What's this master business?" Royland demanded. "If you're grateful, swell, but I don't *own* you."

"My master is pleased to jest," said Li Po. Politely, face-saving and third-personing Royland until hell wouldn't have it, he explained that Royland, having meddled with the Celestial decree that Li Po should, while drunk, roll into the irrigation ditch and drown, now had Li Po on his hands, for the Celestial Ones had washed theirs of him. "As my master of course will recollect in a moment or two." Understandingly he expressed his sympathy with Royland's misfortune in acquiring him as an obligation, especially since he had a hearty appetite, was known to be dishonest, and suffered from fainting fits and spasms when confronted with work.

"I don't *know* about all this," Royland said fretfully. "Wasn't there another Li Po? A poet?"

"Your servant prefers to venerate his namesake as one of the greatest drunkards the Flowery Kingdom has ever known," the Chinese observed. And a moment later he bent over, clipped Royland behind the knees so that he toppled forward and bumped his head, and performed the same obeisance himself, more gracefully. A vehicle went sputtering and popping by on the road as they kowtowed.

Li Po said reproachfully: "I humbly observe that my master is unaware of the etiquette our noble overlords exact. Such negligence cost the head of my insignificant elder brother in his twelfth year. Would my master be pleased to explain how he can have reached his honorable years without learning what babes in their cradles are taught?"

Royland answered with the whole truth. Li Po politely begged clarification from time to time, and a sketch of his mental horizons emerged from his questioning. That "magic" had whisked Royland forward a century or more he did not doubt for an instant, but he found it difficult to understand why the proper *fung shui* precautions had not been taken to avert a disastrous outcome to the God Food experiment. He suspected, from a description of Nahataspe's hut, that a simple wall at right angles to the door would have kept all really important demons out. When Royland described his escape from German territory to Japanese, and why he had effected it, he was very bland and blank. Royland judged that Li Po privately thought him not very bright for having left *any* place to come here.

And Royland hoped he was not right. "Tell me what it's like," he said.

"This realm," said Li Po, "under our benevolent and noble overlords, is the haven of all whose skin is not the bleached-bone hue which indicates the undying curse of the Celestial Ones. Hither flock men of Han like my unworthy self, and the sons of Hind beyond the Tian-Shang, that we may till new soil and raise up sons, and sons of sons to venerate us when we ascend."

"What was that bit," Royland demanded, "about the bleached bones? Do they shoot, ah, white men on sight here, or do they not?"

Li Po said evasively: "We are approaching the village where I unworthily serve as fortune-teller, doctor of *fung shui,* occasional poet, and storyteller. Let my master have no fear about his color. This humble one will roughen his master's skin, tell a circumstantial and artistic lie or two, and pass his master off as merely a leper."

After a week in Li Po's village Royland knew that life was good there. The place was a wattle-and-clay settlement of about two hundred souls on the bank of an irrigation ditch large enough to be dignified by the name of "canal." It was situated nobody knew just where; Royland thought it must be the San Fernando Valley. The soil was thick and rich and bore furiously the year round. A huge kind of radish was the principal crop. It was too coarse to be eaten by man; the villagers understood that it was feed for chickens somewhere up north. At any rate they harvested the stuff, fed it through a great hand-powered shredder, and shade-cured the shreds. Every few days a Japanese of low caste would come by in a truck, they would load tons of the stuff onto it, and wave their giant radish goodbye forever. Presumably the chickens ate it, and the Japanese then ate the chickens.

The villagers ate chicken, too, but only at weddings and funerals. The rest of the time they ate vegetables that they cultivated, a quarter-acre to a family, the way other craftsmen facet diamonds. A single cabbage might receive, during its ninety days from planting to maturity, one hundred work hours from grandmother, grandfather, son, daughter, eldest grandchild, and on down to the smallest toddler. Theoretically the entire family line should have starved to death, for there are not one hundred energy hours in a cabbage; somehow they did not. They merely stayed thin and cheerful and hard-working and fecund.

They spoke English by Imperial decree; the reasoning seemed to be that they were as unworthy to speak Japanese as to paint the Imperial Chrysanthemum Seal on their houses, and that to let them cling to their old languages and dialects would have been politically unwise.

They were a mixed lot of Chinese, Hindus, Dravidians, and, to Royland's surprise, low-caste and outcaste Japanese; he had not known there were such things. Village tradition had it that a samurai named Ugetsu long ago said, pointing at the drunk tank of a Hong Kong jail, "I'll have that lot," and "that lot" had been the ancestors of these villagers transported to America in a foul hold practically as ballast and settled here by the canal with orders to start making their radish quota. The place was at any rate called The Ugetsu Village, and if some of the descendants were teetotallers, others like Li Po gave color to the legend of their starting point.

After a week the cheerful pretense that he was a sufferer from Hansen's disease evaporated and he could wash the mud off his face. He had merely to avoid the upper-caste Japanese and especially the samurai. This was not exactly a stigma; in general it was a good idea for *everybody* to avoid the samurai.

In the village Royland found his first love and his first religion both false.

He had settled down; he was getting used to the oriental work rhythm of slow, repeated, incessant effort; it did not surprise him any longer that he could count his ribs. When he ate a bowl of artfully arranged vegetables, the red of pimiento played off against the yellow of parsnip, a slice of pickled beet adding visual and olfactory tang to the picture, he felt full enough; he *was* full enough for the next day's feeble work in the field. It was pleasant enough to play slowly with a wooden mattock in the rich soil; did not people once buy sand so their children might do exactly what he did, and envy their innocent absorption? Royland was innocently absorbed, then, and the radish truck had collected six times since his arrival, when he began to feel stirrings of lust. On the edge of starvation (but who knew this? for everybody was) his mind was dulled, but not his loins. They burned, and he looked about him in the fields, and the first girl he saw who was not repulsive he fell abysmally in love with.

Bewildered, he told Li Po, who was also Ugetsu Village's go-between. The storyteller was delighted; he waddled off to seek information and returned. "My master's choice is wise. The slave on whom his lordly eye deigned to rest is known as Vashti, daughter of Hari Bose, the distiller. She is his seventh child and so no great dowry can be expected (I shall ask for fifteen kegs toddy but would settle for seven), but all this humble village knows that she is a skilled and willing worker in the hut as in the fields. I fear she has the customary lamentable Hindu talent for concocting curries, but a dozen good beatings at the most should cause her to reserve it to appropriate occasions, such as visits from her mother and sisters."

So, according to the sensible custom of Ugetsu, Vashti came that night to the hut which Royland shared with Li Po, and Li Po visited with cronies by his master's puzzling request. He begged humbly to point out that it would be dark in the hut, so this talk of lacking privacy was inexplicable to say the least. Royland made it an order, and Li Po did not really object, so he obeyed it.

It was a damnably strange night during which Royland learned all about India's national sport and most highly developed art form. Vashti, if she found him weak on the theory side, made no complaints. On the contrary, when Royland woke she was doing something or other to his feet.

"More?" he thought incredulously. "With *feet?*" He asked what she was doing. Submissively she replied: "Worshiping my lord husband-to-be's big toe. I am a pious and old-fashioned woman."

So she painted his toe with red paint and prayed to it, and then she fixed breakfast—curry, and excellent. She watched him eat, and then modestly licked his leavings from the bowl. She handed him his clothes, which she had washed while he still slept, and helped him into them after she helped him wash. Royland thought incredulously: "It's not possible! It must be a show, to sell me on marrying her—as if I had to be sold!" His heart turned to custard as he saw her, without a moment's pause, turn from dressing him to polishing his wooden rake. He asked that day in the field, roundabout fashion, and learned that this was the kind of service he could look forward to for the rest of his life after marriage. If the woman got lazy he'd have to beat her, but this seldom happened more than every year or so. We have good girls here in Ugetsu Village.

So an Ugetsu Village peasant was in some ways better off than anybody from "his time" who was less than a millionaire!

His starved dullness was such that he did not realize this was true for only half the Ugetsu Village peasants.

Religion sneaked up on him in similar fashion. He went to the part-time Taoist priest because he was a little bored with Li Po's current after-dinner saga. He could have sat like all the others and listened passively to the interminable tale of the glorious Yellow Emperor, and the beautiful but wicked Princess Emerald, and the virtuous but plain Princess Moon Blossom; it just happened that he went to the priest of Tao and got hooked hard.

The kindly old man, a toolmaker by day, dropped a few pearls of wisdom which, in his foggy starvation-daze, Royland did not perceive to be pearls of undemonstrable nonsense, and showed Royland how to meditate. It worked the first time. Royland bunged right smack through into a two-hundred-proof state of *samadhi*—the Eastern version of self-hypnotized Enlightenment—that made him feel wonderful and all-knowing and left him without a hangover when it wore off. He had despised, in college, the type of people who took psychology courses and so had taken none himself; he did not know a thing about self-hypnosis except as just demonstrated by this very nice old gentleman. For several days he was offensively religious and kept trying to talk to Li Po about the Eightfold Way, and Li Po kept changing the subject.

It took murder to bring him out of love and religion.

At twilight they were all sitting and listening to the storyteller as usual. Royland had been there just one month and for all he knew would be there forever. He soon would have his bride officially; he knew he had discovered The Truth About the Universe by way of Tao meditation; why should he change? Changing demanded a furious outburst of energy, and he did not have energy on that scale. He metered out his energy day and night; one had to save so much for tonight's love play, and then one had to save so much for tomorrow's planting. He was a poor man; he could not afford to change.

Li Po had reached a rather interesting bit where the Yellow Emperor was declaiming hotly: "Then she shall die! Whoever dare transgress Our divine will—"

A flashlight began to play over their faces. They perceived that it was in the hand of a samurai with kimono and sword. Everybody hastily kowtowed, but the samurai shouted irritably (all samurai were irritable, all the time): "Sit up, you fools! I want to see your stupid faces. I hear there's a peculiar one in this flea-bitten dungheap you call a village."

Well, by now Royland knew his duty. He rose and with downcast eyes asked: "Is the noble protector in search of my unworthy self?"

"Ha!" the samurai roared. "It's true! A big nose!" He hurled the flashlight away (all samurai were nobly contemptuous of the merely material), held his scabbard in his left hand, and swept out the long curved sword with his right.

Li Po stepped forward and said in his most enchanting voice: "If the Heaven-born would only deign to heed a word from this humble—" What he must have known would happen happened. With a contemptuous backhand sweep of the blade the samurai beheaded him and Li Po's debt was paid.

The trunk of the storyteller stood for a moment and then fell stiffly forward. The samurai stooped to wipe his blade clean on Li Po's ragged robes.

Royland had forgotten much, but not everything. With the villagers scattering before him he plunged forward and tackled the samurai low and hard. No doubt the samurai was a Brown Belt judo master; if so he had nobody but himself to blame for turning his back. Royland, not remembering that he was barefoot, tried to kick the samurai's face in. He broke his worshipful big toe, but its untrimmed horny nail removed the left eye of the warrior and after that it was no contest. He never let the samurai get up off the ground; he took out his other eye with the handle of a rake and then killed him an inch at a time with his hands, his feet, and the clownish rustic's traditional weapon, a flail. It took easily half an hour, and for the final twenty minutes the samurai was screaming for his mother. He died when the last light left the western sky, and in darkness Royland stood quite alone with the two corpses. The villagers were gone.

He assumed, or pretended, that they were within earshot and yelled at them brokenly: "I'm sorry, Vashti. I'm sorry, all of you. I'm going. Can I make you understand?

"Listen. You aren't living. This isn't life. You're not making anything but babies, you're not changing, you're not growing up. That's not enough! You've got to read and write. You can't pass on anything but baby stories like the Yellow Emperor by word of mouth. The village is growing. Soon your fields will touch the fields of Sukoshi Village to the west, and then what happens? You won't know what to do, so you'll fight with Sukoshi Village.

"Religion. No! It's just getting drunk the way you do it. You're set up for it by being half-starved and then you go into *samadhi* and you feel better so you think you understand everything. No! You've got to *do* things. If you don't grow up, you die. All of you.

"Women. *That's* wrong. It's good for the men, but it's wrong. Half of you are slaves, do you understand? Women are people, too, but you use them like animals and you've convinced them it's right for them to be old at thirty and discarded for the next girl. For God's sake, can't you try to think of yourselves in their place?

"The breeding, the crazy breeding—it's got to stop. You frugal Orientals! But you aren't frugal; you're crazy drunken sailors. You're squandering the whole world. Every mouth you breed has got to be fed by the land, and the land isn't infinite.

"I hope some of you understood. Li Po would have, a little, but he's dead.

"I'm going away now. You've been kind to me and all I've done is make trouble. I'm sorry."

He fumbled on the ground and found the samurai's flashlight. With it he hunted the village's outskirts until he found the Japanese's buckboard car. He started the motor with its crank and noisily rolled down the dirt track from the village to the highway.

Royland drove all night, still westward. His knowledge of southern California's geography was inexact, but he hoped to hit Los Angeles.

There might be a chance of losing himself in a great city. He had abandoned hope of finding present-day counterparts of his old classmates like Jimmy Ichimura; obviously they had lost out. Why shouldn't they have lost? The soldier-politicians had won the war by happenstance, so all power to the soldier-politicians! Reasoning under the great natural law *post hoc ergo propter hoc,* Tojo and his crowd had decided: fanatic feudalism won the war; therefore fanatic feudalism is a good thing, and it necessarily follows that the more fanatical and feudal it is, the better a thing it is. So you had Sukoshi Village, and Ugetsu Village; Ichi Village, Ni Village, San Village, Shi Village, dotting that part of Great Japan formerly known as North America, breeding with the good old fanatic feudalism and so feudally averse to new thought and innovations that it made you want to scream at them—which he had.

The single weak headlight of his buckboard passed few others on the road; a decent feudal village is self-contained.

Damn them and their suicidal cheerfulness! It was a pleasant trait; it was a fool in a canoe approaching the rapids saying: "Chin up! Everything's going to be all right if we just keep smiling."

The car ran out of gas when false dawn first began to pale the sky behind him. He pushed it into the roadside ditch and walked on; by full light he was in a tumble-down, planless, evil-smelling, paper-and-galvanized-iron city whose name he did not know. There was no likelihood of him being noticed as a "white" man by anyone not specifically looking for him. A month of outdoor labor had browned him, and a month of artistically composed vegetable plates had left him gaunt.

The city was carpeted with awakening humanity. Its narrow streets were paved with sprawled-out men, women, and children beginning to stir and hawk up phlegm and rub their rheumy eyes. An open sewer-latrine running down the center of each street was casually used, ostrich-fashion —the users hid their own eyes while in action.

Every mangled variety of English rang in Royland's ears as he trod between bodies.

There had to be something more, he told himself. This was the shabby industrial outskirts, the lowest marginal-labor area. Somewhere in the city there was beauty, science, learning!

He walked aimlessly plodding until noon and found nothing of the sort. These people in the cities were food-handlers, food-traders, food-transporters. They took in one another's washing and sold one another chop suey. They made automobiles (Yes! There were one-family automobile factories that probably made six buckboards a year, filing all metal parts by hand out of bar stock!) and orange crates and baskets and coffins; abacuses, nails, and boots.

The Mysterious East has done it again, he thought bitterly. The Indians-Chinese-Japanese won themselves a nice sparse area. They could have laid things out neatly and made it pleasant for everybody instead of for a minute speck of aristocracy that he was unable even to detect in this human soup . . . but they had done it again. They had bred irresponsibly just as fast as they could until the land was *full.* Only famines and pestilence could "help" them now.

He found exactly one building that owned some clear space around it and that would survive an earthquake or a flicked cigarette butt. It was the German Consulate.

I'll give them the Bomb, he said to himself. Why not? None of this is mine. And for the Bomb I'll exact a price of some comfort and dignity for as long as I live. *Let* them blow one another up! He climbed the consulate steps.

To the black-uniformed guard at the swastika-trimmed bronze doors he said: *"Wenn die Lichtstärke der von einer Fläche kommenden Strahlung dem Cosinus des Winkels zwischen Strahlrichtung und Flächennormalen proportional ist, so nennen wir die Fläche eine volkommen streunde Fläche."* Lambert's Law, Optics I. All the Goethe he remembered happened to rhyme, which might have made the guard suspicious.

Naturally the German came to attention and said apologetically: "I don't speak German. What is it, sir?"

"You may take me to the consul," Royland said, affecting boredom.

"Yes, sir. At once, sir. Er, you're an *agent* of course, sir?"

Royland said witheringly: *"Sicherheit, bitte!"*

"Yessir. This way, sir!"

The consul was a considerate, understanding gentleman. He was somewhat surprised by Royland's true tale, but said from time to time: "I see; I see. Not impossible. Please go on."

Royland concluded: "Those people at the sulfur mine were, I hope, unrepresentative. One of them at least complained that it was a dreary sort of backwoods assignment. I am simply gambling that there is intelligence in your Reich. I ask you to get me a real physicist for twenty minutes of conversation. You, Mr. Consul, will not regret it. I am in a position to turn over considerable information on—atomic power." So he had not been able to say it after all; the Bomb was still an obscene kick below the belt.

"This has been very interesting, Dr. Royland," said the consul gravely.

"You referred to your enterprise as a gamble. I too shall gamble. What have I to lose by putting you *en rapport* with a scientist of ours if you prove to be a plausible lunatic?" He smiled to soften it. "Very little indeed. On the other hand, what have I to gain if your extraordinary story is quite true? A great deal. I will go along with you, doctor. Have you eaten?"

The relief was tremendous. He had lunch in a basement kitchen with the Consulate guards—a huge lunch, a rather nasty lunch of stewed *Lungen* with a floured gravy, and cup after cup of coffee. Finally one of the guards lit up an ugly little spindle-shaped cigar, the kind Royland had only seen before in the caricatures of George Grosz, and as an afterthought offered one to him.

He drank in the rank smoke and managed not to cough. It stung his mouth and cut the greasy aftertaste of the stew satisfactorily. One of the blessings of the Third Reich, one of its gross pleasures. They were just people, after all—a certain censorious, busybody type of person with altogether too much power, but they were human. By which he meant, he supposed, members of Western Industrial Culture like him.

After lunch he was taken by truck from the city to an airfield by one of the guards. The plane was somewhat bigger than a B-29 he had once seen, and lacked propellers. He presumed it was one of the "jets" Dr. Piqueron had mentioned. His guard gave his dossier to a Luftwaffe sergeant at the foot of the ramp and said cheerfully: "Happy landings, fellow. It's all going to be all right."

"Thanks," he said. "I'll remember you, Corporal Collins. You've been very helpful." Collins turned away.

Royland climbed the ramp into the barrel of the plane. A bucket-seat job, and most of the seats were filled. He dropped into one on the very narrow aisle. His neighbor was in rags; his face showed signs of an old beating. When Royland addressed him, he simply cringed away and began to sob.

The Luftwaffe sergeant came up, entered, and slammed the door. The "jets" began to wind up, making an unbelievable racket; further conversation was impossible. While the plane taxied, Royland peered through the windowless gloom at his fellow-passengers. They all looked poor and poorly.

God, were they so quickly and quietly airborne? They were. Even in the bucket seat, Royland fell asleep.

He was awakened, he did not know how much later, by the sergeant. The man was shaking his shoulder and asking him: "Any joolery hid away? Watches? Got some nice fresh water to sell to people that wanna buy it."

Royland had nothing and would not take part in the miserable little racket if he had. He shook his head indignantly and the man moved on with a grin. He would not last long!—petty chiselers were leaks in the efficient dictatorship; they were rapidly detected and stopped up. Mussolini made the trains run on time, after all. (But naggingly Royland recalled mentioning this to a Northwestern University English professor, one Bevans. Bevans had coldly informed him that from 1931 to 1936 he had lived under Mussolini as a student and tourist guide, and therefore had extraordinary opportunities for observing whether the trains ran on time or not, and could definitely state that they did not; that railway timetables under Mussolini were best regarded as humorous fiction.)

And another thought nagged at him, a thought connected with a pale, scarred face named Bloom. Bloom was a young refugee physical chemist working on WEAPONS DEVELOPMENT TRACK I, and he was somewhat crazy, perhaps. Royland, on TRACK III, used to see little of him and could have done with even less. You couldn't say hello to the man without it turning into a lecture on the horrors of Nazism. He had wild stories about "gas chambers" and crematoria that no reasonable man could believe and was a blanket slanderer of the German medical profession. He claimed that trained doctors, certified men, used human beings in experiments that terminated fatally. Once, to try and bring Bloom to reason, he asked what sort of experiments these were, but the monomaniac had heard that worked out: piffling nonsense about reviving mortally frozen men by putting naked women into bed with them! The man was probably sexually deranged to believe that; he naively added that one variable in the series of experiments was to use women immediately after sexual intercourse, one hour after sexual intercourse, et cetera. Royland had blushed for him and violently changed the subject.

But that was not what he was groping for. Neither was Bloom's crazy story about the woman who made lampshades from the tattooed skin of concentration-camp prisoners; there were people capable of such things, of course, but under no regime whatever do they rise to positions of authority; they simply can't do the work required in positions of authority because their insanity gets in the way.

"Know your enemy," of course—but making up pointless lies? At least Bloom was not the conscious prevaricator. He got letters in Yiddish from friends and relations in Palestine, and these were laden with the latest wild rumors supposed to be based on the latest word from "escapees."

Now he remembered. In the cafeteria about three months ago Bloom had been sipping tea with somewhat shaking hand and rereading a letter.

Royland tried to pass him with only a nod, but the skinny hand shot out and held him.

Bloom looked up with tears in his eyes: "It's cruel, I'm tellink you, Royland, it's cruel. They're not givink them the right to scream, to strike a futile blow, to sayink prayers *Kiddush ha Shem* like a Jew should when he is dyink for Consecration of the Name! They trick them, they say they go to farm settlements, to labor camps, so four-five of the stinkink bastards can handle a whole trainload Jews. They trick the clothes off of them at the camps, they sayink they delouse them. They trick them into room says showerbath over the door and then is too late to sayink prayers; *then goes on the gas.*"

Bloom had let go of him and put his head on the table between his hands. Royland had mumbled something, patted his shoulder, and walked on, shaken. For once the neurotic little man might have got some straight facts. That was a very circumstantial touch about expediting the handling of prisoners by systematic lies—always the carrot and the stick.

Yes, everybody had been so goddamn agreeable since he climbed the Consulate steps! The friendly door guard, the Consul who nodded and remarked that his story was not an impossible one, the men he'd eaten with—all that quiet optimism. "Thanks. I'll remember you, Corporal Collins. You've been very helpful." He had felt positively benign toward the corporal, and now remembered that the corporal had turned around *very* quickly after he spoke. *To hide a grin?*

The guard was working his way down the aisle again and noticed that Royland was awake. "Changed your mind by now?" he asked kindly. "Got a good watch, maybe I'll find a piece of bread for you. You won't need a watch where you're going, fella."

"What do you mean?" Royland demanded.

The guard said soothingly: "Why, they got clocks all over them work camps, fella. Everybody knows what time it is in them work camps. You don't need no watches there. Watches just get in the way at them work camps." He went on down the aisle, quickly.

Royland reached across the aisle and, like Bloom, gripped the man who sat opposite him. He could not see much of him; the huge windowless plane was lit only by half a dozen stingy bulbs overhead. "What are you here for?" he asked.

The man said shakily: "I'm a Laborer Two, see? A Two. Well, my father he taught me to read, see, but he waited until I was ten and knew the score? See? So I figured it was a family tradition, so I taught my own kid to read because he was a pretty smart kid, ya know? I figured he'd have some fun reading like I did, no harm done, who's to know, ya know? But I should of waited a couple of years, I guess, because the kid was too young and got to bragging he could read, ya know how kids do? I'm from St. Louis, by the way. I should of said first I'm from St. Louis, a track maintenance man, see, so I hopped a string of returning empties for San Diego because I was scared like you get."

He took a deep sigh. "Thirsty," he said. "Got in with some Chinks, nobody to trouble ya, ya stay outta the way, but then one of them cops-like seen me and he took me to the Consul place like they do, ya know? Had me scared, they always tole me illegal reading they bump ya off, but they don't, ya know? Two years work camp, how about that?"

Yes, Royland wondered, How about it?

The plane decelerated sharply; he was thrown forward. Could they brake with those "jets" by reversing the stream or were the engines just throttling down? He heard gurgling and thudding; hydraulic fluid to the actuators letting down the landing gear. The wheels bumped a moment later and he braced himself; the plane was still and the motors cut off seconds later.

Their Luftwaffe sergeant unlocked the door and bawled through it: "Shove that goddamn ramp, willya?" The sergeant's assurance had dropped from him; he looked like a very scared man. He must have been a very brave one, really, to have let himself be locked in with a hundred doomed men, protected only by an eight-shot pistol and a chain of systematic lies.

They were herded out of the plane onto a runway of what Royland immediately identified as the Chicago Municipal Airport. The same reek wafted from the stockyards; the row of airline buildings at the eastern edge of the field was ancient and patched but unchanged; the hangars, though, were now something that looked like inflated plastic bags. A good trick. Beyond the buildings surely lay the dreary red-brick and painted-siding wastes of Cicero, Illinois.

Luftwaffe men were yapping at them: "Form up, boys; make a line! Work means freedom! Look tall!" They shuffled and were shoved into columns of fours. A snappy majorette in shiny satin panties and white boots pranced out of an administration building twirling her baton; a noisy march blared from louvers in her tall fur hat. Another good trick.

"Forward march, boys," she shrilled at them. "Wouldn't y'all just like to follow me?" Seductive smile and a wiggle of the rump; a Judas ewe. She strutted off in time to the music; she must have been wearing earstopples. They shuffled after her. At the airport gate they dropped their blue-coated

Luftwaffe boys and picked up a waiting escort of a dozen black-coats with skulls on their high-peaked caps.

They walked in time to the music, hypnotized by it, through Cicero. Cicero had been bombed to hell and not rebuilt. To his surprise Royland felt a pang for the vanished Poles and Slovaks of Al's old bailiwick. There were *German* Germans, French Germans, and even Italian Germans, but he knew in his bones that there were no Polish or Slovakian Germans. . . . And Bloom had been right all along.

Deathly weary after two hours of marching (the majorette was indefatigable), Royland looked up from the broken pavement to see a cockeyed wonder before him. It was a Castle; it was a Nightmare; it was the Chicago Parteihof. The thing abutted Lake Michigan; it covered perhaps sixteen city blocks. It frowned down on the lake at the east and at the tumbled acres of bombed-out Chicago at the north, west, and south. It was made of steel-reinforced concrete grained and grooved to look like medieval masonry. It was walled, moated, portcullised, towered, ramparted, crenellated. The death's-head guards looked at it reverently and the prisoners with fright. Royland wanted only to laugh wildly. It was a Disney production. It was as funny as Hermann Goering in full fig, and probably as deadly.

With a mumbo jumbo of passwords, heils, and salutes they were admitted, and the majorette went away, no doubt to take off her boots and groan.

The most bedecked of the death's head lined them up and said affably: "Hot dinner and your beds presently, my boys; first a selection. Some of you, I'm afraid, aren't well and should be in sick bay. Who's sick? Raise your hands, please."

A few hands crept up. Stooped old men.

"That's right. Step forward, please." Then he went down the line tapping a man here and there—one fellow with glaucoma, another with terrible varicose sores visible through the tattered pants he wore. Mutely they stepped forward. Royland he looked thoughtfully over. "You're thin, my boy," he observed. "Stomach pains? Vomit blood? Tarry stools in the morning?"

"Nossir!" Royland barked. The man laughed and continued down the line. The "sick bay" detail was marched off. Most of them were weeping silently; they knew. Everybody knew; everybody pretended that the terrible thing would not, might not, happen. It was much more complex than Royland had realized.

"Now," said the death's head affably, "we require some competent cement workers—"

The line of remaining men went mad. They surged forward almost touching the officer but never stepping over an invisible line surrounding him. "Me!" some yelled. "Me! Me!" Another cried: "I'm good with my hands, I can learn, I'm a machinist too, I'm strong and young, I can learn!" A heavy middle-aged one waved his hands in the air and boomed: "Grouting and tile-setting! Grouting and tile-setting!" Royland stood alone, horrified. They knew. They knew this was an offer of real work that would keep them alive for a while.

He knew suddenly how to live in a world of lies.

The officer lost his patience in a moment or two, and whips came out. Men with their faces bleeding struggled back into line. "Raise your hands, you cement people, and no lying, please. But you wouldn't lie, would you?" He picked half a dozen volunteers after questioning them briefly, and one of his men marched them off. Among them was the grouting-and-tile man, who looked pompously pleased with himself; such was the reward of diligence and virtue, he seemed to be proclaiming; pooh to those grasshoppers back there who neglected to learn A Trade.

"Now," said the officer casually, "we require some laboratory assistants." The chill of death stole down the line of prisoners. Each one seemed to shrivel into himself, become poker-faced, imply that he wasn't really involved in all this.

Royland raised his hand. The officer looked at him in stupefaction and then covered up quickly. "Splendid," he said. "Step forward, my boy. You," he pointed at another man. "You have an intelligent forehead; you look as if you'd make a fine laboratory assistant. Step forward."

"Please, no!" the man begged. He fell to his knees and clasped his hands in supplication. "Please no!" The officer took out his whip meditatively; the man groaned, scrambled to his feet, and quickly stood beside Royland.

When there were four more chosen, they were marched off across the concrete yard into one of the absurd towers, and up a spiral staircase and down a corridor, and through the promenade at the back of an auditorium where a woman screamed German from the stage at an audience of women. And through a tunnel and down the corridor of an elementary school with empty classrooms full of small desks on either side. And into a hospital area where the fake-masonry walls yielded to scrubbed white tile and the fake flagstones underfoot to composition flooring and the fake pinewood torches in bronze brackets that had lighted their way to fluorescent tubes.

At the door marked RASSENWISSENSCHAFT the guard rapped and a frosty-faced man in a laboratory coat opened up. "You requisitioned a demonstrator, Dr. Kalten," the guard said. "Pick any one of these."

Dr. Kalten looked them over. "Oh, this one, I suppose," he said, indicating Royland. "Come in, fellow."

The Race Science Laboratory of Dr. Kalten proved to be a decent medical setup with an operating table and intricate charts of the races of men and their anatomical, mental, and moral makeups. There were also a phrenological head diagram and a horoscope on the wall, and an arrangement of glittering crystals on wire that Royland recognized. It was a model of one Hans Hoerbiger's crackpot theory of planetary formation, the *Welteislehre*.

"Sit there," the doctor said, pointing to a stool. "First I've got to take your pedigree. By the way, you might as well know that you're going to end up dissected for my demonstration in Race Science III for the Medical School, and your degree of cooperation will determine whether the dissection is performed under anaesthesia or not. Clear?"

"Clear, doctor."

"Curious—no panic. I'll wager we find you're a proto-Hamitoidal hemi-Nordic of at *least* degree five . . . but let's get on. Name?"

"Edward Royland."

"Birthdate?"

"July second, nineteen twenty-three."

The doctor threw down his pencil. "If my previous explanation was inadequate," he shouted, "let me add that if you continue to be difficult I may turn you over to my good friend Dr. Herzbrenner. Dr. Herzbrenner happens to teach interrogation technique at the Gestapo School. *Do—you —now—understand?*"

"Yes, doctor. I'm sorry I cannot withdraw my answer."

Dr. Kalten turned elaborately sarcastic. "How then do you account for your remarkable state of preservation at your age of approximately a hundred and eighty years?"

"Doctor, I am twenty-three years old. I have traveled through time."

"Indeed?" Kalten was amused. "And how was this accomplished?"

Royland said steadily: "A spell was put on me by a satanic Jewish magician. It involved the ritual murder and desanguination of seven beautiful Nordic virgins."

Dr. Kalten gaped for a moment. Then he picked up his pencil and said firmly: "You will understand that my doubts were logical under the circumstances. Why did you not give me the sound scientific basis for your surprising claim at once? Go ahead; tell me all about it."

He was Dr. Kalten's prize; he was Dr. Kalten's treasure. His peculiari-

ties of speech, his otherwise-inexplicable absence of a birth number over
his left nipple, when they got around to it the gold filling in one of his
teeth, his uncanny knowledge of Old America, all now had a simple scientific explanation. He was from 1944. What was so hard to grasp about
that? Any sound specialist knew about the lost Jewish Cabala magic,
golems and such.

His story was that he had been a student Race Scientist under the
pioneering master William D. Pully. (A noisy whack who used to barn-
storm the chaw-and-gallus belt with the backing of Deutsches Neues
Buro; sure enough they found him in Volume VII of the standard *Introduction to a Historical Handbook of Race Science.)* The Jewish fiends had
attempted to ambush his master on a lonely road; Royland persuaded him
to switch hats and coats; in the darkness the substitution was not noticed.
Later in their stronghold he was identified, but the Nordic virgins had
already been ritually murdered and drained of their blood, and it wouldn't
keep. The dire fate destined for the master had been visited upon the
disciple.

Dr. Kalten loved that bit. It tickled him pink that the submen's "revenge" on their enemy had been to precipitate him into a world purged of
the submen entirely, where a Nordic might breathe freely!

Kalten, except for discreet consultations with such people as Old America specialists, a dentist who was stupefied by the gold filling, and a derma-
tologist who established that there was not and never had been a *Geburtsnummer* on the subject examined, was playing Royland close to his vest.
After a week it became apparent that he was reserving Royland for a grand
unveiling that would climax the reading of a paper. Royland did not want
to be unveiled; there were too many holes in his story. He talked with
animation about the beauties of Mexico in the spring, its fair mesas,
cactus, and mushrooms. Could they make a short trip there? Dr. Kalten
said they could not. Royland was becoming restless? Let him study, learn,
profit by the matchless arsenal of the sciences available here in Chicago
Parteihof. Dear old Chicago boasted distinguished exponents of the
World Ice Theory, the Hollow World Theory, Dowsing, Homeopathic
Medicine, Curative Folk Botany—

This last did sound interesting. Dr. Kalten was pleased to take his prize
to the Medical School and introduce him as a protégé to Professor Albiani, of Folk Botany.

Albiani was a bearded gnome out of the Arthur Rackham illustrations
for *Das Rheingold.* He loved his subject. "Mother Nature, the all-bounte-
ous one! Wander the fields, young man, and with a seeing eye in an hour's
stroll you will find the ergot that aborts, the dill that cools fever, the tansy

that strengthens the old, the poppy that soothes the fretful teething babe!"

"Do you have any hallucinogenic Mexican mushrooms?" Royland demanded.

"We may," Albiani said, surprised. They browsed through the Folk Botany museum and pored over dried vegetation under glass. From Mexico there were peyote, the buttons and the root, and there was marihuana, root, stem, seed, and stalk. No mushrooms.

"They may be in the storeroom," Albiani muttered.

All the rest of the day Royland mucked through the storeroom where specimens were waiting for exhibit space on some rotation plan. He went to Albiani and said, a little wild-eyed: "They're not there."

Albiani had been interested enough to look up the mushrooms in question in the reference books. "See?" he said happily, pointing to a handsome color plate of the mushroom: growing, mature, sporing, and dried. He read: " '. . . superstitiously called *God Food*,' " and twinkled through his beard at the joke.

"They're not there," Royland said.

The professor, annoyed at last, said: "There might be some uncatalogued in the basement. Really, we don't have room for everything in our limited display space—just the *interesting* items."

Royland pulled himself together and charmed the location of the department's basement storage space out of him, together with permission to inspect it. And, left alone for a moment, ripped the color plate from the professor's book and stowed it away.

That night Royland and Dr. Kalten walked out on one of the innumerable tower-tops for a final cigar. The moon was high and full; its light turned the cratered terrain that had been Chicago into another moon. The sage and his disciple from another day leaned their elbows on a crenellated rampart two hundred feet above Lake Michigan.

"Edward," said Dr. Kalten, "I shall read my paper tomorrow before the Chicago Academy of Race Science." The words were a challenge; something was wrong. He went on: "I shall expect you to be in the wings of the auditorium, and to appear at my command to answer a few questions from me and, if time permits, from our audience."

"I wish it could be postponed," Royland said.

"No doubt."

"Would you explain your unfriendly tone of voice, doctor?" Royland demanded. "I think I've been completely cooperative and have opened the way for you to win undying fame in the annals of Race Science."

"Cooperative, yes. Candid—I wonder? You see, Edward, a dreadful thought struck me today. I have always thought it amusing that the Jewish attack of Reverend Pully should have been for the purpose of precipitating him into the future and that it should have misfired." He took something out of his pocket: a small pistol. He aimed it casually at Royland. "Today I began to wonder *why* they should have done so. Why did they not simply murder him, as they did thousands, and dispose of him in their secret crematoria, and permit no mention in their controlled newspapers and magazines of the disappearance?

"Now, the blood of seven Nordic virgins can have been no cheap commodity. One pictures with ease Nordic men patrolling their precious enclaves of humanity, eyes roving over every passing face, noting who bears the stigmata of the submen, and following those who do most carefully indeed lest race-defilement be committed with a look or an 'accidental' touch in a crowded street. Nevertheless the thing was done; your presence here is proof of it. It must have been done at enormous cost; hired Slavs and Negroes must have been employed to kidnap the virgins, and many of them must have fallen before Nordic rage.

"This merely to silence one small voice crying in the wilderness? *I— think—not.* I think, Edward Royland, or whatever your real name may be, that Jewish arrogance sent you, a Jew yourself, into the future as a greeting from the Jewry of that day to what it foolishly thought would be the triumphant Jewry of this. At any rate the public questioning tomorrow will be conducted by my friend Dr. Herzbrenner, whom I have mentioned to you. If you have any little secrets, they will not remain secrets long. No, no! Do not move toward me. I shall shoot you disablingly in the knee if you do."

Royland moved toward him and the gun went off; there was an agonizing hammer blow high on his left shin. He picked up Kalten and hurled him, screaming, over the parapet two hundred feet into the water. And collapsed. The pain was horrible. His shinbone was badly cracked if not broken through. There was not much bleeding; maybe there would be later. He need not fear that the shot and scream would rouse the castle. Such sounds were not rare in the Medical Wing.

He dragged himself, injured leg trailing, to the doorway of Kalten's living quarters; he heaved himself into a chair by the signal bell and threw a rug over his legs. He rang for the diener and told him very quietly: "Go to the medical storeroom for a leg U-brace and whatever is necessary for a cast, please. Dr. Kalten has an interesting idea he wishes to work out."

He should have asked for a syringe of morphine—no he shouldn't. It might affect the time distortion.

When the man came back he thanked him and told him to turn in for the night.

He almost screamed getting his shoe off; his trouser leg he cut away. The gauze had arrived just in time; the wound was beginning to bleed more copiously. Pressure seemed to stop it. He constructed a sloppy walking cast on his leg. The directions on the several five-pound cans of plaster helped.

His leg was getting numb; good. His cast probably pinched some major nerve, and a week in it would cause permanent paralysis; who cared about *that?*

He tried it out and found he could get across the floor inefficiently. With a strong-enough bannister he could get downstairs but not, he thought, up them. That was all right. He was going to the basement.

Goddamning the medieval Nazis and their cornball castle every inch of the way, he went to the basement; there he had a windfall. A dozen drunken SS men were living it up in a corner far from the censorious eyes of their company commander; they were playing a game that might have been called Spin the Corporal. They saw Royland limping and wept sentimental tears for poor ol' doc with a bum leg; they carried him two winding miles to the storeroom he wanted, and shot the lock off for him. They departed, begging him to call on ol' Company K any time, bes' fellas in Chicago, doc. Ol' Bruno here can tear the arm off a Latvik shirker with his bare hands, honest, doc! Jus' the way you twist a drumstick off a turkey. You wan' us to get a Latvik an' show you?

He got rid of them at last, clicked on the light, and began his search. His leg was now ice cold, painfully so. He rummaged through the uncataloged botanicals and found after what seemed like hours a crate shipped from Jalasca. Royland opened it by beating its corners against the concrete floor. It yielded and spilled plastic envelopes; through the clear material of one he saw the wrinkled black things. He did not even compare them with the color plate in his pocket. He tore the envelope open and crammed them into his mouth, and chewed and swallowed.

Maybe there had to be a Hopi dancing and chanting, maybe there didn't have to be. Maybe one had to be calm, if bitter, and fresh from a day of hard work at differential equations which approximated the Hopi mode of thought. Maybe you only had to fix your mind savagely on what you desired, as his was fixed now. Last time he had hated and shunned the Bomb; what he wanted was a world without the Bomb. He had got it, all right!

. . . his tongue was thick and the fireballs were beginning to dance around him, the circling circles . . .

Charles Miller Nahataspe whispered: "Close. Close. I was so frightened."

Royland lay on the floor of the hut, his leg unsplinted, unfractured, but aching horribly. Drowsily he felt his ribs; he was merely slender now, no longer gaunt. He mumbled: "You were working to pull me back from this side?"

"Yes. You, you were there?"

"I was there. God, let me sleep."

He rolled over heavily and collapsed into complete unconsciousness.

When he awakened it was still dark and his pains were gone. Nahataspe was crooning a healing song very softly. He stopped when he saw Royland's eyes open. "Now you know about break-the-sky medicine," he said.

"Better than anybody. What time is it?"

"Midnight."

"I'll be going then." They clasped hands and looked into each other's eyes.

The jeep started easily. Four hours earlier, or possibly two months earlier, he had been worried about the battery. He chugged down the settlement road and knew what would happen next. He wouldn't wait until morning; a meteorite might kill him, or a scorpion in his bed. He would go directly to Rotschmidt in his apartment, defy Vrouw Rotschmidt and wake her man up to tell him about 56c, tell him we have the Bomb.

We have a symbol to offer the Japanese now, something to which they can surrender, and will surrender.

Rotschmidt would be philosophical. He would probably sigh about the Bomb: "Ah, do we ever act responsibly? Do we ever know what the consequences of our decisions will be?"

And Royland would have to try to avoid answering him very sharply: "Yes. This once we damn well do."

The Fall of
Frenchy Steiner

Hilary Bailey

Nineteen fifty-four was not a year of progress. A week before Christmas I walked into the bar of the Merrie Englande in Leicester Square, my guitar in its case, my hat in my hand. Two constables were sitting on wooden stools at the counter. Their helmets turned together as I walked in. The place was badly lit by candles, hiding the rundown look but not the rundown smell of home-brew and damp rot.

"Who's he?" said one of the PCs as I moved past.

"I work here," I said. Tired old dialogue for tired old people.

He grunted and sipped his drink. I didn't look at the barman. I didn't look at the cops. I just went into the room behind the bar and took off my coat. I went to the wash-basin, turned the taps. Nothing happened. I got my guitar out of its case, tested it, tuned it, and went back into the bar with it.

"Water's off again," said Jon, the barman. He was a flimsy wisp in black with a thin white face. "Nothing's working today . . ."

"Well, we've still got an efficient police force," I said. The cops turned to look at me again. I didn't care. I felt I could afford a little relaxation. One of them chewed the strap of his helmet and frowned. The other smiled.

"You work here do you, sir? How much does the boss pay you?" He continued to smile, speaking softly and politely. I sneered.

"Him?" I pointed with my thumb up to where the boss lived. "He wouldn't, even if it was légal." Then I began to worry. I'm like that—moody. "What are you doing here, anyway, officer?"

"Making enquiries, sir," said the frowning one.

"About a customer," said Jon. He leaned back against an empty shelf, his arms folded.

"That's right," said the smiling one.

"Who?"

The cops' eyes shifted.

"Frenchy," said Jon.

"So Frenchy's in trouble. It couldn't be something she's done. Someone she knows?"

The cops turned back to the bar. The frowning one said: "Two more. Does he know her?"

"As much as I do," said Jon, pouring out the potheen. The white, cloudy stuff filled the tumblers to the brim. Jon must be worried to pour such heavy ones for nothing.

I got up on to the platform where I sang, flicking the mike, which I knew would be dead as it had been since the middle of the war. I leaned my guitar against the dryest part of the wall and struck a match. I lit the two candles in their wall-holders. They didn't exactly fill the corner with a blaze of light, they smoked and guttered and stank and cast shadows. I wondered briefly who had supplied the fat. They weren't much good as heating either. It was almost as cold inside as out. I dusted off my stool and sat down, picked up my guitar, and struck a few chords. I hardly realised I was playing "Frenchy's Blues." It was one of those corny numbers that come easy to the fingers without you having to think about them.

Frenchy wasn't French, she was a kraut and who liked krauts? I liked Frenchy, along with all the customers who came to hear her sing to my accompaniment. Frenchy didn't work at the Merrie Englande, she just enjoyed singing. She didn't keep boyfriends long or often, she preferred to sing, she said.

"Frenchy's Blues" appealed only to the least sensitive members of our cordial clientele. I didn't care for it. I'd tried to do something good for her, but as with most things I tried to do well, it hadn't come off. I changed the tune. I was used to changing my tune. I played "Summertime" and then I played "Stormy Weather."

The cops sipped the drinks and waited. Jon leaned against the shelves, his narrow, black-clad body almost invisible in the shadow, only his thin face showing. We didn't look at one another. We were both scared—not only for Frenchy, but for ourselves. The cops had a habit of subpoenaing witnesses and forgetting to release them after the trial—particularly if they were healthy men who weren't already working in industry or the police force. Though I didn't have to fear this possibility as much as most, I was still worried.

During the evening I heard the dull sound of faraway bomb explosions, the drone of planes. That would be the English Luftwaffe doing exercises over the still-inhabited suburbs.

Customers came and most of them went after a drink and a squint at the constables.

Normally Frenchy came in between eight and nine, when she came. She didn't come. As we closed up around midnight, the cops got off their stools. One unbuttoned his tunic pocket and took out a notebook and pencil. He wrote on the pad, tore off the sheet, and left it on the bar.

"If she turns up, get in touch," he said. "Merry Christmas, sir," he nodded to me. They left.

I looked at the piece of paper. It was cheap, blotting-paper stuff and one corner was already soaking up spilled potheen. In large capitals the PC had printed: "Contact Det. Insp. Braun, N. Scot. Yd, Ph. WHI 1212, Ext. 615."

"Braun?" I smiled and looked up at Jon. "Brown?"

"What's in a name?" he said.

"At least it's CID. What do you think it's about, Jon?"

"You never can tell these days," said Jon. "Good night, Lowry."

"Night." I went into the room behind the bar, packed my guitar and put on my coat. Jon came in to get his street clothes.

"What do they want her for?" I said. "It's not political stuff, anyway. The Special Branch isn't interested, it seems. What—?"

"Who knows?" said Jon brusquely. "Goodnight—"

" 'Night," I said. I buttoned up my coat, pulled my gloves on, and picked up the guitar case. I didn't wait for Jon since he evidently wasn't seeking the company and comfort of an old pal. The cops seemed to have worried him. I wondered what he was organizing on the side. I decided to be less matey in future. For some time my motto had been simple—keep your nose clean.

I left the bar and entered the darkness of the square. It was empty. The iron railings and trees had gone during the war. Even the public lavatories were officially closed, though sometimes people slept in them. The tall buildings were stark against the night sky. I turned to my right and walked toward Piccadilly Circus, past the sagging hoardings that had been erected around bomb craters, treading on loose paving stones that rocked beneath my feet. Piccadilly Circus was as bare and empty as anywhere else. The steps were still in the center, but the statue of Eros wasn't there any more. Eros had flown from London toward the end of the war. I wish I'd had the same sense.

I crossed the circus and walked down Piccadilly itself, the wasteland of St. James's Park on one side, the tall buildings, or hoardings where they had been, on the other. I walked in the middle of the road, as was the custom. The occasional car was less of a risk than the frequent cosh-merchant. My hotel was in Piccadilly, just before you got to Park Lane.

I heard a helicopter fly over as I reached the building and unlocked the door. I closed the door behind me, standing in a wide, cold foyer un-lighted and silent. Outside the sound of the helicopter died and was replaced by the roar of about a dozen motorbikes heading in the general direction of Buckingham Palace, where Field Marshal Wilmot had his court. Wilmot wasn't the most popular man in Britain, but his efficiency was much admired in certain quarters. I crossed the foyer to the broad staircase. It was marble, but uncarpeted. The bannister rocked beneath my hand as I climbed the stairs.

A man passed me on my way up. He was an old man. He wore a red dressing gown and carried a chamber pot as far away from him as his shaking hand could stand.

"Good morning, Mr. Pevensey," I said.

"Good morning, Mr. Lowry," he replied, embarrassed. He coughed, started to speak, coughed again. As I began on the third flight, I heard him wheeze something about the water being off again. The water was off most of the time. It was news only when it came on. The gas came on three times a day for half an hour—if you were lucky. The electricity was supposed to run all day if people used the suggested ration, but nobody did, so power failures were frequent.

I had an oil stove, but no oil. Oil was expensive and could be got only on the black market. Using the black market meant risking being shot, so I did without oil. I had a place I used as a kitchen, too. There was a bathroom along the corridor. One of the rooms I used had a balcony overlooking the street with a nice view of the weed-tangled park. I didn't pay rent for these rooms. My brother paid it under the impression that I had no money. Vagrancy was a serious crime, though prevalent, and my brother didn't want me to be arrested because it caused him trouble to get me out of jail or one of the transit camps in Hyde Park.

I unlocked my door, tried the light switch, got no joy. I struck a match and lit four candles stuck in a candelabra on the heavy mantelpiece. I glanced in the mirror and didn't like the dull-eyed face I saw there. I was reckless. My next candle allowance was a month off but I'd always liked living dangerously. In a small way.

I put on my tattered tweed overcoat, Burberry's 1938, lay down on the dirty bed, and put my hands behind my head. I brooded.

I wasn't tired, but I didn't feel very well. How could I, on my rations?

I went back to thinking about Frenchy's trouble. It was better than thinking about trouble in general. She must be involved in something, although she never looked as if she had the energy to take off her slouch hat, let alone get mixed up in anything illegal. Still, since the krauts had taken over in 1946 it wasn't hard to do something illegal. As we used to say, if it wasn't forbidden, it was compulsory. Even strays and vagabonds like me were straying under license—in my case procured by brother Gottfried, ex-Godfrey, now Deputy Minister of Public Security. How he'd made it baffled me, with our background. Because obviously the first people the krauts had cleared out when they came to liberate us was the revolutionary element. And in England, of course, that wasn't the tattered, hungry mob rising in fury after centuries of oppression. It was the well-heeled, well-meaning law-civil-service-church-and-medicine brigade who came out of their warm houses to stir it all up.

Anyway, thinking about Godfrey always made my flesh creep, so I pulled my mind back to Frenchy. She was a tall, skinny rake of a girl, a worn-out, battered old twenty in a dirty white mac and a shapeless pull-down hat with the smell of a Cagney gangster film about it. I never noticed what was under the mac—she never took it off. Once or twice she'd gone mad and undone it. I had the impression that underneath she was wearing a dirty black mac. No stockings, muddy legs, shoes worn down to stubs, not exactly Ginger Rogers on the town with Fred Astaire. Still, the customers liked her singing, particularly her deadpan rendering of "Deutschland über Alles," slow, husky, and meaningful, with her white face staring out over the people at the bar. A kraut by nationality, but not by nature, that was Frenchy.

I yawned. Not much to do but go to sleep and try for that erotic dream where I was sinking my fork into a plate of steak and kidney pudding. Or perhaps, if I couldn't get to sleep, I'd try a nice stroll round the crater where St. Paul's had been—my favorite way of turning my usual depression into a really fruity attack of melancholia.

Then there was a knock.

I went rigid.

Late-night callers were usually cops. In a flash I saw my face with blood streaming from the mouth and a lot of black bruises. Then the knock came again. I relaxed. Cops never knocked twice—just a formal rap and then in and all over you.

The door opened and Frenchy stepped in. She closed the door behind her.

I was off the bed in a hurry.

I shook my head. "Sorry, Frenchy. It's no go."

She didn't move. She stared at me out of her dark blue eyes. The shadows underneath looked as though someone had put inky thumbs under them.

"Look, Frenchy," I said. "I've told you there's nothing doing." She ought to have gone before. It was the code. If someone wanted by the cops asked for help you had the right to tell them to go. No one thought any the worse of you. If you were a breadwinner it was expected.

She went on standing there. I took her by the shoulders, about faced her, wrenched the door open with one hand and ran her out on to the landing.

She turned to look at me. "I only came to borrow a fag," she said sadly, like a kid wrongfully accused of drawing on the wallpaper.

The code said I had to warn her, so I shoved her back into my room again.

She sat on my rumpled bed in the guttering candlelight with her beautiful, mud-streaked legs dangling over the side. I passed her a cigarette and lit it.

"There were two cops in the Merrie asking about you," I said. "CID!"

"Oh," she said blankly, "I wonder why? I haven't done anything."

"Passing on coupons, trying to buy things with money, leaving London without a pass—" I suggested. Oh, how I wanted to get her off the premises.

"No. I haven't done anything. Anyhow, they must know I've got a full passport."

I gaped at her. I knew she was a kraut—but why should she have a full passport? Owning one of those was like being invisible—people ignored what you did. You could take what you wanted from who you wanted. You could, if you felt like it, turn a dying old lady out of a hospital wagon so you could have a joyride, pinch food—anything. A sensible man who saw a full-passport holder coming toward him turned round and ran like hell in the other direction. He could shoot you and never be called to account. But how Frenchy had come by one beat me.

"You're not in the government," I said. "How is it you've got an FP?"

"My father's Willi Steiner."

I looked at her horrible hat, her draggled blonde hair, her filthy mac and scruffed shoes. My mouth tightened.

"You don't say?"

"My father's the Mayor of Berlin," she said flatly. "There are eight of us and mother's dead so no one cares much. But of course we've all got full passports."

"Well, what the hell are you shambling around starving in London for?"

"I don't know."

Suspicious, I said: "Let's have a look at it, then."

She opened her raincoat and reached down into whatever it was she had on underneath. She produced the passport. I knew what they looked like because brother Godfrey was a proud owner. They were unforgettable. Frenchy had one.

I sat down on the floor, feeling expansive. If Frenchy had an FP I was safer than I'd ever been. An FP reflected its warm light over everybody near it. I reached under the mattress and pulled out a packet of Woodies. There were two left.

Frenchy grinned, accepting the fag. "I ought to flash it about more often."

We smoked gratefully. The allowance was ten a month. As stated, the penalty for buying on the black market, presuming you could get hold of some money, was shooting. For the seller it was something worse. No one knew what, but they hung the bodies up from time to time and you got some idea of the end result.

"About this police business," I said.

"You don't mind if I kip here tonight," she said. "I'm beat."

"I don't mind," I said. "Want to hop in now? We can talk in bed."

She took off the mac, kicked away her shoes, and hopped in.

I took off my trousers, shoes, and socks, pulled down my sweater, and blew out the candles. I got into bed. There was nothing more to it than that. Those days you either did or you didn't. Most didn't. What with the long hours, short rations, and general struggle to keep half-clean and slightly below par, few people had the will for sex. Also sex meant kids and the kids mostly died, so that took all the joy out of it. Also I've got the impression us English don't breed in captivity. The Welsh and Irish did, but then they've been doing it for hundreds of years. The Highlanders didn't produce either. Increasing the population was something people like Godfrey worried about in the odd moments when they weren't eliminating it, but a declining birthrate is something you can't legislate about. What with the slave labor in the factories, cops round every corner, the jolly lads of the British Wehrmacht in every street, and being paid out in food and clothing coupons so you wouldn't do anything rash with the cash, like buying a razor blade and cutting your throat, you couldn't blame people for losing interest in propagating themselves. There'd been a resistance movement up until three or four years before, but they'd made a mistake and taken to the classic methods—blowing up bridges, the few operating railway lines, and what factories had started up. It wasn't only the reprisals—on the current scale it was twenty men for every German killed, or ten schoolkids or five women—but when people found out they were blowing up boot factories and stopping food trains, a loyal population, as the krauts put it, stamped out the antisocial Judeo-Bolshevik element in their midst.

The birthrate might have gone up if they'd raised the rations after that, but that might cause a population explosion in more ways than one.

Anyhow, it was warmer in there with Frenchy beside me.

"Would you mind," I said, "removing your hat?"

I couldn't see her, but I could tell she was smiling. She reached up and pulled the old hat off and threw it on the floor.

"What about these cops, then?" I asked.

"Oh—I really don't know. Honestly, I haven't done anything. I don't even know anybody who's doing anything."

"Could they be after your full passport?"

"No. They never withdraw them. If they did the passports wouldn't mean anything. People wouldn't know if they were deferring to a man with a withdrawn passport. If you do something like spying for Russia, they just eliminate *you*. That gets rid of your FP automatically."

"Maybe that's why they're after you . . . ?"

"No. They don't involve the police. It's just a quick bullet."

I couldn't help feeling awed that Frenchy, who'd shared my last crusts, knew all this about the inner workings of the regime. I checked the thought instantly. Once you started being interested in them, or hating them, or being emotionally involved with them in any way at all—they'd got you. It was something I'd sworn never to forget—only indifference was safe, indifference was the only weapon that kept you free, for what your freedom was worth. They say you get hardened to anything. Well, I'd had nearly ten years of it—disgusting, obscene cruelty carried out by stupid men who, from top to bottom, thought they were masters of the earth —and I wasn't hardened. That was why I cultivated indifference. And the Leader—Our *Führer*—was no mad genius either. Mad and stupid. That was even worse. I couldn't understand, then, how he'd managed to do what he'd done. Not then.

"I don't know what it can be," Frenchy was saying, "but I'll know tomorrow when I wake up."

"Why?"

"I'm like that," she said roughly.

"Are you?" I was interested. "Like—what?"

She buried her face in my shoulder. "Don't talk about it, Lowry," she said, coming as near to an appeal as a hard case like Frenchy could.

"OK," I said. You soon learned to steer away from the wrong topic. The way things, and people, were then.

So we went to sleep. When I woke, Frenchy was lying awake, staring up at the ceiling with a blank expression on her face. I wouldn't have cared if she'd turned into a marmalade cat overnight. I felt hot and itchy after listening to her moans and mutters all night, and I could feel a migraine coming on.

The moment I'd acknowledged the idea of a migraine, my gorge rose, I got up and stumbled along the peeling passageway. Once inside the lavatory I knew I shouldn't have gone there. I was going to vomit in the bowl. The water was off. It was too late. I vomited, vomited, and vomited. At least this one time the water came on at the right moment and the lavatory flushed.

I dragged myself back. I couldn't see and the pain was terrible.

"Come back to bed," Frenchy said.

"I can't," I said. I couldn't do anything.

"Come on."

I sat on the edge of the bed and lowered myself down. Go away, Frenchy, I said to myself, go away.

But her hands were on that spot, just above my left temple, where the pain came from. She crooned and rubbed and to the sound of her crooning I fell asleep.

I woke about a quarter of an hour later and the pain had gone. Frenchy, mac, hat, and shoes on, was sitting in my old armchair, with the begrimed upholstery and shedding springs.

"Thanks, Frenchy," I mumbled. "You're a healer."

"Yeah," she said discouragingly.

"Do you often?"

"Not now," she said. "I used to. I just thought I'd like to help."

"Well, thanks," I said. "Stick around."

"Oh, I'm off now."

"OK. See you tonight, perhaps."

"No. I'm getting out of London. Coming with me?"

"Where. What for?"

"I don't know. I know the cops want me but I don't know why. I just know if I keep away from them for a month or two they won't want me any more."

"What the bloody hell are you talking about?"

"I said I'd know what it was about when I awoke. Well, I don't—not really. But I do know the cops want me to do something, or tell them something. And I know there's more to it than just the police. And I know that if I disappear for some time I won't be useful any more. So I'm going on the run."

"I suppose you'll be all right with your FP. No problem. But why don't you cooperate?"

"I don't want to," she said.

"Why run? With your FP they can't touch you."

"They can. I'm sure they can."

I gave her a long look. I'd always known Frenchy was odd, by the old standards. But as things were now it was saner to be odd. Still, all this cryptic hide-and-seek, all this prescient stuff, made me wonder.

She stared back. "I'm not cracked. I know what I'm doing. I've got to keep away from the cops for a month or two because I don't want to cooperate. Then it will be OK."

"Do you mean you'll be OK?"

"Don't know. Either that or it'll be too late to do what they want. Are you coming?"

"I might as well," I said. When it came down to it, what had I got to lose? And Frenchy had an FP. We'd be millionaires. Or would we?

"How many FPs in Britain?" I asked.

"About two hundred."

"You can't use it then. If you go on the run using an FP you'd—we'd never go unnoticed. We'll stick out like a searchlight on a moor. And no one will cover for us. Why should they help an FP-holder with the cops after her?"

Frenchy frowned. "I'd better stock up here then. Then we can leave London and throw them off the scent."

I nodded and got up and into the rest of my gear. "I'll nip out and spend a few clothing coupons on decent clothes for you. You won't be so memorable then. They'll just think you're some high-up civil servant. Then I'll tell you who to go to. The cops will check with the dodgy suppliers last. They won't expect FP-holders to use Sid's Foodmart when they could go to Fortnums. Then I'll give you a list of what to get."

"Thanks, boss," she said. "So I was born yesterday."

"If I'm coming with you I don't want any slip-ups. If we're caught you'll risk an unpleasant little telling-off. And I'll be in a camp before you can say Abie Goldberg."

"No," she said bewilderedly. "I don't think so."

I groaned. "Frenchy, love. I don't know whether you're cracked, or Cassandra's second cousin. But if you can't be specific, let's play it sensible. OK?"

"Mm," she said.

I hurried off to spend my clothing coupons at Arthur's.

It was a soft day, drizzling a bit. I walked through the park. It was like a wood, now. The grass was deep and growing across the paths. Bushes and saplings had sprung up. Someone had built a small compound out of barbed wire on the grass just below the Atheneum. A couple of grubby white goats grazed inside. They must belong to the cops. With rations at two loaves a week people would eat them raw if they could get at them. Look what had happened to the vicar of All Saints, Margaret Street. He shouldn't have been so High Church—all that talk about the body and blood of Christ had set the congregation thinking along unorthodox lines.

I walked on in the drizzle. No one around. Nice fresh day. Nice to get out of London.

"Any food coupons?" said a voice in my ear.

I turned sharply. It was a young woman, so thin her shoulder blades and cheekbones seemed pointed. In her arms was a small baby. Its face was blue. Its violet-shadowed eyes were closed. It was dressed in a tattered blue jumper.

I shrugged. "Sorry, love, I've got a shilling—any use?"

"They'd ask me where I'd got it from. What's the good?" she whispered, never taking her eyes off the child's face.

"What's wrong with the kid?"

"They've cut off the dried milk. Unless you can feed them yourself they starve—I'm hungry."

I took out my diary. "Here's the address of a woman called Jessie Wright. Her baby's just died of diphtheria. She may take the kid on for you."

"Diphtheria?" she said.

"Look, love, your kid's half-dead anyway. It's worth trying."

"Thanks," she said. Tears started to run down her face. She took the piece of paper and walked off.

"Hey ho," said I, walking on.

I crossed the Mall and got the usual suspicious stares from the mixed assortment of soldiery that half-filled it. The uniforms were all the same. You couldn't tell the noble Tommy from the fiendish Hun. I looked to my right and saw Buckingham Palace. From the mast flew a huge flag, a Union Jack with a bloody great swastika superimposed on it. I'd never got rid of my loathing for that symbol, conceived as part of their perverted, crazy mysticism. Field Marshal Wilmot had been an officer in the Brigade of St. George—British fascists who had fought with Hitler almost from the start. A shrewd character that Wilmot. He had a little moustache that was identical with the Leader's—but as he was prematurely bald, hadn't been able to cultivate the lock of hair to go with it. He was fat and bloated with drink and probably drugs. He depended entirely on the Leader. If he hadn't been there it might have been a different story.

I walked down Buckingham Gate and turned right into Victoria Street. The Army and Navy Stores had become exactly what it said—only the military elite could shop there.

Arthur was in business in the former foreign-exchange kiosk at Victoria Station. I bunged over the coupons. Sunlight streamed through the shattered canopy of the station. There had been some street fighting around here but it hadn't lasted long.

"I want a lady's coat, hat, and shoes. Are these enough?"

Arthur was small and shrewd. He only had one arm. He put the coupons under his scanner. "They're not fakes." I said impatiently, "Are they enough?"

"Just about, mate—as it's you," he said. He was a thin-faced cockney from the City. His kind had survived plagues, sweatshops, and the depression. He'd survive this, too. I happened to know he'd been one of Mosely's fascists before the War—in fact he'd kicked a thin-skulled Jew in the head in Dalston in 1938, thus saving him from the gas chambers in 1948. Funny how things work out.

But somehow since the virile lads of the Wehrmacht had marched in he seemed to have cooled off the old blood-brotherhood of the Aryans, so I never held it against him. Anyway, being about five foot two and weasely with it, he was no snip for the selective breeding camps.

"What size d'you want?" he asked.

"Oh, God. I don't know."

"The lady should have come herself." He looked suspicious.

"Coppers tore her clothes off," I said. That satisfied him. A cop passed across the station at a distance. Arthur's eyes flicked, then came back to me.

"Funny the way they left them in their helmets and so on," he said. "Seems wrong, dunnit?"

"They wanted you to think they were the same blokes who used to tell you the time and find old Rover for you when he got lost."

"Aren't they?" Arthur said sardonically. "You should have lived 'round where I lived mate. Still, this won't buy baby a new pair of boots. What's the lady look like?"

"About five nine or ten. Big feet."

"Coo—no wonder the coppers fancied her," he jeered jealously. "You must feel all warm and safe with her. Thin or fat?"

"Come off it Arthur. Who's fat?"

"Girls who know cops."

"This one didn't until last night."

"Nothing dodgy is it?" His eyes started looking suspicious again. Trading licenses were hard to come by these days. I thought of telling him about Frenchy's full passport, but dismissed the idea. It would sound like a fantastic, dirty great lie.

"She's OK. She just wants some clothes that's all."

"If she got her clothes torn off why don't she want a dress? That's more important to a lady than a hat—a lady what is a lady that is."

"Give me the coupons, Arthur." I stretched out my hand. "You're not the only clothes-trader around. I came here to buy some gear, not tell you my love life."

"OK, Lowry. One coat, one hat, one pair of shoes, size 7—and God help you if her feet's size 5." Arthur produced the things with a wonderful turn of speed. "And that'll be a quid on top."

I'd expected this. I handed him the pound. As I put the goods in a paper bag I said, "I took the number of that quid, mate. If the cops call on me about this deal I'll be able to tell them you're taking cash off the customers. They may not nick you, of course—but they may soak you hard."

He called me a bastard and added some more specific details, then said, "No hard feelings, Lowry. But I thought all along this was a dodgy deal."

"You mind your business, chum, I'll mind mine," I said. "So long."

"So long," he said. I headed back towards the park.

Frenchy was asleep when I got back. She looked fragile, practically TB. I woke her up and handed her the gear. She put it on.

"Frenchy, love," I said sadly. "I've got to break it to you—you must have a wash. And comb your hair. And haven't you got a lipstick?"

She sulked but I fetched some water. By some accident Pevensey had missed what was left in the taps. She washed, combed her hair with my comb, and we made up her lips with a Swan Vesta.

I stood back. Black coat, a bit short with a fur collar, white beret, and black high-heeled shoes.

"Honestly, French, you look like Marlene Dietrich," I said partly to give her the morale to carry off the FP-ing, partly because it was almost true. It was a pity she looked so undernourished, but perhaps they'd think it was natural.

"Get yourself some makeup while you're at it."

"Here," she said in alarm, "I don't know what to do."

"You mean you've never *used* that passport?" I said.

"You wouldn't if you were me," she replied. For her that was obviously the question you never asked, like "where were you in '45" or "what happened to cousin Fred." Her face was dark.

I passed it off. "You're cracked. Never mind. Just march into the place. Look confident. Tell them what you want. They'll cotton on immediately. You probably won't even need to show it to them. Scoop the stuff up and go. Don't forget they're scared of you."

"OK."

"Here's the list of what we want and where to get it."

"Yeah," she glanced over the list. "Brandy, eh?"

I grinned. "Christmas, after all. You never drink, though."

"No. It does something bad to me."

"Uh huh. Use a slight German accent. That'll convince them."

She left and I went and lay down. I felt tired after all that.

And, lo, another knock at my door. Thinking it was Pevensey wanting me to get him some more quack medicine, I shouted "come in."

He stood in the doorway, a vision of loveliness in his black striped coat and pinstriped trousers. He glanced round fastidiously at my cracked lino, peeling wallpaper, the net curtain that was hanging down on one side of the small greasy window. Well, he had a right. He paid the rent, after all.

I didn't get up. "Hullo, mein Gottfried," I said.

"Hullo, old man." He came in. Sat down on my armchair like a man performing an emergency appendectomy with a rusty razor blade. He lit a Sobranie.

As an afterthought he flung the packet to me. I took one, lit it, and shoved the packet under the mattress.

"I thought I'd look in," he said.

"How sweet of you. It must be two years now. Still, Christmas is the time for the family, isn't it?"

"Well, quite. . . . How are you?"

"Rubbing along, thanks, Godfrey. And you?"

"Not too bad."

The scene galled me. When we were young, before the war, we had been friends. Even if we hadn't been, brothers were still brothers. It wasn't that I minded hating my brother, that's common enough. It was that I didn't hate him the way brothers hate. I hated him coldly and sickly.

At that moment I would have liked to fall on him and throttle him, but only in the cold, satisfied way you rake down a flypaper studded with flies.

Besides I still couldn't see why he had come.

"How's the—playing?" he asked.

"Not bad, you know. I'm at the Merrie Englande these days."

"So I heard."

Hullo, I thought, I see glimmers of light. He saw I saw them—he was, after all, my brother.

"I wondered if you'd like some lunch," he said.

Normally I would have refused, but I knew he might stay and catch Frenchy coming back. So I pretended to hesitate. "All right, hungry enough for anything."

We went down the cracked steps and walked up Park Lane. The drizzle had stopped and a cold sun had come out and made the street look even more depressing. Boarded-up hotels, looted shops, cracked façades, grass growing in the broken streets, bent lamp standards, the park itself a tangled forest of weeds. It was sordid.

"Thinking of cleaning up, ever, Godfrey?" I asked.

"Not my department," he said.

"Someone ought to."

"No manpower, you see," he said. I bet, I thought. Naturally they left it. One look was enough to break anyone's morale. If you were wondering how defeated and broken you were and looked at Park Lane, or Piccadilly, or Trafalgar Square, you'd soon know—completely.

Godfrey took me to a sandwich-and-soup place on the corner. A glance and the man behind the counter knew him for an FP-holder. So the food wasn't bad, although Godfrey picked at it like a man used to something better.

Conversation stopped. The customers bent their shoulders over their plates of sandwiches and munched stolidly. Godfrey didn't seem to notice. He probably never had noticed. I had to face facts—although a member of my own family, Godfrey had always been a kraut psychologically. Always neat, always methodical, jumping his hurdles—exams, tests, and assignments at work—like a trained horse. It wasn't that he didn't care about other people—I can't say I did—he just never knew there was anything to care about.

"How's the department?" I asked, beginning the ridiculous question-

and-answer game again—as if either of us worried about anything to do with the other.

"Going well."

"And Andrea?"

"She's well."

She ought to be, I thought. Fat cow. She'd married Godfrey for his steady civil-service job and made a far better bargain than she'd thought.

"What about you—are you thinking of getting married?"

I stared at him. Who married these days unless they had a steady job at one of the factories or on road transport, or, of course, in the police?

"Not exactly. Haven't really got the means to keep my bride in the accustomed manner."

"Oh," said Godfrey. Watch it, I thought. I knew that expression. "Oh, they said Sebastian'd been riding Celeste's bike, mother." "Oh, father, I thought you'd given Seb *permission* to go out climbing."

"I mentioned it because they told me you were engaged to a singer at the Merrie Englande."

"Who are they?"

"Well, my private secretary, as a matter of fact. He's a customer."

Yeah, I thought, like a rag-and-bone-man's a customer at the Ritz. He'd heard it from some spy.

"Well," I said. "I can't think how he managed to get that idea. I'm not sure there is a regular singer at the Merrie . . ."

"This girl was supposed to be like you—a sort of casual entertainer. A German girl I think he said."

Too specific, chum. That line might just work with a stranger—not with your little brother.

"I think I've met her. In fact I've played for her once or twice. I don't know much about her, though. I'm certainly not engaged to her."

Godfrey bit into a sandwich. I'd closed that line of enquiry. He was wondering how to open another.

"That's a relief. She sounds a tramp."

"Maybe."

"We want to repatriate her—know where she is?"

"Why should I?" I said. "Apart from that, why should I help you? If she doesn't want to be repatriated, that's her business."

"Be realistic, Sebby—anyway, she does want to be, or she would do, if she knew. Her aunt's died and left her a lot of money. The other side has asked us to let her know so she can go home and sort out her affairs."

I went on drinking soup, but I wondered. Perhaps the story was true. Still, I didn't need to put Godfrey on to her—I could tell her myself.

"Well, I'll tell her if I see her. I doubt if I shall. I should leave a message at the Merrie."

"Yes."

He looked up broodingly, staring round in that blank way people have when they're bored with their eating companion.

I followed his gaze. My eyes lit on Frenchy. Loaded with parcels, she was buying food and having a flask filled with coffee at the counter. I went rigid. Frenchy had gained confidence—she was buying like an FP-holder. And anyone with that amount of stuff on them attracted attention anyway. She was attracting it all right. Godfrey was the only man in the room who wasn't looking at her and pretending not to. He was just looking at her. I couldn't decide if he was watching her like a cat or just watching.

"Heard about Freddy Gore," I said.

"No," said Godfrey, not taking his eyes off her.

"He committed suicide," I said.

"Well I'm damned," said Godfrey, looking at me greedily. "Why?"

"It was his wife. He came home one afternoon. . . ." I spoke on hastily. Frenchy was still buying. Half the customers were still pointedly ignoring her—apart from anything else she looked quite good in her new gear. She picked up her stuff and left without showing her FP to the man behind the counter. She left without Godfrey noticing. I brought my tale of lust, adultery, rape, and murder in the Gore family to a speedy close. A horrible thought had struck me. Godfrey was a high-up. He knew about Frenchy and he knew I knew her. There were a lot of cops on the job and he might have fixed it so that some were watching my hotel. Somehow I had to shift him and catch Frenchy before she got back.

"Shocking story," said Godfrey, looking at his watch. "I must be getting back. Like a lift?"

"Not going in that direction," I said. "Thanks all the same."

So he flagged down a passing car and told the sulky driver to take him to Buckingham Palace—the krauts had restored it at huge expense for the Ministry of Security as well as our paternal governor.

I walked slowly down the road, turned off and ran like hell. I caught Frenchy, all burdened with parcels, just in time.

"Better not go back," I gasped. "They may be watching the hotel."

There was a car standing outside a house just down the street. I ran her up to it and tugged at the door. It wasn't locked. I shoved her in, paper bags, flask, and all, and got in the driving seat.

A stocky man ran out of the house. He had a revolver in his hand. I started up. Frenchy had the passport out. I grabbed it and waved it at the man with the gun.

"Full passport!" I yelled.

He stood staring at the back of the car. He didn't even dare snarl.

"What makes you think they're watching the hotel?"

I told her about Godfrey.

She frowned. "I must be right about having to run."

"Are you sure it isn't this legacy they say you've inherited?"

"I've only got one aunt and she's broke. Besides, why should your brother get involved in such a silly little business?"

"Because your father's so important. Or perhaps Papa just wants you home and made up the aunt business to cover up the fact that you're his no-good daughter who's drifting about in occupied territory, dragging the family name in the mud behind her."

"Could be. It's not enough. I'm still not sure—you'll have to believe me. In the past I've been—well—important. It's to do with that, I know."

"What sort of important?"

She began to cry, great, racking sobs that bent her double.

"Don't ask me—oh, don't ask me."

I got hard-hearted. "Come on, Frenchy. Why should I break the law for you?"

"I don't want to remember—I can't remember," she gasped.

"Nuts. You can remember if you want to."

"I can't. I don't want to."

I passed her my handkerchief silently. How important could she have been—at twenty years old? She must have been at school until a couple of years ago.

"Where did you go to school?" I asked, more to pass time than anything.

"I was at the Berlin Gymnasium for Girls. When I was thirteen, I—they took me away."

Then the tears stopped and when I glanced at her, she had fainted. I pushed her back so that she was sitting comfortably, and drove on.

As dark came we reached Histon, just outside Cambridge, and spent the night in the car, parked beside a hedge, inside a field.

When I woke next morning, there was a rifle barrel in my ear.

"Oh, Gawd," I said. "What's this?"

A hand opened the car door and dragged me out. I lay on the ground with the barrel pointing at my belly. Above the barrel was a red face topped by a trilby hat. It wasn't a copper anyway.

I glanced sideways at the car. Inside Frenchy was sitting up. Outside another man pointed a rifle at her temple, through the open window.

"What's all this about?" I said.

"Who're you?" the man said. "Sebastian Lowry and Frenchy Steiner," I said.

"What're you here for?"

"Just riding—"

The gun barrel dropped. The man was looking at his friend.

Then I saw—Frenchy had her passport out.

He touched his hat and retreated quickly, mumbling apologies. So I got back in the car and we snuggled up and back to sleep.

When we woke up, we had coffee from the flask and a sandwich. Then we walked round the field. One or two birds cheeped from the bare hedges and our feet sank into ploughed furrows. It was silent and lonely. We walked round and round, breathing deeply.

We sat down and looked over the big, flat field, sharing a bar of chocolate.

Frenchy smiled at me—a real smile, not her usual tense grin. I smiled back. We sat on. No noise, no people, no grimy, cracked buildings, no cops. A pale sun was high in the sky. The birds cheeped. I took Frenchy's hand. It felt strange, to be holding someone's hand again. It was warm and dry. Her fingers gripped mine. I stared at the pale, pointed profile beside me and the long, messy blonde hair. Then I looked at the field again. We started a second bar of chocolate. Frenchy yawned. The silence went on and on. And on and on.

I was staring numbly across the acres of brown earth when Frenchy's hand clenched painfully on mine.

Slowly, from behind every bush, like the characters in some monstrous, silent film, the cops were rising. On all sides, over the bare bushes came a pair of blue shoulders, topped by a helmet. They rose slowly until they were standing. Then they moved silently forward. They tightened in.

Frenchy and I rose. The circle closed. To keep in the center we had to move over to the road. Slowly they drove us out of the field, past our car, through the gate, and on to the road. No one spoke. All we heard was the sound of their boots on the earth. Their faces were rigid, like cops' faces always are.

Coming through the gate, we saw the reception committee. Three of them. My friend Inspector Braun, all knife-edged creases and polished buttons, and brother Godfrey. And then a short fat man I didn't know. He was wearing a well-cut suit, and power, as they say, was written all over him, from his small, neatly shod feet to his balding head.

Frenchy stepped up to the group. "Hullo, father," she said in German.

"Hullo, Franziska. We've found you at last, I see."

Godfrey smirked. Extra rations for good old Gottfried tomorrow. Maybe the Iron Cross.

So I thought I'd embarrass him. "Hi, Godfrey, old man."

"Morning, Sebastian." How he wished I wasn't shaking his hand. "We're parked up the road. Come on."

So we walked up the road to the shiny blue car that would take us back to God knew where—or what.

How silently they must have moved. What bloody fools we'd been not to get away after those two farmers had copped us. Godfrey and friends had probably had bulletins out for us all morning.

I sat at the back, between Godfrey and the Inspector. Frenchy was in front with her father and the driver.

"It's nice to know officialdom has its more human side," I remarked. "To think that deputy security minister, a CID Inspector and fifty coppers should all come out on a cold winter's morning to see a young girl gets the legacy that's rightfully hers."

Godfrey said nothing. He merely looked important. From the way Braun didn't grip my arm and the driver didn't keep glancing over his shoulder to see who I was coshing, I got the impression this wasn't a hanging charge. There was a sort of alligator grin in the air—cops taking home a naughty under-age couple who had run off to get married—not that cops did that kind of little social-service job these days, but, wistfully, they kept trying to make you think so.

But what *was* the set-up? In front Frenchy had given up talking to her father—he cut every remark off at source. Why? No family rows in public? Frenchy, what I could see of her, looked like a girl on a cart bound for the scaffold. Her father looked like a man determined to knock some sense into his daughter's flighty head as soon as he got her home. Godfrey merely looked pontifical. Braun looked official.

Frenchy tried again. "Father. I *can't* go—"

"Be quiet!" said her father. Godfrey was listening hard. Suddenly I got the picture. *Godfrey and Braun didn't know what it was all about.* And Frenchy's father didn't want them to.

It must be really something, then, I thought.

There was silence all the way back to London. What about me? I thought. I'm just not in this at all. But I bet it's me who takes the rap. The car stopped in Trafalgar Square. Frenchy and her father got out. He hurried her up the steps of the Goering Hotel. Her eyes were burning like coals.

Then Godfrey and Braun pulled me out. "You'll be in a suite here till we decide what to do with you," Godfrey said in a low voice. "Don't worry. I'll do what I can to help."

I won't say tears came to my eyes—I knew just how far he would go to help. I said goodbye to him and Braun led me up the marble steps. The place was crowded with neat soldiery. We were joined by the hotel manager and two coppers. We went up to the top story and I was shown my suite. Three rooms and a bathroom. Quite a nice little shack, although somewhat Teutonically furnished. It was elegant, but there was the smell of loot about it. You kept wondering which bit of furniture covered the bloodstains where they'd bayoneted the Countess and her kids one morning.

Then the two policemen stationed themselves, one at the door and one inside with me. That wasn't so pleasant. I wondered when the cop was going to suggest a hand of nap to while away the time before the execution. I looked about appreciatively, sat down on the blue silk sofa and said "What now?"

A waiter came in with tea and toast. One cup. I asked the cop if he'd like some. He refused. As I went to pour out my second cup I saw why, because the room began to spin. "This hotel isn't what it was," I muttered and fell down.

I woke up next morning in a four-poster. Frenchy, in a red silk nightdress and negligee, was bending over me with a cup of coffee. I hauled myself up, noticing my blue silk pajamas, and took the cup.

She sat down at the Louis XIV table beside the bed. She went on eating rolls and butter. Her hair, obviously washed, cascaded down her back like gold thread.

"Very nice," I said, handing back my cup for a refill. "If I didn't wonder whose Christmas dinner I was being fattened for. Where's the cop?"

"I sent him outside."

I began to glance round. The windows were barred.

"You can't get out. The place is heavily guarded and the cops will shoot you on sight."

"That's new?"

She ignored me. "You're quite safe as long as you're with me. I've told them I've got to have you with me."

"That's nice. How long will you be around?"

"I thought you'd spot a snag."

"Look, Frenchy. I think you'd better tell me what this is about. It's my carcass after all."

"I will," she said calmly. "Prepare yourself for surprises." She seemed very matter of fact, but her face had the calm of a woman who's just had a baby, the pain and shock were over, but she knew this was really only the beginning of the trouble.

"I told you I was at a gymnasium in Berlin until I was thirteen. Then I began seeing visions. Of course, the tutors didn't make much of it at first. It's not too unusual in girls at the beginning of puberty. The trouble was, they weren't the usual kind of visions. I used to see tables surrounded by German officers. I used to overhear conferences. I saw tanks going into battle, burning cities, concentration camps—things I couldn't possibly know about. Then, one night, my roommate heard me talking English in my sleep. I was talking about battle plans, using military terms and English slang I also couldn't possibly have known. She told the House Leader. The House Leader told my father, who was then only a captain in the SS. Father was an intelligent man. He took me to Karl Ossietz, one of the Leader's chief soothsayers. A month later I was installed in a suite at headquarters. I was dressed in a white linen dress, my hair was bound with a gold band. I'd become part of the German myth . . .

"I was the virgin who prophesied to Attila, I was thirteen years old and I lived like a ritual captive for four years, officiating at sacrifices and Teutonic saturnalia, watching goats have their throats cut with gold knives, seeing torchlight on the walls—all that. And I thought it was marvelous, to be helping the cause like that. I went into a kind of mystic dream where I was an Aryan queen helping her nation to victory. And in my midnight conferences with the Leader I prophesied. I told him not to attack Russia—I knew he would be defeated. I told him where to concentrate his forces to use them to their best effect. Oh, and much, much more . . .

"Also only I could soothe him when his attacks of mania came on—by putting my hands on him the way I did for you the other day. I'm not a real healer. I can't cure the body. But I can reach into overtaxed or unstable minds and take away the tightness.

"When the war ended, I just left in a daze. They thought they didn't really need me at that time. There was something in the back of my mind —I don't know what it was—made me come here, with my passport, my safe-conducts, my letters of introduction. . . . When I saw what I had done to you all—what could I do? I tried to kill myself and failed—maybe I wasn't trying hard enough. Then I tried to live with you, simply because I couldn't think of anything else to do. A stronger person might have thought of practical ways to help—but I'd spent four years in an atmosphere of blood and hysteria, calling on the psychic part of me and ignoring the rest. I was unfit for life. I just tried to forget everything that had ever happened to me."

She shrugged. "That's it."

I stared at her, feeling a horrible pity. She knew she had been used to kill millions of people and reduce a dozen nations to slavery. And she had got to live with it.

"What's it all about now?" I asked.

"They need me again. There must be desperate problems to be solved. Or the Leader's madness is getting worse. Or both. That's why I felt if I could disappear for a month it would be all right. By that time no one could have cleared up the mess." She lit a cigarette, passed it to me, and lit one for herself.

"What are you going to do?"

"I don't know. If I don't help they'll torture me until I do. I'm not strong enough to resist. But I can't, can't, *can't* cooperate any more. If I had the guts I'd kill myself but I haven't. Anyway, they've taken away anything I could use to do it. That's why all the windows are barred—it's not to stop you escaping. It's to stop me from throwing myself out. I don't suppose you'd kill me quickly, so I wouldn't know anything about it?"

In a sense the idea was tempting. A chance to get back at the Leader with a vengeance. But I knew I couldn't kill poor, thin Frenchy.

I told her so. "I'm too kindhearted," I said. "If I killed you, how could I go on hoping you'd have a better life?"

"I won't. If I'm needed they'll cage me again. And this time I'll have known freedom. I'll be back in robes, with incense and torchlight and all the time I'll be able to remember being free—walking in the field at Histon, for example." I felt very sad. Then I felt even sadder—I was thinking about myself.

"What happens next?" I said.

"They'll fly me to Germany. You're coming, too."

"Oh, no," I said. "Not Germany. I wouldn't stand a chance."

"What chance do you stand here? If I went and you stayed, you'd be shot the moment I left the building. They can't risk letting you go about with your story."

Her shoulders were bowed. She looked as if she had no inner resources left. "I'm sorry. It's my fault. I should have left you alone. If I'd never made you run away with me you'd be safe now."

That wasn't how I remembered it exactly, but I'd rather blame her than me for my predicament. I agreed, oh, how I agreed. Still, once a gent, always a gent. "Never mind that, I'll come and perhaps we can think of something." I was dubious about that, but by that time I was too far in.

So at eleven that morning we left the hotel for the airport. From Berlin we went by limousine to the Leader's palace. I've never been so afraid in my life. It's one thing to go in daily danger of being shot, or sent to starve in a camp. It's another thing to fly straight into the center of all the trouble. I was so afraid I could hardly speak. Not that anyone wanted to hear from me anyway. I was just a passenger—like a bullock on its way to the abattoir.

During the trip Frenchy's father kept up a nervous machine-gun monologue of demands that she would cooperate and promises of a glorious future for her. Frenchy said nothing. She looked drained.

We arrived in the green courtyard of the palace. On the other side of the wall I heard the rush of a waterfall into a pool. The palace was half old German mansion, half modern Teutonic with vulgar marble statues all over the place—supermen on superhorses. That's the nearest they'd got to the master race, so far. A white-haired old man led the jackbooted party that met us.

Frenchy smiled when she saw him, a child's smile. "Karl," she said. Even her voice was like the voice of a very young girl. I shuddered. The spell was beginning to operate again—that blank face, the voice of the little schoolgirl. Oh, Frenchy, love, I sighed to myself. Don't let them do it to you. She was being led along by Karl Ossietz, across the green courtyard.

We made a peculiar gang. In front, Ossietz, tall and thin, with long white hair, and Frenchy, now looking so frail a breeze might blow her away. Behind them a group of begonged generals, all horribly familiar to me from seeing their portraits on pub signs. Just behind them rolled Frenchy's father, trying to join in. Then me, with two ordinary German cops. I caught myself feeling peeved that if I made a dash for it I'd be shot down by an ordinary cop.

Then Karl turned sharply back, stared at me and said: "Who's that?"

Her father said: "He's an Englishman. She wouldn't come without him."

Karl looked furious and terrified. His face began to crumble. "Are you lovers?" he shouted at Frenchy.

"No, Karl," she whispered. He stared long and deeply into her eyes, then nodded.

"They must be separated," he said to Frenchy's father.

Frenchy said nothing. Suddenly I felt more than concern for her—panic for myself. The only reason I'd come here was because she could protect me. Now she could, but she wasn't interested any more. So instead of being shot in England, I was going to be shot right outside the Leader's front door. Still, dead was dead, be it palace or dustbin.

We entered the huge dark hall, full of figures in ancient armors and dark horrible little doors leading away to who knew where. The mosaic floor almost smelt of blood. My legs practically gave way under me, I saw Frenchy being led up the marble staircase. I felt tears come to my eyes— for her, for me, for both of us.

Then they took me along a corridor and up the back stairs. They shoved me through a door. I stood there for several minutes. Then I looked round. Well, it wasn't a rat-haunted oubliette, at any rate. In fact it was the double of my suite at the Goering Hotel. Same thick carpets, heavy antique furniture, even—I poked my head round the door—the same fourposter. Obviously they picked up their furniture at all the little chateaux and castles they happened to run across on a Saturday-morning march.

In the bedroom torches burned. I took off my clothes and got into bed. I was asleep.

The first thing I saw as I awoke was that the torches were burning down. Then I saw Frenchy, naked as a peeled wand, pulling back the embroidered covers and coming into bed. Then I felt her warmth beside me.

"Do it for me," she murmured. "Please."

"What?"

"Take me," she whispered.

"Eh?" I was somewhat shocked. People like Frenchy and me had a code. This wasn't part of it.

"Oh, please," she said, pressing her long body against me. "It's so important."

"Oh—let's have a fag."

She sank back. "Haven't got any," came her sulky voice.

I found some in my pocket and we lit up. "May as well drop the ash on the carpet," I said. "Not much point in behaving nicely so we'll be asked again." I was purposely being irrelevant. Code or no code the situation was beginning to affect me. I tried to concentrate on my imminent death. It had the opposite effect.

"I don't understand, love," I said, taking her hand.

"I had to crawl over the roof to get here," she said, rather annoyed.

"It can't just be passion," I suggested politely.

"Didn't you hear—?"

"My God," I said. "Ossietz. Do you mean that if you're not a virgin, you can't prophesy?"

"I don't know—he seems to think so. It's my only chance. He'll make me do whatever he wants me to—but if I can't perform, if it seems the power's gone—it won't matter. They may shoot me, but it will be a quick death."

"Don't be so dramatic, love." I put my cigarette out on the bed head and took her in my arms. "I love you, Frenchy." I said. And it was quite true. I did.

That was the best night of my life. Frenchy was sweet, and actually so was I. It was a relief to drop the mask for a few hours. As dawn came through the windows, she lay in our tangled bed like a piece of pale wreckage.

She smiled at me and I smiled back. I gave her a kiss. "A man who would do anything for his country," she grinned.

"How are you going to get back?" I said.

"I thought I'd go back over the roof—but now I'm not sure I'll ever walk again."

I said: "Have I hurt you?"

"Like hell. I'll bluff my way out. The guards will be tired and I doubt if they know anything. Anyway all roads lead to the same destination now."

I began to cry. That's the thing about an armadillo—underneath his flesh is more tender than a bear's. Not that I cared if I cried, or if she cried, or if the whole palace rang with sobs. The torches were guttering out.

She stood naked beside the bed. Then she put on her clothes, said goodbye. I heard her speaking authoritatively outside the door, heels clicking, and then her feet going along the corridor.

I just went on crying. Her meeting with the Leader was in two hours' time. If I went on crying for two hours, I wouldn't have to think about it all.

I couldn't. By the time the guard came in with my breakfast, I was dressed and dry-eyed. He looked through the open door at the bed and gave a wink. He said something in German I couldn't understand, so I knew the words weren't in the dictionary. I stared at the bed and my stomach lurched. It seemed a bit rude to feel lust for a woman who was going to die.

Then I realized my condition was getting critical, so I ate my breakfast to bring me to my senses. The four last things, that was what I ought to be thinking about. What were they?

Suddenly I thought of the woman with the baby in the park. If Frenchy couldn't help the Leader, perhaps he'd go. Perhaps they'd lead a better life.

I paced the floor, wondering what was happening now.

This was what was happening . . .

Frenchy was bathed, dressed in a white linen robe with a red cloak and led down to the great hall.

The Leader was sitting on a dais in a heavy wooden chair. His arms were extended along the arms of the chair, his face held the familiar look of stern command, now a cracking façade covering decay and lunacy.

On his lips were traces of foam. Around him were his advisers, belted and booted, robed and capped or blonde and dressed in subvalkyrie silk dresses. The court of the mad king—the atmosphere was hung with heavy incomprehensibilities. Led by her father and Karl Ossietz, Frenchy approached the dais.

"We—need—you—" the Leader grunted. His court held their places by willpower. They were terrified, and with good reason. The hall had seen terrible things in the past year. There were, too, one or two faces blankly waiting for the outcome. As the old pack-leader sickens, the younger wolves start to plan.

"We—have—sought—you for—half a year," the grating, half-human voice went on. "We need your predictions. We need your—*health!*"

His eyes stared into hers. He leapt up with a cry. "Help! Help! Help!" His voice rang round the hall. More foam appeared at his lips. His face twisted.

"Go forward to the Leader," Karl Ossietz ordered.

Frenchy stepped forward. The court looked at her, hoping.

"Help! Help!" the mad, uncontrollable voice went on. He fell back, writhing on his throne.

"I can't help," she said in a clear voice.

Karl's whisper came, smooth and terrifying, in her ear: "Go forward!"

She went forward, compelled by the voice. Then she stopped again.

"I can't help." She turned to Ossietz. "Can I Karl? You can see?"

He stared at her in horror, then at the writhing man, making animal noises on the dais, then back at Frenchy Steiner.

"You—you—you have fallen . . ." he whispered. "No. No, she cannot help!" he called. "The girl is no longer a virgin—her power has gone!"

The court looked at the Leader, then at Frenchy.

In a moment chaos had broken out. Women screamed—there was a rush to the heavy doors. Men's voices rose, shouted. Then came the crack of the first gun, followed by others. In a moment the hall was milling and ringing with shots, groans, and shouts.

On the dais the Leader lay twisting and uttering guttural moans. The pack was at frenzied war. Those who had considered the Leader immortal —and many had—were bewildered, terrified. Those who had planned to succeed him now hardly knew what to do. Several of them shot themselves there and then.

I was lying on the bed smoking when Frenchy ran in, slammed and bolted the doors behind the guards and her pursuers. Her hair was disheveled, she held the scarlet cloak round her. "Out of the window," she yelled, ripping it off. Underneath her white dress was in ribbons.

I got up on to the windowsill and helped her after me. I looked down toward the courtyard far below. I clung to the sill.

"Go on!"

I reached out and got a grip on a drainpipe. I began to slide down it, the metal chafing my hands. She followed.

At the bottom I paused, helped her down the last few feet, and pointed at a staff car that was parked near the gates. Guards had left the gates and were probably taking part in the indoor festivities. There was only one there and he hadn't seen us. He was looking warily out along the road, as if expecting attack.

We skipped over the lawn and got into the car. I started up.

At the gate the guard, seeing a general's insignia on the car, automatically stepped aside. Then he saw us, did a double-take, and it was too late. We roared down that road, away from there.

The road ahead was clear.

True to form, Frenchy had found and put on an officer's white mac from the back seat.

I slowed down. There was no point in doing eighty toward any danger on the road.

"And have you lost your power?" I asked her.

"Don't know," she gave me an irresponsible grin.

"What was going on below? It sounded like a battlefield."

She told me.

"The Leader's finished. His successors are fighting among themselves. This is the end of the Thousand Year Reich." She grinned again. "I did it."

"Oh, come now," I protested. "Anyway I think we'll try to get back to England?"

"Why?"

"Because if the Empire's crumbling, England will go first. It's an island. They'll withdraw the legions to defend the Empire—it's traditional."

"Can we make it?"

"Not now. We'll get out of Germany and then lie low for a few days until the news leaks out in France. Once things start to break down the organization will disintegrate and we'll get help."

We bowled on merrily, whistling and singing.

Through Road
No Whither

Greg Bear

T he long black Mercedes rumbled out of the fog on the road south from Dijon, moisture running in cold trickles across its windshield. Horst von Ranke moved the military pouch to one side and carefully read the maps spread on his lap, eyeglasses perched low on his nose, while Waffen Schutzstaffel Oberleutnant Albert Fischer drove. "Thirty-five kilometers," von Ranke said under his breath. "No more."

"We are lost," Fischer said. "We've already come thirty-six."

"Not quite that many. We should be there any minute now."

Fischer nodded and then shook his head. His high cheekbones and long, sharp nose only accentuated the black uniform with silver death's heads on the high, tight collar. Von Ranke wore a broad-striped gray suit; he was an undersecretary in the Propaganda Ministry, now acting as a courier. They might have been brothers, yet one had grown up in Czecho-slovakia, the other in the Rhur; one was the son of a coal-miner, the other of a brewer. They had met and become close friends in Paris, two years before.

"Wait," von Ranke said, peering through the drops on the side window. "Stop."

Fischer braked the car and looked in the direction of von Ranke's long finger. Near the roadside, beyond a copse of young trees, was a low thatch-roofed house with dirty gray walls, almost hidden by the fog.

"Looks empty," von Ranke said.

"It is occupied; look at the smoke," Fischer said. "Perhaps somebody can tell us where we are."

They pulled the car over and got out, von Ranke leading the way across a mud path littered with wet straw. The hut looked even dirtier close up. Smoke rose in a darker brown-gray twist from a hole in the peak of the thatch. Fischer nodded at his friend and they cautiously approached. Over the crude wooden door letters wobbled unevenly in some alphabet neither knew, and between them they spoke nine languages. "Could that be Rom?" von Ranke asked, frowning. "It does look familiar—Slavic Rom."

"Gypsies? Romany don't live in huts like this, and besides, I thought they were rounded up long ago."

"That's what it looks like," von Ranke said. "Still, maybe we can share some language, if only French."

He knocked on the door. After a long pause he knocked again, and the door opened before his knuckles made the final rap. A woman too old to be alive stuck her long, wood-colored nose through the crack and peered at them with one good eye. The other was wrapped in a sunken caul of flesh. The hand that gripped the door edge was filthy, its nails long and black. Her toothless mouth cracked into a wrinkled, round-lipped grin. "Good evening," she said in perfect, even elegant German. "What can I do for you?"

"We need to know if we are on the road to Dôle," von Ranke said, controlling his repulsion.

"Then you're asking the wrong guide," the old woman said. Her hand withdrew and the door started to close. Fischer kicked out and pushed her back. The door swung open and began to lean on worn-out leather hinges.

"You do not treat us with the proper respect," he said. "What do you mean, 'the wrong guide'? What kind of guide are you?"

"So *strong*," the old woman crooned, wrapping her hands in front of her withered chest and backing away into the gloom. She wore colorless, ageless gray rags. Worn knit sleeves extended to her wrists.

"Answer me!" Fischer said, advancing despite the strong odor of urine and decay in the hut.

"The maps I know are not for this land," she sang, stopping before a cold and empty hearth.

"She's crazy," von Ranke said. "Let the local authorities take care of her later. Let's be off." But a wild look was in Fischer's eye. So much filth, so much disarray, and impudence as well; these things made him angry.

"What maps do you know, crazy woman?" he demanded.

"Maps in time," the old woman said. She let her hands fall to her side and lowered her head, as if, in admitting her specialty, she was suddenly humble.

"Then tell us where we are," Fischer sneered.

"Come, we have important business," von Ranke said, but he knew it was too late. There would be an end, but it would be on his friend's terms, and it might not be pleasant.

"You are on a through road no whither," the old woman said.

"What?" Fischer towered over her. She stared up as if at some prodigal son returned home, her gums shining spittle.

"If you wish a reading, sit," she said, indicating a low table and three battered wood chairs. Fischer glanced at her, then at the table.

"Very well," he said, suddenly and falsely obsequious. Another game, von Ranke realized. Cat and mouse.

Fischer pulled out a chair for his friend and sat across from the old woman. "Put your hands on the table, palms down, both of them, both of you," she said. They did so. She lay her ear to the table as if listening, eyes going to the beams of light coming through the thatch. "Arrogance," she said. Fischer did not react.

"A road going into fire and death," she said. "Your cities in flame, your women and children shriveling to black dolls in the heat of their burning homes. The death camps are found and you stand accused of hideous crimes. Many are tried and hanged. Your nation is disgraced, your cause abhorred." Now a peculiar light came into her eye. "And many years later, a comedian swaggers around on stage, in a movie, turning your Führer into a silly clown, singing a silly song. Only psychotics will believe in you, the lowest of the low. Your nation will be divided among your enemies. All will be lost."

Fischer's smile did not waver. He pulled a coin from his pocket and threw it down before the woman, then pushed the chair back and stood. "Your maps are as crooked as your chin, hag," he said. "Let's go."

"I've been suggesting that," von Ranke said. Fischer made no move to leave. Von Ranke tugged on his arm but the SS Oberleutnant shrugged free of his friend's grip.

"Gypsies are few, now, hag," he said. "Soon to be fewer by one." Von Ranke managed to urge him just outside the door. The woman followed and shaded her eye against the misty light.

"I am no gypsy," she said. "You do not even recognize the words?" She pointed at the letters above the door.

Fischer squinted, and the light of recognition dawned in his eyes. "Yes," he said. "Yes, I do, now. A dead language."

"What are they?" von Ranke asked, uneasy.

"Hebrew, I think," Fischer said. "She is a Jewess."

"No!" the woman cackled. "I am no Jew."

Von Ranke thought the woman looked younger now, or at least stronger, and his unease deepened.

"I do not care what you are," Fischer said quietly. "I only wish we were in my father's time." He took a step toward her. She did not retreat. Her face became almost youthfully bland, and her bad eye seemed to fill in. "Then, there would be no regulations, no rules—I could take this pistol" —he tapped his holster—"and apply it to your filthy Kike head, and perhaps kill the last Jew in Europe." He unstrapped the holster. The woman straightened in the dark hut, as if drawing strength from Fischer's abusive tongue. Von Ranke feared for his friend. Rashness would get them in trouble.

"This is not our fathers' time," he reminded Fischer.

Fischer paused, the pistol half in his hand, his finger curling around the trigger. "Old woman"—though she did not look half as old, perhaps not even old at all, and certainly not bent and crippled—"you have had a very narrow shave this afternoon."

"You have no idea who I am," the woman half-sang, half-moaned.

"*Scheisse,*" Fischer spat. "Now we will go, and report you and your hovel."

"I am the scourge," she breathed, and her breath smelled like burning stone even three strides away. She backed into the hut but her voice did not diminish. "I am the visible hand, the pillar of cloud by day and the pillar of fire by night."

Fischer's face hardened, and then he laughed. "You are right," he said to von Ranke, "she isn't worth our trouble." He turned and stomped out the door. Von Ranke followed, with one last glance over his shoulder into the gloom, the decay. *No one has lived in this hut for years,* he thought. Her shadow was gray and indefinite before the ancient stone hearth, behind the leaning, dust-covered table.

In the car von Ranke sighed. "You *do* tend toward arrogance, you know that?"

Fischer grinned and shook his head. "You drive, old friend. *I'll* look at the maps." Von Ranke ramped up the Mercedes's turbine until its whine was high and steady and its exhaust cut a swirling hole in the fog behind. "No wonder we're lost," Fischer said. He shook out the Pan-Deutschland map peevishly. "This is five years old—1979."

"We'll find our way," von Ranke said. "I wouldn't miss old Krumnagel's face when we deliver the plans. He fought so long against the antipodal skip bombers. . . . And you delay us by fooling with an old woman."

"It is my way," Fischer said. "I hate disarray. Do you think he will try to veto the Pacific Northwest blitz?"

"He won't dare. He will know his place after he sees the declarations," von Ranke said. The Mercedes whined its way toward Dôle.

From the door of the hut the old woman watched, head bobbing. "I am not a Jew," she said, "but I loved them, too, oh, yes. I loved all my children." She raised her hand as the long black car roared into the fog.

"I will bring you to justice, whatever line you live upon, and all your children, and their children's children," she said. She dropped a twist of smoke from her elbow to the dirt floor and waggled her finger. The smoke danced and drew black figures in the dirt. "As you wished, into the time of your fathers." The fog grew thinner. She brought her arm down, and forty years melted away with the mist.

High above a deeper growl descended on the road. A wide-winged shadow passed over the hut, wings flashing stars, invasion stripes and cannon fire.

"Hungry bird," the shapeless figure said. "Time to feed."

Weihnachtsabend

Keith Roberts

1

The big car moved slowly, nosing its way along narrowing lanes. Here, beyond the little market town of Wilton, the snow lay thicker. Trees and bushes loomed in the headlights, coated with driven white. The tail of the Mercedes wagged slightly, steadied. Mainwaring heard the chauffeur swear under his breath. The link had been left live.

Dials let into the seatback recorded the vehicle's mechanical well-being; oil pressure, temperature, revs, k.p.h. Lights from the repeater glowed softly on his companion's face. She moved, restlessly; he saw the swing of yellow hair. He turned slightly. She was wearing a neat, brief kilt, heavy boots. Her legs were excellent.

He clicked the dial lights off. He said, "Not much farther."

He wondered if she was aware of the open link. He said, "First time down?"

She nodded in the dark. She said, "I was a bit overwhelmed."

Wilton Great House sprawled across a hilltop five miles or more beyond the town. The car drove for some distance beside the wall that fringed the estate. The perimeter defenses had been strengthened since Mainwaring's last visit. Watchtowers reared at intervals; the wall itself had been topped by multiple strands of wire.

The lodge gates were commanded by two new stone pillboxes. The Merc edged between them, stopped. On the road from London the snow had eased; now big flakes drifted again, lit by the headlights. Somewhere, orders were barked.

A man stepped forward, tapped at the window. Mainwaring buttoned it open. He saw a GFP armband, a hip holster with the flap tucked back. He said, "Good evening, Captain."

"Guten Abend, mein Herr. Ihre Ausweiskarte?"

Cold air gusted against Mainwaring's cheek. He passed across his identity card and security clearance. He said, *"Richard Mainwaring. Die rechte Hand des Gesandten. Fräulein Hunter, von meiner Abteilung."*

A torch flashed over the papers, dazzled into his eyes, moved to examine the girl. She sat stiffly, staring ahead. Beyond the security officer Mainwaring made out two steel-helmeted troopers, automatics slung. In front of him the wipers clicked steadily.

The GFP man stepped back. He said, *"Ihre Ausweis wird in einer Woche ablaufen. Erneuen Sie Ihre Karte."*

Mainwaring said, *"Vielen Dank, Herr Hauptmann. Frohe Weihnachten."*

The man saluted stiffly, unclipped a walkie-talkie from his belt. A pause, and the gates swung back. The Merc creamed through. Mainwaring said, *"Bastard . . ."*

She said, "Is it always like this?"

He said, "They're tightening up all round."

She pulled her coat round her shoulders. She said, "Frankly, I find it a bit scary."

He said, "Just the Minister taking care of his guests."

Wilton stood in open downland set with great trees. Hans negotiated a bend, carefully, drove beneath half-seen branches. The wind moaned, zipping round a quarterlight. It was as if the car butted into a black tunnel, full of swirling pale flakes. He thought he saw her shiver. He said, "Soon be there."

The headlamps lit a rolling expanse of snow. Posts, buried nearly to their tops, marked the drive. Another bend, and the house showed ahead. The car lights swept across a façade of mullioned windows, crenellated towers. Hard for the uninitiated to guess, staring at the skillfully weathered stone, that the shell of the place was of reinforced concrete. The car swung right with a crunching of unseen gravel, and stopped. The ignition repeater glowed on the seatback.

Mainwaring said, "Thank you, Hans. Nice drive."

Hans said, "My pleasure, sir."

She flicked her hair free, picked up her handbag. He held the door for her. He said, "OK, Diane?"

She shrugged. She said, "Yes. I'm a bit silly sometimes." She squeezed his hand, briefly. She said, "I'm glad you'll be here. Somebody to rely on."

Mainwaring lay back on the bed and stared at the ceiling. Inside as well as out Wilton was a triumph of art over nature. Here, in the Tudor wing, where most of the guests were housed, walls and ceilings were of wavy plaster framed by heavy oak beams. He turned his head. The room was dominated by a fireplace of yellow Ham stone; on the overmantel, carved in bold relief, the *Hakenkreuz* was flanked by the lion and eagle emblems of the Two Empires. A fire burned in the wrought-iron basket; the logs glowed cheerfully, casting wavering warm reflections across the ceiling. Beside the bed a bookshelf offered required reading: the *Führer's* official biography, Shirer's *Rise of the Third Reich*, Cummings's monumental *Churchill: The Trial of Decadence*. There were a nicely bound set of Buchan novels, some Kiplings, a Shakespeare, a complete Wilde. A side table carried a stack of current magazines: *Connoisseur, The Field, Der Spiegel, Paris Match*. There was a washstand, its rail hung with dark blue towels; in the corner of the room were the doors to the bathroom and wardrobe, in which a servant had already neatly disposed his clothes.

He stubbed his cigarette, lit another. He swung his legs off the bed, poured himself a whisky. From the grounds, faintly, came voices, snatches of laughter. He heard the crash of a pistol, the rattle of an automatic. He walked to the window, pushed the curtain aside. Snow was still falling, drifting silently from the black sky; but the firing pits beside the big house were brightly lit. He watched the figures move and bunch for a while, let the curtain fall. He sat by the fire, shoulders hunched, staring into the flames. He was remembering the trip through London; the flags hanging limp over Whitehall, slow, jerking movement of traffic, the light tanks drawn up outside St. James. The Kensington Road had been crowded, traffic edging and hooting; the vast frontage of Harrod's looked grim and oriental against the louring sky. He frowned, remembering the call he had had before leaving the Ministry.

Kosowicz had been the name. From *Time International;* or so he had claimed. He'd refused twice to speak to him; but Kosowicz had been insistent. In the end he'd asked his secretary to put him through.

Kosowicz had sounded very American. He said, "Mr. Mainwaring, I'd like to arrange a personal interview with your Minister."

"I'm afraid that's out of the question. I must also point out that this communication is extremely irregular."

Kosowicz said, "What do I take that as, sir? A warning, or a threat?"

Mainwaring said carefully, "It was neither. I merely observed that proper channels of approach do exist."

Kosowicz said, "Uh-huh. Mr. Mainwaring, what's the truth behind this rumor that Action Groups are being moved into Moscow?"

Mainwaring said, "Deputy *Führer* Hess has already issued a statement on the situation. I can see that you're supplied with a copy."

The phone said, "I have it before me. Mr. Mainwaring, what are you people trying to set up? Another Warsaw?"

Mainwaring said, "I'm afraid I can't comment further, Mr. Kosowicz. The Deputy *Führer* deplored the necessity of force. The *Einsatzgruppen* have been alerted; at this time, that is all. They will be used if necessary to disperse militants. As of this moment the need has not arisen."

Kosowicz shifted his ground. "You mentioned the Deputy *Führer*, sir. I hear there was another bomb attempt two nights ago; can you comment on this?"

Mainwaring tightened his knuckles on the handset. He said, "I'm afraid you've been misinformed. We know nothing of any such incident."

The phone was silent for a moment. Then he said, "Can I take your denial as official?"

Mainwaring said, "This is not an official conversation. I'm not empowered to issue statements in any respect."

The phone said, "Yeah, channels do exist. Mr. Mainwaring, thanks for your time."

Mainwaring said, "Goodbye." He put the handset down, sat staring at it. After a while he lit a cigarette.

Outside the windows of the Ministry the snow still fell, a dark whirl and dance against the sky. His tea, when he came to drink it, was half cold.

The fire crackled and shifted. He poured himself another whisky, sat back. Before leaving for Wilton he'd lunched with Winsby-Walker from Productivity. Winsby-Walker made it his business to know everything, but had known nothing of a correspondent called Kosowicz. He thought, "I should have checked with Security." But then, Security would have checked with him.

He sat up, looked at his watch. The noise from the ranges had diminished. He turned his mind with a deliberate effort into another channel. The new thoughts brought no more comfort. Last Christmas he had spent with his mother; now, that couldn't happen again. He remembered other Christmases, back across the years. Once, to the child unknowing, they had been gay affairs of crackers and toys. He remembered the scent and texture of pine branches, closeness of candlelight; and books read by torchlight under the sheets, the hard angles of the filled pillowship, heavy at the foot of the bed. Then, he had been complete; only later, slowly, had come the knowledge of failure. And with it, loneliness. He thought, "She wanted to see me settled. It didn't seem much to ask."

The Scotch was making him maudlin. He drained the glass, walked through to the bathroom. He stripped, and showered. Toweling himself, he thought, "Richard Mainwaring, Personal Assistant to the British Minister of Liaison." Aloud he said, "One must remember the compensations."

He dressed, lathered his face, and began to shave. He thought, "Thirty-five is the exact middle of one's life." He was remembering another time with the girl Diane when just for a little while some magic had interposed. Now, the affair was never mentioned between them. Because of James. Always, of course, there is a James.

He toweled his face, applied aftershave. Despite himself, his mind had drifted back to the phone call. One fact was certain: there had been a major security spillage. Somebody somewhere had supplied Kosowicz with closely guarded information. That same someone, presumably, had supplied a list of ex-directory lines. He frowned, grappling with the problem. One country, and one only, opposed the two empires with gigantic, latent strength. To that country had shifted the focus of Semitic nationalism. And Kosowicz had been an American.

He thought, "Freedom, schmeedom. Democracy is Jew-shaped." He frowned again, fingering his face. It didn't alter the salient fact. The tip-off had come from the Freedom Front; and he had been contacted, however obliquely. Now, he had become an accessory; the thought had been nagging at the back of his brain all day.

He wondered what they could want of him. There was a rumor—a nasty rumor—that you never found out. Not till the end, till you'd done whatever was required from you. They were untiring, deadly, and subtle. He hadn't run squalling to Security at the first hint of danger; but that would have been allowed for. Every turn and twist would have been allowed for.

Every squirm on the hook.

He grunted, angry with himself. Fear was half their strength. He buttoned his shirt, remembering the guards at the gates, the wire and pillboxes. Here, of all places, nothing could reach him. For a few days he could forget the whole affair. He said aloud, "Anyway, I don't even matter. I'm not important." The thought cheered him, nearly.

He clicked the light off, walked through to his room, closed the door behind him. He crossed to the bed and stood quite still, staring at the bookshelf. Between Shirer and the Churchill tome there rested a third slim volume. He reached to touch the spine, delicately; read the author's name, Geissler, and the title, *Toward Humanity.* Below the title, like a topless Cross of Lorraine, were the twin linked "F''s" of the Freedom Front.

Ten minutes ago the book hadn't been there.

He walked to the door. The corridor beyond was deserted. From somewhere in the house, faintly, came music: *Till Eulenspiegel.* There were no nearer sounds. He closed the door again, locked it. Turned back and saw the wardrobe stood slightly ajar.

His case still lay on the side table. He crossed to it, took out the Lüger. The feel of the heavy pistol was comforting. He pushed the clip home, thumbed the safety forward, chambered a round. The breech closed with a hard snap. He walked to the wardrobe, shoved the door wide with his foot.

Nothing there.

He let his breath escape with a little hiss. He pressed the clip release, ejected the cartridge, laid the gun on the bed. He stood again looking at the shelf. He thought, "I must have been mistaken."

He took the book down, carefully. Geissler had been banned since publication in every province of the two empires; Mainwaring himself had never even seen a copy. He squatted on the edge of the bed, opened it at random.

The doctrine of Aryan co-ancestry, seized on so eagerly by the English middle classes, had the superficial reasonableness of most theories ultimately traceable to Rosenberg. Churchill's answer, in one sense, had already been made: but Chamberlain, and the country, turned to Hess. . . .

The Cologne settlement, though seeming to offer hope of security to Jews already domiciled in Britain, in fact paved the way for campaigns of intimidation and extortion similar to those already undertaken in history, notably by King John. The comparison is not unapt; for the English bourgeoisie, anxious to construct a rationale, discovered many unassailable precedents. A true Sign of the Times, almost certainly, was the resurgence of interest in the novels of Sir Walter Scott. By 1942 the lesson had been learned on both sides; and the Star of David was a common sight on the streets of most British cities.

The wind rose momentarily in a long wail, shaking the window casement. Mainwaring glanced up, turned his attention back to the book. He leafed through several pages.

In 1940, her Expeditionary Force shattered, her allies quiescent or defeated, the island truly stood alone. Her proletariat, bedevilled by bad leadership, weakened by a gigantic depression, was effectively without a voice. Her aristocracy, like their Junker counterparts, embraced coldly what could no longer be ignored; while after the Whitehall Putsch the Cabinet was reduced to the status of an Executive Council. . . .

The knock at the door made him start, guiltily. He pushed the book away. He said, "Who's that?"

She said, "Me. Richard, aren't you ready?"

He said, "Just a minute." He stared at the book, then placed it back on the shelf. He thought, "That at least wouldn't be expected." He slipped the Lüger into his case and closed it. Then he went to the door.

She was wearing a lacy black dress. Her shoulders were bare; her hair, worn loose, had been brushed till it gleamed. He stared at her a moment, stupidly. Then he said, "Please come in."

She said, "I was starting to wonder. . . . Are you all right?"

"Yes. Yes, of course."

She said, "You look as if you've seen a ghost."

He smiled. He said, "I expect I was taken aback. Those Aryan good looks."

She grinned at him. She said, "I'm half Irish, half English, half Scandinavian. If you have to know."

"That doesn't add up."

She said, "Neither do I, most of the time."

"Drink?"

"Just a little one. We shall be late."

He said, "It's not very formal tonight." He turned away, fiddling with his tie.

She sipped her drink, pointed her foot, scuffed her toe on the carpet. She said, "I expect you've been to a lot of house parties."

He said, "One or two."

She said, "Richard, are they . . .?"

"Are they what?"

She said, "I don't know. You can't help hearing things."

He said, "You'll be all right. One's very much like the next."

She said, "Are you honestly OK?"

"Sure."

She said, "You're all thumbs. Here, let me." She reached up, knotted deftly. Her eyes searched his face for a moment, moving in little shifts and

changes of direction. She said, "There. I think you just need looking
after."

He said carefully, "How's James?"

She stared a moment longer. She said, "I don't know. He's in Nairobi. I
haven't seen him for months."

He said, "I am a bit nervous, actually."

"Why?"

He said, "Escorting a rather lovely blonde."

She tossed her head, and laughed. She said, "You need a drink as well
then."

He poured whisky, said, "Cheers." The book, now, seemed to be burning into his shoulder blades.

She said, "As a matter of fact, you're looking rather fetching yourself."

He thought, "This is the night when all things come together. There
should be a word for it." Then he remembered about *Till Eulenspiegel.*

She said, "We'd honestly better go down."

Lights gleamed in the Great Hall, reflecting from polished boards, dark
linenfold paneling. At the nearer end of the chamber a huge fire burned.
Beneath the minstrels' gallery long tables had been set. Informal or not,
they shone with glass and silverware. Candles glowed amid wreaths of dark
evergreen; beside each place was a rolled crimson napkin.

In the middle of the Hall, its tip brushing the coffered ceiling, stood a
Christmas tree. Its branches were hung with apples, baskets of sweets, red
paper roses; at its base were piled gifts in gay-striped wrappers. Round the
tree folk stood in groups, chatting and laughing. Richard saw Müller, the
Defense Minister, with a striking-looking blonde he took to be his wife;
beside them was a tall, monocled man who was something or other in
Security. There was a group of GFP officers in their dark, neat uniforms,
beyond them half a dozen Liaison people. He saw Hans the chauffeur
standing head bent, nodding intently, smiling at some remark; and
thought as he had thought before, how he looked like a big, handsome ox.

Diane had paused in the doorway, and linked her arm through his. But
the Minister had already seen them. He came weaving through the crowd,
a glass in his hand. He was wearing tight black trews, a dark blue roll-neck
shirt. He looked happy and relaxed. He said, "Richard. And my dear Miss
Hunter. We'd nearly given you up for lost. After all, Hans Trapp is about.
Now, some drinks. And come, do come; please join my friends. Over here,
where it is warm."

She said, "Who's Hans Trapp?"

Mainwaring said, "You'll find out in a bit."

A little later the Minister said, "Ladies and gentlemen, I think we may be seated."

The meal was superb, the wine abundant. By the time the brandy was served Richard found himself talking more easily, and the Geissler copy pushed nearly to the back of his mind. The traditional toasts—King and *Führer*, the provinces, the Two Empires—were drunk; then the Minister clapped his hands for quiet. "My friends," he said, "tonight, this special night when we can all mix so freely, is *Weihnachtsabend*. It means, I suppose, many things to the many of us here. But let us remember, first and foremost, that this is the night of the children. Your children, who have come with you to share part at least of this very special Christmas."

He paused. "Already," he said, "they have been called from their crèche; soon, they will be with us. Let me show them to you." He nodded; at the gesture servants wheeled forward a heavy, ornate box. A drape was twitched aside, revealing the grey surface of a big TV screen. Simultaneously the lamps that lit the hall began to dim. Diane turned to Mainwaring, frowning; he touched her hand, gently, and shook his head.

Save for the firelight the hall was now nearly dark. The candles guttered in their wreaths, flames stirring in some draught; in the hush, the droning of the wind round the great façade of the place was once more audible. The lights would be out, now, all over the house.

"For some of you," said the Minister, "this is your first visit here. For you, I will explain.

"On *Weihnachtsabend* all ghosts and goblins walk. The demon Hans Trapp is abroad; his face is black and terrible, his clothing the skins of bears. Against him comes the Lightbringer, the Spirit of Christmas. Some call her Lucia Queen, some *Das Christkind*. See her now."

The screen lit up.

She moved slowly, like a sleepwalker. She was slender, and robed in white. Her ashen hair tumbled round her shoulders; above her head glowed a diadem of burning tapers. Behind her trod the Star Boys with their wands and tinsel robes; behind again came a little group of children. They ranged in age from eight- and nine-year-olds to toddlers. They gripped each other's hands, apprehensively, setting feet in line like cats, darting terrified glances at the shadows to either side.

"They lie in darkness, waiting," said the Minister softly. "Their nurses have left them. If they cry out, there is none to hear. So they do not cry out. And one by one she has called them. They see her light pass beneath the door; and they must rise and follow. Here, where we sit, is warmth. Here is safety. Their gifts are waiting; to reach them they must run the gauntlet of the dark."

The camera angle changed. Now they were watching the procession from above. The Lucia Queen stepped steadily; the shadows she cast leaped and flickered on paneled walls.

"They are in the Long Gallery now," said the Minister, "almost directly above us. They must not falter, they must not look back. Somewhere, Hans Trapp is hiding. From Hans, only *Das Christkind* can protect them. See how close they bunch behind her light!"

A howling began, like the crying of a wolf. In part it seemed to come from the screen, in part to echo through the Hall itself. The *Christkind* turned, raising her arms; the howling split into a many-voiced cadence, died to a mutter. In its place came a distant huge thudding, like the beating of a drum.

Diane said abruptly, "I don't find this particularly funny."

Mainwaring said, "It isn't supposed to be. Shh."

The Minister said evenly, "The Aryan child must know, from earliest years, the darkness that surrounds him. He must learn to fear, and to overcome that fear. He must learn to be strong. The Two Empires were not built by weakness; weakness will not sustain them. There is no place for it. This in part your children already know. The house is big, and dark; but they will win through to the light. They fight as the Empires once fought. For their birthright."

The shot changed again, showed a wide, sweeping staircase. The head of the little procession appeared, began to descend. "Now, where is our friend Hans?" said the Minister. "*Ah . . .*"

Her grip tightened convulsively on Mainwaring's arm. A black-smeared face loomed at the screen. The bogey snarled, clawing at the camera; then turned, loped swiftly toward the staircase. The children shrieked, and bunched; instantly the air was wild with din. Grotesque figures capered and leaped; hands grabbed, clutching. The column was buffeted and swirled; Mainwaring saw a child bowled completely over. The screaming reached a high pitch of terror; and the *Christkind* turned, arms once more raised. The goblins and werethings backed away, growling, into shadow; the slow march was resumed.

The Minister said, "They are nearly here. And they are good children, worthy of their race. Prepare the tree."

Servants ran forward with tapers to light the many candles. The tree sprang from gloom, glinting, black-green; and Mainwaring thought for the first time what a dark thing it was, although it blazed with light.

The big doors at the end of the Hall were flung back; and the children came tumbling through. Tear-stained and sobbing they were, some bruised; but all, before they ran to the tree, stopped, made obeisance to the strange creature who had brought them through the dark. Then the crown was lifted, the tapers extinguished; and Lucia Queen became a child like the rest, a slim, barefooted girl in a gauzy white dress.

The Minister rose, laughing, "Now," he said, "music, and some more wine. Hans Trapp is dead. My friends, one and all, and children; *frohe Weihnachten!*"

Diane said, "Excuse me a moment."

Mainwaring turned. He said, "Are you all right?"

She said, "I'm just going to get rid of a certain taste."

He watched her go, concernedly; and the Minister had his arm, was talking. "Excellent, Richard," he said. "It has gone excellently so far, don't you think?"

Richard said, "Excellently, sir."

"Good, good. Eh, Heidi, Erna . . . and Frederick, is it Frederick? What have you got there? Oh, very fine. . . ." He steered Mainwaring away, still with his fingers tucked beneath his elbow. Squeals of joy sounded, somebody had discovered a sled, tucked away behind the tree. The Minister said, "Look at them; how happy they are now. I would like children, Richard. Children of my own. Sometimes I think I have given too much. . . . Still, the opportunity remains. I am younger than you, do you realize that? This is the Age of Youth."

Mainwaring said, "I wish the Minister every happiness."

"Richard, Richard, you must learn not to be so very correct at all times. Unbend a little, you are too aware of dignity. You are my friend. I trust you; above all others, I trust you. Do you realize this?"

Richard said, "Thank you, sir. I do."

The Minister seemed bubbling over with some inner pleasure. He said, "Richard, come with me. Just for a moment. I have prepared a special gift for you. I won't keep you from the party very long."

Mainwaring followed, drawn as ever by the curious dynamism of the man. The Minister ducked through an arched doorway, turned right and left, descended a narrow flight of stairs. At the bottom the way was barred by a door of plain gray steel. The Minister pressed his palm flat to a sensor plate; a click, the whine of some mechanism, and the door swung inward. Beyond was a further flight of concrete steps, lit by a single lamp in a heavy well-glass. Chilly air blew upward. Mainwaring realized, with something approaching a shock, they had entered part of the bunker system that honeycombed the ground beneath Wilton.

The Minister hurried ahead of him, palmed a further door. He said, "Toys, Richard. All toys. But they amuse me." Then, catching sight of

Mainwaring's face. "Come, man, come! You are more nervous than the children, frightened of poor old Hans!"

The door gave on to a darkened space. There was a heavy, sweetish smell that Mainwaring, for a whirling moment, couldn't place. His companion propelled him forward, gently. He resisted, pressing back; and the Minister's arm shot by him. A click, and the place was flooded with light. He saw a wide, low area, also concrete-built. To one side, already polished and gleaming, stood the Mercedes, next to it the Minister's private Porsche. There were a couple of Volkswagens, a Ford Executive; and in the farthest corner a vision in glinting white. A Lamborghini. They had emerged in the garage underneath the house.

The Minister said, "My private shortcut." He walked forward to the Lamborghini, stood running his fingers across the low, broad bonnet. He said, "Look at her, Richard. Here, sit in. Isn't she a beauty? Isn't she fine?"

Mainwaring said, "She certainly is."

"You like her?"

Mainwaring smiled. He said, "Very much, sir. Who wouldn't?"

The Minister said, "Good, I'm so pleased. Richard, I'm upgrading you. She's yours. Enjoy her."

Mainwaring stared.

The Minister said, "Here, man. Don't look like that, like a fish. Here, see. Logbook, your keys. All entered up, finished." He gripped Mainwaring's shoulders, swung him round laughing. He said, "You've worked well for me. The Two Empires don't forget their good friends, their servants."

Mainwaring said, "I'm deeply honored, sir."

"Don't be honored. You're still being formal. Richard . . ."

"Sir?"

The Minister said, "Stay by me. Stay by me. Up there . . . they don't understand. But we understand . . . eh? These are difficult times. We must be together, always together. Kingdom and Reich. Apart . . . we could be destroyed." He turned away, placed clenched hands on the roof of the car. He said, "Here, all this. Jewry, the Americans . . . Capitalism. They must stay afraid. Nobody fears an Empire divided. It would fall!"

Mainwaring said, "I'll do my best, sir. We all will."

The Minister said, "I know, I know. But, Richard, this afternoon. I was playing with swords. Silly little swords."

Mainwaring thought, "I know how he keeps me. I can see the mechanism. But I mustn't imagine I know the entire truth."

The Minister turned back, as if in pain. He said, "Strength is Right. It has to be. But Hess . . ."

Mainwaring said slowly, "We've tried before, sir . . ."

The Minister slammed his fist on to metal. He said, "Richard, don't you see? It wasn't us. Not this time. It was his own people. Baumann, von Thaden. . . . I can't tell. He's an old man, he doesn't matter any more. It's an idea they want to kill, Hess is an idea. Do you understand? It's *Lebensraum*. Again. . . . Half the world isn't enough."

He straightened. He said, "The worm, in the apple. It gnaws, gnaws. . . . But we are Liaison. We matter, so much. Richard, be my eyes. Be my ears."

Mainwaring stayed silent, thinking about the book in his room; and the Minister once more took his arm. He said, "The shadows, Richard. They were never closer. Well might we teach our children to fear the dark. But . . . not in our time. Eh? Not for us. There is life, and hope. So much we can do . . ."

Mainwaring thought, "Maybe it's the wine I drank. I'm being pressed too hard." A dull, queer mood, almost of indifference, had fallen on him. He followed his Minister without complaint, back through the bunker complex, up to where the great fire, and the tapers on the tree burned low. He heard the singing mixed with the wind-voice, watched the children rock heavy-eyes, caroling sleep. The house seemed winding down, to rest; and she had gone, of course. He sat in a corner and drank wine and brooded, watched the Minister move from group to group until he too was gone, the hall nearly empty, and the servants clearing away.

He found his own self, his inner self, dozing at last as it dozed at each day's end. Tiredness, as ever, had come like a benison. He rose carefully, walked to the door. He thought, "I shan't be missed here." Shutters closed, in his head.

He found his key, unlocked his room. He thought, "Now, she will be waiting. Like all the letters that never came, the phones that never rang." He opened the door.

She said, "What kept you?"

He closed the door behind him, quietly. The fire crackled in the little room, the curtains were drawn against the night. She sat by the hearth, barefooted, still in her party dress. Beside her on the carpet were glasses, an ashtray with half-smoked stubs. One lamp was burning; in the warm light her eyes were huge and dark.

He looked across to the bookshelf. The Geissler stood where he had left it. He said, "How did you get in?"

She chuckled. She said, "There was a spare key on the back of the door. Didn't you see me steal it?"

He walked toward her, stood looking down. He thought, "Adding another fragment to the puzzle. Too much, too complicated."

She said, "Are you angry?"

He said, "No."

She patted the floor. She said gently, "Please, Richard. Don't be cross."

He sat, slowly, watching her.

She said, "Drink?" He didn't answer. She poured one anyway. She said, "What were you doing all this time? I thought you'd be up hours ago."

He said, "I was talking to the Minister."

She traced a pattern on the rug with her forefinger. Her hair fell forward, golden and heavy, baring the nape of her neck. She said, "I'm sorry about earlier on. I was stupid. I think I was a bit scared, too."

He drank, slowly. He felt like a run-down machine. Hell to have to start thinking again at this time of night. He said, "What were you doing?"

She watched up at him. Her eyes were candid. She said, "Sitting here, listening to the wind."

He said, "That couldn't have been much fun."

She shook her head, slowly, eyes fixed on his face. She said softly, "You don't know me at all."

He was quiet again. She said, "You don't believe in me, do you?"

He thought, "You need understanding. You're different from the rest; and I'm selling myself short." Aloud he said, "No."

She put the glass down, smiled, took his glass away. She hotched toward him across the rug, slid her arm round his neck. She said, "I was thinking about you. Making my mind up." She kissed him. He felt her tongue pushing, opened his lips. She said, *"Mmm. . . ."* She sat back a little, smiling. She said, "Do you mind?"

"No."

She pressed a strand of hair across her mouth, parted her teeth, kissed again. He felt himself react, involuntarily; and felt her touch and squeeze.

She said, "This is a silly dress. It gets in the way." She reached behind her. The fabric parted; she pushed it down, to the waist. She said, "Now, it's like the last time."

He said slowly, "Nothing's ever like last time."

She rolled across his lap, lay looking up. She whispered, "I've put the clock back."

Later in the dream she said, "I was so silly."

"What do you mean?"

She said, "I was shy. That was all. You weren't really supposed to go away."

He said, "What about James?"

"He's got somebody else. I didn't know what I was missing."

He let his hand stray over her; and present and immediate past became confused so that as he held her he still saw her kneeling, firelight dancing on her body. He reached for her and she was ready again; she fought, chuckling, taking it bareback, staying all the way.

Much later he said, "The Minister gave me a Lamborghini."

She rolled on to her belly, lay chin in hands watching under a tangle of hair. She said, "And now you've got yourself a blonde. What are you going to do with us?"

He said, "None of it's real."

She said, "*Oh. . . .*" She punched him. She said, "Richard, you make me cross. It's happened, you idiot. That's all. It happens to everybody." She scratched again with a finger on the carpet. She said, "I hope you've made me pregnant. They you'd have to marry me."

He narrowed his eyes; and the wine began again, singing in his head.

She nuzzled him. She said, "You asked me once. Say it again."

"I don't remember."

She said, "Richard, please . . ."

So he said, "Diane, will you marry me?"

And she said, "Yes, yes, yes."

Then afterward awareness came and though it wasn't possible he took her again and that time was finest of all, tight and sweet as honey. He'd fetched pillows from the bed and the counterpane. They curled close and he found himself talking, talking, how it wasn't the sex, it was shopping in Marlborough and having tea and seeing the sun set from White Horse Hill and being together, together; then she pressed fingers to his mouth and he fell with her in sleep past cold and loneliness and fear, past deserts and unlit places, down maybe to where spires reared gold and tree leaves moved and dazzled and white cars sang on roads and suns burned inwardly, lighting new worlds.

He woke, and the fire was low. He sat up, dazed. She was watching him. He stroked her hair a while, smiling; then she pushed away. She said, "Richard I have to go now."

"Not yet."

"It's the middle of the night."

He said, "It doesn't matter."

She said, "It does. He mustn't know."

"Who?"

She said, "You know who. You know why I was asked here."

He said, "He's not like that. Honestly."

She shivered. She said, "Richard, please. Don't get me in trouble." She smiled. She said, "It's only till tomorrow. Only a little while."

He stood, awkwardly, and held her, pressing her warmth close. Shoeless, she was tiny; her shoulder fitted beneath his armpit.

Halfway through dressing she stopped and laughed, leaned a hand against the wall. *"Oh. . . ."* She said, "I'm all woozy."

Later he said, "I'll see you to your room."

She said, "No, please. I'm all right." She was holding her handbag, and her hair was combed. She looked, again, as if she had been to a party.

At the door she turned. She said, "I love you, Richard. Truly." She kissed again, quickly; and was gone.

He closed the door, dropped the latch. He stood a while looking round the room. In the fire a burned-through log broke with a snap, sending up a little whirl of sparks. He walked to the washstand, bathed his face and hands. He shook the counterpane out on the bed, rearranged the pillows. Her scent still clung to him; he remembered how she had felt, and what she had said.

He crossed to the window, pushed it ajar. Outside the snow lay in deep swaths and drifts. Starlight gleamed from it, ghost-white; and the whole great house was mute. He stood feeling the chill move against his skin; and in all the silence a voice drifted far-off and clear. It came maybe from the guardhouses, full of distance and peace.

"Stille Nacht, heilige Nacht,
alles schläft, einsam wacht . . ."

He walked to the bed, pulled back the covers. The sheets were crisp and spotless, fresh smelling. He smiled, and turned off the lamp.

"Nur das traute, hochheilige Paar.
Holder Knabe mit lochigem Haar. . . ."

In the wall of the room, an inch behind the plasterwork, a complex little machine hummed. A spool of delicate golden wire shook slightly; but the creak of the opening window had been the last thing to interest the recorder, the singing alone couldn't activate its relays. A microswitch tripped, inaudibly; valve filaments faded, and died. Mainwaring lay back in the last of the firelight, and closed his eyes.

> *"Schlaf in himmlischer Ruh,*
> *Schlaf in himmlischer Ruh. . . ."*

2

Beyond drawn curtains, brightness flicks on.

The sky is a hard, clear blue; icy, full of sunlight. The light dazzles back from the brilliant land. Far things—copses, hills, solitary trees—stand sharp-etched. Roofs and eaves carry hummocks of whiteness, twigs a three-inch crest. In the stillness, here and there, the snow cracks and falls, powdering.

The shadows of the riders jerk and undulate. The quiet is interrupted. Hooves ring on swept courtyards or stamp muffled, churning the snow. It seems the air itself has been rendered crystalline by cold; through it the voices break and shatter, brittle as glass.

"Guten Morgen, Hans . . ."

"Verflucht Kalt!"

"Der Hundenmeister sagt, sehr gefahrlich!"

"Macht nichts! Wir erwischen es bevor dem Wald!"

A rider plunges beneath an arch. The horse snorts and curvets.

"Ich wette dir fünfzig amerikanische Dollar!"

"Einverstanden! Heute, habe ich Glück!"

The noise, the jangling and stamping, rings back on itself. Cheeks flush, perception is heightened; for more than one of the riders, the early court-yard reels. Beside the house door trestles have been set up. A great bowl is carried, steaming. The cups are raised, the toasts given; the responses ring again, crashing.

"The Two Empires . . .!"

"The Hunt . . .!"

Now, time is like a tight-wound spring. The dogs plunge forward, six to a handler, leashes straining, choke links creaking and snapping. Behind them jostle the riders. The bobbing scarlet coats splash across the snow. In the house drive an officer salutes; another strikes gloved palms together, nods. The gates whine open.

And across the country for miles around doors slam, bolts are shot, shutters closed, children scurried indoors. Village streets, muffled with snow, wait dumbly. Somewhere a dog barks, is silenced. The houses squat sullen, blind-eyes. The word has gone out, faster than horses could gallop. Today the Hunt will run; on snow.

The riders fan out, across a speckled waste of fields. A check, a questing; and the horns begin to yelp. Ahead the dogs bound and leap, black spots against whiteness. The horns cry again; but these hounds run mute. The riders sweep forward, on to the line.

Now, for the hunters, time and vision are fragmented. Twigs and snow merge in a racing blue; and tree-boles, ditches, gates. The tide reaches a crest of land, pours down the opposing slope. Hedges rear, mantled with white; and muffled thunder is interrupted by sailing silence, the smash and crackle of landing. The View sounds, harsh and high; and frenzy, and the racing blood, discharge intelligence. A horse goes down, in a gigantic flailing; another rolls, crushing its rider into the snow. A mount runs riderless. The Hunt, destroying, destroys itself unaware.

There are cottages, a paling fence. The fence goes over, unnoticed. A chicken house erupts in a cloud of flung crystals; birds run squawking, under the hooves. Caps are lost, flung away; hair flogs wild. Whips flail, spurs rake streaming flanks; and the woods are close. Twigs lash, and branches; snow falls, thudding. The crackling, now, is all around.

At the end it is always the same. The handlers close in, yodelling, waist-high in trampled brush; the riders force close and closer, mounts sidling and shaking; and silence falls. Only the quarry, reddened, flops and twists; the thin high noise it makes is the noise of anything in pain.

Now, if he chooses, the *Jagdmeister* may end the suffering. The crash of the pistol rings hollow; and birds erupt, high from frozen twigs, wheel with the echoes and cry. The pistol fires again; and the quarry lies still. In time, the shaking stops; and a dog creeps forward, begins to lick.

Now a slow movement begins; a spreading-out, away from the place. There are mutterings, a laugh that chokes to silence. The fever passes. Somebody begins to shiver; and a girl, blood glittering on cheek and neck, puts a glove to her forehead and moans. The Need has come and gone; for a little while the Two Empires have purged themselves.

The riders straggle back on tired mounts, shamble in through the gates. As the last enters, a closed black van starts up, drives away. In an hour, quietly, it returns; and the gates swing shut behind it.

Surfacing from deepest sleep was like rising, slowly, through a warm sea. For a time, as Mainwaring lay eyes closed, memory and awareness were confused so that she was with him and the room a recollected, childhood place. He rubbed his face, yawned, shook his head; and the knocking that had roused him came again. He said, "Yes?"

The voice said, "Last breakfast in fifteen minutes, sir."

He called, "Thank you," heard the footsteps pad away.

He pushed himself up, groped on the side table for his watch, held it close to his eyes. It read ten-forty-five.

He swung the bedclothes back, felt air tingle on his skin. She had been with him, certainly, in the dawn; his body remembered the succubus, with nearly painful strength. He looked down smiling, walked to the bathroom. He showered, toweled himself, shaved, and dressed. He closed his door and locked it, walked to the breakfast room. A few couples still sat over their coffee; he smiled a good morning, took a window seat. Beyond the double panes the snow piled thickly; its reflection lit the room with a white, inverted brilliance. He ate slowly, hearing distant shouts. On the long slope behind the house, groups of children pelted each other vigorously. Once a toboggan came into sight, vanished behind a rising swell of ground.

He had hoped he might see her, but she didn't come. He drank coffee, smoked a cigarette. He walked to the television lounge. The big color screen showed a children's party taking place in a Berlin hospital. He watched for a while. The door behind him clicked a couple of times, but it wasn't Diane.

There was a second guests' lounge, not usually much frequented at this time of the year, and a reading room and library. He wandered through them, but there was no sign of her. It occurred to him she might not yet be up; at Wilton there were few hard-and-fast rules for Christmas Day. He thought, "I should have checked her room number." He wasn't even sure in which of the guest wings she had been placed.

The house was quiet; it seemed most of the visitors had taken to their rooms. He wondered if she could have ridden with the Hunt; he'd heard it vaguely, leaving and returning. He doubted if the affair would have held much appeal.

He strolled back to the TV lounge, watched for an hour or more. By lunchtime he was feeling vaguely piqued; and sensing too the rise of a curious unease. He went back to his room, wondering if by any chance she had gone there; but the miracle was not repeated. The room was empty.

The fire was burning, and the bed had been remade. He had forgotten the servants' passkeys. The Geissler copy still stood on the shelf. He took it down, stood weighing it in his hand and frowning. It was, in a sense, madness to leave it there.

He shrugged, put the thing back. He thought, "So who reads book-shelves anyway?" The plot, if plot there had been, seemed absurd now in the clearer light of day. He stepped into the corridor, closed the door, and locked it behind him. He tried as far as possible to put the book from his mind. It represented a problem; and problems, as yet, he wasn't prepared to cope with. Too much else was going on in his brain.

He lunched alone, now with a very definite pang; the process was disquietingly like that of other years. Once he thought he caught sight of her in the corridor. His heart thumped; but it was the other blonde, Müller's wife. The gestures, the fall of the hair, were similar; but this woman was taller.

He let himself drift into a reverie. Images of her, it seemed, were engraved on his mind; each to be selected now, studied, placed lovingly aside. He saw the firelit texture of her hair and skin, her lashes brushing her cheek as she lay in his arms and slept. Other memories, sharper, more immediate still, throbbed like little shocks in the mind. She tossed her head, smiling; her hair swung, touched the point of a breast.

He pushed his cup away, rose. At fifteen hundred patriotism required her presence in the TV lounge. As it required the presence of every other guest. Then, if not before, he would see her. He reflected, wryly, that he had waited half a lifetime for her; a little longer now would do no harm.

He took to prowling the house again: the Great Hall, the Long Gallery where the *Christkind* had walked. Below the windows that lined it was a snow-covered roof. The tart, reflected light struck upward, robbing the place of mystery. In the Great Hall they had already removed the tree. He watched household staff hanging draperies, carrying in stacks of gilded cane chairs. On the Minstrels' Gallery a pile of odd-shaped boxes proclaimed that the orchestra had arrived.

At fourteen hundred hours he walked back to the TV lounge. A quick glance assured him she wasn't there. The bar was open; Hans, looking as big and suave as ever, had been pressed into service to minister to the guests. He smiled at Mainwaring and said, "Good afternoon, sir." Mainwaring asked for a lager beer, took the glass to a corner seat. From here he could watch both the TV screen and the door.

The screen was showing the worldwide link-up that had become hallowed Christmas afternoon fare within the Two Empires. He saw, without particular interest, greetings flashed from the Leningrad and Moscow garrisons, a lightship, an Arctic weather station, a Mission in German East Africa. At fifteen hundred the *Führer* was due to speak; this year, for the first time, Ziegler was preceding Edward VIII.

The room filled, slowly. She didn't come. Mainwaring finished the lager, walked to the bar, asked for another and a packet of cigarettes. The unease was sharpening now into something very like alarm. He thought for the first time that she might have been taken ill.

The time signal flashed, followed by the drumroll of the German anthem. He rose with the rest, stood stiffly till it had finished. The screen cleared, showed the familiar room in the Chancellery; the dark, high panels, the crimson drapes, the big *Hakenkreuz* emblem over the desk. The *Führer*, as ever, spoke impeccably; but Mainwaring thought with a fragment of his mind how old he had begun to look.

The speech ended. He realized he hadn't heard a word that was said.

The drums crashed again. The King said, "Once more, at Christmas, it is my . . . duty and pleasure . . . to speak to you."

Something seemed to burst inside Mainwaring's head. He rose, walked quickly to the bar. He said, "Hans, have you seen Miss Hunter?"

The other jerked round. He said, "Sir *shh* . . . please . . ."

"Have you seen her?"

Hans stared at the screen, and back to Mainwaring. The King was saying, "There have been . . . troubles, and difficulties. More perhaps lie ahead. But with . . . God's help, they will be overcome."

The chauffeur licked his mouth. He said, "I'm sorry, sir. I don't know what you mean."

"Which was her room?"

The big man looked like something trapped. He said, "Please, Mr. Mainwaring. You'll get me into trouble . . ."

"Which was her room?"

Somebody turned and hissed, angrily. Hans said, "I don't understand."

"For God's sake, man, you carried her things upstairs. I saw you!"

Hans said, "No, sir . . ."

Momentarily the lounge seemed to spin.

There was a door behind the bar. The chauffeur stepped back. He said, "Sir. Please . . ."

The place was a storeroom. There were wine bottles racked, a shelf with jars of olives, walnuts, eggs. Mainwaring closed the door behind him, tried to control the shaking. Hans said, "Sir, you must not ask me these things. I don't know a Miss Hunter. I don't know what you mean."

Mainwaring said, "Which was her room? I demand that you answer."

"I can't!"

"You drove me from London yesterday. Do you deny that?"

"No, sir."

"You drove me with Miss Hunter."

"No, sir!"

"Damn your eyes, where is she?"

The chauffeur was sweating. A long wait; then he said, "Mr. Mainwaring, please. You must understand. I can't help you." He swallowed, and drew himself up. He said, "I drove you from London. I'm sorry. I drove you . . . *on your own.*"

The lounge door swung shut behind Mainwaring. He half-walked, half-ran to his room. He slammed the door behind him, leaned against it panting. In time the giddiness passed. He opened his eyes, slowly. The fire glowed; the Geissler stood on the bookshelf. Nothing was changed.

He set to work, methodically. He shifted furniture, peered behind it. He rolled the carpet back, tapped every foot of floor. He fetched a flashlight from his case and examined, minutely, the interior of the wardrobe. He ran his fingers lightly across the walls, section by section, tapping again. Finally he got a chair, dismantled the ceiling lighting fitting.

Nothing.

He began again. Halfway through the second search he froze, staring at the floorboards. He walked to his case, took the screwdriver from the pistol holder. A moment's work with the blade and he sat back, staring into his palm. He rubbed his face, placed his find carefully on the side table. A tiny earring, one of the pair she had worn. He sat a while breathing heavily, his head in his hands.

The brief daylight had faded as he worked. He lit the standard lamp, wrenched the shade free, stood the naked bulb in the middle of the room. He worked round the walls again, peering, tapping, pressing. By the fireplace, finally, a foot-square section of plaster rang hollow.

He held the bulb close, examined the hairline crack. He inserted the screwdriver blade delicately, twisted. Then again. A click; and the section hinged open.

He reached inside the little space, shaking, lifted out the recorder. He stood silent a time, holding it; then raised his arms, brought the machine smashing down on the hearth. He stamped and kicked, panting, till the thing was reduced to fragments.

The droning rose to a roar, swept low over the house. The helicopter settled slowly, belly lamps glaring, downdraught raising a storm of snow. He walked to the window, stood staring. The children embarked, clutching scarves and gloves, suitcases, boxes with new toys. The steps were withdrawn, the hatch dogged shut. Snow swirled again; the machine lifted heavily, swung away in the direction of Wilton.

The Party was about to start.

Lights blaze, through the length and breadth of the house. Orange-lit windows throw long bars of brightness across the snow. Everywhere is an anxious coming and going, the pattering of feet, clink of silver and glassware, hurried commands. Waiters scuttle between the kitchens and the

Green Room where dinner is laid. Dish after dish is borne in, paraded. Peacocks, roasted and gilded, vaunt their plumes in shadow and candleglow, spirit-soaked wicks blazing in their beaks. The Minister rises, laughing; toast after toast is drunk. To five thousand tanks, ten thousand fighting airplanes, a hundred thousand guns. The Two Empires feast their guests royally.

The climax approaches. The boar's head, garnished and smoking, is borne shoulder-high. His tusks gleam; clamped in his jaws is the golden sun-symbol, the orange. After him march the waifs and mummers, with their lanterns and begging-cups. The carol they chant is older by far than the Two Empires; older than the Reich, older than Great Britain.

"Alive he spoiled, where poor men toiled, which made kind Ceres sad . . ."

The din of voices rises. Coins are flung, glittering; wine is poured. And more wine, and more and more. Bowls of fruit are passed, and trays of sweets; spiced cakes, gingerbread, marzipans. Till at a signal the brandy is brought, and boxes of cigars.

The ladies rise to leave. They move flushed and chattering through the corridors of the house, uniformed link-boys grandly lighting their way. In the Great Hall their escorts are waiting. Each young man is tall, each blonde, each impeccably uniformed. On the Minstrels' Gallery a baton is poised; across the lawns, distantly, floats the whirling excitement of a waltz.

In the Green Room, hazed now with smoke, the doors are once more flung wide. Servants scurry again, carrying in boxes, great gay-wrapped parcels topped with scarlet satin bows. The Minister rises, hammering on the table for quiet.

"My friends, good friends, friends of the Two Empires. For you, no expense is spared. For you, the choicest gifts. Tonight, nothing but the best is good enough; and nothing but the best is here. Friends, enjoy yourselves. Enjoy my house. *Frohe Weihnachten . . .!*"

He walks quickly into shadow, and is gone. Behind him, silence falls. A waiting; and slowly, mysteriously, the great heap of gifts begins to stir. Paper splits, crackling. Here a hand emerges, here a foot. A breathless pause; and the first of the girls rises slowly, bare in flamelight, shakes her glinting hair.

The table roars again.

The sound reached Mainwaring dimly. He hesitated at the foot of the main staircase, moved on. He turned right and left, hurried down a flight of steps. He passed kitchens, and the servants' hall. From the hall came the blare of a record player. He walked to the end of the corridor, unlatched a door. Night air blew keen against his face.

He crossed the courtyard, opened a further door. The space beyond was bright-lit; there was the faint, musty stink of animals. He paused, wiped his face. He was shirt-sleeved; but despite the cold he was sweating.

He walked forward again, steadily. To either side of the corridor were the fronts of cages. The dogs hurled themselves at the bars, thunderously. He ignored them.

The corridor opened into a square concrete chamber. To one side of the place was a ramp. At its foot was parked a windowless black van.

In the far wall a door showed a crack of light. He rapped sharply, and again.

"Hundenmeister . . ."

The door opened. The man who peered up at him was as wrinkled and pot-bellied as a Nast Santa Claus. At sight of his visitor's face he tried to duck back; but Mainwaring had him by the arm. He said, *"Herr Hundenmeister,* I must talk to you."

"Who are you? I don't know you. What do you want? . . ."

Mainwaring showed his teeth. He said, "The van. You drove the van this morning. What was in it?"

"I don't know what you mean . . ."

The heave sent him stumbling across the floor. He tried to bolt; but Mainwaring grabbed him again.

"What was in it . . .?"

"I won't talk to you! Go away!"

The blow exploded across his cheek. Mainwaring hit him again, back-handed, slammed him against the van.

"Open it . . .!"

"Wer ist da? Was ist passiert?"

The little man whimpered, rubbing at his mouth.

Mainwaring straightened, breathing heavily. The GFP captain walked forward, staring, thumbs hooked in his belt.

"Wer sind Sie?"

Mainwaring said, "You know damn well. And speak English, you bastard. You're as English as I am."

The other glared. He said, "You have no right to be here. I should arrest you. You have no right to accost *Herr Hundenmeister."*

"What is in that van?"

"Have you gone mad? The van is not your concern. Leave now. At once."

"Open it!"

The other hesitated, and shrugged. He stepped back. He said, "Show him, *mein Herr.*"

The *Hundenmeister* fumbled with a bunch of keys. The van door grated. Mainwaring walked forward, slowly.

The vehicle was empty.

The captain said, "You have seen what you wished to see. You are satisfied. Now go."

Mainwaring stared round. There was a further door, recessed deeply into the wall. Beside it controls like the controls of a bank vault.

"What is in that room?"

The GFP man said, "You have gone too far. I order you to leave."

"You have no authority over me!"

"Return to your quarters!"

Mainwaring said, "I refuse."

The other slapped the holster at his hip. He gut-held the Walther, wrist locked, feet apart. He said, "Then you will be shot."

Mainwaring walked past him, contemptuously. The baying of the dogs faded as he slammed the outer door.

It was among the middle classes that the seeds had first been sown; and it was among the middle classes that they flourished. Britain had been called often enough a nation of shopkeepers; now for a little while the tills were closed, the blinds left drawn. Overnight it seemed, an effete symbol of social and national disunity became the Einsatzgruppenführer; *and the wire for the first detention camps was strung . . .*

Mainwaring finished the page, tore it from the spine, crumpled it and dropped it on the fire. He went on reading. Beside him on the hearth stood a part-full bottle of whisky and a glass. He picked the glass up mechanically, drank. He lit a cigarette. A few minutes later a new page followed the last.

The clock ticked steadily. The burning paper made a little rustling. Reflections danced across the ceiling of the room. Once Mainwaring raised his head, listened; once put the ruined book down, rubbed his eyes. The room, and the corridor outside, stayed quiet.

Against immeasurable force we must pit cunning; against immeasurable evil, faith and a high resolve. In the war we wage, the stakes are high: the dignity of man, the freedom of the spirit, the survival of humanity. Already in that war, many of us have died; many more, undoubtedly, will lay down their lives. But always, beyond them, there will be others; and still more. We shall go on, as we must go on; till this thing is wiped from the earth.

Meanwhile, we must take fresh heart. Every blow, now, is a blow for freedom. In France, Belgium, Finland, Poland, Russia, the forces of the Two Empires confront each other uneasily. Greed, jealousy, mutual distrust; these are the enemies, and they work from within. This the Empires know full well. And, knowing, for the first time in their existence, fear . . .

The last page crumpled, fell to ash. Mainwaring sat back, staring at nothing. Finally he stirred, looked up. It was zero three hundred; and they hadn't come for him yet.

The bottle was finished. He set it to one side, opened another. He swilled the liquid in the glass, hearing the magnified ticking of the clock.

He crossed the room, took the Lüger from the case. He found a cleaning rod, patches, and oil. He sat a while dully, looking at the pistol. Then he slipped the magazine free, pulled back on the breech toggle, thumbed the latch, slid the barrel from the guides.

His mind, wearied, had begun to play aggravating tricks. It ranged and wandered, remembering scenes, episodes, details sometimes from years back; trivial, unconnected. Through and between the wanderings, time after time, ran the ancient, lugubrious words of the carol. He tried to shut them out, but it was impossible.

"Living he spoiled where poor men toiled, which made kind Ceres sad . . ."

He pushed the link pin clear, withdrew the breech block, stripped the firing pin. He laid the parts out, washed them with oil and water, dried and reoiled. He reassembled the pistol, working carefully; inverted the barrel, shook the link down in front of the hooks, closed the latch, checked the recoil spring engagement. He loaded a full clip, pushed it home, chambered a round, thumbed the safety to *Gesichert.* He released the clip, reloaded.

He fetched his briefcase, laid the pistol inside carefully, grip uppermost. He filled a spare clip, added the extension butt and a fifty box of Parabellum. He closed the flap and locked it, set the case beside the bed. After that there was nothing more to do. He sat back in the chair, refilled his glass.

"Toiling he boiled, where poor men spoiled . . ."

The light faded, finally.

He woke, and the room was dark. He got up, felt the floor sway a little. He understood that he had a hangover. He groped for the light switch. The clock hands stood at zero eight hundred.

He felt vaguely guilty at having slept so long.

He walked to the bathroom. He stripped and showered, running the water as hot as he could bear. The process brought him round a little. He dried himself, staring down. He thought for the first time what curious things these bodies were.

He dressed and shaved. He had remembered what he was going to do; fastening his tie, he tried to remember why. He couldn't. His brain, it seemed, had gone dead.

There was an inch of whisky in the bottle. He poured it, grimaced and drank. Inside him was a fast, cold shaking. He thought, "Like the first morning at a new school."

He lit a cigarette. Instantly his throat filled. He walked to the bathroom and vomited. Then again. Finally there was nothing left to come.

His chest ached. He rinsed his mouth, washed his face again. He sat in the bedroom for a while, head back and eyes closed. In time the shaking went away. He lay unthinking, hearing the clock tick. Once his lips moved. He said, "They're no better than us."

At nine hundred hours he walked to the breakfast room. His stomach, he felt, would retain very little. He ate a slice of toast, carefully, drank some coffee. He asked for a pack of cigarettes, went back to his room. At ten hundred hours he was due to meet the Minister.

He checked the briefcase again. A thought made him add a pair of stringback motoring gloves. He sat again, stared at the ashes where he had burned the Geissler. A part of him was willing the clock hands not to move. At five to ten he picked the briefcase up, stepped into the corridor. He stood a moment staring round him. He thought, "It hasn't happened yet. I'm still alive." There was still the flat in Town to go back to, still his office; the tall windows, the telephones, the khaki utility desk.

He walked through sunlit corridors to the Minister's suite.

The room to which he was admitted was wide and long. A fire crackled in the hearth; beside it on a low table stood glasses and a decanter. Over

the mantel, conventionally, hung the *Führer*'s portrait. Edward VIII faced
him across the room. Tall windows framed a prospect of rolling parkland.
In the distance, blue on the horizon, were the woods.

The Minister said, "Good morning, Richard. Please sit down. I don't
think I shall keep you long."

He sat, placing the briefcase by his knee.

This morning everything seemed strange. He studied the Minister curiously, as if seeing him for the first time. He had that type of face once
thought of as peculiarly English: shortnosed and slender, with high, finely
shaped cheekbones. The hair, blonde and cropped close to the scalp, made
him look nearly boyish. The eyes were candid, flat, dark-fringed. He
looked, Mainwaring decided, not so much Aryan as like some fierce nurs-
ery toy; a feral Teddy Bear.

The Minister riffled papers. He said, "Several things have cropped up;
among them, I'm afraid, more trouble in Glasgow. The fifty-first Panzer
division is standing by; as yet, the news hasn't been released."

Mainwaring wished his head felt less hollow. It made his own voice
boom so unnecessarily. He said, "Where is Miss Hunter?"

The Minister paused. The pale eyes stared; then he went on speaking.

"I'm afraid I may have to ask you to cut short your stay here. I shall be
flying back to London for a meeting; possibly tomorrow, possibly the day
after. I shall want you with me, of course."

"Where is Miss Hunter?"

The Minister placed his hands flat on the desktop, studied the nails. He
said, "Richard, there are aspects of Two Empires culture that are neither
mentioned nor discussed. You of all people should know this. I'm being
patient with you; but there are limits to what I can overlook."

*"Seldom he toiled, while Ceres rolled, which made poor kind men
glad . . ."*

Mainwaring opened the flap of the case and stood up. He thumbed the
safety forward and leveled the pistol.

There was silence for a time. The fire spat softly. Then the Minister
smiled. He said, "That's an interesting gun, Richard. Where did you get
it?"

Mainwaring didn't answer.

The Minister moved his hands carefully to the arms of his chair, leaned
back. He said, "It's the Marine model, of course. It's also quite old. Does
it by any chance carry the Erfurt stamp? Its value would be considerably
increased."

He smiled again. He said, "If the barrel is good, I'll buy it. For my private collection."

Mainwaring's arm began to shake. He steadied his wrist, gripping with his left hand.

The Minister sighed. He said, "Richard, you can be so stubborn. It's a good quality; but you do carry it to excess." He shook his head. He said, "Did you imagine for one moment I didn't know you were coming here to kill me? My dear chap, you've been through a great deal. You're overwrought. Believe me, I know just how you feel."

Mainwaring said, "You murdered her."

The Minister spread his hands. He said, "What with? A gun? A knife? Do I honestly look such a shady character?"

The words made a cold pain, and a tightness in the chest. But they had to be said.

The Minister's brows rose. Then he started to laugh. Finally he said, "At last I see. I understood, but I couldn't believe. So you bullied our poor little *Hundenmeister*, which wasn't very worthy; and seriously annoyed the *Herr Hauptmann*, which wasn't very wise. Because of this fantasy, stuck in your head. Do you really believe it, Richard? Perhaps you believe in *Struwwelpeter* too." He sat forward. He said, "The Hunt ran. And killed . . . a deer. She gave us an excellent chase. As for your little Huntress . . . Richard, she's gone. She never existed. She was a figment of your imagination. Best forgotten."

Mainwaring said, "We were in love."

The Minister said, "Richard, you really are becoming tiresome." He shook his head again. He said, "We're both adult. We both know what that word is worth. It's a straw, in the wind. A candle, on a night of gales. A phrase that is meaningless. *Lächerlich.*" He put his hands together, rubbed a palm. He said, "When this is over, I want you to go away. For a month, six weeks maybe. With your new car. When you come back . . . well, we'll see. Buy yourself a girlfriend, if you need a woman that much. *Einen Schatz.* I never dreamed; you're so remote, you should speak more of yourself. Richard, I understand; it isn't such a very terrible thing."

Mainwaring stared.

The Minister said, "We shall make an arrangement. You will have the use of an apartment, rather a nice apartment. So your lady will be close. When you tire of her . . . buy another. They're unsatisfactory for the most part, but reasonable. Now sit down like a good chap, and put your gun away. You look so silly, standing there scowling like that."

It seemed he felt all life, all experience, as a gray weight pulling. He lowered the pistol, slowly. He thought, "At the end, they were wrong.

They picked the wrong man." He said, "I suppose now I use it on my-self."

The Minister said, "No, no, no. You still don't understand." He linked his knuckles, grinning. He said, "Richard, the *Herr Hauptmann* would have arrested you last night. I wouldn't let him. This is between ourselves. Nobody else. I give you my word."

Mainwaring felt his shoulders sag. The strength seemed drained from him; the pistol, now, weighed too heavy for his arm.

The Minister said, "Richard, why so glum? It's a great occasion, man. You've found your courage. I'm delighted."

He lowered his voice. He said, "Don't you want to know why I let you come here with your machine? Aren't you even interested?"

Mainwaring stayed silent.

The Minister said, "Look around you, Richard. See the world. I want men near me, serving me. Now more than ever. Real men, not afraid to die. Give me a dozen . . . but you know the rest. I could rule the world. But first . . . I must rule them. My men. Do you see now? Do you understand?"

Mainwaring thought, "He's in control again. But he was always in control. He owns me."

The study spun a little.

The voice went on, smoothly. "As for this amusing little plot by the so-called Freedom Front; again, you did well. It was difficult for you. I was watching; believe me, with much sympathy. Now, you've burned your book. Of your own free will. That delighted me."

Mainwaring looked up, sharply.

The Minister shook his head. He said, "The real recorder is rather better hidden, you were too easily satisfied there. There's also a TV moni-tor. I'm sorry about it all, I apologize. It was necessary."

A singing started inside Mainwaring's head.

The Minister sighed again. He said, "Still unconvinced, Richard? Then I have some things I think you ought to see. Am I permitted to open my desk drawer?"

Mainwaring didn't speak. The other slid the drawer back slowly, reached in. He laid a telegram flimsy on the desk top. He said, "The addressee is Miss D.J. Hunter. The message consists of one word. *'Acti-vate.'* "

The singing rose in pitch.

"This as well," said the Minister. He held up a medallion on a thin gold chain. The little disc bore the linked motif of the Freedom Front. He said,

"Mere exhibitionism; or a deathwish. Either way, a most undesirable trait."

He tossed the thing down. He said, "She was here under surveillance, of course, we'd known about her for years. To them, you were a sleeper. Do you see the absurdity? They really thought you would be jealous enough to assassinate your Minister. This they mean in their silly little book, when they talk of subtlety. Richard, I could have fifty blonde women if I chose. A hundred. Why should I want yours?" He shut the drawer with a click, and rose. He said, "Give me the gun now. You don't need it any more." He extended his arm; then he was flung heavily backward. Glasses smashed on the side table. The decanter split; its contents poured dark across the wood.

Over the desk hung a faint haze of blue. Mainwaring walked forward, stood looking down. There were blood-flecks, and a little flesh. The eyes of the Teddy Bear still showed glints of white. Hydraulic shock had shattered the chest; the breath drew ragged, three times, and stopped. He thought, "I didn't hear the report."

The communicating door opened. Mainwaring turned. A secretary stared in, bolted at sight of him. The door slammed.

He pushed the briefcase under his arm, ran through the outer office. Feet clattered in the corridor. He opened the door, carefully. Shouts sounded, somewhere below in the house.

Across the corridor hung a loop of crimson cord. He stepped over it, hurried up a flight of stairs. Then another. Beyond the private apartments the way was closed by a heavy metal grille. He ran to it, rattled. A rumbling sounded from below. He glared round. Somebody had operated the emergency shutters; the house was sealed.

Beside the door an iron ladder was spiked to the wall. He climbed it, panting. The trap in the ceiling was padlocked. He clung one-handed, awkward with the briefcase, held the pistol above his head.

Daylight showed through splintered wood. He put his shoulder to the trap, heaved. It creaked back. He pushed head and shoulders through, scrambled. Wind stung at him, and flakes of snow.

His shirt was wet under the arms. He lay face down, shaking. He thought, "It wasn't an accident. None of it was an accident." He had underrated them. They understood despair.

He pushed himself up, stared round. He was on the roof of Wilton. Beside him rose gigantic chimney stacks. There was a lattice radio mast. The wind hummed in its guy wires. To his right ran the balustrade that crowned the façade of the house. Behind it was a snow-choked gutter.

He wriggled across a sloping scree of roof, ran crouching. Shouts sounded from below. He dropped flat, rolled. An automatic clattered. He edged forward again, dragging the briefcase. Ahead, one of the corner towers rose dark against the sky. He crawled to it, crouched sheltered from the wind. He opened the case, pulled the gloves on. He clipped the stock to the pistol, laid the spare magazine beside him and the box of rounds.

The shots came again. He peered forward, through the balustrade. Running figures scattered across the lawn. He sighted on the nearest, squeezed. Commotion below. The automatic zipped; stone chips flew, whining. A voice called, "Don't expose yourselves unnecessarily." Another answered.

"Die kommen mit den Hubschrauber . . ."

He stared round him, at the yellow-gray horizon. He had forgotten the helicopter.

A snow flurry drove against his face. He huddled, flinching. He thought he heard, carried on the wind, a faint droning.

From where he crouched he could see the nearer trees of the park, beyond them the wall and gatehouses. Beyond again, the land rose to the circling woods.

The droning was back, louder than before. He screwed his eyes, made out the dark spot skimming above the trees. He shook his head. He said, "We made a mistake. We all made a mistake."

He settled the stock of the Lüger to his shoulder, and waited.

Thor Meets
Captain America

David Brin

1

Loki's dwarf rolled its eyes and moaned pitifully as the sub leveled off at periscope depth. With stubby fingers the gnarled, neckless creature pulled at its yellow-stained, gray beard, staring up at the creaking pipes.

A thing of dark forest depths and hidden caves, Chris Turing thought as he watched the dwarf. *It wasn't meant for this place.*

Only men *would choose such a way to die, in a leaking steel coffin, on a hopeless attempt to blow up Valhalla.*

But then, it wasn't likely Loki's dwarf had had any choice in being here.

Why, Chris wondered suddenly—not for the first time. *Why do such creatures exist? Wasn't evil doing well enough in the world before they came to help it along?*

The engines rumbled and Chris shrugged aside the thought. Even imagining a world without Aesir and their servants in it was by now as hard as remembering a time without war.

Chris sat strapped in his crash seat—he could hear the swishing of icy Baltic water just behind the tissue-thin bulkhead—and watched the gnome huddle atop a crate of hydrogen-bomb parts. It drew its clublike feet up away from the sloshing brine on the deck, scrunching higher on the black box. Another moan escaped the dwarf as the *Razorfin*'s periscope went up and more water gurgled in through the pressure relief lines.

Major Marlowe looked up from the assault rifle he was reassembling for the thirtieth time. "What's eating the damn dwarf now?" the marine officer asked.

Chris shook his head. "Search me. The fact that he's out of his element, maybe? After all, the ancient Norse thought of the deep as a place for sunken boats and fishes."

"I thought you were some sort of expert on the Aesir. And you aren't even sure why the thing is foaming at the mouth like that?"

Chris could only shrug. "I said I don't know. Why don't you go over and ask him yourself?"

Marlowe gave Chris a sour glance, as if to say that he didn't much care for the joke. "Sidle up to that stench and ask Loki's damn *dwarf* to explain its *feelings?* Hmmph. I'd rather spit in an Aesir's eye."

From his left Chris's assistant, Zap O'Leary, leaned out and grinned at Marlowe. "Dig it, daddyo," O'Leary said to the marine. "There's an Aes over by the scope, dope. Be my guest. Write him runes in his spittoon." The eccentric technician gestured over toward the Navy men, clustered around the sub's periscope. Next to the Skipper stood a hulking figure clad in furs and leather, towering over the submariners.

Marlowe blinked back at O'Leary in bewilderment. The marine did not seem offended as much as confused. "What did he say?" he asked Chris.

Chris wished he weren't seated between the two. "Zap suggests that you test it by spitting in *Loki's* eye."

Marlowe grimaced. O'Leary might as well have suggested he stick his hand into a scram-jet engine. At that moment one of the marines crammed into the passageway behind them made the mistake of dropping a cartridge into the foul leak-water underfoot. Marlowe vented his frustration on the poor grunt in richly inventive profanity.

The dwarf moaned again, eyes darting, hugging his knees against the straps holding him onto the hermetically sealed crate.

Wherever they're from, they aren't used to submarines, Chris thought. *And these so-called dwarves sure don't like water.*

Chris wondered how Loki had managed to persuade this one to come along on this suicide mission.

Probably threatened to turn him into a toad, he speculated. *I wouldn't put it past Loki.*

It was a desperate venture. In late 1962 there was very little time left for what remained of the Alliance against Nazism. If anything at all could be done this autumn to stave off the inevitable, it would be worth the gamble.

Even Loki—bearlike, nearly invulnerable, and always booming forth laughter that sent chills down human spines—had betrayed nerves earlier, as the *Razorfin* dropped from the belly of a screaming B-65, sending their stomachs whirling as the arrow-sub plummeted like a great stone into Neptune's icy embrace.

Chris had to admit that *he* would have been sick, had that brief, seemingly endless fall lasted any longer. The crash and shriek of tortured metal when they hit was almost a relief, after that.

And anything seemed an improvement over the long, screeching trip over the pole, skirting Nazi missiles, skimming mountains and gray waters in lurching zigs and zags, helplessly listening, strapped into place, as the airmen swooped their flying coffins hither and yon, praying that the enemy's Aesir masters weren't patrolling that section of the north that night . . .

Of twenty sub-carriers sent out together from Baffin Island only six had made it all the way to the waters between Sweden and Finland. And both *Cetus* and *Tigerfish* had broken up on impact with the water, tearing like ripped sardine cans and spilling their hapless crews into freezing death.

Only four subs left, Chris thought.

Still, he reminded himself. *Our chances may be slim, but those poor pilots are the real heroes.* He doubted even one of the crews would make it across dark, deadly Europe to Tehran and safety.

"Captain Turing!"

Chris looked up as the Skipper called his name. Commander Lewis had lowered the periscope and moved over to the chart table.

"Be right with you, Commander." Chris unstrapped and stepped down into the brine.

"Tell 'em we're savin' our own hooch for ourselves," O'Leary advised him, sotto voce. "Good pot is too rare to share."

"Shut up, fool," said Marlowe. Chris ignored both of them as he sloshed forward. The Skipper awaited him, standing beside their "friendly adviser," the alien creature calling himself *Loki.*

I've known Loki for years, Chris thought. *I've fought alongside him against his Aesir brothers . . . and he still scares the living hell out of me every time I look at him.*

Towering over everyone else, Loki regarded Chris enigmatically with fierce black eyes. The "god of tricks" looked much like a man, albeit an unnaturally large and powerful one. But those eyes belied the impression of humanity. Chris had spent enough time with Loki, since the renegade Aesir defected to the Allied side, to have learned to avoid looking into them whenever possible.

"Sir," he said, nodding to Commander Lewis and the bearded Aesir. "I take it we're approaching point Y?"

"That's correct," the Skipper said. "We'll be there in about twenty minutes, barring anything unforeseen."

Lewis seemed to have aged over the last twenty hours. The young sub commander knew that his squadron wasn't the only thing considered expendable in this operation. Several thousand miles to the west the better part of what remained of the United States Surface Navy was engaged hopelessly for one reason only—to distract the Kriegsmarine and the SS and especially a certain "god of the sea" away from the Baltic and Operation Ragnarok. Loki's cousin Tyr wasn't very potent against submarines, but unless his attention was drawn elsewhere, he could make life hell for them when their tiny force tried to land.

So tonight, instead, he would be making hell for American and Canadian and Mexican sailors, far away.

Chris shied away from thinking about it. Too many boys were going to their deaths off Labrador, just to keep one alien creature occupied while four subs tried to sneak in through the back door.

"Thank you. I'd better tell Marlowe and my demolition team." He turned to go but was stopped by an outsized hand on his arm, holding him gently but with steellike adamancy.

"Thou must know something more," the being called Loki said in a low, resonant voice. Impossibly white teeth shone in that gleaming smile above Chris. "Thou wilt have a passenger in going ashore."

Chris blinked. The *plan* had been for only his team and their commando escort. . . . Then he saw the pallor of dread on Commander Lewis's face—deeper than any mere fear of death.

Chris turned back to stare at the fur-clad giant. "*You* . . ." he breathed.

Loki nodded. "That is correct. There will be a slight change in plans. I will not accompany the undersea vessels, as they attempt to break out through the Skaggerak. I will go ashore with thee, to Gotland."

Chris kept his face blank. In all honesty there was no way this side of heaven that he or Lewis or anybody else could stop this creature from doing anything it wanted to do. One way or the other the Allies were about to lose their only Aesir friend in the long war against the Nazi plague.

If the word "friend" ever really described Loki—who had appeared one day on the tarmac of a Scottish airfield during the final evacuation of Britain, accompanied by eight small, bearded beings carrying boxes—who led them up to the nearest amazed officer to commandeer the Prime Minister's personal plane to take him the rest of the way to America.

Perhaps an armored battalion might have stopped him. Battle reports had proven that Aesir could be killed, if you were lucky, and pounded one hard and fast enough. But when the local commander realized what was happening, he had decided to take a chance.

Loki had proven his worth over and over again since that day, ten years ago.

Until now, that is.

"If you insist," he told the Aes.

"I do. It is my will."

"Then I'll go explain it to Major Marlowe. Excuse me, please."

He backed away a few meters first, then turned to go. As he sloshed away, that glittering stare seemed to follow him, past the moaning dwarf, past O'Leary's ever-sardonic smile, down the narrow, dank passageway lined with strapped-in marines, all the way to the sabot-launching tubes.

Voices were hushed. All the young men spoke English, but only half were North Americans. Their shoulder patches—Free French, Free Russian, Free Irish, German Christian—were muted in the dim light, but the mixed accents were unmistakable, as well as the way they stroked their weapons and the gleam Chris caught sight of in one or two pairs of eyes.

These were the sort that volunteered for suicide missions, the type—common in the world after thirteen years of horrible war—that had little or nothing left to lose.

Major Marlowe had come back to supervise the loading of the landing boats. He did not take Chris's news well.

"Loki wants to come along? To *Gotland?*" He spat. "The bastard's a *spy.* I knew it all the time!"

Chris shook his head. "He's helped us in a hundred ways, John. Why, just by accompanying Ike to Tokyo, and convincing the Japanese . . ."

"Big deal! We'd already *beaten* the Japs!" The big marine clenched his fist, hard. "Like we'd have *crushed* Hitler, if these monsters hadn't arrived, like Satan's curse, out of nowhere.

"And now he's lived among us for *ten years,* observing our methods, our tactics, and our *technology,* the only real advantage we had left!"

Chris grimaced. How could he explain it to Marlowe? The Marine officer had never been to Tehran, as Chris had, only last year. Marlowe had never seen the capital city of Israel-Iran, America's greatest and most stalwart ally, bulwark of the East.

There, in dozens of armed settlements along the east bank of the Euphrates, Chris had met fierce men and women who bore on their arms tattooed numbers from Treblinka, Dachau, Auschwitz. He had heard their story of how, one hopeless night under barbed wire and the stench of chimneys, the starving, doomed masses had looked up to see a strange vapor fall from the sky. Unbelieving, death-starkened eyes had stared in wonderment as the mists gathered and coalesced into something that seemed almost solid.

Out of that eerie fog a *bridge* of many colors formed . . . a rainbow arch climbing, apparently without end, out of the places of horror into a moonless night. And from the heights each doomed man and woman saw a dark-eyed figure on a flying horse ride down. They felt him whisper to them *inside* their minds.

Come, children, while your tormenters blink unbelievingly in my web of the mind. Come, all, unto my bridge to safety, before my cousins descry my treason.

When they sank to their knees, or rocked in thankful prayer, the figure only snorted in derision. His voice hissed within their heads.

Do not mistake me for your God, who left you here to die! I cannot explain that One's absence to you, or His plan in all this. The All-Father is a mystery even to Great Odin!

Know only that I will take you to safety now, such as there may be in this world. But only if you hurry! Come, and be grateful later, if you must!

Down to the camps, to bleak ghettos, to a city under siege—the bridges formed in a single night, and with dawn were gone like vapor or a dream. Two million people, the old, the lame, women, children, the slaves of Hitler's war factories, climbed those paths—for there was no other choice —and found themselves transported to a desert land, by the banks of an ancient river.

They arrived just in time to take up hasty arms and save a British army fleeing the wreckage of Egypt and Palestine. They fused with the astonished Persians, and with refugees from crippled Russia, and together they built a new nation out of chaos.

That was why Loki appeared on the tarmac in Scotland, shortly after that night of miracles. He could not return to Europe, for the fury of his Aesir kin would be savage. In returning to Gotland, today, he was certainly in as much peril as the commandos.

"No, Marlowe. Loki's not a spy. I haven't any idea what on God's green Earth he *is*. But I'd bet my life he's not a spy."

2

The sabots gurgled and rocked as they shot free of the submarine and bobbed to the surface of the cold sea. The outer shells broke away, and the sailors dipped their oars. The men all took their first breath of clean air in more than a day.

Loki's dwarf seemed little relieved. He looked across the dark waters to the west, where the thin, reddish line of sunset outlined the hills of a great Baltic island, and muttered gutturally in a language like nothing earthly.

Which was only natural. Like most Americans Chris was convinced that these beings were as much the ancient Norse gods—recalled into the modern world—as *he* was Sandy Koufax, or that they didn't play baseball in Brooklyn.

Aliens—that was the official line . . . the story broadcast by Allied Radio all through the Americas and Japan and what remained of Free Asia. Creatures from the stars had arrived, as in those stories by Chester Nimitz, the famous science-fiction author.

It wasn't hard to imagine why they might want to be looked on as gods. And it explained why they had chosen to side with the Nazis. After all, the ruse would not have worked in the West, where, no matter how great their guests' powers, Euro-American scientists would have probed and queried and people would have asked questions.

But in the Teutonic madness of Nazism, the "Aesir" had found fertile ground.

Chris had read captured German SS documents. Even back in the thirties and early forties, before the arrival of the Aesir, they had been filled with mumbo jumbo and pseudo-religious mysticism—nonsense about ice moons falling from the sky and the romantic spirit of the Aryan super-race.

A Nazi-conquered world would *belong* to the Aesir, whoever and whatever they were. They would be gods indeed. Much as he understood the logic of a rat or a hyena, Chris could follow the aliens' reasons for choosing the side they had, goddamn them.

Silhouettes of pines outlined the hilltops, serrating the faintly glowing western sky. The two lead boats were crammed with marines, who were to take the beachhead and move inland to scout. The flankers were Navy teams, who were supposed to prepare the boats for a getaway . . . as if anyone believed that would ever happen.

The last two craft held most of Chris's demolition team.

Loki knelt on one knee at the prow of Chris's boat, and stared ahead with those black, glittering eyes. Dark as he was, he nevertheless looked at that moment like something straight out of a Viking saga.

Good verisimilitude, Chris thought. Or maybe the creatures actually *believed* they were what they said they were. Who could tell?

All Chris knew for sure was that they had to be defeated, or for humanity there would be nothing but darkness, from now on.

He checked his watch and looked up at the sky, scanning the broad, starry openings in the clouds.

Yes, there it was. The Satellite. Riding Newton's wings more than two hundred miles up, circling the globe every ninety minutes.

When it had appeared, the Nazis had gone into paroxysms, proclaiming it an astrological portent. For some unknown bureaucratic reason officials in the Pentagon had sat on the secret until half the world believed Goebbels's propaganda. Then, at last, Washington revealed the truth. That American Space-Argonauts were circling the Earth.

For two months the world had seemed turned around. This new technological wonder would be more important than the atom bomb, many thought.

Then the invasion of Canada began.

Chris turned his mind away from what was happening now, out in the Atlantic. He wished he had one of those new *laser* communicators, so he could tell the men up in the Satellite how things were progressing. But the light amplification devices were so secret, as yet, that the Chiefs of Staff had refused to allow any to be taken into the enemy heartland.

Supposedly the Nazis were working on a way to shoot down the Satellite. It was still a mystery why, with aliens to help them, the enemy had let their early lead in rocketry slip so badly. Chris wondered why the Aesir had allowed the American spacecraft to fly up there as long as this.

Perhaps they can't really operate up there, anymore . . . just as they haven't been able to crush our submarine forces.

But does that make sense? Could aliens have lost the ability to destroy such a crude spacecraft?

Chris shook his head.

Not that it matters all that much, he thought. *Tonight the Atlantic fleet is dying. This winter, we'll probably be forced to use the big bombs to hold the line in Canada . . . wrecking the continent even if we slow them down.*

He looked at the figure in the boat's prow. *How can cleverness or industry or courage prevail against such power?*

Those fur-covered shoulders were passive now. But Chris had seen him tear down buildings with his bare hands. And Loki had admitted to being one of the *weakest* of these "gods."

"Loki," he said quietly.

As often as not, the Aes would ignore any human who spoke to him without his leave. But this time the dark-haired figure turned and regarded Chris. Loki's expression was not warm, but he did smile.

"Thou art troubled, youngling. I spy it in thy heart." He seemed to peer into Chris. "It is not fear, I am glad to see, but only a great perplexity."

Fitting their assumed roles as the fabled lords of Valhalla, courage was the one human attribute most honored by the Aesir. Even by the god of trickery and treachery.

"Thank you, Loki." Chris nodded respectfully. *You could've fooled me. I thought I was scared spitless!*

Loki's eyes were pools glittering with starlight. "On this fateful eve it is meet to grant a brave worm a boon. Therefore I will favor thee, mortal. Ask three questions. These will Loki answer truthfully, by his very life."

Chris blinked, for the moment stricken speechless. He was unprepared for anything like this! Everyone from President Marshall and Admiral Heinlein on down to the lowliest Brazilian draftee had hungered for answers. Imperious and aloof, their one Aesir ally had doled out hints and clues, had helped to foil Nazi schemes and slow the implacable enemy advance, but he had never made a promise like this!

Chris could sense O'Leary tense behind him, trying to seem invisible. For once the beatnik's mouth was firmly sealed.

Pine forests loomed above them as the boat entered shallows out of the evening wind. He could smell the dark woods. There was so little time! Chris groped for a question.

"I . . . who *are* you, and where did you *come* from?"

Loki closed his eyes. When he opened them, the black orbs were filled with dark sadness.

> "*Out of the body of Ymir, slain by Odin, poured the Sea.*
> "*Gripping the body of Ymir, Yggdrasil, the great tree.*
> "*Sprung from salt and frost, the Aesir, tremble Earth!*
> "*Borne of Giant and man, Loki, bringer of mirth.*"

The creature stared at Chris. "This has always been my home," he said. And Chris knew that he meant the Earth. "I remember ages and everything spoken of in the Eddas—from the chaining of Fenris to the lies of Skrymnir. And yet . . ." Loki's voice was faintly puzzled, even hushed. "And yet there is something about those memories . . . something *laid over,* as lichen lays upon the frost."

He shook himself. "In truth I cannot say for certain that I am older than thee, child-man."

Loki's massive shoulders shrugged. "But make haste with your next question. We are approaching the Gathering Place. *They* will be here and we must stop them from their scheming, if it is not already too late."

Reminded suddenly of the present, Chris looked up at the wilderness all around them on the shadowed hillsides. "Are you sure about this plan—taking on so many of the Aesir in one place?"

Loki smiled. And Chris realized at once why. Like some idiot out of a fairy tale, he had squandered a question in a silly quest for comfort! But reassurance was not one of Loki's strong suits.

"No, I am *not* sure, impertinent mortal!" Loki laughed and the rowing sailors briefly lost their stride as they looked up at the ironic, savage sound. "Thinkest thou that only men may win honor by daring all against death? Here does Loki show his courage, to face Odin's spear and Thor's hammer if he must, tonight!" He turned and shook a ham-sized fist toward the west. The dwarf whimpered and crouched beside his master.

Chris saw that the marines had already landed. Major Marlowe made quick hand gestures sending the first skirmishers fanning out into the forest. The second row of boats shipped oars and were carried by momentum toward the gravelly shore.

He hurried to take advantage of the remaining time.

"Loki. What is happening in Africa?"

Since '49 the Dark Continent had been dark indeed. From Tunis to the Cape of Good Hope fires burned, and rumors of horror flowed.

Loki whispered softly.

> *"Surtur must needs have a home, before the time of raging.*
> *"There, in torment, men cry out, screaming for an ending."*

The giant shook his great head. "In Africa and on the great plains of Russia terrible magics are being made, small one, and terrible woe."

Back in Israel-Iran Chris had seen some of the refugees—blacks and high-cheeked Slavs—lucky escapees who had fled the fires in time. Even they had not been able to tell what was happening in the interior. Only people who had seen the earlier horrors—whose arms bore stenciled numbers from the first wave of chimney camps—could imagine what was happening in the silent continents. And those fierce men and women kept their silence.

It struck Chris that Loki did not seem to speak out of pity, but matter-of-factly, as if he thought a *mistake* were being made, but not any particular evil.

"Terrible magics . . ." Chris repeated. And suddenly he had a thought. "You mean the purpose isn't *only* to slaughter people? That something else is going on, as well? Is it related to the reason why you saved those people from the first camps? Was something being *done* to them?"

Chris had a sense that there was something important here. Something ultimately crucial. But Loki smiled, holding up three fingers.

"No more questions. It is time."

The boat scraped bottom. Sailors leaped out into the icy water to drag it up to the rocky shore. Shortly Chris was busy supervising the unloading of their supplies, but his mind was a turmoil.

Loki was hiding something, laughing at him for having come so close and yet missing the target. There was more to this, tonight, than an attempt to kill a few alien gods.

High in the dark forest canopy, a crow cawed. The dwarf, laden under enough boxes to crush a man, rolled his eyes and moaned softly, but Loki seemed not to notice.

"Reet freaking hideaway, daddyo," O'Leary muttered as he helped Chris shoulder the bomb's fuse mechanism. "A heavy-duty scene."

"Right," Chris answered, feeling sure he understood the beatnik this time. "A heavy-duty scene." They set out, following the faint blazings laid by the marine scouts.

As they climbed a narrow trail from the beach, Chris felt a sense of anticipation growing within him . . . a feeling of being, right then, at the navel of the world. For well or ill this place was where the fate of the world hung. He could think of no better end than to sear this island clean of all life. And if that meant standing beside the bomb and triggering it himself, well, few men ever had the chance to trade their lives so well.

They were deep under the forest canopy, now. Chris caught sight of flickering movements under the trees, marine flankers guarding them and their precious cargo. According to prewar maps they had only to top one rise, then another. From that prominence any place to plant the bomb would be as good as any other.

Chris started to turn, to look back at Loki . . . but at that very moment the night erupted with light. Flares popped and fizzed and floated slowly through the branches on tiny parachutes. Men dove for cover as tracer bullets sent their shadows fleeing. There was sudden gunfire up ahead, and loud concussions. Men screamed.

Chris sought cover behind a towering fir as mortars began pounding the forest around him.

From high up the hillside—even over the explosions—they heard booming laughter.

Clutching the roots of a tree, Chris looked back. A dozen yards away

the dwarf lay flat on his back, a smoking ruin where a mortar round must
have landed squarely.

But then he felt a hand on his shoulder. O'Leary pointed up the hill
and whispered, goggle-eyed, "Dig it, man."

Chris turned and stared upslope at the huge, manlike being striding
down the hillside, followed by dark-cloaked, armed men. The figure carried a giant bludgeon that screamed whenever he threw it, crushing trees
and marines without prejudice. Giant conifers exploded into kindling and
men were turned into jam. Then the weapon swept back into the red-
bearded Aesir's hand.

Not mortars. Chris realized. *Thor's hammer.*

Of Loki himself there was no sign at all.

3

"There, there, Hugin. Fear not the dark Americans. They shall not hurt
thee."

The one-eyed being called Odin sat upon a throne of ebony, bearing
upon his upraised left hand a raven the color of night. A jewel set in the
giant's eye patch glittered like an orb more far-seeing than the one he had
lost, and across his lap lay a shining spear.

On both sides stood fur-clad figures nearly as imposing, one blond, with
a great ax laid arrogantly over his shoulder, the other red-bearded, leaning
lazily on a hammer the size of a normal man.

Guards in black leather, twin lightning strokes at their collars, stood at
attention around the hall of rough-hewn timbers. Even their rifles were
polished black. The only spot of color on their SS uniforms was a red
swastika armband.

The being called Odin looked down at the prisoners, chained together
in a heap on the floor of the great hall.

"Alas. Poor Hugin has not forgiven you, my American guests. His
brother, Munin, was lost when Berlin burned under your Hellfire bombs."

The Aesir chief's remaining eye gleamed ferally. "And who can blame
my poor watch-bird, or fail to understand a father's grief, when that same
flame deluge consumed my bright boy, my far-seeing Heimdallr."

The survivors of the ill-fated raiding party lay on the dry stone floor,
exhausted. The unconscious, dying Major Marlowe was in no condition to
answer for them, but one of the Free British volunteers stood up, rattling
his chains, and spat on the floor in front of the manlike creature.

"Higgins!" O'Leary tried to pull on the man's arm, but was shrugged off as the Brit shook his fist.

"Yeah, they got your precious boy in Berlin. An' you killed *everyone* in London an' Paris in revenge! I say the Yanks were too soft, lettin' that stop 'em. They should'a gone ahead, *whatever* the price, an' fried every last Aryan bitch an' cub . . ."

His defiance was cut off as a Gestapo officer knocked him down. SS troopers brought their rifle butts down hard, again and again.

Finally Odin waved them back.

"Take the body to the center of the Great Circle, to be sent to Valhalla."

The Gestapo officer looked up sharply, but Odin rumbled in a tone that assumed obedience. "I want that brave man with me, when Fimbul-Winter blows," the creature explained. And obviously he thought that settled the matter. As the black-uniformed guards cut the limp form free, the chief of the Aesir chucked his raven under the beak and offered it a morsel of meat. He spoke to the huge redhead standing beside him.

"Thor, my son. These other things are thine. Poor prizes, I admit, but they did show some prowess in following the Liar this far. What will thou do with them?"

The giant stroked his hammer with gauntlets the size of small dogs. Here, indeed, was a creature that made even Loki seem small.

He stepped forward and scanned the prisoners, as if searching for something. When his gaze alighted on Chris, it seemed to shimmer. His voice was as deep as the growling of earthquakes.

"I will deign to speak with one or two of them, Father."

"Good." Odin nodded. "Have them cast into a pit, somewhere," he told the SS general nearby, who clicked his heels and bowed low. "And await my son's pleasure."

The Nazis hauled Chris and the other survivors to their feet and pulled them away, single file. But not before Chris overheard the elder Aesir tell his offspring, "Find out what you can about that wolf-spawn, Loki, and then give them all over to be used in the sacrifice."

4

Poor Major Marlowe had been right about one thing. The Nazis would never have won without the Aesir, or something like them. Hitler and his gang must have believed from the start that they could somehow call forth the ancient "gods," or they'd surely never have dared wage such a war, one certain to bring in America.

Indeed, by early 1944 it had seemed all but over. There was hell yet to pay, of course, but nobody back home feared defeat anymore. The Russians were pushing in from the east. Rome was taken, and the Mediterranean was an Allied lake. The Japanese were crumbling—pushed back or bottled up in island after island—while the greatest armada in history was gathering in England, preparing to cross the Channel and lance the Nazi boil for good and all.

In factories and shipyards across America the Arsenal of Democracy was pouring forth more materiel in any given month than the Third Reich had produced in its best year. Ships rolled off the ways at intervals of hours. Planes every few minutes.

Most important of all, in Italy and in the Pacific, a rabble of farmers and city boys in soldier suits had been tempered and become warriors in a great army. Man to man, they were now on a par with their experienced foe. And the enemy was outnumbered as well.

Already there was talk of the postwar recovery, of plans to help in the rebuilding, and of a *United Nations* to keep the peace forever.

Chris had been only a child in knee pants, back in '44, devouring Chet Nimitz novels and praying with all his might that there would be something half as glorious to do in his adulthood as what his uncles were achieving overseas right then. Maybe there would be adventures in space, he hoped, for after this, the horror of war would surely never be allowed again.

Then came the rumors . . . tales of setbacks on the eastern front . . . of reeling Soviet armies sent into sudden and unexpected retreat. The reasons were unclear . . . mostly, what came back were superstitious rumblings that no modern person credited.

Voices on a streetcorner.

Damn Russkies. . . . I knew all along they didn' have no stayin' power. . . . Alla time yammerin' 'bout a "second front." . . . Well, we'll give 'em a second front! Save their hash. . . . Don't fret, Ivan, Uncle Sam's coming. . . .

June, and the Norman sky was filled with planes. Ships covered the Channel Sea. . . .

Sitting against a cold stone wall in an underground cell, Chris pinched his eyes shut and tried to crush away the memory of the grainy black-and-white films he had been shown. But he failed to keep the images out.

Ships, as far as one could see . . . the greatest armada of free men ever assembled . . .

It was not until he joined the OSS that Chris actually saw photographs never shown to the public. In all the years since then he wished *he* had not seen them, either.

D-Day . . . D for disaster.

Cyclones, hundreds of them, spinning like horrible tops, rising out of the dawn mists. They grew and climbed until the dark funnels appeared to stretch beyond the sky. And as they approached the ships, it seemed one could see flying figures on their flanks, driving the storms faster and faster with their beating wings . . .

"Marlowe's come up aces and eights, man." O'Leary sighed heavily as he sagged down next to Chris. "You're the big cheese now, dad."

Chris closed his eyes. *All men die,* he thought, reminding himself that he hadn't really liked the dour marine all that much, anyway.

He mourned nonetheless, if for no other reason than that Marlowe had been his insulation, protecting him from that bitch called "command."

"So what gives now, chief?"

Chris looked at O'Leary. The man was really too old to be playing kids' games. There were lines at the edges of those doelike eyes, and the baby fat was turning into a double chin. The Army recognized genius, and put up with a lot from its civilian experts. But Chris wondered how this escapee from Greenwich Village ever came to be in a position of responsibility.

Loki chose him. That was the real answer. *As he chose me. So much for the god of cleverness.*

"What *gives* is that you damp down the beat-rap, O'Leary. Making only every third sentence incomprehensible should be enough to provide your emotional crutch."

O'Leary winced, and Chris at once regretted the outburst.

"Oh, never mind." He changed the subject. "How are the rest of the men doing?"

"Copasetic, I guess. . . . I mean, they're OK, for guys slated for ritual shortening in a few hours. They all knew this was a suicide mission. Just wanted to take a few more of the bastards with them, is all."

Chris nodded. *If we'd had another year or two . . .*

By then the missile scientists would have had rockets accurate enough to go for a surgical strike, making this attempt to sneak in bombs under the enemy's noses unnecessary. The Satellite was just the beginning of the possibilities, if they had had time.

"Higgins was right, man," O'Leary muttered as he collapsed against the wall next to Chris. "We shoulda pasted them with everything we had. Melted Europe to slag, if that's what it took."

"By the time we had enough bombs to do much more than slow them down they had atomic weapons, too," Chris pointed out.

"So? After we fried Peenemünde, their delivery systems stagnated. And they haven't got a clue how to go thermonuclear! Why even if they *did* manage to disassemble our bomb—"

"—God forbid!" Chris blinked. His heart raced, even considering the possibility. If the Nazis managed to make the leap from A-bombs to fusion weapons . . ."

The tech shook his head vigorously. "I scoped. . . . I mean I checked out the destruct triggers myself, Chris. Anyone pokes around to try to see how a U.S. of A. type H-bomb works will be in for a nasty surprise."

That had, of course, been a minimum requirement before being allowed to attempt this mission. Had they been able to assemble the weapon near the "Great Circle" of Aesgard, the course of the war might have been changed. Now, all they could hope was that the separate components would melt to slag as they were supposed to when their timers expired.

O'Leary persisted. "I still think we should have launched everything we had back in '52."

Chris knew how the man felt. Most Americans believed the exchange would have been worth it. A full scale strike at Hitler's homeland would sear the heart out of it. The monster's retaliation, with cruder rockets and fissile bombs would be a price worth paying.

When he had learned the real reason, at first he had refused to believe it. Chris assumed that Loki was lying . . . that it was an Aesir trick.

But since then he had seen the truth. America's arsenal of bombs was a two-edged sword. Unless used carefully, it would cut both ways.

There was a rattling of keys. Three SS guards stepped in, looking down their noses at the dejected allied raiders.

"The great Aes, Thor, would deign speak wit' your leader," the officer said in thickly accented English. When no one moved, his gaze fell upon Chris and he smiled. "This one. This strayed sheep. Our lord asked for him, especially."

He snapped his fingers and the guards grabbed Chris by the arms. "Cool as glass, dad," O'Leary said. "Drive 'em crazy, baby."

Chris glanced back from the door. "You, too, O'Leary."

He was pushed through and the dungeon gate slammed shut behind him.

5

"You are a Dane, are you not?"

Chris was tied firmly to a beam pillar in front of a crackling fireplace. The Gestapo official had peered at Chris from several angles before asking his question.

"Danish by ancestry. What of it?" Chris shrugged under his bonds.

The Nazi clucked. "Oh, nothing in particular. It is just that I never cease to be amazed when I find specimens of clearly superior stock fighting against their own divine heritage."

Chris lifted an eyebrow. "Do you interrogate a lot of prisoners?"

"Oh yes, very many."

"Well then you must be amazed all the time."

The Gestapo man blinked, then smiled sourly. He stepped back to light a cigarette, and Chris noticed that his hands were trembling.

"But doesn't your very blood cry out, when you find yourself working with, going into battle alongside racial scum, mongrels . . ."

Chris laughed. He turned his head and regarded the Nazi icily.

"Why are you even here?" he asked.

"I—what do you mean?" The fellow blinked again. "See here now, I am in charge of interrogation of—"

"You're in charge of a jail detail," Chris sneered. "The priests of the Aesir run everything now. The mystics in the SS control the Reich. Hitler's a tottering old syphilitic they won't let out of Berchtesgarten. And you old-fashioned Nazis are barely tolerated anymore."

The officer sucked at his cigarette. "What do you mean by that remark?"

"I mean that all that racial claptrap was just window dressing. An excuse to set up the death camps. But the SS would've been just as happy to use *Aryans* in them, if that was the only way to—to . . ."

"Yes?" The Gestapo man stepped forward. "To do what? If the purpose of the camps was not the elimination of impure stock, then what, smart man? *What?*"

There was a brittle, high-pitched edge to the man's laughter. "You do not know, do you? Even Loki did not tell you!"

Chris could have sworn that there was *disappointment* in the officer's eyes . . . as if he had hoped to learn something from Chris, and was let down to find out that his prisoner was as much in the dark as he was.

No, I wasted a question, and Loki did not tell me about the camps. Chris looked at the other man's trembling hands—hands that had, no doubt, wreaked more hell on broken bodies and spirits than bore contemplating —all, apparently, in a cause that was no longer even relevant to the winning side.

"Poor obsolete national socialist," Chris said. "Your dreams, mad as they were, were human ones. How does it feel to have it all taken over by aliens? To watch it all change beyond recognition?"

The Gestapo man reddened. Fumbling, he picked up a truncheon from a table near the wall and smacked it into his gloved left hand.

"I will change something *else* beyond recognition," he growled menacingly. "And if I am obsolete, at least I am still allowed the pleasure of my craft."

He approached, smiling with a thin film on his lips. Chris braced himself as the arm swung back, raising the bludgeon high. But at that moment the leather curtains parted and a large shadow fell across the rug. The Gestapo officer paled and snapped to attention.

The red-bearded Aesir named Thor nodded briefly as he shrugged out of his furred cloak. "You may go," he rumbled.

Chris did not even look at the Nazi as the interrogator tried to meet his eye. Chris watched the coals in the fireplace until the curtains swished again and he was alone with the alien.

Thor sat down, cross-legged, on a thick rug and spent a few minutes joining Chris in contemplation of the flickering flames. When he used his hammer to prod the logs, heat brought out fine, glowing designs in the massive iron head.

"Fro sends word from Vinland . . . from the sea thou callest Labrador. There has been a slaughter of many brave men."

Thor looked up.

"Those cowards' tools—submarines—did much harm to our fleet. But in the end Fro's tempests were masterful. The landing is secured."

Chris controlled the sinking feeling in his stomach. This was expected. Worse was to come, this winter.

Thor shook his head. "This is a bad war. Where is the honor, when thousands die unable even to show valor?"

Chris had more experience than most Americans in holding conversation with gods. Still, he took a chance, speaking without permission.

"I agree, Great One. But you can't blame *us* for that."

Thor's eyes glittered as he inspected Chris. "No, brave worm. I do not blame you. That you have used your flame weapons as little as you have speaks well for the pride of thy leaders. Or perhaps they know what our wrath would be, if they were so cowardly as to use them wantonly."

I never should have been allowed on this mission. I know too much, Chris realized. Loki had been the one to overrule High Command and insist that Chris come along. But that made him the only one here who knew the *real* reason the H-bombs had been kept leashed.

Dust from atom blasts, and soot from burning cities—those were what allied High Command feared, far more than radiation or Nazi retaliation. Already, from limited use of nuclear weapons so far, the weather had chilled measurably.

And the Aesir were so much stronger in winter! Scientists verified Loki's story, that careless use of the Allied nuclear advantage would lead to catastrophe, no matter how badly they seared the other side.

"We, too, prefer a more personal approach," Chris said, hoping to keep the Aesir believing his own explanation. "No man wishes to be killed by powers beyond his understanding, impossible to resist or fight back against."

Thor's rumble, Chris realized, was a low laughter. "Well said, worm. Thou dost chastise as Freyr does, with words that reap, even as they sow."

The Aes leaned forward a little. "You would earn merit in my eyes, small one, if you told me how to find the Brother of Lies."

Those gray eyes were like cold clouds, and Chris felt his sense of reality begin to waver as he looked into them. It took a powerful effort of will to tear his gaze away. Shutting his eyes, he spoke with a dry mouth.

"I . . . don't know what you're talking about."

The rumbling changed tone, deepening a little. Chris felt a rough touch and opened his eyes to see that Thor was brushing his cheek with the leather-bound haft of the great war hammer.

"Loki, youngling. Tell me where the Trickster may be found, and you may yet escape your doom, and even find a place by my side. In the world to come there will be no greater place for a man."

This time Chris steeled himself to meet the hypnotic pools of Thor's eyes. Their power reached out for his soul, as a magnet for native iron. But Chris fought back with the savage heat of hatred.

"Not . . . for all the valkyries in your fucking, alien pantheon," he whispered. "I'd rather run with wolves."

The smile vanished. Thor blinked, and for a moment Chris thought he saw the Aesir's image waver just a little, as if . . . as if he were looking through a man-shaped *fold* in space.

"Courage will not save thee from the wages of disrespect, worm," the shape growled, and solidified again into a fur-clad giant.

All at once Chris was glad to have known O'Leary.

"Don't you dig it yet, daddyo? I don't fucking *believe* in you! Wherever you're from, baby, they probably kicked you out! You may be mean enough to wreck our world, but everything about you screams that you're the *dregs*, man. Leaky squares. Probably burned out papa's stolen saucer just gettin' here!"

He shook his head. "I just refuse to believe in you, man."

The icy gray eyes blinked once. Then Thor's surprised expression faded into a smile. "I did not ken your other insults. But for calling me a *man*, you shall die before the morning sun."

He stood up and placed a hand on Chris's shoulder, as if emparting a friendly benediction, but even the casual power of that touch felt viselike.

"I add only this, little one. We Aesir have come *invited*, and we arrived not in ships—even ships between the stars—but on the wings of Death itself. This much, this boon of knowledge I grant thee, in honor of your defiance."

Then, in a swirl of furs and displaced air, the creature was gone, leaving Chris alone again to watch the coals flicker slowly and turn into ashes.

6

The Teutonic priests were resplendent in red and black, their robes traced in gold and silver. Platinum eagles' wings rose from their top-heavy helms as they marched around a great circle of standing stones, chanting in a tongue that sounded vaguely German, but which Chris knew was much, much older.

An altar, carved with gaping dragons' mouths, stood beside a raging bonfire. Smoke rose in a turbulent funnel, carrying bright sparks upward toward a full moon. The heat blazed at the ring of prisoners, each chained to his own obelisk of rough-hewn rock.

They faced southward, looking from a Gotland prominence across the Baltic toward a shore that had once been Poland, and for a little while after that had been the "Thousand Year Reich."

The waters were unnaturally calm, almost glassy, reflecting a nearly perfect image of the bonfire alongside the moon's rippling twin.

"Fro must be back from Labrador," O'Leary commented loudly enough for Chris to hear him over the chanting and the pounding drums. "That'd explain the clear night. He's th' god of tempests."

Chris glanced at the man sourly, and O'Leary grinned back, apologetically. "Sorry, man. I mean he's th' little green alien who's in charge of weather control. Make you feel any better?"

I had that coming, Chris thought. He smiled dryly and shrugged. "I don't suppose it matters all that much, now."

O'Leary watched the Aryan Brothers march by again, carrying a giant swastika alongside a great dragonlike totem. The technician started to say something, but then he blinked and seemed to mumble to himself, as if trying to catch a drifting thought. When the procession had passed, he turned to Chris, a mystified expression on his face. "I just remembered something."

Chris sighed. "What is it now, O'Leary?"

The beatnik frowned in puzzlement. "I can't figure why it slipped my mind until now. But back when we were on the beach, unloading the bomb parts, Old Loki pulled me aside. It was all so hectic, but I could swear I saw him palm th' H-bomb trigger mechanism, Chris. That means . . ."

Chris nodded. "That means he knew we were going to be captured. I'd already figured that out, O'Leary. At least the Nazis won't get the trigger."

"Yeah. But that's not all I just remembered, Chris. Loki told me to *tell* you something for him. He said you'd asked him a question, and he told me to relay an answer he said you might understand."

O'Leary shook his head. "I don't know why I forgot to tell you about it until now."

Chris laughed. Of course the renegade Aes had put the man under a posthypnotic command to recall the message only later . . . perhaps only in a situation like this.

"What is it, O'Leary? What did he say to tell me?"

"It was just one word, Chris. He said to tell you—*necromancy.* And then he clammed up. Wasn't much after that that the SS jumped us. What'd he mean by that, Captain? What was your question, anyway? What does the answer mean?"

Chris did not reply. He stared at the funnel of sparks climbing toward the moon.

With his last question he had asked Loki about the camps—about the awesome, horrible, concentrated effort of death that had been perpetrated, first in Europe and then in Russia and Africa. What were they *for?* There had to be more to it than a plan to eliminate some bothersome minorities.

Moreover, why had Loki, who normally seemed so oblivious to human life, acted to rescue so many from the death factories, at so great a risk to himself?

Necromancy. That was Loki's delayed reply to his final question. And

Loki had told it in such a way that Chris might have his answer, but never be able to tell anyone who mattered.

Necromancy . . .

The word stood for the performance of magic . . . but magic of a special, terrible kind. In legend a necromancer was an evil wizard who used the concentrated field created by the death agony of human beings in order to drive his spells.

But that was just superstitious nonsense!

Lightheaded, Chris looked out across the sand at the hulking Aesir, seated on their gilded thrones, heard the chanting of the priests, and wished he could dismiss the idea as easily as he once would have.

Was that the reason the Nazis had dared to wage a war they otherwise could never have won? Because they believed that they could create such concentrated, distilled horror that ancient spells would actually work?

It explained so much. Other nations had gone insane, in human history. Other movements had been evil. But none had perpetrated its crimes with such dedication and efficiency. The horror must have been directed not so much at death itself, but at some hideous goal beyond death!

"They . . . *made* . . . the Aesir. That's what Loki meant by thinking that, maybe, his own memories were false . . . when he suspected that he was actually no older than I . . . ."

"What was that, Cap'n?" O'Leary leaned as far as his chains would allow. "I couldn't follow . . . ."

But the procession chose that moment to stop. The High Priest, carrying a golden sword, held it before Odin's throne. The "father of the gods" touched it and the Aesir's rumbling chant could be heard, lower than human singing, like a growl that trembled within the Earth.

One of the chained Allies—a Free Briton—was dragged, numbed with dread, from his obelisk toward the fire and the dragon altar.

Chris shut his eyes, as if to hold out the screams. "Jesus!" O'Leary hissed.

Yes. Chris thought. *Invoke Jesus. Or Allah or God of Abraham. Wake up, Brahma! For your dream has turned into a nightmare.*

He understood clearly now why Loki had not told him his answer while there was even an infinitesimal chance that he might ever make it home again alive.

Thank you, Loki.

Better America and the Last Alliance should go down fighting honorably than even be tempted by this knowledge . . . to have its will tested by this *way out.* For if the Allies ever tried to adopt the enemy's methods, there would be nothing left in the soul of humanity to fight for.

Who would we conjure, Chris wondered. *If we ever did use those spells? Superman? or Captain Marvel? Oh, they'd be more than a match for the Aesir, certainly! Our myths were boundless.*

He laughed, and the sound turned into a sob as another scream of agony pierced the night.

Thank you, Loki, for sparing us that test of our souls.

He had no idea where the renegade "trickster god" had gone, or whether this debacle had only been a cloak for some deeper, more secret mission.

Could that be? Chris wondered. He knew that it was possible. Soldiers seldom ever saw the big picture, and President Marshall did not have to tell his OSS captains everything. This mission could just have been a feint, a minor piece in a greater plan.

Lasers and satellites . . . they could be just part of it. There might be a silver bullet . . . a sprig of mistletoe, yet.

Chains rattled to his right. He heard a voice cursing in Portuguese and footsteps dragging the latest prisoner off.

Chris looked up at the sky, and a thought suddenly occurred to him, as if out of nowhere.

Legends begin in strange ways, he realized.

Someday—even if there was no silver bullet—the horror would have to ebb at last. When humans grew scarce, perhaps, and the Aesir were less plump and well-fed on the death manna they supped from charnel houses.

Then there would come a time when human heroes would count for something again. Perhaps in secret laboratories, or in exile on the moon, or at the bottom of the sea, free men and women would work and toil to build the armor, the weapons, maybe the heroes themselves . . .

This time the scream was choked, as if the Brazilian ranger was trying to defy his enemies, and broke only to show his agony at the last.

Footsteps approached. To his amazement Chris felt feather-light, as if gravity were barely enough to keep him on the ground.

"So long, O'Leary," he said, distantly.

"Yeah, man. Stay cool."

Chris nodded. He offered the black-and-silver-clad SS his wrists as they unchained him, and said to them softly, in a friendly tone of voice, "You know, you look pretty silly for grown men."

They blinked at him in surprise. Chris smiled and stepped between them, leading the way toward the altar and the waiting Aesir.

Someday men will challenge these monsters, he thought, knowing that the numb, lightheaded feeling meant that he would not scream . . . that nothing they could do would make him take more than casual notice.

Loki had made certain of this. *This* was why the Trickster had spent so much time with Chris, this last year . . . why he had insisted that Chris come along on this mission.

Our day will come. Revenge will drive our descendants. Science will armor them. But those heroes will need one more thing, he realized. *Heroes need inspiration. They need legends.*

On their way toward the humming Aesir they passed before a row of human "dignitaries" from the Reich, a few with faces glazed in excitement, but others sitting numbly, as if lost. He felt he could almost read the despair in those darkened, mad eyes. They were aware that something they had wrought had gone long, long out of their control.

Thor frowned as Chris flashed him a smile. "Hi, how'ya doin'?" he said to the Aesir, interrupting their grumbling music in a muttering of surprise. Where curses and screams had only resonated with the chant, his good-natured sarcasm broke up the ritual.

"Move, swine!" An SS guard pushed Chris, or tried to, but stumbled instead on empty air where the American had been. Chris ducked underneath the jangling, cumbersome uniform, between the Nazi's legs, and swatted the fellow's behind with the flat of his hand, sending him sprawling.

The other guard reached for him, but crumpled open-mouthed as Chris bent his fingers back and snapped them. The third guard he lifted by the belt buckle and tossed into the bonfire, to bellow in sudden horror and pain.

Hysterical strength, of course, Chris realized, knowing what Loki had done to him. Four onrushing underpriests went down with snapped necks. No human could do these things without being used up, Chris knew, distantly, but what did it matter? This was far more fun than he had expected to be having, at this moment.

A golden flash out of the corner of his eye warned him. . . . Chris whirled and ducked, catching Odin's spear with one sudden snatch.

"Coward," he whispered at the hot-faced "father of the gods." He flipped the heavy, gleaming weapon about and held it in two hands before him . . .

God, help me . . .

. . . and with a cry he broke the legendary spear over his knee. The pieces fell to the sand.

Nobody moved. Even Thor's whirling hammer slowed and then dropped. In the sudden silence Chris was distantly aware of the fact that his femur was shattered—along with most of the bones in his hands—leaving him perched precariously on one leg.

But Chris's only regret was that he could not emulate an aged Jew he had heard of, from one of the concentration-camp survivors. Standing in front of the grave he had been forced to dig for himself, the old man had not begged, or tried to reason with the SS, or slumped in despair. Instead the prisoner had turned away from his murderers, dropped his pants, and said aloud in Yiddish as he bent over, *Kish mir im toches . . .*

"Kiss my ass," Chris told Thor as more guards finally ran up and grabbed his arms. As they dragged him to the altar, he kept his gaze on the red-bearded "god." The priests tied him down, but Chris met the Aesir's gray eyes.

"I don't believe in you," he said.

Thor blinked, and the giant suddenly turned away.

Chris laughed out loud then, knowing that nothing in the world would suppress this story. It would spread. There would be no stopping it.

Loki, you bastard. You used me, and I suppose I should thank you. But rest assured, Loki, someday we'll get you, too.

He laughed. Chris watched the dismayed High Priest fumble with the knife, and found it terrifically funny. A wide-eyed assistant jiggled and dropped his swastika banner. Chris roared.

Behind him he heard O'Leary's high-pitched giggle. Then another of the prisoners barked, and another. It was unstoppable.

Across the chilly Baltic an uncertain wind blew. And overhead a recent star sailed swiftly where the old ones merely drifted across the sky.

Moon of Ice

Brad Linaweaver

If you gaze long into an abyss, the abyss will gaze back into you.
                                     NIETZSCHE, *Beyond Good and Evil*

To all doubts and questions, the new man of the first German Empire has only one answer: Nevertheless, I will!
                          ALFRED ROSENBERG, *The Myth of the Twentieth Century*

I have seen the man of the future; he is cruel; I am frightened by him.
                                     ADOLF HITLER TO HERMANN RAUSCHNING

ENTRIES FROM THE DIARY
OF DR. JOSEPH GOEBBELS, NEW BERLIN

Translated into English by Hilda Goebbels

April 1965

Today I attended the state funeral for Adolf Hitler. They asked me to give the eulogy. It wouldn't have been so bothersome except that Himmler pulled himself out of his thankful retirement to advise me on all the things I mustn't say. The old fool still believes that we are laying the foundation for a religion. Acquainted as he is with my natural skepticism, he never ceases to worry that I will say something in public not meant for the consumption of the masses. It is a pointless worry on his part; not even early senility should enable him to forget that I am the propaganda expert. Still, I do not question his insistence that he is in rapport with what the masses feel most deeply. I leave such matters to one who is uniquely qualified for the task.

I suppose that I was the last member of the entourage to see Hitler alive. Speer had just left, openly anxious to get back to his work with the Von Braun team. In his declining years he has taken to involving himself full-time with the space program. This question of whether the Americans or we will reach the moon first seems to me a negligible concern. I am convinced by our military experts that the space program that really matters is in terms of orbiting platforms for the purpose of global intimidation. Such a measure seems entirely justified if we are to give the *Führer* his thousand-year Reich (or something even close).

The *Führer* and I talked of Himmler's plans to make him an SS saint. "How many centuries will it be," he asked in a surprisingly firm voice, "before they forget I was a man of flesh and blood?"

"Can an Aryan be any other?" I responded dryly, and he smiled as he is wont to do at my more jestful moments.

"The spirit of Aryanism is another matter," he said. "The same as destiny or any other workable myth."

"Himmler would ritualize these myths into a new reality," I pointed out.

"Of course," agreed Hitler. "That has always been *his* purpose. You and I are realists. We make use of what is available." He reflected for a moment and then continued: "The war was a cultural one. If you ask the man in the street what I really stood for, he would not come near the truth. Nor should he!"

I smiled. I'm sure he took that as a sign of assent. This duality of Hitler, with its concern for exact hierarchies to replace the old social order—and what is true for the *Volk* is not always what is true for us—seemed to me just another workable myth, often contrary to our stated purposes. I would never admit that to him. In his own way Hitler was quite the bone-headed philosopher.

"Mein Führer," I began, entirely a formality in such a situation but I could tell that he was pleased I had used the address, "the Americans love to make fun of your most famous statement about the Reich that will last one thousand years, as though what we have accomplished now is an immutable status quo."

He laughed. "I love those Americans. I really do. They believe their own democratic propaganda . . . so obviously what we tell our people must be what we believe! American credulity is downright refreshing at times, especially after dealing with Russians."

On the subject of Russians Hitler and I did not always agree, so there was no point in continuing that line of dialogue at this late date. Before he died I desperately wished to ask him some questions that had been haunting me. I could see that his condition was deteriorating. This would be my last opportunity.

The conversation rambled on for a bit, and we again amused ourselves over how Franklin Delano Roosevelt had plagiarized National Socialism's Twenty-five Points when he issued his own list of economic rights. How fortunate for us that when FDR borrowed other of our policies, he fell flat on his face. War will always be the most effective method for disposing of surplus production, although infinitely more hazardous in a nuclear age. We never thought that FDR could push America into using our approach for armaments production.

Hitler summed up: "Roosevelt fell under the influence of the madman Churchill; that's what happened!"

"Fortunately our greatest enemy in America was impeached," I said. The last thing we'd needed was a competing empire-builder with the resources of the North American continent. I still fondly recalled the afternoon the American Congress was presented with evidence that FDR was a traitor on the Pearl Harbor question.

"I've never understood why President Dewey didn't follow FDR's lead, *domestically,*" Hitler went on. "They remained in the war, after all. My God, the man even released American-Japanese from those concentration camps and insisted on restitution payments! And this during the worst fighting in the Pacific!"

"That was largely the influence of Vice President Taft," I reminded Hitler. His remarkable memory had suffered these last years.

"Crazy Americans," he said, shaking his head. "They are the most unpredictable people on earth. They pay for their soft hearts in racial pollution."

We moved on into small talk, gossiping about various wives, when that old perceptiveness of the *Führer* touched me once again. He could tell that I wasn't speaking my mind. "Joseph, you and I were brothers in Munich," he said. "I am on my deathbed. Surely you can't be hesitant to ask me *anything.* Speak, man. I would talk in my remaining hours."

And how he could talk. I remember one dinner party for which an invitation was extended to my two eldest daughters, Helga and Hilda. Hitler entertained us with a brilliant monologue on why he hated modern architecture anywhere but factories. He illustrated many of his points about the dehumanizing aspect of giant cities with references to the film *Metropolis.* Yet despite her great love for the cinema Hilda would not be brought out by his entreaties. Everyone else enjoyed the evening immensely.

On this solemn occasion I asked if he had believed his last speech of encouragement in the final days of the war when it seemed certain that we would be annihilated. Despite his words of stern optimism there was quite literally no way of his knowing that our scientists had at that moment solved the shape-charge problem. Thanks to Otto Hahn and Werner Heisenberg working together, we had developed the atomic bomb first. Different departments had been stupidly fighting over limited supplies of uranium and heavy water. Speer took care of that, and then everything began moving in our direction. After the first plutonium came from a German atomic pile it was a certain principle that we would win.

I still viewed that period as miraculous. If Speer and I had not convinced the army and air force to cease their rivalry for funds, we never would have developed the V-3 in time to deliver those lovely new bombs.

In the small hours of the morning one cannot help but wonder how things might have been different. We'd been granted one advantage when the cross-Channel invasion was delayed in 1943. But 1944 was the real turning point of the war. Hitler hesitated to use the nuclear devices, deeply fearful of the radiation hazards to our side as well as the enemy. If it had not been for the assassination attempt of July 20th, he might not have found the resolve to issue the all-important order: destroy Patton and his Third Army before they become operational, before they invade Europe like a cancer. What a glorious time that was for all of us, as well as my own career. For the Russians there were to be many bombs, and many German deaths among them. It was a small price to stop Marxism cold. Even our concentration camps in the East received a final termination order in the form of the by-now familiar mushroom clouds.

If the damned Allies had agreed to negotiate, all that misery could have been avoided. Killing was dictated by history. Hitler fulfilled Destiny. He never forgave the West for forcing him into a two-front war, when he, the chosen one, was their best protection against the Slavic hordes.

How he'd wanted the British Empire on our side. How he'd punished them for their folly. A remaining V-3 had delivered The Bomb on London, fulfilling a political prophecy of the *Führer*. He had regretted that; but the premier war criminal of our time, Winston Churchill, had left him no alternative. They started unrestricted bombing of civilians; well, we finished it. Besides, it made up for the failure of Operation Sea Lion.

Right doesn't guarantee might. The last years of the war taught us that. How had Hitler found the strength to fill us all with hope when there was no reason for anything but despair? Could he really foretell the future?

"Of course not," he answered. "I had reached the point where I said we would recover at the last second with a secret weapon of invincible might . . . *without believing it at all!* It was pure rhetoric. I had lost hope long ago. The timing on that last speech could not have been better. Fate *was* on our side."

So at last I knew. Hitler had bluffed us all again. As he had begun, so did he end: the living embodiment of *will.*

I remembered his exaltation at the films of nuclear destruction. He hadn't been that excited, I'm told, since he was convinced of the claim for Von Braun's rockets—and it took a film for that, as well.

At each report of radiation dangers, he had the more feverishly buried himself in the *Führerbunker,* despite assurances of every expert that Berlin was safe from fallout. Never in my life have I known a man more concerned for his health, more worried about the least bit of a sore throat after a grueling harangue of a speech. And the absurd lengths he went to for his diet, limited even by vegetarian standards. Yet his precautions had brought him to this date, to see himself master of all Europe. Who was in a position to criticize *him?*

He had a way of making me feel like a giant. "I should have listened to you so much earlier," he now told me, "when you called for Totalization of War on the homefront. I was too soft on Germany's womanhood. Why didn't I listen to you?" Once he complimented a subordinate, he was prone to continue. "It was an inspiration, the way you pushed that morale-boosting joke: 'If you think the war is bad, wait until you see the peace, should we lose.' " He kept on, remembering to include my handling of the foreign press during *Kristalnacht,* and finally concluding with his favorite of all my propaganda symbols: "Your idea to use the same railway carriage from the shameful surrender of 1918, to receive France's surrender in 1940, was the greatest pleasure of my life." His pleasure was contagious.

He propped himself up slightly in bed, a gleam of joy in his eyes. He looked like a little boy again. "I'll tell you something about my thousand years. Himmler invests it with the mysticism you'd expect. Ever notice how Jews, Muslims, Christians, and our very own pagans have a predilection for millennia? The number works a magic spell on them."

"Pundits in America observe that also. They say the number is merely good psychology, and point to the longevity of the ancient empires of China, Rome, and Egypt for similar numerical records. They say that Germany will never hold out that long."

"It won't," said Hitler, matter-of-factly.

"What do you mean?" I asked, suddenly not sure of the direction he was moving. I suspected it had something to do with the cultural theories,

but of his grandest dreams for the future Hitler had always been reticent
. . . even with me.

"It will take at least that long," he said, "for the New Culture to take
root on earth. For the New Europe to be what I have foreseen."

"If Von Braun has his way, we'll be long gone from earth by then! At
least he seems to plan passages for many Germans on his spaceships."

"Germans!" spat out Hitler. "What care I for Germans or Von Braun's
space armada? Let the technical side of Europe spread out its power in
any direction it chooses. Speer will be *their* god. He is the best of that
collection. But let the other side determine the values, man. The values,
the spiritual essence. Let them move through the galaxy for all I care, so
long as they look homeward to me for the guiding cultural principles. And
Europe will be the eternal monument to that vision. I speak of a Reich
lasting a thousand years. It will take that long to finish the job, to build
something that will then last for the rest of eternity."

The old fire was returning. His voice was its old, strong hypnotic self.
His body quivered with the glory of his personal vision, externalized for
the whole of mankind to touch, to worship . . . or to fear. I bowed my
head in the presence of the greatest man in history.

He fell back for a minute, exhausted, lost in the phantasms behind his
occluded eyes. Looking at the weary remains of this once-human dynamo,
I was sympathetic, almost sentimental. I said: "Remember when we first
met through our anti-Semitic activities? It was an immediate bond between us."

He chuckled. "Oh, for the early days of the Party again. At the beginning you thought me too bourgeois."

He was dying in front of me, but his mind was as alert as ever. "Few
people understand why we singled out the Jew, even with all the Nazi
literature available," I continued.

He took a deep breath. "I was going to turn all of Europe into a canvas
on which I'd paint the future of humanity. The Jew would have been my
severest and most obstinate critic." The *Führer* always had a gift for the
apt metaphor. "Your propaganda helped keep the populace inflamed.
That anger was only fuel for the task at hand."

We had discussed on previous occasions the fundamental nature of the
Judeo-Christian ethic, and how the Christian was a spiritual Semite (as
any pope would observe). The Jew had made an easy scapegoat. There was
such a fine old tradition behind it. But once the Jew was for all practical
purposes removed from Europe, there remained the vast mass of Christians, many Germans among them. Hitler had promised strong measures
in confidential statements to high officials of the SS. Martin Bormann had

been the most ardent advocate of the *Kirchenkampf*, the campaign against the churches. In the ensuing years of peace and the nuclear stalemate with the United States little had come of it. I brought up the subject again.

"It will take generations," he answered. "The Jew is only the first step. And please remember that Christianity will by no means be the last obstacle, either. Our ultimate enemy is an idea dominant in the United States in theory, if not in practice. Their love of the individual is more dangerous to us than even mystical egalitarianism. In the end the decadent idea of complete freedom will be more difficult to handle than all the religions and other imperial governments put together." He lapsed back into silence, but only for a moment. "We are the last bastion of true Western civilization. America is always a few steps from anarchy. They would sacrifice the state to the individual! But Soviet communism—despite an ideology—was little better. Its state was all muscles and no brain. It forbade them to get the optimum use out of their best people. Ah, only in the German Empire, and especially here in New Berlin, do we see the ideal at work. The state uses most individuals as the sheep they were meant to be. More important is that the superior individual is allowed to use the state."

"Like most of the *Gauleiters?*" I asked, again in a puckish mood.

He laughed in a loud and healthy voice. "Good God," he said. "Nothing's perfect . . . except the SS, and the work you did in Berlin."

I did not have the heart to tell him that I thought he had been proved soundly mistaken on one of his predictions for the United States. With the nuclear stalemate and the end of the war—America having used its atomic bombs in the Orient, and riveting the world's attention in the same fashion as we—the isolationist forces in that country had had a resurgence. In a few years they had moved the country back to the foreign policy it held before the Spanish-American War. Hitler had predicted grim consequences for that country's economy. The reverse unobligingly came true. This was in part because the new isolationists didn't believe in economic isolation by any means; they freed American corporations to protect their own interests.

The latest reports I had seen demonstrated that the American Republic was thriving, even as our economy was badly suffering from numerous entanglements that go hand-in-gauntlet with an imperial foreign policy. We had quite simply overextended ourselves. New Berlin, after all, was modeled on the old Rome . . . and like the Roman Empire we were having trouble financing the operation and keeping the population amused. There are times I miss our old slogan: Gold or Blood?

I'm as dedicated a National Socialist as ever, but I must admit that America does not have our problems. What it has is a lot of goods, a willingness to do business in gold (our stockpile of which increased mark-edly after the war), and paper guarantees that we would not interfere in their hemisphere. We keep our part of the bargain fairly well: all adults understand that Latin America is fair game.

There is, of course, no censorship for the upper strata of Nazi Germany. The friends and families of high Reich officialdom can openly read or see anything they want. I still have trouble with this modification in our policy. At least I keep cherished memories of 1933, when I personally gave the order to burn the books at the Franz Joseph Platz outside Berlin University. I have never enjoyed myself more than in the period when I perfected an acid rhetoric as editor of *Der Angriff*, which more often than not inspired the destruction of writings inimical to our point of view. It was a pleasure putting troublesome editors in the camps. Those days seem far away now. Many enjoy *All Quiet on the Western Front!*

Hitler would not have minded a hearty exchange on the subject of censorship. He likes any topic that relates at some point to the arts. He would have certainly preferred such a discussion to arguing about capitalist policy in America. I didn't pursue either. I am satisfied to leave to these diary pages my conclusion that running an empire is a lot more expensive than having a fat republic, sitting back, and collecting profits. The British used to understand. If they hadn't forgotten, we probably wouldn't be where we are today.

Ironically for someone reputed to be a political and military genius, Hitler has spent the entirety of his retirement (he holds his title for life) ignoring both subjects and concentrating on his cultural theories. He be-came a correspondent with the woman who chairs the anthropology de-partment of New Berlin University (no hearth and home for her) and behaved almost as though he were jealous of her job. Lucky for her that he didn't stage a *putsch*. Besides, she was a fully accredited Nazi.

I think that Eva took it quite well. *Kinder, Küche, Kirche!*

As I stood in Hitler's sickroom, watching the man to whom I had devoted my life waning before me, I felt an odd ambivalence. On one hand I was sorry to see him go. On the other hand I felt a kind of—I'm not sure how to put it—release. It was as though, when he died, I would at last begin my true retirement. The other years of supposed resignation from public life did not count. Truly Adolf Hitler had been at the very center of my life.

I wish that he had not made his parting comment. *"Herr Dr. Goeb-bels,"* he said, and the returned formality made me uncharacteristically adopt a military posture, "I want to remind you of one thing. Shortly before his death Goering agreed with me that our greatest coup was the secrecy with which we handled the Jewish policy. The atom-bombing of camps was a bonus. Despite the passage of time I believe this secret should be preserved. In fact, there may come a day when no official in the German government knows of it. Only the hierarchy of the SS will preserve the knowledge in their initiatory rites."

"Allied propaganda continues to speak of it, *mein Führer*. Various Jewish organizations in America and elsewhere continue to mourn the lost millions every year. At least Stalin receives his share of blame."

"Propaganda is one thing. Proof is another. You know this as well as anyone. I'd like to hear you agree that the program should remain a secret. As for Stalin's death camps, talk that up forever."

I was taken aback that he would even speak of it. "Without question, I agree!" I remembered how we had exploited in our propaganda the Russian massacre of the Poles at Katyn. The evidence was solid . . . and there is such a thing as world opinion. I could see his point. At this late date there was little advantage in admitting to our vigorous policy for the Jews. The world situation had changed since the war.

Nevertheless his request seemed peculiar and unnecessary. In the light of later events I cannot help but wonder whether or not Hitler really was psychic. Could he have known of the personal disaster that would soon engulf members of my family?

The conversation kept running through my mind on the way to the funeral. As we traveled under Speer's Arch of Triumph, I marveled for—I suppose—the hundredth time at his architectural genius. Germany would be paying for this city for the next fifty years, but it was worth it. Besides, we had to do something with all that Russian gold! What is gold, in the end, but a down payment on the future, be it the greatest city in the world or buying products from America?

The procession moved at a snail's pace, and considering the distance we had to cover I felt it might be the middle of the night by the time we made it to the Great Hall. The day lasted long enough, as it turned out.

The streets were thronged with sobbing people, Hitler's beloved *Volk*. The swastika flew from every window; I thought to conceive a poetic image to describe the thousands of fluttering black shapes, but when all I could think of was a myriad of spiders, I gave up. *Leave poetry to those more qualified,* I thought—*copywriting is never an ode.*

Finally we were moving down the great avenue between Goering's Palace and the Soldier's Hall. The endless vertical lines of these towering structures always remind me of Speer's ice-cathedral lighting effects at

Nuremberg. Nothing he has done in concrete has ever matched what he
did with pure light.

God, what a lot of white marble! The glare hurts my eyes sometimes.
When I think of how we denuded Italy of its marble to accomplish all
this, I recognize the Duce's one invaluable contribution to the Greater
Reich.

Everywhere you turn in New Berlin there are statues of heroes and
horses; horses and heroes. And flags, flags, flags. Sometimes I become just
a little bored with our glorious Third Reich. Perhaps success must lead to
excess. But it keeps beer and cheese on the table, as my wife, Magda,
would say. I am an author of it. I helped to build this gigantic edifice with
my ideas as surely as the workmen did with the sweat of their brows and
the stones from the quarries. And Hitler, dear, sweet Hitler—he ate up
little inferior countries and spat out the mortar of this metropolis. Never
has a man been more the father of a city.

The automobiles had to drive slowly to keep pace with the horses in the
lead, pulling the funeral caisson of the *Führer*. I was thankful when we
reached our destination.

It took a while to seat the officialdom. As I was in the lead group, and
seated first, I had to wait interminably while everyone else ponderously
filed in. The hall holds thousands upon thousands. Speer saw to that. I had
to sit still and watch what seemed like the whole German nation enter and
take seats.

Many spoke ahead of me. After all, when I was finished with the official
eulogy, there would be nothing left but to take him down and pop him in
the vault. When Norway's grand old man, Quisling, rose to say a few
words, I was delighted that he only took a minute. Really amazing. He
praised Hitler as the destroyer of the Versailles penalties, and that was
pretty much it.

The only moment of interest came when a representative of the sover-
eign nation of Burgundy stood in full SS regalia. A hush fell over the
audience. Most Germans have never felt overly secure at the thought of
Burgundy, a nation given exclusively to the SS . . . and outside the juris-
diction of German law. It was one of the wartime promises Hitler made
that he kept to the letter. The country was carved out of France (which
I'm sure never noticed—all they ever cared about was Paris, anyway).

The SS man spoke of blood and iron. He reminded us that the war had
not ended all that long ago, although many Germans would like to forget
that and merely wallow in the proceeds from the adventure. This feudalist
was also the only speaker at the funeral to raise the old specter of the
International Zionist Conspiracy, which I thought was a justifiable piece

of nostalgia, considering the moment. As he droned on in a somewhat monotonous voice, I thought about Hitler's comment regarding the secret death camps. Of course, there are still Jews in the world, and Jewish organization in America worth reckoning with, and a group trying to reestablish Israel—so far unsuccessfully—and understandably no group of people would rather see us destroyed. What I think is important to remember is that the Jew is hardly the only enemy of the Nazi.

By the time he was finished the crowd was seething in that old, pleasing, violent way . . . and I noticed that many of them restrained themselves with good Prussian discipline from cheering and applauding the speaker (which would not be entirely proper at a funeral). If they had broken protocol, however, I would have gladly joined in!

It seemed that an eternity had passed by the time I stood at the microphone to make my oration. I was surrounded by television cameras. How things have changed since the relatively simple days of radio. I'm sure that many of my ardent supporters were disappointed that I did not give a more rousing speech. I was the greatest orator of them all, even better than Hitler (if I may say so). My radio speeches are universally acclaimed as having been the instrumental factor in upholding German morale. I was more than just the Minister of Propaganda—I was the soul of National Socialism.

Toward the end of the war I made the greatest speech of my career, and this in the face of total disaster. I had no more believed at the time that we could win than Hitler had when he made his final boast about a mysterious secret weapon still later in the darkest of dark hours. My friends were astonished that after my emotional speech I could sit back and dispassionately evaluate the effect I had had upon my listeners. Such is the nature of a good propagandist.

Alas for the nostalgia buffs, there was no fire or fury in my words that day. I was economical of phrase. I listed his most noteworthy achievements; I made an objective statement about his sure and certain place in history; I told the mourners that they were privileged to have lived in the time of this man. That sort of thing, you know.

I finished on a quiet note. I said: "This man was a symbol. He was an inspiration. He took up a sword against the enemies of a noble idea that had almost vanished. He fought small and mean notions of man's destiny. Adolf Hitler restored the beliefs of our strong ancestors. Adolf Hitler restored the sanctity of our"—and I used the loaded term—"race." (I could feel the stirring in the crowd. It works every time.) "Adolf Hitler is gone. But what he accomplished will never die . . . *if*"—I gave them my best stare—"you work to make sure that his world is your world."

I was finished. The last echoes of my voice died to be replaced by the strains of *Die Walküre* from the Berlin Philharmonic.

On the way to the vault I found myself thinking about numerous things, none of them having to do directly with Hitler. I thought of Speer and the space program; I philosophized that Jewry is an *idea;* I reveled in the undying pleasure that England had become the Reich's "Ireland"; I briefly ran an inventory of my mistress, my children, my wife; I wondered what it would be like to live in America, with a color television and bomb shelter in every home.

The coffin was deposited in the vault, behind a bulletproof sheet of glass. His waxen-skinned image would remain there indefinitely, preserved for the future. I went home, then blissfully to bed and sleep.

October 1965

Last night I dreamed that I was eighteen years old again. I remembered a Jewish teacher I had at the time, a pleasant and competent fellow. What I remember best about him was his sardonic sense of humor.

Funny how after all this time I still think about Jews. I have written that they were the inventor of the lie. I used that device to powerful effect in my propaganda. (Hitler claimed to have made this historic "discovery.")

My so-called retirement keeps me busier than ever. The number of books on which I'm currently engaged is monumental. I shudder to think of all the unfinished works I shall leave behind at my death. The publisher called the other day to tell me that the Goebbels war memoirs are going into their ninth printing. That is certainly gratifying. They sell quite well all over the world.

My daughter Hilda, besides being a competent chemist, is serious about becoming a writer as well, and if her letters are any sign I have no doubt but that she will succeed on her own merits. Alas, her political views become more dangerous all the time, and I fear she would be in grave trouble by now were it not for her prominent name. The German Freedom League, of which she is a conspicuous member, is composed of sons and daughters of approved families and so enjoys its immunity from prosecution. At least they are not rabble-rousers (not that I would mind if they had the proper Nazi ideas). They are purely intellectual critics and as such are accommodated. We are embracing a risk.

It was not too many years after our victory before the charter was passed allowing for freedom of thought for the elite of our citizenry. I laugh to think how I initially opposed the move, and remember all too well Hitler's surprising indifference to the measure. After the war he was a tired man, willing to leave administration to party functionaries, and the extension of ideology to the SS in Burgundy. He became frankly indolent in his new lifestyle.

Anyway, it doesn't matter now. "Freedom of thought" for the properly indoctrinated Aryan appears harmless enough. So long as he benefits from the privilege of real personal power at a fairly early age, the zealous desire for reform is quickly sublimated into the necessities of intelligent and disciplined management.

Friday's *New Berlin Post* arrived with my letter in answer to a question frequently raised by the new crop of young Nazis, not the least of whom is my own son Helmuth, currently under apprenticeship in Burgundy. I love him dearly, but what a bother he is sometimes. What a family! Those six kids were more trouble than the French underground. But I digress.

These youngsters are always asking why we didn't launch an A-bomb attack on New York City when we had the bomb before America did. If only they would read more! The explanation is self-evident to anyone acquainted with the facts. Today's youth has grown up surrounded by a phalanx of missiles tipped with H-bomb calling cards. They have no notion of how close we were to defeat. The Allies knew about Peenemünde. The V-3 was only finished in the nick of time. As for the rest, the physicists were not able to provide us with a limitless supply of A-bombs. There wasn't even time to test one. We used all but one against the invading armies; the last we threw at London, praying that some sympathetic Valkyrie would help guide it on its course so it would come somewhere near the target. The result was more than we anticipated.

The letter explained all this and also went into considerable detail on the technical reasons preventing a strike on New York. Admittedly we had developed a long range bomber for the purpose. It was ready within a month of our turning back the invasion. But there were no more A-bombs to be deployed at that moment. Our intelligence reported that America's Manhattan project was about to bear its fiery fruit. That's when the negotiations began. We much preferred the Americans teaching Japan (loyal ally though it had been) a lesson rather than making an atomic deposit on our shores. Besides, the war between us had truly reached a stalemate, our U-boats against their aircraft carriers; and each side's bombers against the other's. One plan was to deliver an atomic rocket from a submarine against America . . . but by then both sides were suing for peace. I still believe we made the best policy under the circumstances.

What would the young critics prefer? Nuclear annihilation? They may not appreciate that we live in an age of detente, but such are the cruel realities. We Nazis never intended to subjugate decadent America anyway.

Ours was a European vision. Dominating the world is fine, but actually
trying to administer the entire planet would be clearly self-defeating. Nobody could be that crazy . . . except for a Bolshevik, perhaps.

Facts have a tendency to show through the haze of even the best propaganda, no matter how effectively the myth would screen out unpleasant-
ries. So it is that my daughter, the idealist of the German Freedom
League, is not critical of our Russian policy. Why should it be otherwise?
She worries about freedom for citizens, and gives the idea of freedom for a
serf no more thought than the actual Russian serf gives it. Which is to say
none at all. Here is one of the few areas where I heartily agree with the
late Alfred Rosenberg.

Once again my *Führer* calls me. And I was so certain all that was over.
They want me at the official opening of the Hitler Memoriam at the
museum. His paintings will be there, along with his architectural sketches.
And his stuffed Shepherd dogs. And his complete collection of Busby
Berkeley movies from America. Ah well, I will have to go.

There is just enough time before departing for me to shower, have some
tea, and listen to Beethoven's Pastorale.

December 1965

I loathe Christmas. It is not that I mind being with my family, but the
rest of it is so commercialized, or else syrupy with contemptible Christian
sentiments. Now if they could restore the vigor of the original Roman
holiday. Perhaps I should speak to Himmler. . . . What am I saying?
Never Himmler! Too bad Rosenberg isn't around.

Helga, my eldest daughter, visited us for a week. She is a geneticist.
Currently she is working on a paper to show the limitations of our eugenic
policies, and to demonstrate the possibilities opened up by genetic engineering. All this is over my head. DNA, RNA, microbiology, and *literal*
supermen in the end? When Hitler said to let the technical side move in
any direction it chooses, he was not saying much. There seems no way to
stop them.

There is an old man in the neighborhood who belongs to the Nordic
cult, body and soul. He and I spoke last week, all the time watching
youngsters ice skating under a startlingly blue afternoon sky. There was
almost a fairy-tale-like quality about the scene, as this old fellow told me in
no uncertain terms that this science business is so much fertilizer. "The
only great scientist I've ever seen was Horbiger," he announced proudly.
"And he was more than a scientist. He was of the true blood, and held the
true historical vision."

I didn't have the heart to tell him that the way in which Horbiger was more than a scientist was in his mysticism. Horbiger was useful to us in his day, and one of Himmler's prophets. But the man's cosmogony was utterly discredited by our scientists. Speer's technical Germany has a low tolerance for hoaxes.

This old man would hear none of it at any rate. He still believed every sacred pronouncement. "When I look up at the moon," he told me in a confidential whisper, "I know what I am seeing." *Green cheese,* I thought to myself, but I was aware of what was coming next.

"You still believe that the moon is made of ice?" I asked him.

"It is the truth," he announced gravely, suddenly affronted as though my tone had given me away. "Horbiger proved it," he said with finality. *Horbiger said it,* I thought to myself. So that's all you need for "proof." I left the eccentric to his idle speculations on the meaning of the universe. I had to get back to one of my books. It had been languishing in the typewriter too long.

Frau Goebbels was in a sufficiently charitable mood come Christmas to invite the entire neighborhood over. I felt that I was about to live through another endless procession of representatives of the German nation—all the pomp of a funeral without any fun. The old eccentric was invited as well. I was just as happy that he did not come. Arguing about Horbiger is not my favorite pastime.

Speer and his wife dropped by. Mostly he wanted to talk about Von Braun and the moon project. Since we had put up the first satellite, the Americans were working around the clock to beat us to Luna and restore their international prestige. As far as I was concerned, propaganda would play the deciding role on world opinion (as always). This was an area in which America had always struck me as deficient.

I listened politely to Speer's worries, and finally pointed out that the United States wouldn't be in the position it currently held if so many of our rocketry people hadn't defected at the end of the war. "It seems to be a race between their German scientists and ours," I said with a hearty chuckle.

Speer did not seem amused. He replied with surprising coldness that Germany would be better off if we hadn't lost so many of our Jewish geniuses when Hitler came to power. I swallowed hard on my bourbon, and perhaps Speer saw consternation on my face, because he was immediately trying to smooth things over with me. Speer is no idealist, but one hell of an expert in his field. I look upon him as I would a well-kept piece of machinery. I hope no harm ever comes to it.

Speer always seems to have up-to-date information on all sorts of interesting subjects. He had just learned that an investigation of many years had been dropped with regard to a missing German geneticist, Richard Dietrich. Since this famous scientist had vanished only a few years after the conclusion of the war, the authorities supposed he had either defected to the Americans in secret or had been kidnapped. After two decades of fruitless inquiry, a department decides to cut off funds for the search. I'm sure that a few detectives had made a lucrative career out of the job. Too bad for them.

Magda and I spent part of the holidays returning to my birthplace on the Rhineland. I like to see the old homestead from time to time. I'm happy it hasn't been turned into a damned shrine as happened with Hitler's childhood home. Looking at reminders of the past in a dry, flaky snowfall—brittle, yet seemingly endless, the same as time itself—I couldn't help but wonder what the future holds. Space travel. Genetic engineering. Ah, I am an old man. I feel it in my bones.

May 1966

I have been invited to Burgundy. My son Helmuth has passed his initiation and is now a fully accredited student of the SS, on his way to joining the inner circle. Naturally he is in a celebratory mood and wants his father to witness the victory. I am proud, of course, but just a little wary of what his future holds in store. I remain the convinced ideologue, and critical of the bourgeois frame of mind. (Our revolution was against that sort of sentimentality.) But I don't mind some bourgeois comforts. My son will live a hard and austere life that I hope will not prove too much for him.

No sooner had I been sent the invitation than I also received a telegram from my daughter Hilda, whom I had not seen since Yuletide, when she stopped by for Christmas dinner. Somehow she had learned of the invitation from Helmuth and insisted that I must see her before leaving on the trip. She told me that I was in danger! The message was clouded in mystery because she did not even offer a hint of a reason. Nevertheless I agreed to meet her at the proposed rendezvous because it was conveniently on the way. And I am always worried that Hilda will find herself in jail for going too far with her unrealistic views.

The same evening I was cleaning out a desk when I came across a letter Hilda had written when she was seventeen years old—from the summer of 1952. I had the urge to read it again:

Dear Father:
    I appreciate your last letter and its frankness, although I don't understand

the point you made. Why have you not been able to think of anything to say to me for nearly a year? I know that you and Mother have found me to be your most difficult daughter. An example comes to mind: Helga, Holly, and Hedda never gave Mother trouble about their clothes. I didn't object to the dresses she put on me, but could I help it if they were torn when I played? It simply seemed to me that more casual attire suited climbing trees and hiking and playing soccer.

From the earliest age I can remember, I've always thought boys had more fun than girls because they get to play all those wonderful games. I didn't want to be left out! Why did that make Mother so upset that she cried?

Ever since Heide died in that automobile accident, Mother has become very protective of her daughters. Only Helmuth escaped that sort of overwhelming protectiveness, and that's just because he's a boy.

At first I wasn't sure that I wanted to be sent to this private school, but a few weeks here convinced me that you had made the right decision. The mountains give you room to stretch your legs. The horses they let us have are magnificent. Wolfgang is mine and he is absolutely the fastest. I'm sure of it.

Soon I will be ready to take my examinations for the university. Your concern that I do well runs through your entire letter. Now we have something to talk about again. At this point it is too late to worry. I'm sure I'll do fine. I've been studying chemistry every chance I get and love it.

My only complaint is that the library is much too small. My favorite book is the unexpurgated Nietzsche, where he talks about the things the Party forbade as subjects of public discussion. At first I was surprised to discover how pro-Jewish he was, not to mention pro-freedom. The more I read of him, the more I understand his point of view.

One lucky development was a box of new books that had been confiscated from unauthorized people (what you would call the wrong type for intellectual endeavor, Father). Suddenly I had in front of me an orgy of exciting reading material. I especially enjoyed the Kafka . . . but I'm not sure why.

Some other students here want to form a club. They are in correspondence with others of our peer group who are allowed to read the old forbidden books. We have not decided on what we would call the organization. We are playing with the idea of the German Reading League. Other titles may occur to us later.

Another reason I like it better in the country than in the city is that there are not as many rules out here. Oh, the school has its curfews and other nonsense but they don't really pay much attention and we can do as we please most of the time. Only one of the teachers doesn't like me and she called me a little reprobate. I suspect she might make trouble for me except that everyone knows that you're my Father. That has always helped.

I was becoming interested in a boy named Franz but it came to the dean's attention and she told me that he was not from a good enough family for me to pursue the friendship. I ignored the advice but within a month Franz had left without saying a word. I know that you are against the old class boundaries, Father, but believe me when I say that they are still around. The people must not know that Hitler socialized them.

Now that I think about it, there are more rules out here than I first realized. Why must there be so many rules?

Why can't I just be me without causing so much trouble?

Well, I don't want to end this letter with a question. I hope you and Mother are happy. You should probably take that vacation you keep telling everyone will be any year now! I want to get those postcards from Hong Kong!

Love,
Hilda

I sat at the desk and thought about my daughter. I had to admit that she was my favorite and always had been. Where had I gone wrong with her? How had her healthy radicalism become channeled in such an unproductive direction? There was more to it than just the books. It was something in her. I was looking forward to seeing her again.

On a Wednesday morning I boarded a luxury train; the power of the rocket engines is deliberately held down so that passengers may enjoy the scenery instead of merely rushing through. I would be meeting Hilda in a small French hamlet directly in line with my final destination. I took along a manuscript—work, always work—this diary, and, for relaxation, a mystery novel by an Englishman. What is it about the British that makes this genre uniquely their own?

Speaking of books, I noticed a rotund gentleman—very much the Goering type—reading a copy of my prewar novel, *Michael.* I congratulated him on his excellent taste and he recognized me immediately. As I was autographing his copy, he asked if I were doing any new novels. I explained that I found plays and movie scripts a more comfortable form with which to work and suggested he see my filmed sequel to *The Wanderer* the next time he was in New Berlin. The director was no less than Leni Riefenstahl! I've never had any trouble living with the fact that my name is a household word. It makes of me a toastmaster much in demand. My most requested lecture topic remains *the* film, *Kolberg.*

I contemplated the numerous ways in which my wife's social calendar would keep her occupied in my absence. Since the children have grown up and left home, she seems more active than before! It's amazing the number of things she can find to do in a day. I would have liked to attend the Richard Strauss concert with her but duty calls.

The food on the train was quite good. The wine was only adequate, however. I had high hopes that that French hamlet would live up to its reputation for prime vintages.

The porter on the train looked Jewish to me. Probably is. There are people of Jewish ancestry living in Europe. It doesn't matter, so long as the practicing Jew is forever removed. God, we made the blood flow to cleanse this soil. Of course, I'm speaking figuratively. But what could one *do* with Jews, Gypsies, Partisans, homosexuals, the feebleminded, racemixers, and all the rest?

We reached the station at dusk and my daughter was waiting for me. She is such a lovely child, except that she is no child any longer! I can see why she has so many admirers. Her political activities (if they even deserve such a label) have not made her any the less attractive. She has the classic features. On her thirtieth birthday I once again brought up the subject of why she had never married. Oh, I am aware that she has many lovers. Not as many as her father, but still a respectable number. The question is: Can that be enough? That she may never reproduce vexes me greatly. As always her deep-throated laugh mocks my concern.

A few seconds after I disembarked she was pulling at my sleeve and rushing me to a cab. I had never seen her looking so agitated. We virtually ran through the lobby of my hotel, and I felt as though I were under some type of house arrest as she bustled me up to my room and bolted the door behind us.

"Father," she said almost breathlessly. "I have terrible news." I found the melodramatic derring-do a trifle annoying. After all, I had put those days firmly behind me (or so I thought). Leave intrigues to the young, I always say . . . suddenly remembering in that case my daughter still qualifies for numerous adventures. If only she would leave me out of it!

"My darling," I said, "I am tired from my trip and in want of a bath. Surely your message can wait until after I am changed? Over dinner we may . . ."

"No," she announced sternly. "It can't wait."

"Very well," I said, recognizing that my ploy had failed miserably and surrendering to her—shall we say—blitzkrieg. "Tell me," I said as I sat in a chair.

"You must not go to Burgundy," she began, and then paused as though anticipating an outburst from me. I am a master at that game. I told her to get on with it.

"Father, you may think me mad when I am finished, but I must tell you!" *A chip off the old block,* I thought. I nodded assent, if only to get it over with.

She was pacing as she spoke: "First of all, the German Freedom League has learned something that could have the worst consequences for the future of our country." I did not attempt to mask my expression of disgust but she plowed on regardless. "Think whatever you will of the League, but facts are facts. And we have uncovered the most diabolical secret."

"Which is?" I prompted her, expecting something anticlimactic.

"I am sure that you have not the slightest inkling of this, but during the war millions of Jews were put to death in horrible ways. What we thought were concentration camps suffering from typhus infections and lacking supplies, were in reality death camps at which was carried out a systematic program of *genocide.*" I could not believe she'd used Raphael Lemkin's smear word!

The stunned expression on my face was no act. My daughter interpreted it as befitted her love for me—she took it, if you will, at face value.

"I can see that you're shocked," she said. "Even though you staged those public demonstrations against the Jews, I realize that was to force the Nazi Party's emigration policy through. I detest that policy, but it wasn't murder."

"Dear," I said, trying to keep my voice even, "what you are telling me is nothing more than thoroughly discredited Allied propaganda. We shot Jewish Partisans, but there's no evidence of systematic—"

"There is now," she said, and I believe that my jaw dropped at the revelation. She went on, oblivious to my horror: "The records that were kept for those camps are all forgeries. A separate set of records, detailing the genocide, has been uncovered by the League."

What a damnably stupid German thing to do. To keep records of *everything.* I knew it had to be true. It was as if my daughter disappeared from the room at that second. I could still see her, but only in a fuzzy way. A far more solid form stood between us, the image of the man who had been my life. It was as if the ghost of Adolf Hitler stood before me then, in our common distress, in our common deed. I could hear his voice and remember my promise to him. Oh God, it was my own daughter who was to provide the test. I really had not the least desire to see her eliminated. I liked her.

What I said next was not entirely in keeping with my feigned ignorance, and if she had been less upset she might have noticed the implications of my remark as I asked her: "Hilda, how many people have you told?"

She answered without hesitation. "Only members of the League and now you." I heaved a sigh of relief.

"Don't you think it would be a good idea to keep this extreme theory to yourself?" I asked.

"It's no theory. It's a fact. And I have no intention of advertising this. It would make me a target for those lunatics in the SS."

So that was the Burgundy connection! I still didn't see why I should be in any danger during my trip to Burgundy. Even if I were innocent of the truth—which every SS official knew to be absurd, since I was an architect of our policy—my sheer prominence in the Nazi Party would keep me safe from harm in Burgundy.

I asked my daughter what this fancy of hers had to do with my impending trip. "Only everything," she answered.

"Are you afraid that they will suspect I've learned of this so-called secret, which is nothing more than patent nonsense to begin with?"

She surprised me by answering, "No." There was an executioner's silence.

"What then?" I asked.

"It is not this crime of the past that endangers you," came the sound of her voice in portentous tones. "It is a crime of the future."

"You should have been the poet of the family."

"If you go to Burgundy, you risk your life. They are planning a new crime against humanity that will make World War II and the concentration camps, on both the Allied and Axis sides, seem like nothing but a prelude. And you will be one of the first victims!"

Never have I felt more acutely the pain of a father for his offspring. I could not help but conclude that my youngest daughter's mind had only a tenuous connection to reality. Her political activities must be to blame! On the other hand I regarded Hilda with a genuine affection. She seemed concerned for my welfare in a manner I supposed would not apply to a stranger. The decadent creed she had embraced had not led to any disaffection from her father.

I thought back to the grand old days of intrigue within the Party and the period in the war years when I referred most often to that wise advice of Machiavelli: "Cruelties should be committed all at once, as in that way each separate one is less felt, and gives less offense." We had come perilously close to *Götterdämmerung* then, but in the end our policy proved sound. I was beyond all that. The state was secure, Europe was secure . . . and the only conceivable threat to my safety would come from foreign sources. Yet here was Hilda, her face a mixture of concern and anger and—perhaps love? She was telling me to beware the Burgundians. She had as much as accused them of plotting against the Reich itself!

I remember how they had invited me to one of the conferences to decide the formation of the new nation of Burgundy. Those were hectic times in the postwar period. As *Gauleiter* of Berlin (one of the *Führer's* few appointments of that title with which I always approved) I had been primarily concerned with Speer's work to build New Berlin. The film industry was flowering under my personal supervision, I was busy writing my memoirs, and I was involved heavily with diplomatic projects. I hadn't really given Burgundy much thought. I knew that it had been a country in medieval times, and had read a little about the Duchy of Burgundy. I remembered that the historical country had traded in grain, wines, and finished wool.

They announced at the conference that the historical Burgundy would be restored, encompassing the area to the south of Champagne, east of Bourbonais, and north and west of Savoy. There was some debate on whether or not to restore the original place-names or else borrow from Wagner to create a series of new ones. In the end the latter camp won out. The capital was named Tarnhelm, after the magic helmet in the *Nibelungenlied* that could change the wearer into a variety of shapes.

Hitler did not officially single out any of the departments that made up the SS: Waffen, Death's Head, or General SS. We in his entourage realized, however, that the gift was to those members of the inner circle who had been most intimately involved with both the ideological and practical side of the extermination program. The true believers! Given the Reich's policy of secrecy, there was no need to blatantly advertise the reasons for the gift. Himmler, as *Reichsführer* of the SS and Hitler's adviser on racial matters, was naturally instrumental in this transfer of power to the new nation. His rival, Rosenberg, met his death.

The officials who would oversee the creation of Burgundy were carefully selected. Their mission was to make certain that Burgundy became a unique nation in all of Europe, devoted to certain chivalric values of the past, and the formation of pure Aryan specimens. It was nothing more than the logical extension of our propaganda, the secularizing of the myths and legends with which we had kept the people fed during the dark days of lost hope. The final result was a picturesque fairy-tale kingdom that made its money almost entirely out of the tourist trade. America loves to boast of its amusement parks but it has nothing to match this.

Hilda interrupted my reverie by asking me in a voice bordering on sternness: "Well, what are you going to do?"

"Unless you make sense, I will continue on my journey to Tarnhelm to see Helmuth." He was living at the headquarters of the SS leaders, the territory that was closed off to outsiders, even during the tourist season. Yet it was by no means unusual for occasional visitors from New Berlin to be invited there. My daughter's melodramatics had not yet given cause to worry. All I could think of was how I'd like to get my hands around the throat of whoever put these idiotic notions in her pretty head.

She was visibly distressed, but in control. She tossed her hair back and said, "I am not sure that the proof I have to offer will be sufficient to convince you."

"Aren't you getting ahead of yourself?" I asked. "You haven't even made a concrete accusation yet! Drop this pose. Tell me what you think constitutes the danger."

"They think you're a traitor," she said.

"What?" I was astounded to hear such words from anyone for any reason. "To Germany?"

"No," she answered. "To the true Nazi ideal."

I laughed. "That's the craziest thing I've ever heard. I'm one of the key—"

"You don't understand," she interrupted. "I'm talking about the religion."

"Oh, Hilda, is that all? You and your group have stumbled upon some threatening comments from the Thule Society, I take it?"

Now it was her turn to be surprised. She sat upon the bed. "Yes," she answered. "But then you know . . . ?"

"The specifics? Not at all. They change their game every few months. Who has the time to keep up? Let me tell you something. The leaders of the SS have always had ties to an occult group called the Thule Society, but there is nothing surprising about that. It is a purely academic exercise in playing with the occult, the same as the British equivalent—The Golden Dawn. I'm sure you're aware that many prominent Englishmen belonged to that club!

"These people are always harmless eccentrics. Our movement made use of the type without stepping on pet beliefs. It's the same as dealing with any religious person whom you want to be on your side. If you receive cooperation, it won't be through insulting his spiritual beliefs."

"What about the messages we intercepted?" she went on. "The threatening tone, the almost deranged—"

"It's how they entertain themselves!" I insisted. "Listen, you're familiar with Horbiger, aren't you?" She nodded. "Burgundians believe that stuff. Even after the launching of Von Braun's satellite, which in no way disturbed the eternal ice, as that old fool predicted! His followers don't care about facts. Hell, they still believe the moon in our sky is the fourth moon this planet has had, that it is made of ice like the other three, that all of the cosmos is an eternal struggle of fire and ice. Even our *Führer* toyed with those ideas in the old days. The Burgundians no more want to give up their sacred ideas merely because modern science has exploded them than fundamentalist Baptists in America want to listen to Darwin."

"I know," she said. "You are acting as though they aren't dangerous."

"They're not."

"Soon Helmuth will be accepted into the inner circle."

"Why not? He's been working for that ever since he was a teenager."

"But the inner circle," she repeated with added emphasis.

"So he'll be a Hitler Youth for the rest of his life. He'll never grow up."

"You don't understand."

"I'm tired of this conversation," I told her bluntly. "Do you remember several years ago when your brother went on that pilgrimage to Lower Saxony to one of Himmler's shrines? You were terribly upset but you didn't have a shred of reason why he shouldn't have gone. You had nightmares. Your mother and I wondered if it was because as a little girl you were frightened by Wagner."

"Now I have reasons."

"Mysterious threatening messages! The Thule Society! It should be taken with a grain of salt. I saw Adolf Hitler once listen to a harangue from an especially unrealistic believer in the Nordic cult, bow solemnly when the man was finished, enter his private office—where I accompanied him—and break out in laughter that would wake the dead. He didn't want to offend the fellow. The man was a good Nazi, at least."

My daughter was fishing around in her purse as I told her these things. She passed me a piece of paper when I was finished. I unfolded it and read:

JOSEPH GOEBBELS MUST ARRIVE ON SCHEDULE FOR THE RITUAL
HE WILL NEVER TELL ANYONE

"What is this?" I asked her. I was becoming angry.

A member of the Freedom League intercepted a message from Burgundy to someone in New Berlin. It was coded, but we were able to break it."

"To whom was the message addressed?"

"To Heinrich Himmler."

Suddenly I felt very, very cold. I had never trusted *der treue Heinrich.*

Admittedly I didn't trust anything that came from the German Freedom League, with a contradiction built into its very title. Nevertheless something in me was clawing at the pit of my stomach. Something told me that maybe, just maybe, there was danger after all. Crazy as Himmler had been during the war years, he had become much worse in peacetime. At least he was competent regarding his own industrial empire.

"How do I know that this note is genuine?" I asked.

"You don't," she answered. "I had to take a great risk in bringing it to you, if that helps you to believe."

"The Burgundians would have stopped you?"

"If they knew about it. I was referring to the German Freedom League. They hate you as much as the rest of them."

My face flushed with anger and I jumped to my feet so abruptly that it put an insupportable strain on my clubfoot. I had to grab for a nearby lamp to keep from stumbling. "Why," I virtually hissed, "do you belong to that despicable bunch of bums and poseurs?"

She stood also, picking up her purse as she did so. "Father, I am going. You may do with this information as you wish. I will offer one last suggestion. Why don't you take another comfortable passenger train back to New Berlin, and call Tarnhelm to say that you will be one day late? See what their reaction is? You didn't manage to attend my college graduation and I'm none the worse for it. Would it matter so much to my brother were you to help him celebrate after the ceremony?"

She turned to go. "Wait," I said. "I'm sorry I spoke so harshly. You mean well."

"We've been through this before," she answered, her back still to me.

"I don't see any harm in doing what you suggest. If it will make you happy, I'll delay the trip."

"Thank you," she said, and walked out. I watched the closed door for several minutes, not moving, not really thinking.

A half-hour later I was back at the railroad station, boarding an even slower passenger train back to New Berlin. I love this sort of travel. The rocket engines were held down to their minimum output. The straining hum they made only accentuated the fact of their great power held in check. Trains are the most human form of mass transportation.

With my state of mind in such turmoil I could not do any serious work. I decided to relax and resumed reading the English mystery novel. I had narrowed it down to three suspects, all members of the aristocracy, naturally—all highly offensive people. The servant I had ruled out as much too obvious. As is typical of the form, a few key sentences give up the solution if you know what they are. I had just passed over what I took to be such a phrase, and returned to it. Looking up from my book to contemplate the puzzle, I noticed that the woman sitting across from me was also reading a book, a French title that seemed vaguely familiar: *Le Théosophisme, histoire d'une pseudo-religion,* by René Guenon.

I looked back to my book when I suddenly noticed that the train was slowing down. There was no reason for it, as we were far from our next stop. Looking out the window, I saw nothing but wooded landscape under a starry night sky. A tall man up the aisle was addressing the porter. His rather lengthy monologue boiled down to a simple question: Why was there the delay? The poor official was shaking his head with bewilderment and indicated that he would move forward to inquire. That's when I noticed the gas.

It was yellow. It was seeping in from the air-conditioning system. Like everyone else I started to get up in hopes of finding a means of egress. Already I was coughing. As I turned to the window, with the idea of releasing the emergency lock, I slipped back down into the cushions as consciousness fled. The last thing I remember was seriously regretting that I had not found the time to sample a glass of wine from that hamlet.

I must have dreamed. I was standing alone in the middle of a great lake, frozen over in the dead of winter. I was not dressed for the weather but had on only my Party uniform. I looked down at the icy expanse at my feet and noticed that my boots were freshly shined, the luster already becoming covered by flakes of snow. I heard the sound of hoofbeats echoing hollowly on the ice, and looked up to see a small army on horseback approaching. I recognized them immediately. They were the Teutonic Knights. The dark armor, the stern faces, the great, black horses, the bright lances and swords and shields. They could be nothing else.

They did not appear to be friendly. I started walking away from them. The sound of their approach was a thunder pounding at my brain. I cursed my lameness, cursed my inability to fly, suddenly found myself suspended in the air, and then I had fallen on the ice, skinning my knees. Struggling to turn over, I heard a bloodcurdling yell and they were all around me. There was a whooshing of blades in the still, icy air. I was screaming. Then I was trying to reason with them.

"I helped Germany win the war . . . I believe in the Aryan race . . . I helped destroy the Jews. . . ." But I knew it was to no avail. They were killing me. The swords plunged in deeply.

I awakened aboard a small jet flying in the early dawn. For a moment I thought I was tied to my seat. When I glanced to see what kind of cords had my wrists bound to the arms of the chair, I saw that I was mistaken.

The feeling of constriction I attributed to the effects of the gas. Painfully I lifted a hand . . . then with even more anguish I raised my head, noticing that the compartment was empty except for me. The door to the cockpit was closed.

The most difficult task that confronted me was to turn my head to the left so that I could have a better view of our location. A dozen tiny needles pricked at the muscles in my neck but I succeeded. I was placed near the wing and could see a good portion of the countryside unfolding like a map beneath it. We were over a rundown railroad station. One last bit of track snaked on beyond it for about half a mile—we seemed flying almost parallel to it—when it suddenly stopped, blocked off by a tremendous oak tree, the size of which was noticeable even from the great height.

I knew where we were immediately. We had just flown over the eastern border of Burgundy.

I leaned back in my seat, attempting to have my muscles relax, but met with little success. They stubbornly insisted on having their way despite my *will* that they be otherwise. I was terribly thirsty. I assumed that if I stood I would have a serious dizzy spell, so I called out instead: "Steward!" No sooner was the word out of my mouth than a young, blonde man in a spotless white jacket came up behind me holding a small, fancy menu.

"What would you like?" he asked.

"An explanation."

"I'm afraid that is not on this menu. I'm sure you will find what you seek when we reach our destination. In the meantime would you care to dine?"

"No," I said, relapsing back into the depths of my seat, terribly tired again.

"Some coffee?" the steward asked, persisting.

I assented to this. It was very good coffee and soon I was feeling better. Looking out the window again, I observed that we were over a lake. There was a long-ship plying the clear, blue water—its dragon's head glared at the horizon. My son had written me about the Viking Club when he first took up residence in Burgundy. This had to be one of their outings.

Thirty minutes and two cups of coffee later the intercom announced that we would be landing at Tarnhelm. From the air the view was excellent: several monasteries—now devoted to SS training as *Ordensbürgen*—were situated near the village that housed the Russian serfs. Beyond that was still another lake and then came the imposing castle in which I knew I would find my son.

There was a narrow landing strip within the castle grounds and the pilot was every bit the professional. We hadn't been down longer than five minutes when who should enter the plane but my son Helmuth! I looked at him. He had blonde hair and blue eyes. The only trouble was that my son did not have blonde hair and blue eyes. Of course, I knew that the hair could be dyed, but somehow it looked quite authentic. As for the eyes, I could think of no explanation but for contact lenses. Helmuth had also lost weight and never appeared more muscular or healthy than he did now.

Here I was, surrounded by mystery—angry, bewildered, unsettled. And yet the first thing that escaped my lips was: "Helmuth, what's happened to you?" He guessed my meaning.

"This is real blonde hair," he said proudly. "And the eye color is real as well. I regret that I am not of the true genotype, any more than you are. I was given a hormone treatment to change the color of my hair. A special radiation treatment took care of the eyes."

As he was saying this, he was helping me to my feet, as I was still groggy. "Why?" I asked him. He would say no more about it.

The sun hurt my eyes as we exited down the ramp from the plane. Two tall, young men—also blonde-haired and blue-eyed—joined my son and helped to usher me inside the castle. They were dressed in Bavarian hunting gear, with large knives strapped on at their waists. Their clothes had the smell of freshest leather.

We had entered from the courtyard of the inner bailey. The hall we traversed was covered in plush red carpets and was illuminated by torches burning in the walls; this cast a weird lighting effect over the numerous suits of armor standing there. I could not help but think of the medieval castles Speer drew for his children every Christmas.

It was a long trek before we reached a stone staircase that we immediately began to ascend. I was not completely recovered from the effects of the gas and wished that we could pause. My clubfoot was giving me considerable difficulty. I did not want to show any weakness to these men, and I knew that my sturdy son was right behind me. I took those steps without slowing down the pace.

We finally came out on a floor that was awash in light from fluorescent tubes. A closed-circuit television console dominated the center of the room, with pictures of all the other floors of the castle, from the keep to the highest tower. There was also a portrait of Meister Eckhart.

"Wait here," Helmuth announced, and before I could make any protestations he and the other two had gone the way we had come, with the door locked behind them. I considered the large window on the right side of the room with a comfortable couch beside it. I gratefully sat there and surveyed my position from the new vantage point. Below me was another courtyard. In one corner was what could be nothing else but an unused funeral pyre. Its height was staggering. There was no body upon it. Along the wall that ran from the pyre to the other end of the compound were letters inscribed of a size easy to read even from such distance. It was a familiar quotation: ANY DESCRIPTION OF ORGANIZATION, MISSION, AND STRUCTURE OF THE SS CANNOT BE UNDERSTOOD UNLESS ONE TRIES TO CONCEIVE IT INWARDLY WITH ONE'S BLOOD AND HEART. IT CANNOT BE EXPLAINED WHY WE CONTAIN SO MUCH STRENGTH THOUGH WE NUMBER SO FEW. Underneath the quote in equally large letters was the name of its author: HEINRICH HIMMLER.

"A statement that you know well," came a low voice behind me and I turned to face Kurt Kaufmann, the most important man in Burgundy. I had met him a few times socially in New Berlin.

Smiling in as engaging a manner as I could (under the circumstances), I said, "Kurt," stressing that I was not addressing him formally, "I have no idea why you have seemingly kidnapped me, but there will be hell to pay!"

He bowed. "What you fail to appreciate, Dr. Goebbels, is that I will receive that payment."

I studied his face—the bushy blonde hair and beard, and of course the bright blue eyes. The monocle he wore over one of them seemed quite superfluous. I knew that he had 20/20 vision.

"I have no idea what you are talking about."

"You lack ideas, it is true," he answered. "Of facts you do not lack. We knew your daughter contacted you . . ."

Even at the time this dialogue struck me as remarkably melodramatic. Nevertheless it was happening *to me*. At the mention of my daughter I failed to mask my feelings. Kaufmann had to notice the expression of consternation on my face. The whole affair was turning into a hideous game that I feared I was losing.

I stood. "My daughter's associations with a subversive political group are well known." There was no reason to mince words with him. "I was attempting to dissuade her from a suicidal course. Why would you be spying on that?"

The ploy failed miserably. "We bugged the room," he said softly.

"You dare to spy on *me?* Have you any idea of the danger?"

"Yes," he said. "You don't."

I made to comment but he raised a hand to silence me. "Do not continue. Soon you will have more answers than you desire. Now I suggest you follow me."

The room had many doors. We left through one at the opposite end from my original point of entry. I was walking down yet another hall. This one, however, was lit by electricity, and at the end of it we entered an elevator. The contrast between modern technology and Burgundian simplicity was becoming more jarring all the time. Like most Germans who had visited the country I only knew it firsthand as a tourist. The reports I had once received on their training operations were not as detailed as I would have liked but certainly gave no hint of dire conspiracy against the Fatherland. The thought was too fantastic to credit. Even now I hoped for a denouement more in keeping with the known facts. Could the entire thing be an elaborate practical joke? Who would run the risk of such a folly?

The elevator doors opened and we were looking out onto the battlements of the castle. I followed Kaufmann onto the walk, and noticed that the view was utterly magnificent. To the left I saw the imported Russian serfs working in the fields; to the right I saw young Burgundians doing calisthenics in the warm morning air. I was used to observing many blonde heads in the SS. Yet here there was nothing but that suddenly predictable homogeneity.

We looked down at the young bodies. Beyond them other young men were dressed in chain-mail shirts and helmets. They were having at one another with the most intensive swordplay I had ever witnessed.

"Isn't that a bit dangerous?" I asked Kaufmann, gesturing at the fencing.

"What do you mean?" he said, as one of the men ran his sword through the chest of another. The blood spurted out in a fountain as the body slumped to the ground. I was aghast, and Kaufmann's voice seemed to be far away as I dimly heard it say: "Did you notice how the loser did not scream? That is what I call discipline." It occurred to me that the man might have simply died too quickly to express his opinion.

Kaufmann seemed wryly amused by my wan expression. "Dr. Goebbels, do you remember the *Kirchenkampf?*"

I recovered my composure. "The campaign against the churches? What about it?"

"Martin Bormann was disappointed in its failure," he said.

"No more than I. The war years allowed little time for less important matters. You know that the economic policies we established after the war helped to undermine the strength of the churches. They have never been weaker. European cinema constantly makes fun of them."

"They still exist," said Kaufmann evenly. "The gods of the Germanic tribes are not fools—their indignation is as great as ever." I stared at this man with amazement as he continued to preach: "The gods remember how Roman missionaries built early Christian churches on the sacred sites, believing that the common people would still climb the same hills they always had to worship . . . only now they would pay homage to a false god!"

"The masses are not easily cured of the addiction," I pointed out.

"You compare religion to a drug?"

"It was one of the few wise statements of Marx," I said, with a deliberate edge in my voice. Kaufmann's face quickly darkened into a scowl. "Not all religions are the same," I concluded in an ameliorative tone. I had no desire to argue with him about the two faiths of Burgundy, the remnants of Rosenberg's Gnostics, and the majority of Himmler's Pagans.

"You say that, but it is only words. Let me tell you a story about yourself, Herr Goebbels." I did not consider the sudden formality a good sign, not the way he said it. He continued: "You always prided yourself on being the true radical of the Nazi Party. You hammered that home whenever you could. Nobody hated the bourgeoisie more than Goebbels. Nobody was more ardent about burning books than Goebbels. As *Reichspropagandaminister* you brilliantly staged the demonstrations against the Jews."

Now the man was making sense. I volunteered another item to his admirable list: "I overheard some young men humming the Horst Wessel song down there during calisthenics." Manufacturing a martyr to give the party its anthem was still one of my favorites. My influence was still on the Germanic world, including Burgundy.

Kaufmann had been surveying rows of men doing pushups . . . as well as the removal of the corpse from the tourney field. Now his stone face turned in my direction, breaking into an unpleasant smile. I preferred his frown. "You misunderstand the direction of my comments, Herr Doktor. I will clarify it. I was told a story about you once. I was only a simple soldier at the time but the story made an indelible impression. You were at a party, showing off for your friends by making four brief political speeches: the first presented the case for the restoration of the monarchy; the second sung the praises of the Weimar Republic; the third proved how communism could be successfully adopted by the German Reich; the fourth was in favor of National Socialism, at last. How relieved they were. How tempted they had been to agree with each of the other three speeches."

I could not believe what I was hearing. How could this dull oaf be in charge of anything but a petty bureaucratic department? Had he no sense of humor, no irony? "I was demonstrating the power of propaganda," I told him.

"In what do you believe?" he asked.

"This is preposterous," I nearly shouted. "Are you impugning—"

"It is not necessary to answer," he said consolingly. "I'm aware that you have only believed in one thing in your life: a man, not an idea. With Hitler dead, what is left for you to believe?"

"This is insane," I replied, not liking the shrill sound of my own voice in my ears. "When I was made Reich Director for Total War, I demonstrated my genius for understanding and operating the mechanisms of a dictatorship. I was crucial to the war effort then."

He completely ignored my point and continued on his solitary course: "Hitler was more than a man. He was a living part of an idea. He did not always recognize his own importance. He was chosen by the Vril Society, the sacred order of the Luminous Lodge, the purest, finest product of the believers in the Thule. Adolf Hitler was the medium. The Society used him accordingly. He was the focal point. Behind him were powerful magicians. The great work has only begun. Soon it will be time for the second step. Only the true man deserves *Lebensraum.*"

Kaufmann was working himself up, I could see that. He stood close to me and said, "You are a political animal, Goebbels. You believe that politics is an end in itself. The truth is that governments are nothing in the face of destiny. We are near the cleansing of the world. You should be proud. Your own son will play an important part. The finest jest is that modern scientific method will also have a role."

He turned to go. I had no recourse but to follow him. There was nowhere else to go but straight down to sudden death.

We reentered the elevator. "Have I been brought here to witness an honor bestowed on my son?" I asked.

"In part. You will also have a role. You saw the telegram!"

That was enough. There could no longer be any doubt. I was trapped amidst madmen. Having made up my mind what to do, I feigned an attack of pain in my clubfoot and crouched at the same time. When Kaufmann made to offer aid, I struck wildly, almost blindly. I tried to knee him in the groin but—failing that—brought my fist down on the back of his neck. The fool went out like a light, falling hard on his face. I congratulated myself on such prowess for an old man.

No sooner had the body slumped to the floor than the elevator came to a stop and the doors opened automatically. I jumped out into the hall. Standing there was a naked seven-foot giant who reached down and lifted me into the air. He was laughing. His voice sounded like a tuba.

"They call me Thor," he said. I struggled. He held.

Then I heard the voice of my son: "That, Father, is what we call a true Aryan."

I was carried like so much baggage down the hall, hearing voices distantly talking about Kaufmann. I was tossed on to the hard floor of a brightly lit room and the door was slammed behind me. A muscle had been pulled in my back and I lay there, gasping in pain like a fish out of water. I could see that I was in some sort of laboratory. In a corner was a humming machine the purpose of which I could not guess. A young woman was standing over me, wearing a white lab smock. I could not help but notice two things about her straightaway: she was a brunette, and she was holding a sword at my throat.

As I look back, the entire affair has an air of unreality about it. Events were becoming more fantastic in direct proportion to the speed with which they occurred. It had all the logic of a dream.

As I lay upon the floor, under that sword held by such an unlikely guardian (I had always supported military service for women, but when encountering the real thing I found it a bit difficult to take seriously), I began to take an inventory of my pains. The backache was subsiding so long as I did not move. I was becoming aware, however, that the hand with which I had dispatched Kaufmann felt like a hot balloon of agony, expanding without an upper limit. My vision was blurred and I shook my head trying to clear it. I dimly heard voices in the background, and then a particularly resonant one was near at hand, speaking with complete authority: "Oh, don't be ridiculous. Help him up."

The woman put down the sword, and was suddenly assisted by a young Japanese girl gingerly lifting me off the floor and propelling me in the direction of a nearby chair. Still I did not see the author of that powerful voice.

Then I was sitting down and the females were moving away. He was standing there, his hands on his hips, looking at me with the sort of analytical probing I always respect. At first I didn't recognize him, but had instead the eerie feeling that I was in a movie. The face made me think of something too ridiculous to credit . . . and then I knew who it really was: Professor Dietrich, the missing geneticist. I examined him more closely. My first impression had been more correct than I thought. The man hardly resembled the photographs of his youth. His hair had turned white and he had let it grow. Seeing him in person, I could not help but notice how angular were his features . . . how much like the face of the late actor Rudolf Klein-Rogge in the role of Dr. Mabuse, Fritz Lang's character that had become the symbol of a super-scientific, scheming Germany to the rest of the world. Although the later films were banned for the average German, the American-made series (Mabuse's second life, you could say) had become so popular throughout the world that Reich officials considered it a mark of distinction to own copies of all twenty. We still preferred the original series, where Mabuse was obviously Jewish.

Since the death of Klein-Rogge other actors had taken over the part, but always the producers looked for that same startling visage. This man Dietrich was meant for the role. Thea von Harbou would approve.

"What are you staring at?" he asked. I told him. He laughed. "You chose the right profession," he continued. "You have a cinematic imagination. I am flattered by the comparison."

"What is happening?" I asked.

"Much. Not all of it is necessary. This show they are putting on for your benefit is rather pointless, for instance."

I was becoming comfortable in the chair, and my back had momentarily ceased to annoy me. I hoped that I would not have to move for still another guided tour of something I wasn't sure that I wanted to see. To my relief Dietrich pulled up a chair, sat down across from me and started talking:

"I expect that Kaufmann meant to introduce you to Thor when the elevator doors opened and then enjoy your startled expression as you were escorted down the hall to my laboratory. They didn't think you'd improvise on the set! Well, they're only amateurs and you are the expert when it comes to good, silly melodrama."

"Thor . . ." I began lamely, but could think of nothing to say.

"He's not overly intelligent. I'm impressed that he finished the scene with such dispatch. I apologize for my assistant. She had been watching the entire thing on one of our monitors and must have come to the conclusion that you are a dangerous fellow. In person, I mean. We all know what you are capable of in an official capacity."

As we talked, I took in my surroundings. The size of the laboratory was tremendous. It was like being in a scientific warehouse. Although without technical training myself, I noticed that there seemed to be a lack of systematic arrangement: materials were jumbled together in a downright sloppy fashion, even if there were a good reason for the close proximity of totally different apparatuses. Nevertheless I realized that I was out of my depth and I might be having nothing more than an aesthetic response.

"They closed the file on you," I said. "I thought you had been kidnapped by American agents."

"That was the cover story."

"Then you were kidnapped by the Burgundians?"

"A reasonable deduction, but wrong. I volunteered."

"For what?"

"Dr. Goebbels, I said that you have a cinematic imagination. That is good. It will help you to appreciate this." He snapped his fingers and the Japanese girl was by his side so swiftly that I didn't see where she had come from. She was holding a small plastic box. He opened it and showed me the interior: two cylinders, each with a tiny suction cup on the end. He took one out. "Examine this," he said, passing it to me.

"One of your inventions?" I asked, noticing that it was as light as if it were made out of tissue paper. But I could tell that whatever the material was, it was sturdy.

"A colleague came up with that," he told me. "He's dead now, unfortunately. Politics." He retrieved the cylinder, did something with the untipped end, then stood. "It won't hurt," he said. "If you will cooperate, I promise a cinematic experience unlike anything you've ever sampled."

There was no point in resisting. They had me. Whatever their purpose, I was in no position to oppose it. Nor is there any denying that my curiosity was aroused by this seeming toy.

Dietrich leaned forward, saying, "Allow me to attach this to your head and you will enjoy a unique production of the Burgundian Propaganda Ministry, if you will—the story of my life."

Without further ado he pressed the small suction cup against the center of my forehead. There was a tingling sensation and then my sight began to dim! I knew that my eyes were still open and I had not lost consciousness. For a moment I feared that I was going blind.

There were new images. I began to dream while wide awake, except that they were not my dreams. They were someone else's!

I was someone else!

I was Dietrich . . . as a child.

I was buttoning my collar on a cold day in February before going to school. The face that looked back from the mirror held a cherubic— almost beautiful—aspect. I was happy to be who I was.

As I skipped down cobbled streets, it suddenly struck me with solemn force that I was a Jew.

My German parents had been strict, orthodox, and humorless. An industrial accident had taken them from me. I was not to be alone for long. An uncle in Spain had sent for me and I went to live there. He had become a gentile (not without difficulty) but was able to take a child from a practicing Jewish family into his household.

It did not take more than a few days at school for the beatings to begin, whereupon they increased with ferocity. There was a bubbling fountain in easy distance of the schoolyard where I went to wash away the blood.

One day I watched the water turn crimson over the rippling reflection of my scarred face. I decided that whatever it was a Jew was supposed to be, I surely didn't qualify. I had the same color blood as my classmates, after all. Therefore I could not be a real Jew.

I announced this revelation the next day at school and was nearly killed for my trouble. One particularly stupid lad was so distressed by my logic that he expressed his displeasure with a critique made up of a two-by-four. Yet somehow in all this pain and anguish—as I fled for my life—I did not think to condemn the attackers. My conclusion was that surely the Jew must be a monstrous creature indeed to inspire such a display. Cursing the memory of my parents, I felt certain that through some happy fluke I was not really of their flesh and blood.

Amazing as it seems, I became an anti-Semite. I took a Star of David to the playground and in full view of my classmates destroyed it. A picture of a rabbi I also burned. Some were not impressed by this display, but others restrained them from resuming the beatings. For the first time I knew security in that schoolyard. None of them became any friendlier; they did not seem to know how to take it.

Suddenly the pictures of Dietrich's early life disappeared into a swirling darkness. I was confused, disoriented.

Time had passed. Now I was Dietrich as a young man back in Germany, dedicating myself to a life's work in genetic research. I joined the Nazi Party on the eve of its power, not so much out of vanity as out of a pragmatic reading of the *Zeitgeist*. Naturally I used my Spanish gentile pedigree, and entertained my new "friends" with a little-known quotation from the canon of Karl Marx, circa 1844: "Once society has succeeded in abolishing the empirical essence of Judaism—huckstering and its preconditions—the Jew will have become impossible."

The Nazis were developing their eugenic theories at the time. To say the basis of their programs was at best pseudo-scientific would still be to compliment it. At best, the only science involved was terminology borrowed from the field of eugenics.

I was doing real research, however, despite the limitations I faced due to Party funding and propaganda requirements. My work involved negative eugenics, the study of how to eliminate defective genes from the gene pool through selective breeding. Assuming an entire society could be turned into a laboratory, defective genes could be eliminated in one generation, although the problem might still crop up from time to time because of recessive genes (easily handled).

The decision to breed something out of the population having been made, the door was opened as to what to breed *for,* or positive eugenics. Now, so long as we were restricting ourselves to a question of a particular genetic disease, we could do something. But even then there were problems. What if some invaluable genius had such a genetic disability? Would you throw out the possibility of his having intelligent offspring just because of one risk?

Add to this valid concern the deranged, mystical ideas of the Nazi with regard to genetics, and the complications really set in. They wanted to breed for qualities that in many cases fell outside the province of real genetics—because they fell outside reality in the first place.

During this period in my life I made another discovery. I was no longer a racist. My anti-Semitism vanished as in a vagrant breeze. I had learned that there was no scientific basis for it. The sincere Nazi belief that the Jew was a creature outside of nature was so much rot. As for the cultural/mystical ideas that revolved around the Jew, the more I learned of how the Nazis perceived this, the more convinced I became that Hitler's party was composed of the insane. (An ironic note was that many European Jews were not even Semitic, but that is beside the point. The Nazis had little concern with, say, Arabs. It was the European Jew they were after, for whatever reasons were handy.)

Although I had come full circle on the question of racism, something else had happened to me in the interim. My hatred for one group of humanity had *not* vanished. My view of the common heritage of *Homo sapiens* led me to despise all of the human race. The implications of this escaped me at the time, but it was the turning point of my life.

Even at the peak of their popularity the world of genetics was only slightly influenced by Nazi thinking. Scientists are scientists first, ideologues second, if at all. To the extent that most scientists have a philosophy it is a general sort of positive humanism: so it was with my teacher in genetics, a brilliant man—who happened to fit the Aryan stereotype coincidentally—and his collaborator, a Jew who was open about his family background, unlike me.

They were the first to discover the structure of DNA. No, they are not in the history books. By then Hitler had come to power. The Nazis destroyed many of their papers when they were judged enemies of the state —for political improprieties having nothing to do with the research. But I was never found guilty of harboring any traitorous notions. Long before the world heard of it, I continued this work with DNA. Publishing this information was the last thing I wanted to do. I had other ideas. By giving the Nazis gobbledygook to make their idiot policies sound good, I remained unmolested. There would be a place for me in the New Order. I remembered when Einstein said that should his theory of relativity prove untrue, the French would declare him a German, and the Germans call him a Jew. At least I knew my place in advance.

Through the haze of Dietrich's memories I could still think; could reflect on what I was assimilating directly from a pattern taken from another's mind. I was impressed that such a man existed, working in secret for decades on what had only recently riveted the world's attention. Only last year had a news story dealt with micro-biologists doing gene splicing. Yet he had done the same sort of experimentation decades earlier.

What had been a trickle suddenly turned into a torrent of concepts and formulae beyond my comprehension. I felt the strain. With quivering fingers I reached for the cylinder and . . .

The images stopped; the words stopped; the kaleidoscope exploding inside my head stopped; the pressure stopped . . .

"You have not finished the program, Dr. Goebbels," said Dietrich. "It was at least another ten minutes before the 'reel change.'" He was holding the other cylinder in his hand, tossing it lightly into the air and catching it as though it were of no importance.

"It's too much," I gasped, "to take all at once. Hold on, I've just remembered something: Thor, in the hallway . . . is it possible?" I thought back over what I had experienced. Dietrich had left simple eugenic breeding programs far behind. His search was for the chemical mysteries of life itself, like some sort of mad alchemist seeking the knowledge of a Frankenstein. "Did you—" I paused, hardly knowing how to phrase it. "Did you create Thor?"

He laughed. "Don't I wish!" he said, almost playfully. "Do you have any idea what you are talking about? To find the genetic formula for human beings would require a language I do not possess."

"A language?"

"You'd have to break the code, be able to read the hieroglyphic wonders of not just one, but millions of genes. It's all there, in the chromosomes, but I haven't been able to find it yet. No one has." He put his face near to mine, grinning, eyes wide and staring. "But I will be the first. Nobody can beat me to it, because only I can do it!"

For a moment I thought I was back in the presence of Hitler. This man was certainly a visionary. Moreover he was dangerous in a fashion beyond any politician.

"Why are you here?" I asked.

"They finance me well. Look at these toys," he said, pointing at what he told me was an atmosphere chamber. "The work is expensive. Do you know how to invade the hidden territory of life itself? With radiation and poison to break down the structures and begin anew. To build! I can never live long enough, never receive enough sponsorship. It is the work of many lifetimes. If only I had more subtle tools . . ."

Before I lost him to a scientist's reverie, I changed the subject: "My son's hair and eyes have changed."

"That's nothing but cosmetics," he said disdainfully.

"The SS wants you to do that?"

"It is considered a mark of distinction. My beautician there"—he pointed at the Japanese girl—"provides this minor and unimportant service."

Only a few blonde-haired, blue-eyed people were working in the laboratory. I asked why everyone had not undergone the treatment. The reason was because the few I had just seen were authentic members of that genotype. Dietrich was blunt: "We don't play SS games in here."

He showed me his workshop, treating the technicians as no more than expensive equipment. I wondered how Speer would react to all this. The place was even larger than I had first thought. I wondered what Holly would make of it all, cramped in her small cubbyhole at the university.

The seemingly endless walk activated my pains again. My host noticed this distress and suggested we sit down again. He had not misplaced the other cylinder. Somehow I was not surprised when he suggested that I sample its contents.

"Did I really share in your memories?" I asked him.

"A carefully edited production, but yes."

"Is there more of the same in this other one?"

"I hold in my hand images from a different point of view. I believe that you might find these even more interesting." He put the thing on my palm. "Do you want it?"

"I have a thousand unanswered questions."

"This will help."

Shrugging, I placed it to the same point on my forehead and . . . *I did not know who I was.*

In vain I searched for the identity into which I had been plunged. What there was of me seemed to be a disembodied consciousness floating high above the European continent. It was like seeing in all directions at once. The moon above was very large, very near the earth—it was made of ice.

Horbiger's *Welteislehre!* It was a projection of one of his prophecies, when the moon would fall toward the earth, causing great upheavals in the crust—and working bizarre mutations on the life of the planet.

There was a panorama unfolding like the Worm Ouroboros: ancient epochs and the far future were melded together in an unbreakable circle. The world and civilization I knew were nothing but a passing aberration in the history of the globe.

I saw ancient Atlantis, not the one spoken of by Plato, but from a time when men were not supposed to exist. The first Atlantis, inhabited by great giants who preceded man and taught the human race all its important knowledge: I beheld Prometheus as real.

Then I was shown that the pantheon of Nordic gods also had a basis in this revelation. Fabled Asgard was not a myth, but a legend—a vague memory of the giant cities that once thrived on earth.

Humanity was incredibly older than the best estimates of the scientists. More startling than that was the tapestry flickering in myriad colors to depict a faraway but inevitable future. All of the human race had perished but for a remnant of Aryans. And these last men, these idealized Viking types, were happily preparing for their own extermination—making way for the *Übermenschen* who had nothing in common with them but for superficial appearances. The human race—as I knew it—was not really "human" at all. The Aryan was shown as that type closest to True Man, but when mutations caused by the descending moon brought back the giants, then the Aryan could join his fellows in welcome oblivion. The masters had returned. They would cherish this world, and perform the rites on the way to the next apocalypse, the *Ragnarök* when the cycle would start again—for the moon of ice would have at last smashed into the earth.

These images burned into my brain: gargantuan cities with spires threatening the stars; science utterly replaced by a functional magic that was the central power of these psychokinetic supermen who needed little else; everything vast, endless, bright . . . so bright that it blinded my sight and my mind . . .

With a scream I ripped the device from my perspiring skin. "This is madness!" I said, putting my head in my hands. "It can't be really true. The SS religion . . . no!"

Dietrich put a comforting hand on my shoulder, much to my surprise. "Of course it is not true," he said. There must have been tears in my eyes. My expression was a mask of confusion. He went on: "What you have seen is no more true than one of your motion pictures, or a typical release from the Ministry of Propaganda. It is more convincing, I'll admit. Just as the first cylinder allowed you to peer into the contents of one mind—my own—this other one has given you a composite picture of what a certain group believes; a collaborative effort, you could say."

"Religious fanatics of the SS," I muttered.

"They have a colorful prediction there, a hypothetical history, a faith. Of course, it is not as worthwhile as my autobiography."

"What has one to do with the other?" I asked. "What does your story have to do with theirs?"

Dietrich stood, and put his hands behind his back. He was appearing to be more like Dr. Mabuse all the time. His voice sounded different somehow, as though he was speaking to a very large audience: "They have hired me to perform a genetic task. In this laboratory a virus is being developed that will spare only blonde, blue-eyed men and women. Yes, Dr. Goebbels, the virus would kill you—with your dark hair and brown eyes—and myself, as readily as my Japanese assistant. It means your son would die also, because his current appearance is, after all, only cosmetic. It means most members of the Nazi Party would perish as not being 'racially' fit by this standard.

"I am speaking of the most comprehensive genocide program of all time. A large proportion of the populations in Sweden and Denmark and Iceland will survive. Too bad for the SS that virtually all those people think these ideas are purest folly, even evil. You know that much of the world's folk have rather strict ethical systems built into their quaint little cultures. That sort of thing gave the Nazis a difficult time at first, didn't it?"

I started to laugh. It was the sort of laughter that is not easy to control. I became hysterical. My concentration was directed at trying to stop the crazy sounds coming out of my mouth and I didn't notice anything else. Suddenly I was surprised to find myself on the floor. Arms were pulling me up and the professor was putting a hypodermic needle in my flesh. As the darkness claimed me, I wondered why there were no accompanying pictures. Didn't this cylinder touching my arm have a story to tell?

It felt as if I had been asleep for days but I came to my wits a few minutes later, according to my watch at least. I was lying on a cot and *he* was standing over me. I knew who he really was: Dr. Mabuse.

"Goebbels, I thought you were made of sterner stuff," came his grim voice.

"You are a lunatic," I told him hoarsely.

"That's unfair. What in my conduct strikes you as unseemly?"

"You said you had been anti-Semitic. Then you told me that you had rejected racism. Now you are part of a plot that takes racism farther than anything I've ever heard of!"

"You've been out of touch."

"The whole mess is a shambles of contradictions!"

"You hurt me deeply," was his retort, but the voice sounded inhuman. "I expected more from a thoughtful Nazi. My sponsors want a project carried out for racist reasons. I do not believe in their theories, religion, or pride. This pure blonde race they worship has never existed, in fact; it was simply a climatological adaptation in Northern Europe, never as widely distributed as Nazis think. It was a trait in a larger population group. I don't believe in SS myths. My involvement in the project is for other reasons."

"There cannot be any other reason."

"You forget what you have learned. Remember that I came to hate all of the human race. This does not mean that I gave up my reason or started engaging in wishful thinking. If the Burgundians enable me to wipe out most of humanity, with themselves exempt from the holocaust, I'll go along with it. The piper calls the tune."

"You couldn't carry on your work. You'd be dead!"

Sometimes one has the certainty of having been led down a primrose path, with the gate being locked against any hope of retreat, only *after* the graveyard sound of the latch snapping shut. Knowledge has a habit of coming too late. Such was the emotion that held me in an iron grip as soon as those words escaped my lips. Dr. Mabuse could never be a fool. It was impossible. Even as he spoke, I could anticipate the words: "Oh, I *am* sorry. I forgot to tell you that a few people outside the fortunate category may be saved. I can make them immune. In this sense, I'll be a Noah, collecting specimens for a specialist's ark. Anyone I consider worthy I will claim."

"Why do you hate the human race?" I asked him.

"To think that a Nazi has the gall to ask that question. Why do you hate the Jews?" he shot back. I could think of nothing to say. He continued: "There's little difference between us, morally. I know what you advocated during World War II, Goebbels. The difference between us is that I've set my sights higher. So what if Nazi Germany is annihilated? By what right can a Nazi criticize me?"

I remained insistent on one theme: "Why do it at all? You won't have destroyed all mankind. Burgundy will remain."

"Then Burgundy and I will play a game with each other," he said.

"What in God's name are you talking about?"

Another voice entered the conversation: "In Odin's name. . . ." It was Kaufmann, walking over to join us. I was pleased that he had a bandage on his head, and his face was drained of color. I wanted to strike him again! He made me think of Himmler at his worst.

It is my firm belief that the mind never ceases working, not even in the deepest slumber. While I had been unconscious the solution to the last part of the puzzle had presented itself. I didn't need to ask Mabuse about this part.

It is certainly understandable that expedient agreement is possible between two parties having nothing in common but one equally desired objective. There was the pact between Germany and Russia early in the war, for instance. The current case was different in one important respect: I doubted this particular alliance could last long enough to satisfy either party. I was certain that this was the Achilles' heel.

A comic-opera kingdom with a mad scientist! If my daughter had known of this, why had she not told me more? Or had she only been guessing in the dark herself?

The knight in armor and the man in the laboratory: the two simply didn't mix! Since the founding of Burgundy, there had been an antiscience, antitechnology attitude at work. Even French critics who never had good things to say about the Reich managed to praise Burgundy for its lack of modern technique. (The French could never be made to shut up altogether, so we allowed them to talk about nearly everything except practical politics. The skeptics and cynics among them could always be counted on to come up with a rationale for their place in postwar Europe, stinging though it was to their pride. What else could they do?)

Here was a geneticist more advanced than anyone else in the field making common cause with a nation devoted to the destruction of science. That the Burgundians trusted his motives was peculiar; that he could trust theirs was even more bizarre.

The explanation that had come to me was this: unlike scientists who belonged to the humanist tradition and believed that genetic engineering could be made to improve the life of human beings (naive healers, but useful to a statesman such as myself), Dr. Mabuse wished to find the secret of manipulating the building blocks of life so that he could create something nonhuman. This creature he had in mind might very well be mistaken by a good Burgundian as one of the New Men or *Übermenschen*, and viewed as an object of worship. Where others might oppose these new beings, the Burgundians—trained from birth in religious acceptance of superior beings in human form—would present no obstacle.

As for the Burgundians, such leaders as Kaufmann had to believe that wicked modern science had produced at least one genius who was the vehicle of higher mysteries: a puppet of Destiny.

I looked in the faces of these two men, such different faces, such different minds. There was something familiar there—a fervor, a wild devotion to The Cause, and a lust to practice sacrificial rites. As Minister of Propaganda I had sought to inculcate that look in the population with regard to Jews.

It was evident that I had not been made privy to their machinations carelessly. Either I would be allowed to join them or I would die. As for the possibility of the former, I did not consider it likely. Perhaps the forebodings engendered in me by Hilda were partly to blame, but in fact I knew that I could not be part of such a scheme against the Fatherland. Could I convince them that I would be loyal? No, I didn't believe it. Could I have convinced them if I had inured myself against shock and displayed nought but enthusiasm for their enterprise? I doubted it.

The question remained why I had been chosen for the privilege. The message Hilda had shown me was rife with unpleasant implications. I took a gamble by sitting up, pointing at Mabuse, and shouting to Kaufmann: "This man is a Jew!"

I could tell that that was a mistake by the exchange of expressions between the two. Of course, they had to know. No one could keep a secret in the SS's own country. If they overlooked Dr. Mabuse's ideas and profession, they could overlook anything. This was one occasion when traditional Jew-baiting would not help a Nazi! I didn't like the situation. I didn't want to be on the receiving end.

The voice of Mabuse seemingly spoke to me, but the words appeared to be for Kaufmann's benefit: "It is too bad that you will not be able to work with the new entertainment technology. I was hoping we could transfer your memories of the affair with Lida Barova. As she was your most famous scandal, it would have made for a good show."

Before I could answer this taunt, Kaufmann's gruff voice announced: "Don't keep your son waiting."

"He should wait for me, not the other way around!"

Kaufmann was oblivious: "He is with his fellows. Come." Mabuse helped me get off the cot and then we were marching down the corridor again. I was dizzy on my feet, my hand hurt, and my head felt as though it were stuffed full of cotton. So many random thoughts swirling in my mind, easily displaced by immediate concern for my future welfare . . .

Twilight was fast approaching as we entered the courtyard I had noticed earlier in Kaufmann's office. The large funeral pyre was still there, unused. Except that now there was a bier next to it. We were too far away to see whose body was on it, but with every step we drew nearer.

A door beside the pyre opened and a line of young men emerged, dressed in black SS regalia. In the lead was my son. They proceeded remorselessly in our direction. Helmuth gave Kaufmann the Nazi salute. He answered with the same. Quite obviously I was in no mood to reciprocate.

"Father," said Helmuth gravely, "I have been granted the privilege of overseeing this observance. Please approach the body."

Such was the formality of his tone that I hesitated to intercede with a fatherly appeal. The expression on his face was blank to my humanity. I did as requested.

Not for a moment did I suspect the identity of the body. Yet as I gazed at that familiar, waxen face, I knew that it fit the Burgundian pattern. It had to be his body. Once more I stood before Adolf Hitler!

"It was an outrage," said Kaufmann, "to preserve his body as though he were Lenin. His soul belongs in Valhalla. We intend to send it there today." My mouth was open with a question that would not be voiced as I turned to Kaufmann. He bowed solemnly. "Yes, Herr Goebbels. You were one of his most loyal deputies. You will accompany him."

There are times when no amount of resolve to be honorable and brave will suffice; I made to run, but many strong hands were on me in an instant. Helmuth placed his hand on my shoulder. "Don't make it worse," he whispered. "It has to be. Preserve your dignity. I want to be proud of you."

There was nothing to say. Nothing to do but contemplate a horrible death. I struggled in vain, doing my best to ignore the existence of Helmuth. It was no surprise that he had been selected for this honor. It made perfect sense in the demented scheme of things.

They brought out an aluminum ramp. Two husky SS men began to carry Hitler's body up the incline, while Helmuth remained behind, no doubt with the intention of escorting me up that unwelcome path.

"The manner of your death will remain a state secret of Burgundy," said Kaufmann. "We were able to receive good publicity from your Ministry when we executed those two French snoopers for trespassing: Louis Pauwels and Jacques Bergier. This is different." He paused, then added: "Soon publicity won't matter anymore."

My options were being reduced to nothing. Even facing death I could not entirely surrender. The years I had spent perfecting the art of propaganda had taught me that no situation is so hopeless that nothing may be salvaged from it. I reviewed the facts: despite their temporary agreement Kaufmann and the new Mabuse were really working at cross-purposes. If I could only exploit those differences, I could sow dissension in their ranks. Mabuse held the trump card, so I decided to direct the ploy at Kaufmann.

"I suppose I'm free to talk," I said to Kaufmann's back as he watched the red ball of the sun setting beyond the castle walls. The sky was streaked with orange and gold—the thin strands of cumulus clouds that seemed so reassuringly distant. There were a million other places I could have been at that moment, but for a vile twist of fate. There had to be some way of escape!

No one answered my query and I continued: "You're not a geneticist, are you, Kaufmann? How would you know if you can trust Dietrich?" He was Dietrich to them, but to me he would always be Mabuse. "What if he is lying? What if his process can't be made specific enough to exclude any group from the virus?"

Mabuse laughed. Kaufmann answered without turning around: "For insurance's sake he will immunize everyone in Burgundy as well as his assistants. If something goes wrong, it will be a shame to lose all those excellent Aryan specimens elsewhere in the world."

"Nothing will go wrong," said Mabuse.

I wouldn't give up that easily and struck back with: "How do you know he won't inject you with poison when the time comes? It would be like a repetition of the Black Plague that ravaged Burgundy in 1348."

"I applaud your inventive suggestion," said Mabuse.

"We have faith," was Kaufmann's astounding reply.

"A faith I will reward," boomed out Mabuse's monster voice. "They are not stupid, Goebbels. Some true believers have sufficient medical training to detect an attempt at the stunt you suggest."

In desperation I spoke again to my son: "Do you trust this?"

"I am here," came his answer in a low voice. "I have taken the oath."

"It's no good," taunted Mabuse. "Stop trying to save yourself."

They had Hitler's body at the top of the ramp. The SS men stood at attention. Everyone was waiting. The setting sun seemed to me at that moment to be pausing in its descent, waiting.

"Father," said Helmuth, "Germany has become decadent. It has forgotten its ideals. That my sister Hilda is allowed to live is proof enough. Look at you. You're not the man you were in the grand old days of the genocide."

"Son," I said, my voice trembling, "what is happening in Burgundy is not the same thing."

"Oh yes it is," said Dr. Mabuse.

Kaufmann strolled over to where I was standing and craned his neck to look at the men at the top of the ramp with the worldly remains of Adolf Hitler. He said, "Nazis were good killers during the war. Jews, Gypsies, and many others fell by the sword, even when it exacted a heavy price from other elements of the war program. Speer always wanting his slave labor for industrial requirements. Accountants always counting pennies. The mass murder was for its own sake, a promise of better things to come!

"After the war only Burgundy seemed to care any longer. Rulings that came out of New Berlin were despicable, loosening up the censorship laws and not strictly enforcing the racial standards. Do you know that a taint of

Jewishness is considered to be sexually arousing in Germany's more deca- dent cabarets of today? Even the euthanasia policy for old and unfit citi- zens was never more than words on paper, after the Catholics and Luther- ans interfered. The Party was corrupted from within. It let the dream die."

The kind of hatred motivating this Burgundian leader was no stranger to me. Never in my worst nightmares did it occur to me that I could be a victim of this kind of thinking.

Kaufmann gestured to the men on the ramp and they placed Hitler's body on top of the pyre. "It is time," mourned Helmuth's voice in my ear. Other young SS men surrounded me, Helmuth holding my arm. We began to walk.

Other SS men had appeared around the dry pyramid of kindling wood and straw. They were holding burning torches. Kaufmann gestured and they set the pyre aflame. The crackling and popping sounds plucked at my nerves as whitish smoke slowly rose. It would take a few minutes before the flame reached the apex to consume Hitler's body . . . and whatever else was near. My only consolation was that they had not used lighter fluid —dreadful modern stuff—to hasten the inferno.

Somewhere in that blazing doom Odin and Thor and Freyja were wait- ing. I was in no hurry to greet them.

I wondered at how the SA must have felt when the SS burst in on them, barking guns ripping out their lives in bloody ruins. Perhaps I should have thought of Magda, but I did not. Instead all my whimsies were directed to miracles and last-minute salvations. How I had preached hope in the final hours of the war before our luck had turned. I had fed Hitler on stories of Frederick the Great's diplomatic coup in the face of a military debacle. I had compared the atom bomb—when we got it—to the remarkable change in fortunes in the House of Brandenburg. Now I found myself pleading with the cruel fates for a personal victory of the same sort.

I was at the top of the ramp. Helmuth's hands were set firmly against my back. To him had fallen the task of consigning his father's living body to the flames. They must have considered him an adept pupil to be trusted with so severe a task.

So completely absorbed was I in thoughts of a sudden reprieve that I barely noticed the distant explosion. Someone behind me said, "What was that?" I heard Kaufmann calling from the ground but his words were lost in a louder explosion that occurred nearby.

A manic voice called out: "We must finish the rite!" It was Helmuth. He pushed me into empty space. I fell on Hitler's corpse, and grabbed at the torso to keep from falling into an opening beneath which raged the impersonal executioner.

"Too soon," one of my son's comrades was saying. "The fire isn't high enough. You'll have to shoot him or . . ."

Already I was rolling onto the other side of Hitler's body as I heard a gunshot. Out of the corner of my eye I could see Helmuth clutching his stomach as he fell into the red flames.

Shouts. Gunfire. More explosions. An army was climbing over the wall of the courtyard. A helicopter was zooming in overhead. My first thought was that it must be the German army come to save me. I was too delighted to care how that was possible.

The conflagration below was growing hotly near. Smoke filling my eyes and lungs was about to choke me to death. I was contemplating a jump from the top—a risky proposition at best—when I was given a better chance by a break in the billowing fumes. The men had cleared the ramp for being ill protected against artillery.

Once again I threw myself over Hitler's body and hit the metal ramp with a thud. What kept me from falling off was the body of a dead SS man, whose leg I was able to grasp as I started to bounce back. Then I lifted myself and ran as swiftly as I could, tripping a quarter of the way from the ground and rolling bruisedly the rest of the way. The whizzing bullets missed me. I lay hugging the dirt, for fear of being shot if I rose.

Even from that limited position I could evaluate certain aspects of the encounter. The Burgundians had temporarily given up their penchant for fighting with swords and were making do with machine guns instead. (The one exception was Thor, who ran forward in a berserker rage, wielding an ax. The bullets tore him to ribbons.) The battle seemed to be going badly for them.

Then I heard the greatest explosion of my life. It was as if the castle had been converted into one of Von Braun's rockets as a sheet of flame erupted from underneath it and the whole building quaked with the vibrations. The laboratory must have been destroyed instantly.

"It's Goebbels," a voice sang out. "Is he alive?"

"If he is, we'll soon remedy that."

"No," said the first voice. "Let's find out."

Rough hands turned me over . . . and I expected to look once more into faces of SS men. These were young men, all right, but there was something disturbingly familiar about them. I realized that they might be Jews! The thought, even then, that my life had been saved by Jews was too much to bear. But those faces, like the faces that I've thought about too many times to count.

"Blindfold him," one said. It was done, and I was being pushed through the courtyard blind, the noises of battle echoing all around. Once we stopped and crouched behind something. There was an exchange of shots. Then we were running and I was pulled into a conveyance of some sort. The whirring sound identified it instantly as a helicopter revving up; and we were off the ground, and we were flying away from that damned castle. A thin, high whistling sound went by—someone must have still been firing at us. And then the fight faded away in the distance.

An hour later we had landed. I was still blindfolded. Low voices were speaking in German. Suddenly I heard a scrap of Russian. This in turn was followed by a comment in Yiddish; and there was a sentence in what I took to be Hebrew. The different conversations were interrupted by a deep voice speaking in French announcing the arrival of an important person. After a few more whisperings—in German again—my blindfold was removed.

Standing in front of me was Hilda, dressed in battle fatigues. "Tell me what has happened," I said, adding as an afterthought—"if you will."

"Father, you have been rescued from Burgundy by a military operation of combined forces."

"You were only incidental," added a lean, dark-haired man by her side.

"Allow me to introduce this officer," she said, putting her hand on his arm. "We won't use names, but this man is with the Zionist Liberation Army. My involvement was sponsored by the guerrilla arm of the German Freedom League. Since your abduction the rest of the organization has gone underground. We are also receiving an influx of Russians into our ranks."

If everything else that had happened seemed improbable, this was sufficient to convince me that I had finally lost my sanity and was enmeshed in the impossible. "There is no Zionist Liberation Army," I said. "I would have heard of it."

"You're not the only one privy to secrets," was her smug reply.

"Are you a Zionist now?" I asked my daughter, thinking that nothing else would astound me. I was wrong again.

"No," she answered. "I don't support statism of any kind. I'm an anarchist."

What next? Her admission stunned me to the core. A large Negro with a beard spoke: "There is only one requirement to be in this army, Nazi. You must oppose National Socialism, German or Burgundian."

"We have communists as well, Father," my daughter went on. "The small wars Hitler kept waging well into the 1950s, always pushing deeper into Russia, made more converts to Marx than you realize."

"But you hate communism, daughter. You've told me so over and over." In retrospect it was not prudent for me to say this in such a company, but I no longer cared. I was emotionally exhausted, numb, empty.

She took the bait. "I hate all dictatorships. In the battle of the moment I must take what comrades I can get. You taught me that."

I could not stop myself talking, despite the risk. I sensed that this was the last chance I would have to reach my daughter. "The Bolsheviks were worse statists than we ever were. Surely the War Crimes Trials we held at the end of hostilities taught you that, even if you wouldn't learn it from your own father."

She raised her voice: "I know the evil that was done. What else would you expect from your darling straight-A princess than I can still recite the names of the Russian death camps: Vorkuta, Karaganda, Dalstroi, Magadan, Norilsk, Bamlag, and Solovki. But it has only lately dawned on me that there is something hypocritical about the victors trying the vanquished. You didn't even try to find judges from neutral countries."

"What do you expect from Nazis?" added the Negro.

My daughter reminded me of myself, as she continued to lecture all of us, captors and captive alike: "The first step on the road to anarchy is to realize that all war is a crime; and that the cause is statism." Before I could get in a word edgewise, other members of the group began arguing among themselves; and I knew that I was in the hands of real radicals. The early days of the Party were like this. And whether Hilda was an anarchist or not, it was clear that the leader of this ad-hoc army—enough of a state for me—was the thin, dark-haired Jew.

He leaned into my face, and vomited up the following: "Your daughter's personal loyalty prevents her from accepting the evidence we have gathered about your involvement in the mass murder of Jews. You're as bad as Stalin."

My dear, sweet daughter. Reaching out to embrace her, I not only caused several guns to be leveled on my person, but received a rebuff from her. She slapped me! Her words were acid as she said, "Fealty only goes so far. Whatever your part in the killing of innocent civilians, the rest of your career is an open book. You are an evil man. I can't lie to myself about it any longer."

There was no room for anger. No room left for anything but a hunger for security. I was ready to happily consign my entire family to Hitler's funeral pyre, if by so doing I could return home to New Berlin. The demeanor of these freelance soldiers told me that they bore me no will that was good.

Hilda must have read my thoughts. "They are going to let you go, this time, as a favor to me. We agreed in advance that Burgundy was the priority. Everything else had to take a back seat, including waking up about my . . . parents."

"When may I leave?"

"We're near the Burgundian border. My friends will disappear, until a later date when you *may* see them again. As for me, I'm leaving Europe for good."

"Where will you go?" I didn't expect an answer to that.

"To the American Republic. My radical credentials are an asset over there."

"America," I said listlessly. "Why?"

"Just make believe you are concocting another of your ideological speeches. Do this one about individual rights and you'll have your answer. They may not be an anarchist utopia, but they are paradise compared with your Europe. Goodbye, Father. And farewell to Hitler's ghost."

I was blindfolded again. Despite mixed feelings I was grateful to be alive. They released me at the great oak-tree I had observed when flying into Burgundy. As I removed the blindfold, I heard the helicopter take off behind me. My eyes focused on the plaque nailed to the tree that showed how SS men had ripped up the railway and transplanted this tremendous oak to block that evidence of the modern world. It had taken a lot of manpower.

How easily manpower can be reduced to dead flesh.

Turning around, I saw the flowing green hills of a world I had never fully understood stretched out to the horizon. With a shudder I looked away, walked around the tree, and began following the rusty track on the other side. It would lead me to the old station where I would put in a call to home . . . to what I thought was home.

POSTSCRIPT BY HILDA GOEBBELS

SPIRIT STATION
(The Charles A. Lindbergh
Experimental Orbital Community)
January 1, 2000

From this point on my father's diaries become incoherent. He must have recorded his Burgundian experiences shortly after returning to New Berlin. However much he had been the public demagogue he was surprisingly frank in his diaries. It must have been galling to him when they assigned psychiatric help. They knew what had happened. They sent in a full strike force to clean out Burgundy. They also came down on the underground shortly after I escaped. What a time that was. When the dust settled, Father had lost his influence.

Sometimes I try to decode Father's final entries, scrawled out in the last year of his life. He was a broken man in 1970, unhinged by the Burgundian affair, afraid of reprisals by the underground, unable to fathom why his favorite child hated him so. One consistent pattern of his last writings is that his recurring nightmare of Teutonic Knights had been displaced by a Jewish terror: an army of Golems concocted by Dr. Mabuse, who, after all, would work for anyone. Although there was no reason to believe that Dietrich survived our attack that afternoon, Father went to his grave believing the man to be immortal.

Images that crop up in these sad pages include a landscape of broken buildings, empty mausoleums, bones, and other wreckage that shows he never got over his obsession with The War. As for Mother leaving him at long last, he makes no comment but *das Nichts*. Even at the end he retained the habits of a literary German. One moment he is taking pleasure from the "heart attack" suffered by Himmler on the eve of Father's return—and there are comments here about how Rosenberg has finally been avenged. This material is interspersed with grocery bills from the days of the Great Inflation, problems he had with raising money for the Party in the mid-thirties, and a tirade against Horbiger. Before I can make heads or tails of this, he's off on a tangent about Nazis who believed in the hollow earth, and pages of minute details about Hitler's diet.

Those of my critics who believe I am suppressing material are welcome to these pages any time they ask. The only material of value was made available in the first appendix to *Final Entries;* to wit, Father's realization that they had substituted another body in Hitler's tomb—hotly denied by New Berliners to this day.

After all these years it is a strange feeling to look at the diary pages again. He accurately described me as the young and headstrong girl I was, although I wonder if he realized that I was firmly in the underground by the time I was warning him about Burgundy. If he could only see the crotchety old woman I have become.

I would have enjoyed speaking to him on his deathbed, as he did with Hitler. The main question I would have asked would be how he thought Reich officials would ever allow his diaries, from 1965 on, to appear in Europe? The early, famous entries, from 1933 to 1963, had been published as part of the official German record. The entries beginning with

1965 would have to be buried, and buried *deep*, by any dictatorship. Father's idea that no censorship applied to the privileged class—of his supposedly classless society—did not take into account sensitive state documents, such as his record of the Burgundy affair, or his highly sensitive discussion with Hitler. If the real *Final Entries* had not been smuggled out of Europe as one of the last acts of the underground, and delivered to me in New York, I never would have been in a position to come to terms with memories of my Father. Nor would I have had the book that launched my career. Americans love hearing of Nazi secrets.

Now as I begin a new life of semiretirement up here in America's first space city, haunted by equal portions of earthlight and moonlight, I wish to reconsider this period of history. Besides, if I don't write a new book, I believe I will go out of my mind.

Yesterday they had me speak to an audience of five hundred about my life as a writer. They wanted to know how much research I had put into the series about postwar Japan and China. They wanted to know how I deal with writer's block. But most of all they wanted to hear about Nazis, Nazis, Nazis.

A handsome young Japanese boy saved me by asking what I considered the greatest moment of my life. I told him it was that I had been a successful thief. Once the audience of dedicated free-enterprisers had stopped gasping like fish out of water, I explained. Back in the eighties, the specter of cancer was finally put to rest, thanks to new work derived from original research by Dr. Richard Dietrich. Yes, the most pleasant irony I've ever tasted was that "Mabuse's" final achievement was for life instead of death; I made it possible. It was I who delivered his papers into the hands of American scientists.

I must take repeated breaks in writing this addendum. My back gives me nothing but trouble, and I spend at least three times a day in zero-g therapy. How Hitler would have loved that. After the last bomb attempt on him his central concern became the damage to his *Sieg Heiling* arm, and his most characteristic feature—his ass. To think my Father literally worshiped that man! I guess if Napoleon had succeeded in unifying Europe he'd be just as popular.

Now I'm reclining on a yellow couch in Observation 10A. There is a breathtaking view of Europe spread out to my right, although I can't make out Germany. The Fatherland is hidden beneath a patch of clouds. What I can see of the continent is cleaner than any map: there are no borderlines.

Who could have predicted the ultimate consequence of Hitler's war? Certainly not myself. I recognized what Nazi Germany was, because I grew up there. It was an organization in the most modern meaning of the word. It was a conveyor belt. Hitler's ideology was the excuse for operating the controls, but that mechanism had a life of its own. Horrors were born of that machine; but so were fruits. Medals and barbed wire; diplomas and death sentences—they were all the same to the machine. The monster seemed unstoppable. In the belly of such a state it was easy to become an anarchist. The next step was just as easy—join a gang of your own, to fight the gang you hate. None of us on any side, not the Burgundians, not the underground, not the Reich itself, could see what was really happening. Only a few pacifists grasped the point.

Adolf Hitler achieved the exact opposite of all his long-term goals, and he did this by winning World War II. Economic reality subverted National Socialism.

The average German used to defend Hitler by saying that he got us out of the Depression, without bothering to note that the way the glorious *Führer* paid off all the classes of Germany was by looting foreigners. This was not the friendliest method of undoing the harm of Versailles. But as Europe began to remove age-old barriers to commerce, economic benefits began to spread. A thriving black market ensured that all would benefit from the new plenty, and ideology be damned. While the Burgundians actually tried to implement Hitlerian ideas, the rest of Europe enjoyed the new prosperity.

Father was intelligent enough to notice this trend, but he carefully avoided drawing the obvious conclusion: Nazi Germany was becoming less National Socialist with every passing decade. For all the talk of Race Destiny, it was the technical mind of Albert Speer that ran the German Empire. Our sideshow bigots provided the decoration. Hitler was going to achieve permanent race segregation; his New Order lasted only long enough to knock down the barriers to racial separation, and economics did the rest. There is more racial intermarriage today than ever, thanks to Adolf Hitler.

Today Germany is seeing a flowering of historical revisionists who are debunking the Hitler myth. They are showing his feet of clay. They are asking why Germany used a nuclear weapon against a civilian population, while President Dewey restricted his atomic bombs to Japanese military targets in the open sea. Even a thick-headed German may get the point after a while. The Reich's youth protests against the treatment of Russians by Rosenberg's Cultural Bureaus, and they are no longer shot, no longer arrested . . . and who knows but that they may accomplish something? If this keeps up, maybe my books, including *Final Entries of Dr. Joseph Goebbels,* will become available in the open market, instead of merely being black-market bestsellers already. America is still the only uncensored society.

More than anything else I am encouraged by what happens when German and American scientists and engineers work together. The magnificent new autobahns of Africa demonstrate this. But nothing is more beautiful than the space cities—the American and German complexes, the Japanese one, and finally, Israel. I've received an invitation to visit. I'm looking forward to setting foot inside a colony that proves *Der Jude* could not be stopped by a mere *Führer*. They have returned to their Holy Land, but at an unexpected altitude.

What would Father make of this sane new world? His final testament was the torment of a soul that had seen his victory become something alien and unconcerned with its architects. His life was melodrama, but his death a cheap farce. They didn't even know what to say at his funeral, he, the great orator of National Socialism. Without his guiding hand, they could not give him a Wagnerian exit.

The final joke is on him, and its practitioner is Dr. Mabuse. Father sincerely believed that in Adolf Hitler, long-awaited Zarathustra, the new man, had descended from the mountain. This above all others, was the greatest lie of Joseph Goebbels's life.

The new man will ascend from the test tube. I pray that he will be wiser than his parents.

Hilda Goebbels

PAUL JOSEPH GOEBBELS
BORN OCTOBER 29, 1897
DIED MARCH 15, 1970

Reichs-Peace

Sheila Finch

Greta spotted her contact as soon as she entered Walgreen's Drug Store. Though he wore a golf shirt and wide-bottom cords like every other male in Indianapolis on a Sunday in June, there was no mistaking that ramrod back, the suggestion of boots under the table. She slid into the booth across from him, setting the shoulder purse down beside her, but keeping an arm linked through the strap. She tugged at her skirt to prevent her thighs sticking to the vinyl seat. The sharp aroma of coffee burning on a hotplate mingled with the gentler scent of Ivory soap, defeating the efforts of the air-conditioner to reduce all smells to anonymity.

"The humidity already exceeds last year's record for this time of year." Nervousness constricted her throat, and the phrase her Irish friend had carefully rehearsed with her came out too high-pitched.

He raised his eyes from the chocolate malt and nodded briefly. *"Gruss Gott, Fräulein Bradford."*

He was in his sixties, with short, steel-gray hair and a deep, rich baritone. She'd known what the response was to be; even so, she felt an irrational fear. But the jukebox was vibrating with the latest big-band sound, and if any of her colleagues from the Lilly labs were around, the chance was slim they'd have heard.

"I'd prefer we spoke English," she said.

"As you wish." His accent was impeccably British. "And yes, it is exceedingly humid!"

She could have told him the exact humidity factor, the barometric pressure, the temperature highs and lows, the percentage of probability for rain before sundown—everything she ever read stayed firmly in her mind, even trivia. She recognized the nervous desire to escape into just such trivia and squashed it.

The soda-fountain jerk came round the counter toward their booth. "What's it to be?"

He was frowning at her skirt, Greta noticed. She hastily placed a paper napkin over the exposed knees. It was stupid to have worn such a short one—hadn't she just finished reading this morning's editorial about the connection between fashion and immorality? *Ominous trend of the eighties,* the paper had called it. *A challenge to our deepest values of family and church.*

"Coffee," she said. "No—make that Coke."

The man turned away and she looked at the German.

"What am I to call you?"

"Mr. Smith will do," he said blandly.

She had an irrational desire to get it over with. Never mind the agony of soul she'd gone through since O'Hara first called her. She had to get out of the States now. She couldn't pass up the opportunity that had come at such a critical time. This man represented her best chance of crossing the borders without a passport—which no one in her division at Lilly had a chance of getting.

The German was observing her beneath a raised eyebrow. "You seem ill at ease."

"I've got what you want."

The eyebrow lifted rather higher, and she thought: *He's a character out of an old movie. He ought to wear a monocle.* Then she realized he was aiming for that effect.

"And what may that be, Miss Bradford?"

"Don't play with me, Mr. Smith," she said fiercely.

"I ask out of curiosity only. It would seem more logical for information to flow the other way. After all, America is unable to launch a weather satellite that works for more than a couple of months, but the *Führer's* son walks on the moon."

They were both silent while the soda jerk pushed the Coca-Cola glass toward her. "That'll be fifty cents."

"Allow me." The German set the coins down with military precision.

When they were alone again she said, "I'll need guarantees."

"Of course."

"Safe passage immediately to England, or I won't consider it."

"Ah." He leaned back against the booth and folded his arms. "Later, perhaps. But first, a necessary detour to Munich."

"Why?" she demanded.

It hadn't been difficult to guess what they wanted, though nothing had been said. Nor had she had much trouble deciding to give it to them— only a fool or a martyr would not agree her own welfare came first, and she was neither. She'd thought this out carefully. Either one would be price-less to him, but the papers could go anywhere while she only wanted to go to London.

He held out a gold case. "Cigarette?" She shook her head. He put it away without taking one for himself. "I believe you left the Fatherland at an early age?"

"In '41. When I was two years old. What's that got to do with—"

"Then you'll enjoy a brief visit of reacquaintance."

"Reawaken a lot of bad memories, you mean?"

He regarded her calmly. "Feeling as you do, Miss Bradford, why are you accepting our help?"

It wasn't as if she hadn't considered this, too. But she had to get out before it was too late, before the hand of the Alliance of Protestant Churches tightened over all aspects of American life and crushed her. Already the missionary visits had begun, though for the moment they merely urged her politely to attend church. The sprawling Pan-European Federation seemed the best refuge. Germany was its most powerful state; she wasn't surprised it recognized the value of what she knew.

She didn't reply.

"My apology," he said. "A tasteless question. One can only imagine the terror of living in fear of the coming pogroms against those with your abilities."

She glanced around Walgreen's. The other customers—mostly men— counted dimes for the jukebox, or sipped their sodas, propping the funnies against the napkin-holders. "What do you mean?"

"The psi gifts you must surely have inherited, Miss Bradford."

"My what?"

In turn, he seemed genuinely puzzled. "You can't imagine we don't know about your *Zigeuner* blood?"

Of course, she thought. As early as 1946 Germany had begun to make its peace with the expatriated Jews, offering generous settlements and a public display of contrition. This was even in American history books that seldom took account of anything outside the boundaries of the forty-eight states. Now, apparently, it was the turn of the Romanies—what there were left of them. Well, if they wanted to put on the sackcloth and ashes for a Gypsy brat whose parents had died in a Bavarian work camp, she supposed she could tolerate it for a few days. But a ticket to London was the prize she wanted in return for her information on the research projects of the Eli Lilly Pharmaceutical Company.

She clutched the shoulder purse tightly and took a deep breath, willing her hands to stop trembling. "How soon can you arrange it?"

It wasn't as if she had anyone or anyplace here to regret leaving. She'd had two broken marriages, and homes in more than a dozen states over the years. One side effect of an overzealous memory was a restless need to escape. But itinerant, double-divorcées weren't exactly popular in America these days.

"Shall we say right away, Miss Bradford?" He stood up. "Of course, there's time to finish your Coke first!"

Early-morning fog lay over the small airstrip outside Munich when they landed. Somewhere a cow mooed as Greta emerged sleepily from the private jet they'd transferred to in neutral Ireland. The air was cool and heavy with the scents of clover and fresh-ploughed earth; she was glad of the felt cape Mr. Smith had lent her. He caught her arm, turning her toward the waiting Volkswagen limousine. The shoulder purse banged against her side, bulging with the small stack of Euromarks she'd picked up in Ireland, where O'Hara had advised her she'd get a better rate for her dollars. Everything she owned in the world was now in that purse. But some of it was so valuable, she'd never miss the rest.

The limousine's uniformed chauffeur snapped to attention as they approached, giving a stiff, high salute her blood remembered in a rush of cold foreboding.

"We're almost there, Fräulein." Mr. Smith held the door for her. "A twenty-minute drive, no more."

From the chauffeur's radio came a raucous song with a heavy beat.

"One of the oldest English rock groups," he said, catching her frown. "Very popular here. The Beatles, they're called. Have you heard of them in America? No, I suppose not."

He slid the glass partition across, shutting the harsh sounds in with the driver.

The interior smelled of leather and polished wood, and lilies of the valley in a small crystal vase attached to the back of the driver's seat. She pressed her cheek to the window and watched the gray-wreathed fields slip by, the huddled villages still asleep, their onion-domed churches catching the first bright rays of sun through the mist, the cows waiting to be milked, the sleek, gleaming spiderweb of robot harvesters crouched over the vegetable fields. The sixteenth and the twentieth centuries coexisted peacefully here.

And America? she thought. America had retreated to a dream of the nineteenth.

Except in one area.

At the edge of the neat fields, as if at the edge of consciousness itself, the forest loomed, *ur-wald,* where generations of her ancestors had stopped their wagons and made camp—until the laws that declared them undesirable, a threat to the progress of Aryan destiny. A pale crescent of moon was still visible above the pines.

"Sad memories?" Mr. Smith enquired. "The work camps were admittedly a blot on the Fatherland's record. I hate to think what might have happened if the truce hadn't been signed in '42. I've always felt that if he'd waited until late June of '41 to start Barbarossa, as he'd originally planned, the *Führer* would have repeated Napoleon's mistake of taking on the winter climate as well as the Russian army. It was a trade-off, of course. Less time to prepare—and some bad feeling with Mussolini, who had other plans—but better weather. Who can guess what he might have done in that cold January of 1942, instead of forging the beginnings of European unification? May his soul find rest in Valhalla, but the *Führer* was inclined to rather wasteful racial policies!"

"I remember nothing of my parents, Herr Schmidt," she said coldly, emphasizing the German form of the code name he'd given her. "I was smuggled out to an English family in Essex, and then on to New York just before the peace in Europe."

He gazed at her thoughtfully a moment before turning away to his own window.

"My mother was English—both nations go back to the same Folk, you know. But here we are!"

The limousine had been traveling up a winding, cobblestone road. Now it stopped on the crown of the low hill before an imposing, square-built mansion. Rows of tall windows along the front flashed in the sunlight; flags snapped crisply on their poles; geraniums bloomed tidily beside a driveway.

"Where are we?"

"*Das Dachauer Schloss*—the old palace at Dachau dating back to the sixteenth century," he said, as the chauffeur opened the door. "But you won't be uncomfortable. It's been modernized."

He led her inside into the high-ceilinged hall. She was aware of dark, polished floors and thick, oriental rugs, the gleam of pewter on mahogany tables, the tapestry depictions of Valkyries and Wagnerian heroes lining the walls. Warmth rose from a discreet radiator under a mullioned window, taking the chill off the smaller room she was ushered into. The room was dominated by a magnificent set of antlers over the fireplace, whose flames were more ornamental than necessary. Hunting horns, elaborately painted beer steins, bundles of partridge feathers tied with faded ribbons, gave the room the air of a pagan shrine. A brocaded armchair stood by the window to take advantage of the fine view over the formal gardens.

"Bitte, warten Sie hier, Fräulein," Herr Schmidt said. "But I'm sorry! I keep forgetting it's painful."

He went out.

Greta hugged the shoulder purse to her breast like a baby about to be torn from her grasp. For whom was she waiting? A scientist would be logical if they knew the importance of what she carried. Germany's physical sciences had boomed under the return of great men like Einstein and Von Braun. Europe was busy in space, pushing out to the moon and beyond. But space science was something the American government hadn't encouraged in the wave of isolationism that gripped the country after two years alone against Japan. Most Americans hadn't wanted to be drawn into the war in the first place; being left alone to finish it was particularly galling. Even victory itself had not been enough to dispel the disillusionment with former allies. The Pacific Rim Treaty, signed in Hawaii in '44, had been followed by a national distaste for war and weapons and the physical science that produced them.

But America had been quietly pioneering a biological revolution, the dimensions of which were about to buy freedom for Dr. Greta Bradford.

On a sudden impulse she took the wad of notes and diagrams out of her purse and stuffed them under the brocade cushion.

She had barely replaced the cushion when the door opened and a plump, white-haired woman in her seventies, wearing a green-and-gold dirndl, came in. A gold swastika suspended on a fine chain nestled in the lace of her blouse. The old face had a peasant's simplicity to it, without the signs of the peasant's hard life. She leaned on a cane and reached out a hand to Greta before Schmidt, coming behind, could introduce her.

"Die gnädige Frau, Eva Hitler," he said.

"I am so glad you are here," the *Führer's* widow said in careful English.

Embarrassed, Greta mumbled, "I understand *Deutsch,* I'm just rusty—"

"Think nothing of it! I like the chance to practice." She smiled conspiratorially at Greta. "It helps me hold my own when I visit the Queen in London. Those Saxe-Coburgs were always such snobs! Shall we sit?"

A long-haired dachshund—as old in dog years as its mistress—came to sit at her feet. Schmidt withdrew, almost colliding with a fresh-faced young girl bringing a tray of coffee.

A hint of lavender cologne drifted from the old woman as she moved. "Do take that low chair over there, it is more comfortable. This is my favorite, by the window." Frau Hitler seated herself, apparently unaware of the new tilt to the seat cushion. "Have some coffee."

She sounded nervous. Odd, Greta thought; she was the one who should feel awkward. Spies and defectors weren't usually treated to audiences with great men's widows. She sat clumsily, dropping the shoulder bag by her feet, and accepted coffee in a delicate Rosenthal cup. The coffee was dark and thick on the tongue.

Frau Hitler nodded at her. "Turkish. Everybody in Europe drinks Turkish coffee now. Even the English!"

Greta added more sugar. The old lady chattered on about the fresh air in this part of Bavaria—she couldn't take the capital in summer, "the *Föhn*, you know"—the cost of heating a Baroque palace, the deplorable opera season just over in Munich, the decline of good breeding among the wives of Europe's new leaders. Greta listened in silence, nodding occasionally, while tension knotted her stomach. She was impatient to get down to business, but this garrulous old woman was not the one who could appreciate the importance of what she had to offer.

Frau Hitler broke off in mid-sentence. She motioned Greta to close the door the serving girl had left ajar.

"Bradford was not the name I once knew you by."

Greta jumped, rattling the small cup on its saucer. "I—the family in England—"

"I know. They gave you their name. Do you know what yours was?" The old lady gazed out the window, the linen napkin twisted round and round in arthritic fingers. "Tshurkurka, I think. Though I could be wrong after all these years. They all had such dreadful names."

She said this with such quiet simplicity, Greta was overwhelmed. The sense of something about to be revealed tightened her chest.

"Your mother's name was Rupa. She read my palm, more than once. She was just about twenty when you last saw her. A dark, scrawny little thing Rupa was—much like you, only even thinner."

Greta's head was starting to pound. "Why are you telling me this?"

"I could not save her, you see." Frau Hitler turned from the window, her eyes catching the light so that they seemed luminous. *"Der Führer* was a very stubborn man, and I had no influence in those days. There were so many crazy people surrounding him, demanding his attention. He was always difficult to deal with, swinging between extroverted confidence—the Adolf I fell in love with—and paranoia. Later, the doctors controlled these moods with their medicines. He was a manic-depressive, you see."

The little fire crackled and spat a small spark onto the hearth. Frau Hitler sipped her coffee. Greta waited, her own coffee forgotten like the papers under the cushion.

"Once, she gave me a warning for Adolf—she'd read it in the cards. The coming winter would be the worst in memory, she said. I didn't know why that might be important, but I told him. I think it was the only time he ever listened to me, and even then I practically had to go down on my knees! Well. But I managed to save Rupa's children. And she smiled at me, before she went."

"Children?" she breathed.

"You had a brother—a baby," Frau Hitler said, her attention back on the misty *Hofgarten* again. "You know, I kept track of what happened to you, even after you were sent on to America."

"But why?"

"I thought it might be useful some day. A Romany, you see? But you do not, of course." She was silent for a moment. Then she picked up the *Suddeutsche Zeitung* that had been lying on a footstool by her side. "Have you seen the paper? My son makes a name for himself in space."

She held it out so Greta could see the front-page headline: *Wolfgang macht die Mondexpedition.* There was a blurry newsphoto accompanying the text. The pounding in her head was becoming a full-scale migraine.

"The paper does not tell everything. Wolfli has gone off on his own, away from the moon base. He did not take a radio with him—he has something of Adolf's impetuosity in him, I think. Or perhaps he is just always trying to live up to the legend of a great man. Well. There has been no communication with him for more than four days. That would not be so alarming—Wolfli is brave and competent!—but something else has occurred."

Her face was a mask of grief; lines that Greta had overlooked on meeting her now stood out like the moon's own rifts and valleys.

"Wolfli must be told of the danger he faces from sudden sunspot activity our scientists have monitored."

"And Wolfli—" Greta said, slipping without thinking into the diminutive form of the name.

"—is your brother. I never could have children, you see. Oh, I did not tell Adolf! I do not think he would have understood, even afterward, when

Mr. Churchill had talked sense into him. He thought the baby was his own son—he was much too busy in those days to keep track of everything! —and so he married me."

She gazed at Greta, seeking understanding. Greta returned the look stonily, in the grip of shock and disbelief through which anger darted. *My brother?*

Frau Hitler sighed and looked wistfully through the window as if she'd rather be strolling down the tunnel formed by the tall trees than revealing long-kept secrets. "Today, *Führer* is almost a bad word. It is all Chancellor and Prime Minister now."

"Why am I here?" Greta asked harshly.

"You are Romany," Frau Hitler said. "Romany have the Gift. I need you. Wolfli needs you."

She gaped. "You think I'm *psychic?*"

Hitler's widow nodded. "No one else can reach him. But you have a chance! An English gypsy once told me the bond is strong between Romany bloodkin."

"That's absurd!" Greta started to laugh. Here, in the world center of science, *this?* "I'm a scientist, Frau Hitler. Tell me you're joking."

"No. Herr Schmidt will take you to Von Braun Space Communications Center in Munich immediately. He does not know what I have just told you—nobody does!—but he will do as I ask. They have equipment there. I do not know how to describe it, but it will augment your Gift in some way. And you will reach Wolfli and save him."

Greta stared at the old woman. Was that love or craziness or both that burned in her eyes? "Look. I was brought here to sell secrets, biological secrets—gene-splicing techniques—" She broke off. This old woman was too simple to understand in any case. "Things Germany could use to its advantage. But not *this!*"

"So you may suppose. Herr Schmidt is so secretive, he would not have told you! However, you came because I gave the order to have you picked up. Because Wolfli's life depends on you. And your safety depends on me, just as my secret depends on you. A karmic situation all round, *nicht wahr?*"

"I appreciate your being a good mother to him," Greta said in gentler tone. "But I'm not telepathic."

The liquid old eyes held hers steadily. "You are still a citizen of that benighted country, you see. If you do not save Wolfli, I shall have you returned."

The highest point of the new space communications building on the west bank of the Isar, a few kilometers past the government offices of the Pan-European Federation outside Munich, was crowned with its ritual fir-tree. German mythology seemed cozily at home with German science in this countryside.

Schmidt led the way through the maze of corridors that connected the labs, offices, and conference rooms. One such bend led to the commissary, she guessed, her nose wrinkling at the pungent odor of sauerkraut being prepared for lunch. Passes were demanded and displayed several times. Guard dogs eyed them suspiciously, jaws working in anticipation. Each time they were waved further inside. The sound of their feet rang hollowly down the corridors.

Greta had not chosen to reply to the small talk he'd felt obliged to make on the drive down, and he'd given up the attempt. She'd insisted on a detour, to the small cemetery cupped in low hills on the outskirts of Dachau, where the concentration camp's victims had been buried. Here, where the scent of lilac hung like incense, under the icons of a Christian religion they'd scorned, lay her parents, anonymously with a few hundred others. Gypsies, Jews, and political undesirables shared a common grave, unfortunates who'd not survived the hard work and malnutrition of the camp between 1933 and 1942. Unbidden, the statistics of death, read long ago in an unguarded moment, rose in her mind. She stooped and tore a weed from its place in the smooth velvet of the lawn. Somewhere not far off a cuckoo called.

Hypocrite! she thought savagely. How would what she was willing to traffic in lead to any better outcome? But she felt no sense of responsibility toward the nation she'd just left, no ties of duty or loyalty, only to herself. Perhaps that was what it meant to be a Gypsy? Disowned by every country, at home nowhere and everywhere.

She turned away. She couldn't mourn for these people, for she'd hardly known who they were. Her true parents had been the second-generation German immigrants in New York who'd raised her and sent her to university. And if she hadn't been capable of loving them, at least she'd honored them. Now they were dead too, severing the only flimsy bond she'd ever felt. A hard anger rose in her, along with something else, an emotion she couldn't at first name.

She'd made Schmidt make a second detour before they left Dachau, to a jeweler's, where she used a large number of her new Euromarks. Now she smoothed her dark hair, feeling the swing of heavy gold hoops in her earlobes. He'd made no comment about her new image.

Schmidt held open a steel door, gesturing for her to enter. A dull confusion of sound flowed out to her—murmur of voices, a low whine of machinery, unidentifiable clicks and whirs, the occasional rasp of a steel chair across a tiled floor. She stopped on the threshold, hardly believing what she saw. The banked computers and display screens lining one complete wall of the room were beyond the wildest imagination of a Hoosier biochemist, both in number and complexity. By comparison the pharmaceutical scientists might as well have been working with abacus and slide rule. She suffered a full minute of gut-wrenching envy; then she remembered what she'd brought with her.

A short, white-haired man in a lab smock was waiting patiently for her to complete her inspection.

"Josef Krantzl, Fräulein." He bowed. *"Einkommen, bitte."*

He led the way through the chamber of technological wonders to a smaller, sparsely furnished room. The lighting here was soft. On a low table beside a reclining leather chair lay an oval contraption of straps and wires. A small computer sat discreetly against a wall.

"Der Apparat—" Krantzl began, waving a hand at the helmet.

Behind her Schmidt asked, "Would you like me to translate?"

Greta stared icily at him.

"As you wish."

Krantzl launched himself into a long passionate explanation of his work, the theories that underpinned it, the apparatus he'd built, the niche in the German space program into which it fitted. The longer he talked, the more he lapsed from the *Hochdeutsch* she'd learned from her foster parents, the vowels broadening, the consonants slurring together in the Bavarian dialect she barely recognized as German. But she was not about to admit this to Schmidt. The man stood with the expectant air of someone with a lifeline, waiting for a drowning victim to throw it to.

German physical science, Krantzl explained, was founded on the works of three masters: Einstein, Jung, and Freud. Intercepting her puzzled expression at this odd coupling, he spoke eloquently of the mating of inner and outer space, the role of Mind in the universe, the effects of the quantum-mechanical revolution on the theory of psionics. Along the way he invoked the mystical role the Fatherland must play in the world's destiny, and the cosmological repercussions of the heirs of Siegfried planting their footprints in the ur-dust of the moon.

She was exhausted trying to follow this twisted logic. She'd heard some bizarre scientific theories proposed over a glass too many of Kentucky bourbon—nothing like this! A glance at Schmidt's impassive face showed Greta that if Krantzl was mad, it was a madness shared by his compatriots.

"Unfortunately," Krantzl came to the end of his dissertation on German psychic science, "that segment of the population which possesses these gifts in extraordinary measure is in short supply, due to the unfortunate circumstances of the recent past."

"He refers to the mistake the *Führer* made about the Romanies," Schmidt said.

She would have laughed, but it wasn't funny. "Mistake, was it? And what am I supposed to do? Soothe your consciences by cooperating in this charade of crystal-ball reading?"

Krantzl's expression was pained. "If you had time to read the literature, Fräulein Bradford—"

"Time is the one element we don't have," Schmidt said sharply. "A man's life is at stake."

The scientist pursed his lips, but was silent.

"By the way," Greta said slowly, "that's Fräulein Doktor Bradford."

"The French have a word for it, I believe," Schmidt said. "*Touché*, Fräulein Doktor Bradford!"

"If you can only reach Herr Hitler," Krantzl pleaded. "Warn him of the solar-radiation danger—get him back to the base—"

And then, a thought she'd been suppressing since the interview in the Baroque splendor of Eva Hitler's summer home surfaced. The man whose life was in danger was her brother. In comparison to the mystical mumbo jumbo she'd just heard it was a simple fact, no more fantastic than the knowledge of her own survival. And there was one thing about the Romanies she knew—the ties of family were all-important.

Tshurkurka. Wolfgang und Greta Tshurkurka. Bloodkin.

She pushed away her scientific reluctance. So what if she didn't believe in telepathy? She owed it to her brother to try. She sat in the reclining chair and lifted the helmet, its wires trailing over her lap.

"Ready when you are, Doktor Krantzl."

Hours later—

Perhaps days? The passage of time was not noticeable in this quiet room—

She developed a cramp in her neck. Reaching up, she started to unfasten the straps of the heavy helmet.

"Please!" Krantzl turned in agitation from the screen he was monitoring. "We haven't made contact yet."

"I have to take a break."

"We're so close!" he mourned.

Greta doubted that. She massaged her neck, her head feeling fantastically light without the helmet. It had been an odd experience, trying to do something all her scientific training told her was nonsense. She placated this part of herself with the thought that she had little choice but to do as they ordered if she ever hoped to get to England. She'd had enough gallivanting around; now she was ready to settle in some quiet Essex village. Near enough to London for work, and perhaps the theater, but—

The wheels of Krantzl's chair squealed as he fidgeted, impatient to resume work.

To gain time she said, "Explain to me again how this contraption is supposed to function."

She regretted it immediately, for the little man waxed eloquent at once. The unfamiliar terms washed over her—nuclear-magnetic-resonance tomography—mapping the complicated microcircuitry of the brain—particle-beam tomographic stimulation, augmenting and transferring the psi-specific waves of her neural activity into space.

Some of this had the ring of good science, though her background, limited as it was to biology and chemistry, was not sufficient for her to separate the physics from the psychic. She wondered if American physicists even dreamed how far advanced the Germans were, or if they cared.

"This explanation would've been unnecessary, Fräulein Doktor Bradford," Schmidt said, "if the United States hadn't lost interest in physical research. They were as far advanced as we in the race to split the atom before the war ended. So, from small decisions mighty histories grow!"

"Of course," Krantzl said hesitantly, "so many of your best physicists were Jews who accepted the *Führer*'s offer to help them settle in Palestine when—"

"Even so!" Schmidt said, and Krantzl subsided.

Greta shut her eyes, banishing the man and the hint of menace that lay under the oily manners of his personality. Worry about the papers left in Frau Hitler's study nagged her. Now that she knew that hadn't been what they wanted, what would she do with them?

If she ever retrieved them.

Greta sighed. The experience itself had been frustrating, for she had no idea what she should do while under the transmitting helmet. Nor had Krantzl offered suggestions. Her Romany blood was supposed to tell her how to do it.

She'd tried sending subvocalized messages—*Wolfli, can you hear me? Wolfli can you hear me?*—but tired of this quickly. Visualizing the man whose attention she hoped to attract didn't work either, for her only image of him was the grainy photo in the newspaper Frau Hitler had showed her. She should have thought to ask for a more intimate picture, maybe a baby portrait, something her own subconscious might recognize and respond to.

Back to work.

She thought of the moon itself—man's first outpost in space—the silver disc by whose waxing and waning the Romanies measured the passage of time—

She couldn't concentrate.

Her mind drifted away from the task, not only rejecting the idea of telepathic communication, but emptying of all thoughts. Once she slid into a light sleep, only to be jolted awake by an indignant Krantzl, who saw the telltale change of brain waves on his screen.

"We waste time, Fräulein Doktor Bradford," Schmidt's voice interrupted harshly. The man was growing more objectionable by the hour. Greta studied the hard lines of his face.

"What're *you* getting out of this—rescuing Frau Hitler's son? Why is it so important?"

"We are a sentimental race," he said, unperturbed. "The son of a great man—"

"Bullshit."

He allowed himself a small, dim smile. "Europe has had forty years of peace—wonderful, isn't it? But peace is not necessarily good for people. They grow fat and lazy. They lose the inner strength that made the Fatherland invincible. Some of us see the necessity of rectifying the matter, directing the feet of our nation back to the narrow path of German destiny. We are called upon to be leaders of the world, Fräulein! Not merchants haggling over the price of cheese and sausage on the London stock exchange."

"You're planning to break up the Federation?"

"The Federation already suffers from inaction. It allows the Slavic states —always a hotbed of crazy political ideas, and paranoid at best!—to dream of separation. And too much peace has encouraged the Greeks to remember a Homeric past that they mutter about restoring. Il Duce was right; we should have taught them a lesson long ago! Without a common goal to fire men's imaginations the Federation will destroy itself. No, you American farmers have been looking to Asia for so long you don't see the European future marching up to your gates."

"War against the States, then."

"Perhaps not at first."

It was unthinkable, but terribly possible. "And where does Wolfgang fit into this?"

"*Hitler,*" he said. "A name to conjure with."

They had the technology to do it, too, she thought.

"But you are procrastinating, Fräulein Doktor Bradford. Please, put the helmet back on voluntarily."

She had a momentary urge to tell him the truth.

Across the room Krantzl glanced up nervously. "This is a scientific endeavor, *Kamerad!*"

Greta lifted the helmet.

It worked no better this time. She forced herself to repeat his name like a mantra, summoned up fantastic images of a moonbase from science fiction she'd read as a child in Brooklyn, before it was banned. She held the gaudy pictures like asymmetric mandalas in her mind, searching for some hidden magic in her inheritance that eluded conscious grasp.

Nothing.

The headache she'd been fighting off pulsed, a spreading ache.

"Look—this won't work! I don't know what you expect from Romany genes, but—"

She shrieked as Schmidt caught her arm, twisting it up behind her back. A purple haze of pain clouded thinking. She expected any minute to hear the bone snap.

He hissed at her. *"Es muss Erfolg haben!* Try again!"

Gasping for breath, she tried to call Wolfgang's name in her head.

"Again!" He jerked her arm.

"Perhaps—" Krantzl began tentatively.

"Again!"

Tears burned behind her closed lids. She fought them back. Her mother had given up her children to safety and gone to the concentration camp smiling. That was bravery. She could do no less.

"You're not trying hard enough, Fräulein!"

She screamed as her arm slid out of its socket. The gold hoops banged against her neck as she writhed in his grip.

Rupa's children—used and abused as countless generations of Romanies before them. The bright caravans hounded from border to border. The smiling, hidden treachery of honest burghers. And always the fear of the dogs, the knives in the long, cold night under an enemy moon.

In the gray wash of agony that blotted out thought Greta was aware only of a pair of dark eyes behind a curve of glass, and a searing point of contact, a skein of spider silk slung across the void.

When she came to, she was lying on a couch under a tapestry she'd seen before. Maidens rose full-breasted out of the Rhine, their arms cradling the fabled gold of the Nibelung. The fire's cheerful flicker played over the woven scenery in the twilit room. Her own arm was strapped securely against her chest, and a dull ache floated somewhere at the edge of attention. Someone was sponging her brow with something cool and fragrant.

"Thank goodness," Eva Hitler said. "I cannot imagine what came over Herr Schmidt! He knows I abhor violence. I used to say to Adolf—"

Greta sat up, ignoring Frau Hitler's protests. The little room spun for a moment. "Wolfgang—"

"—contacted us almost immediately!" she replied happily. "He said he had a hunch something was not right! He got back safely to moonbase."

Greta lay back and closed her eyes. Coincidence? Probably. Wolfgang was a trained astronaut, after all.

"Good! Now, let me work again with the *Kolnischewasser*—"

She couldn't believe in telepathy, no matter what blood she'd inherited. Many strange things in life owed themselves to coincidence. Jung's principle of synchronicity, Krantzl would have called it. She pushed this thought away.

There was a knock at the door—but without waiting for an answer, Schmidt entered. The dachshund scuttled to safety behind its mistress.

"Hans!" Frau Hitler said with displeasure. "You might have—"

"What more do you want from me?" Greta said. "You have your next *Führer* safe and sound."

She tried to sit up, but Frau Hitler's swollen fingers, fragrant with the cologne she'd been using, gently pushed her back.

"You have more talents than we suspected, Fräulein. I ran a check on the work you were doing at Lilly Labs." He nodded thoughtfully at her. He had her shoulder bag in his hand. "There was something you thought important. Something you hoped to bargain with when I picked you up. Your ticket to England, I believe."

"You chose a different currency," she said. "I've kept my part of the bargain."

"And if I choose again, how will you prevent me? Come, Fräulein, where are the papers you brought with you? They weren't in your bag. I've no time for gypsy tricks." He tossed the bag contemptuously on the rug.

"What are you talking about, Hans?" Frau Hitler demanded.

"All weapons are useful in war," he said. "Especially biological ones that call down the plagues of hell, twisting the bodies of man and beast, even destroying minds—am I not right, Fräulein?—leaving one's own forces unharmed. Appropriate, isn't it, that a nation of farmers should be the first to learn how to poison the harvest? Oh, yes! We knew the Lilly company was working on recombinant DNA, an area we'd neglected. We were only a little slow acting on that intelligence. We indulged ourselves in the security of knowing your country was not pursuing the more profitable avenues of nuclear fission. Then this occurred, and you fell into our hands most fortunately."

Her skin crawled as he spoke. This was what she had intended to do, so why the sudden reluctance? The man aroused a primeval fear in her. He was the hunter, the man with a knife in the night—

"There will be no more war!" the old lady said imperiously. "It contradicts Adolf's vision for Europe. On his deathbed he spoke of the thousand years of peace—"

"The so-called *Reichs-Peace!*" Schmidt said, mouthing the words with obvious distaste. "A bastard concept, like the phrase itself! A new Hitler will see things differently."

She could tell him the truth about Wolfgang Tshurkurka, and then perhaps he'd be discouraged.

And an old woman's heart would be broken. It shouldn't have mattered to Greta Tshurkurka, Gypsy, but somehow she found that it did.

She said nothing.

"If the *Führer* hadn't agreed to peace when he did, if he'd pursued the advantage that was all his," Schmidt said, "there might've been a German Empire today, not a Federation of shopkeepers! We are the only major European nation that has been denied an empire. Now there's a second chance."

"Yes," Frau Hitler said. "An empire in space!"

He gazed up at the voluptuous Rhine maidens in the full bloom of their triumph. "I regret now that I went with Rudolf Hess to England in the spring of '41—parachuting like a couple of romantic schoolboys into a Scottish glen! Of course, I *was* hardly more than a boy—Hess understood the English fascination with the Young Poet image I could project so well! I think to myself, if only I hadn't been so eloquent, if only the mission had failed and we had not persuaded the stubborn British to join forces with us against the communist threat. How differently things might have turned out then!"

"But the war would have dragged on, Hans—"

"And Germany would have won! We wouldn't have needed sniveling treaties, promising to love each other and get along like so many peasants at a wedding."

How could she be sure about Wolfgang Tshurkurka, born a Gypsy, raised a Nazi? She might never know, and not knowing might make a terrible mistake.

Frau Hitler said—as if she, rather than Greta, possessed the Gift of the

Romanies—"Wolfli is not like that. I did not raise him to be so. He will conquer the stars, not people."

The old woman radiated a strength beyond her size, Greta thought. In that instant she was willing to believe she was right.

Schmidt made an impatient noise in his throat.

Frau Hitler looked down at Greta for a long moment, her expression thoughtful. "You have kept your side of the bargain twice over, Fräulein Bradford. Germany will remember that."

She turned to the fireplace, withdrawing something from a pocket in the embroidered apron over the voluminous folds of her dirndl. Flames leaped up as the first sheets reached them.

Schmidt crossed the room in three strides. *"Gott in Himmel! Was tun Sie?"*

"Do not touch me, Hans!" Frau Hitler stood, back to the fireplace, protecting it with her upraised cane. "You have no right to prevent me disposing of trash I find in my own home."

Gone. Her ticket to England vanished in a shower of sparks.

But the formulas for destruction, the equations themselves that led to twisted minds and grotesque bodies were etched on her brain for as long as she lived.

Schmidt cursed loudly in German and English.

"Leave us now, Hans," Frau Hitler said as smoke billowed into the room from the last of the pages. "I will overlook this impoliteness, for today you are overwrought."

"You may succeed in delaying us, *gnädige Frau,* but you can't stop us!" He clicked his heels and lunged out of the room.

Greta lay back against the pillow. How long had she been without sleep? Since Indianapolis—sometime soon she'd have to think what she was going to do here in Germany. Her only skill was as a biochemist—there would be other nations anxious to buy what she knew, if she were willing to sell . . .

The shoulder began to throb.

She was aware of the old woman's arthritic fingers laid on her brow, and made an effort to swallow down fatigue. "I'm glad you burned them."

Frau Hitler smiled. "Do you not suppose I had enough talk of genetic selection, years ago? It is our destiny and our danger to be always thinking of improving the race, you see! But not this way."

Greta exhaled. If it had only been that simple—

She felt the pull of the painkillers and tranquilizers they had obviously pumped into her. Schmidt suspected her of the wrong mental powers. He hadn't guessed what templates for disaster were really locked in her brain.

Worthless treasure, like the rest of the trivia, for she knew she could never bring herself to use it now.

Perversely she felt only a great relief.

"Perhaps the time has come for me to tell Wolfli my secret. He has children of his own—he will understand now. Besides, a little insurance against Herr Schmidt might be useful. Ach! We are in for interesting times again. How tiresome."

Lethargically Greta opened her eyes again and saw the old woman's hands with their swollen knuckles. One of the formulas someone else at Lilly had been working on had promised relief for arthritis—she'd seen it once, but hadn't paid much attention, absorbed as she was then in her own deadly equations. If she worked hard enough, she could reconstruct it, or at least enough of it to give somebody else a clue.

Greta sighed. "Tomorrow, I'll—"

"You will stay in Germany long enough to welcome Wolfli home?"

"No, I—what?"

"I need a companion to accompany me to London next month. The Queen's garden parties are always such fun, but exhausting for a woman of my age! I had hoped you would come."

Tears that Schmidt had not been able to command spilled over now.

Frau Hitler settled back in her favorite chair, the dachshund on her lap. "And I would not be offended if you did not return with me, you see."

Behind her, Greta glimpsed the bright moon framed in the mullioned window—a promise that the Reichs-Peace would be kept a little while longer.

"Rupa's children bless you, Eva Hitler," Greta said. "And so does History."

Never Meet Again

Algis Budrys

The breeze soughed through the linden trees. It was warm and gentle as it drifted along the boulevard. It tugged at the dresses of the girls strolling with their young men and stirred their modishly cut hair. It set the banner atop the government buildings to flapping, and it brought with it the sound of a jet aircraft—a Heinkel or a Messerschmitt —rising into the sky from Tempelhof Aerodrome. But when it touched Professor Kempfer on his bench, it brought only the scent of the Parisian perfumes and the sight of gaily colored frocks swaying around the girls' long, healthy legs.

Doctor Professor Kempfer straightened his exhausted shoulders and raised his heavy head. His deep, strained eyes struggled to break through their now habitual dull stare.

It was spring again, he realized in faint surprise. The pretty girls were eating their lunches hastily once more, so that they and their young men could stroll along Unter Den Linden, and the young men in the broad-shouldered jackets were clear-eyed and full of their own awakening strength.

And of course Professor Kempfer wore no overcoat today. He was not quite the comic pedant who wore his galoshes in the sunshine. It was only that he had forgotten, for the moment. The strain of these last few days had been very great.

All these months—these years—he had been doing his government-subsidized research and the other thing, too. Four or five hours for the government, and then a full day on the much more important thing no one knew about. Twelve, sixteen hours a day. Home to his very nice government apartment, where Frau Ritter, the housekeeper, had his supper ready. The supper eaten, to bed. And in the morning; cocoa, a bit of pastry, and to work. At noon he would leave his laboratory for a little while, to come here and eat the slice of black bread and cheese Frau Ritter had wrapped in waxed paper and put in his pocket before he left the house.

But it was over, now. Not the government sinecure—that was just made work for the old savant who, after all, held the Knight's Cross of the Iron Cross for his work with the antisubmarine radar detector. That, of course, had been fifteen years ago. If they could not quite pension him off, still no one expected anything of a feeble old man puttering around the apparatus they had given him to play with.

And they were right, of course. Nothing *would* ever come of it. But the other thing . . .

That was done, now. After this last little rest he would go back to his laboratory in the Himmlerstrasse and take the final step. So now he could let himself relax and feel the warmth of the sun.

Professor Kempfer smiled wearily at the sunshine. The good, constant sun, he thought, that gives of itself to all of us, no matter who or where we are. Spring . . . April 1958.

Had it really been fifteen years—and sixteen years since the end of the war? It didn't seem possible. But then one day had been exactly like another for him, with only an electric light in the basement where his real apparatus was, an electric light that never told him whether it was morning, noon, or night.

I have become a cave-dweller! he thought with sudden realization. I have forgotten to think in terms of serial time. What an odd little trick I have played on myself!

Had he *really* been coming here, to this bench, every clear day for *fifteen* years? Impossible! But . . .

He counted on his fingers. 1940 was the year England had surrendered, with its air force destroyed and the Luftwaffe flying unchallenged air cover for the swift invasion. He had been sent to England late that year, to supervise the shipment home of the ultra-shortwave radar from the Royal Navy's antisubmarine warfare school. And 1941 was the year the U-boats took firm control of the Atlantic. 1942 was the year the Russians lost at

Stalingrad, starved by the millions, and surrendered to a Wehrmacht fed on shiploads of Argentinian beef. 1942 was the end of the war, yes.

So it *had* been that long.

I have become an indrawn old man, he thought to himself in bemusement. So very busy with myself . . . and the world has gone by, even while I sat here and might have watched it, if I'd taken the trouble. The world . . .

He took the sandwich from his coat pocket, unwrapped it, and began to eat. But after the first few bites he forgot it, and held it in one hand while he stared sightlessly in front of him.

His pale, mobile lips fell into a wry smile. The world—the vigorous young world, so full of strength, so confident . . . while I worked in my cellar like some Bolshevik dreaming of a fantastic bomb that would wipe out all my enemies at a stroke.

But what I have is not a bomb, and I have no enemies. I am an honored citizen of the greatest empire the world has ever known. Hitler is thirteen years dead in his auto accident, and the new chancellor is a different sort of man. He has promised us no war with the Americans. We have peace, and triumph, and these create a different sort of atmosphere than do war and desperation. We have relaxed, now. We have the fruit of our victory— what do we not have, in our empire of a thousand years? Western civilization is safe at last from the hordes of the East. Our future is assured. There is nothing, no one to fight, and these young people walking here have never known a moment's doubt, an instant's question of their place in an endlessly bright tomorrow. I will soon die, and the rest of us who knew the old days will die soon enough. It will all belong to the young people—all this eternal world. It belongs to them already. It is just that some of us old ones have not yet gotten altogether out of the way.

He stared out at the strolling crowds. How many years can I possibly have left to me? Three? Two? Four? I could die tomorrow.

He sat absolutely still for a moment, listening to the thick old blood slurring through his veins, to the thready flutter of his heart. It hurt his eyes to see. It hurt his throat to breathe. The skin of his hands was like spotted old paper.

Fifteen years of work. Fifteen years in his cellar, building what he had built—for what? Was his apparatus going to change anything? Would it detract even one trifle from this empire? Would it alter the life of even one citizen in that golden tomorrow?

This world would go on exactly as it was. Nothing would change in the least. So, what had he worked for? For himself? For this outworn husk of one man?

Seen in that light, he looked like a very stupid man. Stupid, foolish—monomaniacal.

Dear God, he thought with a rush of terrible intensity, am I now going to persuade myself not to use what I have built?

For all these years he had worked, worked—without stopping, without thinking. Now, in this first hour of rest, was he suddenly going to spit on it all?

A stout bulk settled on the bench beside him. "Jochim," the complacent voice said.

Professor Kempfer looked up. "Ah, Georg!" he said with an embarrassed laugh, "You startled me."

Doctor Professor Georg Tanzler guffawed heartily. "Oh, Jochim, Jochim!" he chuckled, shaking his head. "What a type you are! A thousand times I've found you here at noon, and each time it seems as if it surprises you. What do you think about, here on your bench?"

Professor Kempfer let his eyes stray. "Oh, I don't know," he said gently. "I look at the young people."

"The girls—" Tanzler's elbow dug roguishly into his side. "The girls, eh, Jochim?"

A veil drew over Professor Kempfer's eyes. "No," he whispered. "Not like that. No."

"What, then?"

"Nothing," Professor Kempfer said dully. "I look at nothing."

Tanzler's mood changed instantly. "So," he declared with precision. "I thought as much. Everyone knows you are working night and day, even though there is no need for it." Tanzler resurrected a chuckle. "We are not in any great hurry now. It's not as if we were pressed by anyone. The Australians and Canadians are fenced off by our navy. The Americans have their hands full in Asia. And your project, whatever it may be, will help no one if you kill yourself with overwork."

"You know there is no project," Professor Kempfer whispered. "You know it is all just busy work. No one reads my reports. No one checks my results. They give me the equipment I ask for, and do not mind, as long as it is not too much. You know that quite well. Why pretend otherwise?"

Tanzler sucked his lips. Then he shrugged. "Well, if you realize, then you realize," he said cheerfully. Then he changed expression again, and laid his hand on Professor Kempfer's arm in comradely fashion. "Jochim. It has been fifteen years. Must you still try to bury yourself?"

Sixteen, Professor Kempfer corrected, and then realized Tanzler was not thinking of the end of the war. Sixteen years since then, yes, but fifteen since Marthe died. Only fifteen?

I *must* learn to think in terms of serial time again. He realized Tanzler was waiting for a response, and mustered a shrug.

"Jochim! Have you been listening to me?"

"Listening? Of course, Georg."

"Of course!" Tanzler snorted, his moustaches fluttering. "Jochim," he said positively, "it is not as if we were young men, I admit. But life goes on, even for us old crocks." Tanzler was a good five years Kempfer's junior. "We must look ahead—we must live for a future. We cannot let ourselves sink into the past. I realize you were very fond of Marthe. Every man is fond of his wife—that goes without saying. But fifteen years, Jochim! Surely, it is proper to grieve. But to *mourn*, like this—this is not *healthy!*"

One bright spark singed through the quiet barriers Professor Kempfer had thought perfect. "Were *you* ever in a camp, Georg?" he demanded, shaking with pent-up violence.

"A camp?" Tanzler was taken aback. "I? Of course not, Jochim! But— but you and Marthe were not in a real *Lager*—it was just a . . . a . . . Well, you were under the State's protection! After all, Jochim!"

Professor Kempfer said stubbornly: "But Marthe *died.* Under the State's protection."

"These things *happen*, Jochim! After all, you're a reasonable man— Marthe—tuberculosis—even sulfa has its limitations—that might have happened to *anyone!*"

"She did not have tuberculosis in 1939, when we were placed under the State's protection. And when I finally said yes, I would go to work for them, and they gave me the radar detector to work on, they promised me it was only a little congestion in her bronchiae and that as soon as she was well they would bring her home. And the war ended, and they did *not* bring her home. I was given the Knight's Cross from Hitler's hands, personally, but they did *not* bring her home. And the last time I went to the sanitorium to see her, she was *dead.* And they paid for it all, and gave me my laboratory here, and an apartment, and clothes, and food, and a very good housekeeper, but Marthe was *dead.*"

"Fifteen *years*, Jochim! Have you not forgiven us?"

"No. For a little while today—just a little while ago—I thought I might. But—no."

Tanzler puffed out his lips and fluttered them with an exhaled breath. "So," he said. "What are you going to do to us for it?"

Professor Kempfer shook his head. "To you? What should I do to you? The men who arranged these things are all dead, or dying. If I had some means of hurting the Reich—and I do not—how could I revenge myself on these children?" He looked toward the passersby. "What am I to them, or they to me? No—no, I am going to do nothing to you."

Tanzler raised his eyebrows and put his thick fingertips together. "If you are going to do nothing to us, then what are you going to do to yourself?"

"I am going to go away." Already, Professor Kempfer was ashamed of his outburst. He felt he had controverted his essential character. A man of science, after all—a thinking, *reasoning* man—could not let himself descend to emotional levels. Professor Kempfer was embarrassed to think that Tanzler might believe this sort of lapse was typical of him.

"Who am I," he tried to explain, "to be judge and jury over a whole nation—an empire? Who is one man, to decide good and evil? I look at these youngsters, and I envy them with all my heart. To be young; to find all the world arranged in orderly fashion for one's special benefit; to have been placed on a surfboard, free to ride the crest of the wave forever, and never to have to swim at all? Who am I, Georg? Who am I?

"But I do not like it here. So I am going away."

Tanzler looked at him enigmatically. "To Carlsbad. For the radium waters. Very healthful. We'll go together." He began pawing Professor Kempfer's arm with great heartiness. "A splendid idea! I'll get the seats reserved on the morning train. We'll have a holiday, eh, Jochim?"

"No!" He struggled to his feet, pulling Tanzler's hand away from his arm. *"No!"* He staggered when Tanzler gave way. He began to walk fast, faster than he had walked in years. He looked over his shoulder, and saw Tanzler lumbering after him.

He began to run. He raised an arm. "Taxi! *Taxi!"* He lurched toward the curb, while the strolling young people looked at him wide-eyed.

He hurried through the ground-floor laboratory, his heart pumping wildly. His eyes were fixed on the plain gray door to the fire stairs, and he fumbled in his trousers pocket for the key. He stumbled against a bench and sent apparatus crashing over. At the door he steadied himself and, using both hands, slipped the key into the lock. Once through the door he slammed it shut and locked it again, and listened to the hoarse whistle of his breath in his nostrils.

Then, down the firestairs he clattered, open-mouthed. Tanzler. Tanzler would be at a telephone, somewhere. Perhaps the State Police were out in the streets, in their cars, coming here, already.

He wrenched open the basement door, and locked it behind him in the darkness before he turned on the lights. With his chest aching he braced himself on widespread feet and looked at the dull sheen of yellow light on

the racks of gray metal cabinets. They rose about him like the blocks of a
Mayan temple, with dials for carvings and pilot lights for jewels, and he
moved down the narrow aisle between them, slowly and quietly now, like a
last, enfeebled acolyte. As he walked he threw switches, and the cabinets
began to resonate in chorus.

The aisle led him, irrevocably, to the focal point. He read what the dials
on the master panel told him, and watched the power demand meter inch
into the green.

If they think to open the building circuit breakers!

If they shoot through the door!

If I was wrong!

Now there were people hammering on the door. Desperately weary, he
depressed the firing switch.

There was a galvanic thrum, half pain, half pleasure, as the vibratory
rate of his body's atoms was changed by an infinitesimal degree. Then he
stood in dank darkness, breathing musty air, while whatever parts of his
equipment had been included in the field fell to the floor.

Behind him he left nothing. Vital resistors had, by design, come with
him. The overloaded apparatus in the basement laboratory began to
stench and burn under the surge of full power, and to sputter in Georg
Tanzler's face.

The basement he was in was not identical with the one he had left.
That could only mean that in this Berlin, something serious had happened
to at least one building on the Himmlerstrasse. Professor Kempfer
searched through the darkness with weary patience until he found a door,
and while he searched he considered the thought that some upheaval,
manmade or natural, had filled in the ground for dozens of meters above
his head, leaving only this one pocket of emptiness into which his apparatus had shunted him.

When he finally found the door, he leaned against it for some time, and
then he gently eased it open. There was nothing but blackness on the
other side, and at his first step he tripped and sprawled on a narrow flight
of stairs, bruising a hip badly. He found his footing again. On quivering
legs he climbed slowly and as silently as he could, clinging to the harsh,
newly sawed wood of the bannister. He could not seem to catch his
breath. He had to gulp for air, and the darkness was shot through with red
swirlings.

He reached the top of the stairs, and another door. There was harsh
gray light seeping around it, and he listened intently, allowing for the
quick suck and thud of the pulse in his ears. When he heard nothing for a

long time, he opened it. He was at the end of a long corridor lined with doors, and at the end there was another door opening on the street.

Eager to get out of the building, and yet reluctant to leave as much as he knew of this world, he moved down the corridor with exaggerated caution.

It was a shoddy building. The paint on the walls was cheap, and the linoleum on the floor was scuffed and warped. There were cracks in the plastering. Everything was rough—half finished, with paint slapped over it, everything drab. There were numbers on the doors, and dirty rope mats in front of them. It was an apartment house, then—but from the way the doors were jammed almost against each other, the apartments had to be no more than cubicles.

Dreary, he thought. Dreary, dreary—who would live in such a place? Who would put up an apartment house for people of mediocre means in this neighborhood?

But when he reached the street, he saw that it was humpy and cobble-stoned, the cobbling badly patched, and that all the buildings were like this one—gray-faced, hulking, ugly. There was not a building he recognized—not a stick or stone of the Himmlerstrasse with its fresh cement roadway and its sapling trees growing along the sidewalk. And yet he knew he must be on the exact spot where the Himmlerstrasse had been—was—and he could not quite understand.

He began to walk in the direction of Unter Den Linden. He was far from sure he could reach it on foot, in his condition, but he would pass through the most familiar parts of the city, and could perhaps get some inkling of what had happened.

He had suspected that the probability world his apparatus could most easily adjust him for would be one in which Germany had lost the war. That was a large, dramatic difference, and though he had refined his work as well as he could, any first model of any equipment was bound to be relatively insensitive.

But as he walked along, he found himself chilled and repelled by what he saw.

Nothing was the same. Nothing. Even the layout of the streets had changed a little. There were new buildings everywhere—new buildings of a style and workmanship that had made them old in atmosphere the day they were completed. It was the kind of total reconstruction that he had no doubt the builders stubbornly proclaimed was "Good as New," because to say it was as good as the old Berlin would have been to invite bitter smiles.

The people in the streets were grim, gray-faced, and shoddy. They stared blankly at him and his suit, and once a dumpy woman carrying a string bag full of lumpy packages turned to her similar companion and muttered as he passed that he looked like an American with his extravagant clothes.

The phrase frightened him. What kind of war had it been, that there would still be Americans to be hated in Berlin in 1958? How long could it possibly have lasted, to account for so many old buildings gone? What had pounded Germany so cruelly? And yet even the "new" buildings were genuinely some years old. Why an American? Why not an Englishman or Frenchman?

He walked the gray streets, looking with a numb sense of settling shock at this grim Berlin. He saw men in shapeless uniform caps, brown trousers, cheap boots, and sleazy blue shirts. They wore armbands with *Volkspolizei* printed on them. Some of them had not bothered to shave this morning or to dress in fresh uniforms. The civilians looked at them sidelong and then pretended not to have seen them. For an undefinable but well-remembered reason, Professor Kempfer slipped by them as inconspicuously as possible.

He grappled at what he saw with the dulled resources of his overtired intellect, but there was no point of reference with which to begin. He even wondered if perhaps the war was somehow still being fought, with unimaginable alliances and unthinkable antagonists, with all resources thrown into a brutal, dogged struggle from which all hope of both defeat and victory were gone, and only endless straining effort loomed up from the future.

Then he turned the corner and saw the stubby military car, and soldiers in baggy uniforms with red stars on their caps. They were parked under a weatherbeaten sign that read, in German above a few lines in unreadable Cyrillic characters: *Attention! You Are Leaving the USSR Zone of Occupation. You Are Entering the American Zone of Occupation. Show Your Papers.*

God in heaven! he thought, recoiling. The Bolsheviks. And he was on their side of the line. He turned abruptly, but did not move for an instant. The skin of his face felt tight. Then he broke into a stumbling walk, back the way he had come.

He had not come into this world blindly. He had not dared bring any goods from his apartment, of course. Not with Frau Ritter to observe him. Nor had he expected that his Reichsmarks would be of any use. He had provided for this by wearing two diamond-set rings. He had expected to have to walk down to the jewelry district before he could begin to settle into this world, but he had expected no further difficulty.

He had expected Germany to have lost the war. Germany had lost another war within his lifetime, and fifteen years later it would have taken intense study for a man in his present position to detect it.

Professor Kempfer had thought it out, slowly, systematically. He had not thought that a Soviet checkpoint might lie between him and the jewelry district.

It was growing cold, as the afternoon settled down. It had not been as warm a day to begin with, he suspected, as it had been in his Berlin. He wondered how it might be, that Germany's losing a war could change the weather, but the important thing was that he was shivering. He was beginning to attract attention not only for his suit but for his lack of a coat.

He had now no place to go, no place to stay the night, no way of getting food. He had no papers, and no knowledge of where to get them or what sort of maneuver would be required to keep him safe from arrest. If anything could save him from arrest. By Russians.

Professor Kempfer began to walk with dragging steps, his body sagging and numb. More and more of the passersby were looking at him sharply. They might well have an instinct for a hunted man. He did not dare look at the occasional policeman.

He was an old man. He had run today, and shaken with nervous anticipation, and finished fifteen years' work, and it had all been a nightmarish error. He felt his heart begin to beat unnaturally in his ears, and he felt a leaping flutter begin in his chest. He stopped, and swayed, and then he forced himself to cross the sidewalk so he could lean against a building. He braced his back and bent his knees a little, and let his hands dangle at his sides.

The thought came to him that there was an escape for him into one more world. His shoulder blades scraped a few centimeters downward against the wall.

There were people watching him. They ringed him in at a distance of about two meters, looking at him with almost childish curiosity. But there was something about them that made Professor Kempfer wonder at the conditions that could produce such children. As he looked back at them, he thought that perhaps they all wanted to help him—that would account for their not going on about their business. But they did not know what sort of complications their help might bring to them—except that there would certainly be complications. So none of them approached him. They gathered around him, watching, in a crowd that would momentarily attract a *Volkspolizier.*

He looked at them dumbly, breathing as well as he could, his palms flat against the wall. There were stocky old women, round-shouldered men, younger men with pinched faces, and young girls with an incalculable wisdom in their eyes. And there was a birdlike older woman, coming quickly along the sidewalk, glancing at him curiously, then hurrying by, skirting around the crowd . . .

There was one possibility of his escape to this world that Professor Kempfer had not allowed himself to consider. He pushed himself away from the wall, scattering the crowd as though by physical force, and lurched toward the passing woman.

"Marthe!"

She whirled, her purse flying to the ground. Her hand went to her mouth. She whispered, through her knuckles: "Jochim . . . Jochim. . . ." He clutched her, and they supported each other. "Jochim . . . the American bombers killed you in Hamburg . . . yesterday I sent money to put flowers on your grave . . . Jochim . . ."

"It was a mistake. It was all a mistake. Marthe . . . we have found each other . . ."

From a distance she had not changed very much at all. Watching her move about the room as he lay, warm and clean, terribly tired, in her bed, he thought to himself that she had not aged half as much as he. But when she bent over him with the cup of hot soup in her hand, he saw the sharp lines in her face, around her eyes and mouth, and when she spoke he heard the dry note in her voice.

How many years? he thought. How many years of loneliness and grief? *When* had the Americans bombed Hamburg? How? What kind of aircraft could bomb Germany from bases in the Western Hemisphere?

They had so much to explain to each other. As she worked to make him comfortable, the questions flew between them.

"It was something I stumbled on. The theory of probability worlds—of alternate universes. Assuming that the characteristic would be a difference in atomic vibration—minute, you understand; almost infinitely minute—assuming that somewhere in the gross universe every possible variation of every event *must* take place—then if some means could be found to alter the vibratory rate within a field, then any object in that field would automatically become part of the universe corresponding to that vibratory rate . . .

"Marthe, I can bore you later. Tell me about *Hamburg*. Tell me how we lost the war. Tell me about Berlin."

He listened while she told him how their enemies had ringed them in— how the great white wastes of Russia had swallowed their men, and the British fire bombers had murdered children in the night. How the Wehrmacht fought, and fought, and smashed their enemies back time after time, until all the best soldiers were dead. And how the Americans with their dollars, had poured out countless tons of equipment to make up for their inability to fight. How, at the last, the vulture fleets of bombers had rumbled inexhaustibly across the sky, killing, killing, killing, until all the German homes and German families had been destroyed. And how now the Americans, with their hellish bomb that had killed a hundred thousand Japanese civilians, now bestrode the world and tried to bully it, with their bombs and their dollars, into final submission.

How? Professor Kempfer thought. How could such a thing have happened?

Slowly he pieced it together, mortified to find himself annoyed when Marthe interrupted with constant questions about his Berlin and especially about his equipment.

And, pieced together, it still refused to seem logical.

How could anyone believe that Goering, in the face of all good sense, would turn the Luftwaffe from destroying the RAF bases to a ridiculous attack on English cities? How could anyone believe that German electronics scientists could persistently refuse to believe ultra-shortwave radar was practical—refuse to believe it even when the Allied hunter planes were finding surfaced submarines at night with terrible accuracy?

What kind of nightmare world was this, with Germany divided and the Russians in control of Europe, in control of Asia, reaching for the Middle East that no Russian, not even the dreaming czars, had seriously expected ever to attain?

"Marthe—we must get out of this place. We must. I will have to rebuild my machine." It would be incredibly difficult. Working clandestinely as he must, scraping components together—even now that the work had been done once, it would take several years.

Professor Kempfer looked inside himself to find the strength he would need. And it was not there. It simply was gone, used up, burnt out, eaten out.

"Marthe, you will have to help me. I must take some of your strength. I will need so many things—identity papers, some kind of work so we can eat, money to buy equipment. . . ." His voice trailed away. It was so much, and there was so little time left for him. Yet, somehow, they must do it.

A hopelessness, a feeling of inevitable defeat, came over him. It was this world. It was poisoning him.

Marthe's hand touched his brow. "Hush, Jochim. Go to sleep. Don't worry. Everything is all right, now. My poor Jochim, how terrible you look! But everything will be all right. I must go back to work, now. I am hours late already. I will come back as soon as I can. Go to sleep, Jochim."

He let his breath out in a long, tired sigh. He reached up and touched her hand. "Marthe . . ."

He awoke to Marthe's soft urging. Before he opened his eyes he had taken her hand from his shoulder and clasped it tightly. Marthe let the contact linger for a moment, then broke it gently.

"Jochim—my superior at the Ministry is here to see you."

He opened his eyes and sat up. "Who?"

"Colonel Lubintsev, from the People's Government Ministerium, where I work. He would like to speak to you." She touched him reassuringly. "Don't worry. It's all right. I spoke to him—I explained. He's not here to arrest you. He's waiting in the other room."

He looked at Marthe dumbly. "I—I must get dressed," he managed to say after a while.

"No—no, he wants you to stay in bed. He knows you're exhausted. He asked me to assure you it would be all right. Rest in bed. I'll get him."

Professor Kempfer sank back. He looked unseeingly up at the ceiling until he heard the sound of a chair being drawn up beside him, and then he slowly turned his head.

Colonel Lubintsev was a stocky, ruddy-faced man with gray bristles on his scalp. He had an astonishingly boyish smile. "Doctor Professor Kempfer, I am honored to meet you," he said. "Lubintsev, Colonel, assigned as adviser to the People's Government Ministerium." He extended his hand gravely, and Professor Kempfer shook it with a conscious effort.

"I am pleased to make your acquaintance," Professor Kempfer mumbled.

"Not at all, Doctor Professor. Not at all. Do you mind if I smoke?"

"Please." He watched the colonel touch a lighter to a long cigarette while Marthe quickly found a saucer for an ashtray. The colonel nodded his thanks to Marthe, puffed on the cigarette, and addressed himself to Professor Kempfer while Marthe sat down on a chair against the far wall.

"I have inspected your dossier," Colonel Lubintsev said. "That is," with a smile, "our dossier on your late counterpart. I see you fit the photographs as well as could be expected. We will have to make a further identification, of course, but I rather think that will be a formality." He smiled again. "I am fully prepared to accept your story. It is too fantastic not to be true. Of course, sometimes foreign agents choose their cover stories with that idea in mind, but not in this case, I think. If what has happened to you could happen to any man, our dossier indicates Jochim Kempfer might well be that man." Again, the smile. "In any counterpart."

"You have a dossier," Professor Kempfer said.

Colonel Lubintsev's eyebrows went up in a pleased grin. "Oh, yes. When we liberated your nation, we knew exactly what scientists were deserving of our assistance in their work, and where to find them. We had laboratories, project agendas, living quarters—everything!—all ready for them. But I must admit, we did not think we would ever be able to accommodate you."

"But now you can."

"Yes!" Once more Colonel Lubintsev smiled like a little boy with great fun in store. "The possibilities of your device are as infinite as the universe! Think of the enormous help to the people of your nation, for example, if they could draw on machine tools and equipment from such alternate places as the one you have just left." Colonel Lubintsev waved his cigarette. "Or if, when the Americans attack us, we can transport bombs from a world where the revolution is an accomplished fact, and have them appear in North America in this."

Professor Kempfer sat up in bed. "Marthe! Marthe, why have you done this to me?"

"Hush, Jochim," she said. "Please. Don't tire yourself. I have done nothing to you. You will have care, now. We will be able to live together in a nice villa, and you will be able to work, and we will be together."

"Marthe—"

She shook her head, her lips pursed primly. "Please, Jochim. Times have changed a great deal, here. I explained to the Colonel that your head was probably still full of the old Nazi propaganda. He understands. You will learn to see it for what it was. And you will help put the Americans back in their place." Her eyes filled suddenly with tears. "All the years I went to visit your grave as often as I could. All the years I paid for flowers, and all the nights I cried for you."

"But I am *here*, Marthe! I am here! I am not dead."

"Jochim, Jochim," she said gently. "Am I to have had all my grief for nothing?"

"I have brought a technical expert with me," Colonel Lubintsev went on as though nothing had happened. "If you will tell him what facilities you will need, we can begin preliminary work immediately." He rose to his feet. "I will send him in. I myself must be going." He put out his cigarette, and extended his hand. "I have been honored, Doctor Professor Kempfer."

"Yes," Professor Kempfer whispered. "Yes. Honored." He raised his hand, pushed it toward the colonel's, but could not hold it up long enough to reach. It fell back to the coverlet, woodenly, and Professor Kempfer could not find the strength to move it. "Goodbye."

He heard the colonel walk out with a few murmured words for Marthe. He was quite tired, and he heard only a sort of hum.

He turned his head when the technical expert came in. The man was all eagerness, all enthusiasm:

"Jochim! This is amazing! Perhaps I should introduce myself—I worked with your counterpart during the war—we were quite good friends —I am Georg Tanzler. Jochim! How *are* you!"

Professor Kempfer looked up. He saw through a deep, tightening fog, and he heard his heart preparing to stop. His lips twisted. "I think I am going away again, Georg," he whispered.

Do Ye Hear the
Children Weeping?

Howard Goldsmith

It began with an ad in the classified section of *Der Spiegel*. It said, in German:

FURNISHED HOUSE FOR RENT. Remodeled brownstone, 2 floors.
Sacrifice at DM 600. Inquire at Mühlenbergstrasse 31.

I was struck by the DM 600 figure. It must be a misprint. More like DM 800 or 900 probably. I snatched up the phone and dialed the number of *Der Spiegel*. Someone in the Classified Department confirmed the accuracy of the ad. It had been placed the previous evening.

My wife, Ellen, and I had our sights set on a house rental ever since we arrived in Germany a few weeks before. I worked for a long-established German jeweler in the United States. As I was in Munich to set up a branch office, the firm would pick up the tab. But houses were scarce.

"Ellen," I called. "There's an ad I think we ought to investigate."

My bride of two months sauntered in from the bedroom wearing an inquisitive expression. "Let's see," she said, nuzzling her chin on my shoulder. "Hmm . . ." she murmured, scanning the ad. "Sounds too good to be true. A whole house. *Lebensraum.*" She spread her arms wide apart.

I winced. "That's what Hitler demanded, you'll recall."

"Jawohl, mein Herr," she replied, snapping to attention with a sharp click of her heels.

I chuckled. "Just don't do your SS imitation in public," I cautioned, pulling her down on my lap. "You'll get us chucked into prison as subversives."

She laughed and wound her arms about my neck. "Prison would, at least, be a change of scene. This hotel room is making me claustrophobic."

"So let's check out the ad," I said.

Ellen bounced up and bounded to the door. "Mühlenbergstrasse, here we come."

Tucking *Der Spiegel* in one pocket and a street map in the other, I darted after her.

The building rose before us, old and gaunt, with mottled bricks and shuttered windows. Two gargoyles glared with frozen ferocity from their perch above the entrance. At the side of the building a weathered sign swung loose from a rusty nail: JOHANN KLEIST, ARZT.

Ellen let out a sigh of disappointment. I gave her waist an encouraging squeeze. Her body sagged against me.

"This wasn't included in the marriage vows."

"It was your idea to rent a house," I reminded her gently.

"A house, not a mausoleum."

"At least we can take a look inside." I pressed the doorbell.

The door inched open. Two small, close-set eyes peered out. The door widened to reveal a thick-set man with large, heavy features. Gray stubble stippled his face. He was dressed in a crumpled tweed suit. A cigar dangled from a corner of his mouth.

"Doctor Kleist?" I said uncertainly.

He nodded with an indistinct grumble of assent. *"Amerikaner?"*

"Ja. Mein Namen ist Paul Konig—"

"Your accent is impenetrable. It will be simpler if we speak English."

"Fine. We've come about the ad. May we see the house?"

"What is your business in Munich?"

"I work for a firm of jewelers."

"Ah. This your wife?" he asked, puffing out a plume of smoke.

"Yes."

"Come in."

I clasped Ellen's hand. As we stepped into the dimly lit hallway, a vague, lurking sense of uneasiness stirred inside me. I could see that Ellen was affected the same way. The house had a chill, musty air. An acrid smell, as of formaldehyde—or embalming fluid—pervaded the place.

Dr. Kleist ushered us into the living room. It was full of heavy mahogany furniture. The adjoining room was empty. "I used this as my office," Dr. Kleist explained. "I'm just retired."

He showed us the dining room and kitchen, then conducted us upstairs to the bedrooms. The furnishings were spare and unadorned, the wallpaper blotchy and discolored.

"I'm in something of a hurry," said Dr. Kleist. "I was packing when you arrived. If you could give me your decision . . ."

"The rent is 600 DM?" I said.

He nodded.

I glanced at Ellen. She licked her upper lip thoughtfully. I could tell she was weighing the possibilities of the house against its present condition. In the end the scarcity of houses decided the issue. "I guess we'll take it," Ellen said.

As we descended the stairs we heard a noise as if a number of people were pattering with their bare feet upon the floor. Dr. Kleist glanced sharply over his shoulder. His face turned very pale, and an odd light shone in his eyes.

"Are there mice in the attic?" Ellen asked with alarm.

"Mice?" Dr. Kleist said distractedly. "No, no, it's just the boards creaking." He hurried down the stairs with a furtive air, plunging into a stream of rapid, disconnected speech. "I have to leave. Take it or leave it. Where is my luggage? Oh, yes. . . ." He moved bulkily toward the living room.

He snatched up two suitcases and carried them out to his car. As he returned the same pattering sound issued from upstairs, as of mice scurrying about with small, rapid steps. A glassy, hunted look sprang into Dr. Kleist's eyes. He backed toward the door, wrenched it open, and plunged forward into the street. "I'll pick up the other suitcases in a day or two," he croaked hoarsely. "That is, if you still want the house."

I whispered into Ellen's ear. "It's just some mice. Some people have a morbid terror of them."

"Including me," said Ellen.

"We'll hire an exterminator. Don't worry about it. Trust me, OK?" Ellen nodded gamely.

"We'll take it," I said.

Dr. Kleist squeezed his bulk into the car. His features were more composed. "I'll need a . . . how you say?"

"A deposit."

"Yes, a deposit."

I wrote a check. He pocketed it, handed me the keys to the house, and drove off.

Ellen and I returned to the hotel and checked out. We took a cab back to the house and unpacked our luggage.

"Honey," I said, "I have to get back to the office. I'll be home by six. Will you be all right?"

"I suppose so," said Ellen, "I'll get acquainted with the mice." She gave a slight shudder.

"Look, maybe there aren't any mice. Old houses do creak a lot. We'll see about it tomorrow, OK?"

In reply Ellen began to nibble on my ear.

"Hey!"

"I come from a long line of rodents," Ellen whispered. "Uncle Harry was known as the biggest rat in Orange County."

"Now you tell me!"

At four o'clock I received a call at the office. It was from Ellen. "Paul, there's something terribly wrong about this house." Her voice quivered on the edge of panic.

I felt a sudden chill at the base of my spine. "Wrong?"

"Objects keep moving about in the kitchen. Spoons, forks. A knife went flying through the air! And there's a blood stain in the doctor's office. It won't come off!"

"Take it easy, Ellen. You're letting your imagination run away with you. I shouldn't have left you alone in a strange house the first day."

"Don't patronize me, Paul. I'm not a little girl."

"Of course not, Ellen. Look, I'll come right home and we'll talk it over."

As she hung up Ellen seemed to be sobbing without tears, making a dry, breathless sound.

I hailed a taxi and made it home in fifteen minutes. Ellen met me at the door. "Do you hear it?" she exclaimed in a hoarse whisper. Her eyes darted about the house.

"What, Ellen?"

"Listen!"

From a distance I heard a sound that resembled the wail of a lost child. Or was it just the high thin whine of the wind? I listened tensely. The broken, squalling cry of an infant shrieked out into the gloom.

Ellen stared at me in a dazed way. "It's been going on all afternoon."

"It must be the neighbor's baby," I said.

"I've checked with them," Ellen said, a note of anguish in her voice. "They have no baby."

"Then it must be coming from the backyard."

"Come, I'll show you something," she said, taking my hand. She led me to a rear window. It looked out upon a high brick wall. There was no backyard.

"Do you want to know something else?" said Ellen. "Dr. Kleist was a leading medical researcher on concentration-camp prisoners during World War II. His specialty was pregnant women, injecting fetuses with various drugs that resulted in stillbirths or monstrosities. The Dachau camp is close by. Some of those experiments probably took place in his own office. *In this building!*"

"The neighbors told you that?"

She nodded. "After the war the *Führer* awarded him the Medal of Honor for his scientific contributions."

"The bastard."

"Shhh!" Ellen glanced reflexively from side to side, out of cautious habit. She had even more reason to fear being overheard in Germany, though Nazi agents were almost as vigilant in the States.

"Then why his great hurry to leave now?"

"The house is haunted, Paul!"

There was no point in arguing with Ellen in her present state. I wondered when we would see Dr. Kleist again. We had only his word that he would return for his suitcases. We resisted the temptation to open them. Or were we perhaps afraid of what we might find?

In any case I hated the thought of moving back into the hotel. And I'd never known Ellen to be superstitious. Perhaps it would all blow over. Maybe it was an alley cat we'd heard. Then I reminded myself that there was no alley.

We settled down to a forlorn dinner, picking idly at the food. Afterward we sat on the sofa, with the radio turned up high. I cradled Ellen in my arms, smoothing back her silky hair, immersed in the depths of her hazel eyes.

Perhaps Bach's sonatas for flute and harpsichord had lulled our poltergeists into inactivity. At least nothing untoward happened that evening.

We went to bed early, both of us feeling the strain of a hectic day. I dozed fitfully and suddenly found myself lying awake, Ellen sitting up beside me. Her eyes were riveted on the opposite wall. A thin stream of moonlight fell across it, framing a wavering silhouette. It was a face with contorted, embryonic features and narrow piglike slits for eyes. I felt an inward shrinking and revulsion. My flesh began to creep.

I turned toward Ellen. Her face was twisted with fear. I didn't trust myself to speak. The tension dried my throat. I snapped on the light and the figure disappeared.

Ellen shivered in a cold sweat. "It's still there," she exclaimed in a terrified whisper.

"It was nothing, Ellen. Just the play of shadows."

"I tell you it's still there. Turn out the lights and you'll see it."

I switched off the light.

"Look! *It's crawling over the side of the bed!*"

"Where, Ellen? I don't see it."

"It's creeping up the blanket. My God! It's on my breast—sucking at my nipple! Get it off!"

"It's your imagination, Ellen! I don't see a damned thing."

She leaped up, flinging the blanket aside. Her leg got caught in the bedding. She clawed at it desperately. "It's twisting around my thigh. Oh God! *It's at my groin!*"

I ripped frantically at the blanket, finally managing to untangle it, and tossed it across the room.

Ellen threw her arms about me, uttering short little staccato gasps.

"It's OK; it's all right, honey." I lowered her gently against the pillows.

"I felt something when I first woke up, Paul—a suffocating feeling. Hands were squeezing my throat. *Small* hands."

"It wasn't *hands*, Ellen," I snapped, then felt like a heel for my impatience. I opened the window. "It *is* pretty close in here. Try to go back to sleep. Would you like a sleeping pill?"

She gave me a blank, hollow stare. I opened a drawer and removed a medicine bottle. As I went for a glass of water, Ellen sat up and cried, "Don't leave me!"

"I'm just going into the bathroom for some water, Ellen."

I slipped into the bathroom and returned with the water. Ellen swallowed the pill in a sort of trance. She lay in bed with her eyes wide open. Her eyelids gradually began to flutter and close, her breathing becoming deep and regular.

I turned over on my side and attempted to sleep, but thoughts continued to nag. Then a sound brought me up with a start. The cry of a baby, as if in pain, rang out from the hallway. It was like a signal for a chorus of shrieks and cries that rose in a tide of savage force. I crossed the room to the door. As I drew it open a strident uproar swept along the corridor.

Ellen shot bolt upright in bed. Frantically she pressed her hands to her ears. I slammed the door and ran back to the bed.

"They're trying to kill us, Paul!" Her facial muscles quivered in a spasm of terror.

"Kill us?"

"The infants that Dr. Kleist murdered."

"Ellen!" She was raving, scared out of her wits.

"We have to confront them, Paul."

I shook my head in disbelief. "Ellen, I realize this whole experience is unnerving, and I have no explanation for it, but—"

She broke in sharply. "Don't you see, Paul? They're seeking vengeance. We have to show them we're not butchers like Kleist."

She rose from the bed and pulled me toward the door. I followed, as if in a dream. There was a moment's silence as she opened the door, then a furious roar of sound—a clamor of shrill, raucous voices. Out of the dark mouth of the corridor emerged a hideous army of infants trailing umbilical cords. A pale, phosphorescent light played upon their frightfully contorted features. Only their eyes seemed alive, burning intensely with an accusing glare. Their ranks deepened and pressed more closely together. They came hobbling forward with disconcerting rapidity.

A shriek of terror burst from Ellen's lips. "Dr. Kleist isn't here," she screamed. "Leave us alone!"

They shuffled forward, arms outstretched, their pale, pudgy hands clenching and unclenching spasmodically.

"We're Americans!"

I swept Ellen into the bedroom and slammed the door. A pandemonium of cries exploded along the corridor, followed by a rapid scurrying on the staircase.

"They're going down to Kleist's office," Ellen gasped. "Searching for him."

We sat in bed, rooted to the spot, too stunned to move. I was long past offering rational explanations. The house grew deathly still. Minutes ticked away. An hour passed. Still we sat, wide awake, till the gray light of dawn dispersed the last, lingering shadows.

We went downstairs and searched the rooms. They were empty.

"Do you think Kleist will ever return?" Ellen asked.

"I suspect he will—during the daytime. I'd like you to go back to the hotel, Ellen. I'll wait here till the evening, then join you. I want to settle scores with Kleist."

"But why? What business is it of yours?"

"I'm making it my business."

"But you're not Jewish."

I lowered my head. "My maternal grandfather was Jewish. I'm sorry I never told you before."

Ellen swallowed. "It wouldn't have mattered one bit. The point is *no one knows.* Even I never suspected. Why dredge it up?"

"It's something personal, Ellen. Intensely personal."

She searched my face. "Then I'll wait with you."

"But Kleist may not even return today."

"We'll wait as long as we have to—with the others."

"The others," I repeated numbly.

"Their grudge isn't against us. I don't think we'll be disturbed."

For want of anything better to do Ellen and I spent the day cleaning up the house. She was right about the blood stain in the office. No amount of scouring would remove it.

Toward evening we were rewarded by the ringing of the doorbell. Dr. Kleist stood outside, shifting uncomfortably from one leg to the other. Ellen admitted him. He entered the hallway with slow, worried steps. As he stepped into the light, dark circles showed under his eyes. A shock of hair straggled untidily over his forehead.

"Come in," Ellen urged.

"I came for my bags," rasped Dr. Kleist. "Would your husband mind carrying them out?"

I stepped forward. "I'd like to have a few words with you, Dr. Kleist." He flinched back.

"Just a few words over a cup of coffee."

"No thank you. I'm in a hurry. If you'll just let me have my bags—"

"I insist you stay, Dr. Kleist."

Kleist shot a nervous glance about him. "What is this?" he demanded, lowering his voice to a rumbling growl.

"Surely you won't refuse the hospitality of a cup of coffee."

"You Americans make a religious institution of your bloody coffee breaks. I told you, I have to leave!" He spun on his heels.

"Ellen, bolt the door."

Ellen stationed herself between Kleist and the door. He shouldered past her with a hard, set face.

"Not so fast," I said, swinging him around.

Ellen turned the bolt in the lock.

"What do you want?" Kleist demanded, his face dark with anger and worry, his lips curving in an ugly scowl.

"Come into the dining room," I said, taking him by the arm.

His shoulders collapsed in a helpless shrug. "All right, if you insist. But just for a few minutes."

I drew up a chair next to the table. "Have a seat."

He slumped into the chair with a gesture of resignation.

"Now tell us everything about this house."

He half rose to his feet. "What do you mean? I displayed the house yesterday."

"Tell us about the others."

"The others? What others?" His eyes dilated with alarm. A nerve twitched in the corner of his mouth.

He cocked his head, swiveling sharply in his chair. "Do you hear it? The footsteps? They're coming. Hurry, we must leave!"

"Who's coming?"

Footsteps slowly descended the stairs.

Kleist ran a trembling hand through his hair. *"There's no time to explain."* A dark flush spread over his face. "Come, let's go!"

I grasped his shoulders tightly, as he struggled frantically in his chair. *"Lass mich gehen!* Let me go!" he cried. *"Amerikanisch hund!* I'll have you shot!"

From the gloomy shadows of the hallway came a procession of infants with angelic yet curiously tainted and twisted faces.

They blundered forward with a jerky, determined gait, their steps small but quite deliberate. As they approached Kleist, their eyes ignited with concentrated hate and fury.

Kleist started violently. The whites of his eyes shone wildly. He sprang to his feet with a choking cry, his arms flung out against the specters.

"Weggeh!" he screamed, his voice breaking in a painful gasp.

"Bereuen sich!" came a shrill, keening cry. "Repent!" The words swirled around us, booming in volume and urgency. *"Bereuen sich!"* The chant grew to a ritual chorus reverberating on all sides as the figures drew steadily closer.

"Get away, you stinking whoreslime! Filthy Jewvermin! You want me to repent? I rejoice that I killed you—you and your bitchslut mothers. I did it for the Fatherland. I'd do it over again. I'd do it now!"

Kleist drew himself erect with military bearing, tugging reflexively at the coattails of a phantom uniform. He felt a sudden infusion of audacity and delight in his unexpected defiance. "You're all freaks: twisted, gnarled little beasts. Back to Munchkinland with you! Ha, ha, ha!" He launched into a fit of ringing, hysterical laughter, his head rocking back and forth on his bloated stump of a neck.

With a sudden look of terror he clutched wildly at his collar, his breath coming in hideous, stertorous gasps. Purple blotches sprang out on his face and neck as he collapsed into his chair.

"*Achhh. . . .*" He gave a violent convulsive jerk and slumped forward, his eyes fixed in a steady, sightless stare. They were the lifeless, cavernous eyes of a dead man.

"Look at his throat!" Ellen screamed.

There were burn marks, like those made by a rope—or an umbilical cord!

The infants so palpably present just moments before had dispersed like a ghostly brigade, leaving a trail of mist.

We heard the front door open and close. Ellen and I ran to the window and looked out. A large panel truck stood at the opposite curb, its motor running. Upon its side was written:

HOLOCAUST CIRCUS OF HORRORS
FEATURING THE DACHAU DWARFS
MASTERS OF ILLUSION

The next hour passed in a daze. Somehow I managed to phone for an ambulance. The SS arrived soon thereafter. We told them, simply, that Kleist had suddenly collapsed. They inspected our papers and took us in for questioning.

"You're both American," SS *Standartenführer* Wilhelm Richter said, examining our passports.

"Yes," I answered.

"You work for a jewelry firm?"

"Yes. It was founded by a German, Bernhard Froebel, in 1912."

"Ah. Did you see a van in the vicinity?"

"A van?"

"A van used by a touring company of Jewish freaks. They're permitted to live solely for their entertainment value to the troops."

Ellen and I said we hadn't seen a van.

Richter wheeled on me. "How do you explain the burn marks on Dr. Kleist's neck?" he shot out.

I looked puzzled. "Burn marks?"

"Marks of a rope."

"I don't know. He was clutching at his collar, fighting for breath."

"Are you keeping anything back?" he demanded.

"Nothing. Why should I keep anything back?"

"And you?" he asked, eyeing Ellen sharply.

"It happened just as my husband described it. I've nothing to add; except perhaps the burn marks were from a previous injury."

Richter held us a little longer while his staff checked our papers. Then he released us. There was no motive to link us with Kleist's death. He had a cardiac history, which lent plausibility to a sudden attack. Two SS men drove us back to the house.

The ownership of the house passed to an heir. Ellen and I remained for several months before returning home. As for "the others," it was the last we ever saw of them.

Enemy
Transmissions

Tom Shippey

They make jokes about the Adolf Hitler schools, you know. Like the one where the London policeman comes on this little boy with his black shirt and shorts on, sobbing his heart out on the pavement. "What's the matter, sonny?" asks the policeman. "I'm lo-o-ost," the little boy wails. "Well, where do you come from?" "I come from *Chiswick.*" "Well, what are you doing all the way over here in Bow?" "Oh," he says, starting to cry all over again, "I've just been to a leadership conference."

It's all in good humor, though. People really recognize that we Hitlerchildren are taught to be self-reliant so that we are more free to serve the nation and the community. That's what National Socialism is all about. That's what I was telling myself, anyway, as my train finally drew in to Oxford this afternoon.

I admit that I had started the journey from "Garterhouse" in Church Stretton in a much worse mood. I'd been furious when they hauled me off the glider range just before I got my turn. When *Onkel* Eric the Director told me to pack my bag and go to Oxford, I'd have to finish my course later, well, I was thunderstruck.

Two things changed my mind. One was the growing realization that even passing out as a full member of the Hitler Order might be less important than being selected for training as a Dreamer. The other, though, the incident that changed my feelings right round, was what happened at Worcester.

Our train was just a little local cross-country job, so I paid no attention when they pulled us over to a siding at Worcester station. But then I realized people were coming out of the houses along the line, and out of the waiting rooms and the stationmaster's office, and calling to their friends to hurry, so I walked over and stuck my head out of the window of my empty compartment.

This enormous train was coming toward me at a fast walking pace. Everything about it was silver, even the wheels and bogies, except for the giant black diesel pulling it. Marked alternately all down the line of wagons were the violet trefoil for radiation and the black swastika for the Party. It was an Atom Service train taking nuclear waste up from the powerplant at Bristol, I'd guess, to the disposal areas in the Scottish highlands.

As the train started to come through the station, a whistle blew and the troopers of the Atom Service came smartly out of their cabooses and down on to the bottom step. People were cheering and waving to them, and they grinned and waved back. They all had machine-pistols slung over their shoulders, and there was a Bugeye spotter plane looping very slowly overhead, as there would be every inch of the journey. All strictly speaking unnecessary, of course, since there has never been *any* injury, accident, loss, or theft at any point of the whole nuclear-power project in all of Europe. But the secret behind that record is simply thoroughness: and dedication. Running the whole thing as if every part of it were a Swiss watch. That's what we Germans are good at. Anyone who doesn't believe it can just look the other side of the Atlantic.

Well, I thought, if those men can spend their lives sitting on piles of plutonium, I can report for Dreamer training. And when it comes to it, there can hardly be any more important or honorable occupation. It is the most Germanic science, the one that marks us out from all other races. I've even heard it said that without *Traumtechnik* Adolf Hitler would not have steered us Germans—us Greater Germans, that is—through to coalition and victory over the East and America in 1946! It sounds a bit disloyal even to think that. But what I mean is that it was a fantastic achievement for the *Führer* to pick his way through all the things that could have gone wrong to the one right path, the best of all possible worlds. Yet he did it, and it's not disloyal at all to recognize that achievement.

So, by the time the train throbbed into Oxford station and I piled out with my bag and the address of the Institute for Dream Technology, I was in a much better frame of mind. I was beginning to think maybe I was someone special.

The man at the "dreamtank" seemed to think so, too. His name was Raven—Dr. Edward Raven, he told me—made Director of Dream Analysis on secondment from his Oxford college. He was quite a young man, born I should think just about the time of the second *Anschluss* between Britain and Germany. He had all my file in front of him.

"Your name's Grenville," he said. "Isn't that a French name?" Of course, people always try that one on.

"It's a Norman name," I told him. "It shows that a town in Normandy was held by a Viking called Grani in personal fief. That shows I've had good blood for a thousand years."

"And you are a Lifeswell boy," he went on.

"Yes. My mother decided it was her duty to the *Führer* to give him her first child. So she went to the 'Lifeswell' foundation in Clerkenwell and conceived by an accredited father there. That was in 1964." I didn't rub it in that my mother did it for the first *Führer* personally, not for a successor, though she was always proud of being one of the last who could say that.

Then he went on through my career as a Hitlerchild and my progress through the Party, but we both knew the point was made. You couldn't get better stock than me. Even so I was surprised they thought I was a Dreamer.

"Germanic science," he told me, "has shown that having prophetic dreams is a strongly inherited quality. It is a matter of mental coordination." Actually he used the German word *Gleichschaltung,* which I think is better. "Coordination" is a feeble Latin word with no heart in it. But if you are *gleichgeschaltet,* you are "like-connected," switched through, like a telephone call zooming all the way down the line. And some minds, Raven said—preeminently the *Führer's*—are switched through all the way to the future.

"What would have happened," Raven asked me as he got excited, "if Hitler had not realized this in 1941 from his intensive study of the works of Carl Jung? He might not have rushed on the Me 262, the jet fighter! He could have wasted money on Von Braun and his ridiculous no-punch cruising bombs. He might have tried to continue the *Blitzkrieg* on and on into Russia, instead of adopting the 'East Goth' policy and allowing the Ukraine to qualify for Germanization. He might not have seen the potential of the schnorkel device and so allowed Churchill's clique to hang onto power in this country. But all those things, all those policies or inventions, were adopted entirely as a result of *Traumtechnik.*

"And I'm telling you, Grenville," he went on, lowering his voice a bit. "Matters are just as critical now. We may not seem to be at war. But the pace of research and change has been heating up steadily. If we do the wrong thing now—well, all I'll say is that the Germanic countries, the *Europverein,* could fall behind the Americans and their mongrel allies in very serious ways.

"Fortunately they have only material science, where we have psychic science, too. That's why we've been testing the population as a whole. We're sure both your parents are *Träumer,* and as far as we can tell your grandparents also showed flashes of the ability. You have it all through your genes, and you're the right age to develop and utilize it. And here at Oxford we have trained analysts like myself, with years of experience at the IAA in Berlin, to pick out what's vital."

I felt slightly funny as all this explanation was going on, because it seemed so *right.* He told me about the drugs and the recording devices and the way they have of trying to guide the dreams into set areas, but when he'd finished I asked him if all that was necessary for a really talented Dreamer. Because the fact was that I'd had a very odd dream recently, and it seemed to be about a war, a future war—not one I'd ever heard of. He was very interested straight away, and got a tape recorder and asked me to tell him all about it.

Dream Transcript, RAG(i)
12th June 1985, Oxford

I was in a big metal compartment, like a hangar. I'm pretty sure I was in a ship—there was that faint sort of vibration through the metal, though it must have been a big ship because I didn't notice any rolling. But the real reason I think it was a ship was that I felt terribly conscious of what was outside, and how thin the walls were. This is the surprising thing about the dream—I was afraid in it, really frightened. Even in the dream I thought this was peculiar. I've never been in a war, but I've always assumed I could manage as well as the next man, and I've never been frightened in training for anything. But in this dream I was cold, and sweating, and shaking all over, and I didn't want to talk to anyone. I kept thinking how thin the walls were, and how something could smash through them any moment and let the sea in.

I was expecting something to do that, because we were at war. I was wearing a coverall with a hood, in some sort of antiflash fabric, and I had something strapped round me like a lifejacket. I had the impression that everything had been going well, but now there was trouble.

The main thing that actually happened in the dream was this: not very far away, like a deck or a couple of compartments distant, I heard a growl. Not a bang or a crash, but a growl that rose from nothing to very loud in about two seconds, and then faded into the distance. I knew that was a missile launch. It made me even more scared, because I knew it was a defensive missile launch, to intercept something hostile—a plane maybe, but I thought it was another missile. I knew they didn't always work.

The other thing I had in my head was the idea of "chaff," or maybe "window." I meant clouds of metal strips launched to confuse an attacker's radar and divert their missiles. Someone had fired this, but I wondered how long it would stay up and whether you had to keep on firing it.

That's really all I can say about the dream—it was more a state than an action. But it's bothered me ever since I had it four weeks ago because it just doesn't sound like anything I ever heard of. The ship was a thin-skinned surface vessel, I think an aircraft carrier, and we don't have any now. What use would they be, with the Atlantic and Pacific entirely covered by satellites and subs? But it can't have been a carrier from the An-schluss war, because she was firing missiles, and they didn't have them then. The dream just doesn't fit any situation I've ever heard about. And it wasn't me in that dream. The person in the dream was a coward: or anyway he was a civilian inside, completely untrained.

The only other thing I can remember is a voice saying very softly, "South Atlantic." Next day I looked at a map and thought about the Falkland Islands. But there hasn't been a battle there since 1914, and they didn't have missiles then. I can't make sense of it, sir, strategically. Who would want to send a war fleet to the Falklands?

A few days later I was in a bar in Oxford with this girl Else, also a trainee Dreamer. It was one of those places with a big TV screen over the bar itself, and the sound coming from individual speakers in the booths that you can turn up or down as you want. They were showing a news program about Ethiopia, with the young Emperor opening up a giant irrigation complex, stage number seventy-something in the whole "Green Africa" plan. Else was a bit puzzled about it.

"Didn't Mussolini conquer Ethiopia?" she asked.

"Yes, but the English threw him out, and after we changed sides the *Führer* decided not to depose Haile Selassie all over again. So the Ethiopians got their independence a bit before the rest of Africa and Asia. Under European hegemony, of course. It was all part of the policy of *Konflikt-losigkeit.*" You still can't quite say "conflictlessness" in English.

"All part of *Traumtechnik,* too," said Else, and she was dead right. It just goes to show . . . if you want any proof of what a good idea limited independence for backward countries is you only have to look over at the US client states in South America. Of course, the Yankees don't call them "backward," they say they're "developing," instead, but what developing can they do when all their money is sucked away and their independence is only good for fighting each other? Giant airports built with American aid. No roads between the airports because they have no industrial infrastructure. *Hacienda* owners and shanty cities. Tanks and planes, but no sewers. Drought and plague and starvation. We Europeans just wouldn't let our neighbors perish like that.

Just about then the program on the TV changed as most of the customers in the bar pressed their buttons to show they wanted the Olympic Games coverage from Peking, with Diego Pereira running for the Germanic Federation—he comes from Andalusia, of course, and has Vandal blood just as I have Norman. Else and I pressed our buttons to show we wanted Channel 1 back, but we were outvoted. Of course, the bar could have put individual screens in with the speakers, but that wouldn't have been *völkisch*. Under National Socialism we all have to muck in, and fair enough.

So I turned over to the real job, which was pumping Else. Not physically pumping her, though I had that on my mind, too—she was very ethnic and attractive with her braided hair and her tan, and I knew she'd been a member of the Maiden's League, known to one and all as "the Mattresses." But it was up to her to make the first move, of course, and anyway I wanted her to talk. She'd been dreaming under controls for a couple of weeks already, while I was to start that night.

"The drugs are pretty mild," she told me. "They don't want you to sleep deeply at all. It feels to me—I don't know. As if you have to be at just the right *level*, not too far down, not so near the surface that you just dream about what happened during the day. The hard part is when they wake you up and you have to start talking right off. You have to get the whole experience of the dream across, because you never know what bit of information is most vital—that's the analyst's job. But you mustn't go all disciplined and military about it, because then there's a danger of organizing and interpreting the facts yourself instead of letting them flow through."

"Have *you* had any foresight dreams?" I asked.

"I think so. They won't tell you. Of course, they don't know for sure till much later. But I think you can *feel* a true dream. There's always something rough-edged about it."

She clammed up after that, and told me I'd learn soon enough. I expect she was right. She was a good comrade after all, as girls are allowed to be nowadays. So we bought each other a couple of beers, and fortunately after that she decided to take me back to the compound and demonstrate her mattress-technique till it was time for the *Traumtank*.

It was her night off, so she didn't come with me. As I walked out of the room, she said, "Watch out, Richard. They call it the traumatank, too." She didn't mean to be unnerving, I'm sure.

Dream Transcript, RAG 1
22nd June 1985, Oxford

It's black, black dark, and the whole place smells. Some of it is hay, and a horsey smell, but also dirt and sweat. The whole place smells poor, some-how, as if the people in it—there are three or four others round me—haven't eaten anything solid for a long time and couldn't hold it if they did. Their sweat smells bad.

I'm lying on very prickly straw, and wearing a complete suit of clothes. It's odd, because it's night, and anyway I'm wearing a suit, a formal suit, with jacket and trousers and a collarless shirt. It's all filthy dirty. I need a shave.

But the main thing is I have this dreadful erection. It is dreadful, it makes me feel sick down at the bottom of my stomach, and I keep going cold. Why is that? All I know is that I'm really frightened that the door over there is going to creak open and let in just a little light, and then—then the Frau will be there. And what do I do then? I know I'll have to go with her. But I know that will be absolutely terrible. The other men know, too, but they passionately want me to go. Something tells me I am the youngest.

I can see the door outline now and there's someone outside. My stomach feels so bad I pull my knees up and groan just once, and my penis sticks straight up along my belly. It's the only thing about me that feels fat. It's as if—I want to go because I'm young and I keep getting terrible fantasies about bending the Frau over her armchair and screwing her till she calls to God for mercy. But I know I mustn't, I mustn't give way, there's no chance at all I'll get away with it. But the other men won't let me back out, though they know there's no chance, too. They won't snigger at me, they'll be terribly grateful tomorrow, when we get a little extra ration and less work, but they won't leave me alone for a second, they won't let me use my hand on it, because—

The door is open now. There's a shape in the dark outside, with a candle.
"Komm," she says, just that. There are hands pushing me. I'm on my feet.
As I go to the door, there's something in my head again, a kind of tree
with three branches, and a village square and a little crowd watching. God,
God, if I had only been born a woman . . .

Raven didn't make much of that dream, I'm pretty sure. I asked him
what it was about—telling the dreams seems to fix them in your memory
—but all he did was grunt and say *"Pölnische Wirtschaft."* That means
"Polish management," which is what people used to say for chaos, or a
complete cock-up. Maybe that's the connection? Anyway there aren't any
Poles now, they've all either qualified for Germanization or been sent east
across the Urals. One thing I am sure of, though. That was a true dream.
Not one of mine. Like the South Atlantic one, the character in it just was
not me.

Raven is still pretty dissatisfied. There is an air of tension throughout
the Institute now, with more trainee Dreamers appearing every day, and a
whole string of portable cabins set up for them to dream in, and no one
allowed to go into Oxford when they're off duty. We all have to keep up
with the news and world situation, and work through the papers every day,
and read *Neuer Wissenschaftler* and *Scientific Europe.* We attend lectures
and discussions with outside speakers, too, and every now and then we are
called in to give our conscious understanding of the world situation to one
of the staff members. Someone has got the University Engineering computer to write "Chance only favors the prepared mind" in giant Gothic
script on a banner, which is now hung over the high table in messhall.
Else finds all this hilarious.

I told them all at one of these briefings that my understanding of the
world situation was this. There were three nuclear powers in the world—
the Germanic Federation, the United States of America, and Japan, in
about that order of strength. Each has a hinterland of subject states, with
differing degrees of independence. Ours is Africa and the East as far as
India, the USA has Canada and the whole of South America, Japan has
China and the Asiatic seaboard, and all the Asian islands. Nobody bothers
about the central Asiatic landmass, which is sheer barbarism. The big
powers are all separated from each other by the Atlantic, Pacific, and
Indian oceans.

Now, ever since Rolls-Royce developed the ramscoop for hydrox engines, and everyone else pinched the idea, manned satellites have been in
use for observation, so these oceans are completely covered. They're alive
with hunter-killer submarines, too, so there's no chance of any power

reaching another by plane or ship. We can all hit each other with ICBMs, and to this there is no known defense. *But,* there is a strong feeling that someone is just on the edge of one. We are in space. Could we fix it to knock down the ICBMs at the top of their trajectory, with lasers, or maybe ball-bearings? Could we strafe all the American bases at once with space-launched missiles? Could we be sure they wouldn't retaliate from space on our cities? If we do attack, instead of defend, we have to be absolutely sure of a clean sweep.

That's what they want us to dream about. After I'd said all that, Raven got up at the back and said Grenville had expressed the state of opinion about as far as a *Beobachter* leader-writer could go (which is quite a compliment, I think, though he meant it to be insulting). But we had to remember things never turned out like that. What I'd said had built into it the notion that the edge of human technology could be decisive. But edges are too risky, too complicated, and at the same time too familiar for practical politics. You should either be a little back from the edge, for reliability, or a good way past it, for surprise. The war of German Unification, he pointed out, was won by two devices, the German atom bomb, which was completely unexpected, and the Me 262 jet fighter, which was based on a device the Royal Air Force could have had in the 1930s, but paid no attention to. The A-bomb made England change sides and throw out the Yanks, but no one could use an A-bomb on Germany or Japan because the 262s had complete air domination over the Allied bombers. We need something like that combination now, he told us. There are things known already that the mere material scientists have missed. And there are "blue sky" projects everywhere, which no one knows if they will work.

That was his grammar, not mine. He talks like that sometimes to show he's *völkisch,* but also he was very excited, glaring round as if we were all on trial. I think he is the one on trial. No results, no Institute. And they want results quick.

"What we want from you," he wound up, "is a sword and a shield."

"Won't just a shield do?" asked one of the new boys. He is not a Hitlerchild, but went to one of those decadent institutions the Party hasn't put a stop to, like Harrow or Winchester.

"We need a sword as well," Raven ground at him. "It is not in the nature of the Germanic race to sit passively."

"Then you need something in addition," the aristo told him. "You'll need a pretext."

Dream Transcript, RAG 7
1st July 1985, Oxford

Holy Woden, but I get tired of the clothes they keep giving me in these dreams! And the people. This time I am putting on a uniform, perfectly familiar, it's feldgrau and I can tell I'm a sergeant of infantry in summer field order. But the blockhead in the uniform can't cope with it all. He buttons the tunic the wrong way round, he doesn't know what the buckles on the webbing are for, and damn me if he doesn't try to get his boots on the wrong feet. All the time I'm sitting about a foot above his right shoulder shouting at him what to do, and some of it even gets through, but slow and wrong and clumsy.

Then we're out of the barracks and walking, a line of us with me in front, along the edge of a wood. It's dark, but the sky is paling to my right, that must be the East. Someone has given me a rifle that I'm carrying with two hands across my body. I can't see if it's an auto, or if it's loaded, and I keep yelling at smearsack to lift it up, but all he does is fumble round the breech as if he's looking for something. He keeps stopping and glancing back, and the rest of the men stop, too, and look around, but then they seem to be shunted on, and blunder forward, not spaced out or even bunched up or in any formation soldiers would take, just like a herd of cows walking along a hedge. These are very peculiar soldiers, especially German soldiers. How could doodlekopf get to be a sergeant?

He's noticed something. There are more people over to his right, all in uniform, too, with weapons in their hands. Behind them, as the sky lightens, I can see towers rising, and wire between the towers, it looks like a radio station, some kind of old radio station, or is that a radar dish . . .

But dimbulb is pleased, terribly pleased, he's running forward to the men in the brown uniforms as if he's recognized someone, they're all calling out to each other, maybe twenty yards apart. I smell a rat somehow, I try to turn him round and lift the rifle, the other men have caught on, too, and they're all starting to scatter. There's a winking from the wood behind and I see the men in the brown uniforms start to fall over, but the towers are winking, too, and there's an enormous long bra-a-ang sound under my feet and I'm lifting up in the air, turning slowly, and I'd like to flip-somersault and land on my feet like we do at vaulting, but what can I do with dumm-stumm here, he's too stiff and slow and . . .

That's that.

Raven is furious with me, but it's a kind of controlled fury, and it's also as if he really likes me, and knows I like him, and just wants me to do something I easily could, if only I could get the hang of it. "We know you're a true Dreamer, Richard," he says. "I won't tell you how we know, but this is a science not just a parlor game, and I can tell from your readings you're picking something up. But all you want to use your talent for is this *Suppentopfschnüffelei*, this snuffling into other people's soup pots. There's nothing important there. That dream you had about the aircraft carrier and the missiles growling, I think that was a really good one. You know, for a while we wondered if you'd been in a spaceship, not a sea-going vessel at all, and I had people checking on sound effects and whether you could have worn something in space that your conscious mind would interpret as a lifejacket. If you'd had that dream here we could have got something vital out of it, something that could have given a hint to the whole War Council. But since then it's all been trivial. I don't know what you're picking up. You remember what I told you about *Gleichschaltung*, well, what you need is some *Selbstgleichschaltung*. Coordinate yourself. Switch yourself through."

Then he went off to shout at someone else, but I have to admit he's right. I went off after our interview and found Else, who has picked up with the aristo from Winchester who talked back to Raven, whose name is Charlie Kent. Now that we are all shut in the compound all the time, relationships are getting very intense, and also changing very fast. Not that I am offended by Else. In fact, I can even understand what she sees in Kent. He is an awkward *kerl* and he speaks his mind, but at least he has got one.

I caught them reading the *Times* and the *Beobachter*, as per orders, and asked them what they thought of it. Kent told me straight off he thought we were edging toward a war. "How can we have a war?" I asked him. "There's nowhere to fight it. There's no chance of a revolt against us in Africa, or in Arabia. How could the natives defy European troops? And the Americans couldn't reinforce anyone in our hinterlands any more than we could smuggle soldiers into Brazil. They can push a submarine over now and then to test out our sea-patrols, but that's the only theater of conflict."

"There's space," he said. "But the real trouble is that I was wrong about needing a pretext. It's got past that. Both sides—leaving out the Japanese—are a match now, but both are just on the edge of a decisive superiority, it has to strike while things are equal. Or else surrender. No one thinks they can stay equal for long."

"What is the American edge?" I asked.

"They are better than us at electronic countermeasures," he said, straight out. "Also at computing. Maybe they would be capable of taking out all our warhead guidance systems with magnetic pulses. Then we might hit America, but we wouldn't hit what we aimed at. And the trend has been to smaller and smaller warheads with more precise guidance systems."

"What's our edge?" I asked.

"We are," he said. "If you look at the record, Germany has shown astonishing ability to win with inferior resources ever since 1939. That's because nothing has been wasted and effort has always gone into the right place, which was rarely where educated opinion said it should."

"That's because we have a divine destiny," said Else, her eyes shining. Kent looked at the sunflower pattern on her tunic, and at the glory-rune on my bracelet, which my father gave me at the youth dedication ceremony when I was a baby, and raised his eyebrows, like these aristos do. I think his family must still be Christians of the old sort, not neopagans or even Aryan Christians.

I was still interested in what he said. There must be a dingstbrums in the works somewhere. A neutron resonator, to make warheads blow up on site? A radiation sniffer that could guide light projectiles down from space to every single silo, even if all they did was jam the doors? Something wilder than that. I sat and read for a while about the HEIMDALL project, to build a really gigantic telescope in space, with such advanced light-gathering and coordinating properties that you could even see planets round other stars. It's named after the god in the Edda who could see the grass growing and the breath from a fish's mouth. But if you turned that round the other way . . . you could see every missile site in America, that's for certain sure, and there'd be no risky edge-of-technology stuff in that.

And then there's RATATOSKR, named after the squirrel in the Edda who runs up and down the branches of the world-ash, passing messages to all and sundry. They say that the joint Swiss Universities satellite has put considerable effort into listening for alien communications. If anything came through on that, what might we get? Contragravity? Psychic amplifiers? Have they tried transmitting dream-waves, I wondered? Or listening for them?

I nearly fell asleep during the day, which is very verboten indeed, thinking about the whiskers of the squirrel reaching out across space to pick up what we have to know. I hope I am getting myself *gleichgeschaltet* now.

Dream Transcript, RAG 8
4th July 1985, Oxford

This person is carrying grief around like a dead fetus. It sits there at the base of her abdomen, not shifting or moving or trying to get out, but pulling her forward all the time with its weight. It's there even when she's forgotten what she's grieving for. And then she remembers, and all she wants to do is sit and let the grief pull her face down to the table so she can weep.

But she doesn't do that, ever, instead she squares her shoulders and holds her head up and walks down the street listening to the other women and answering them back, "Yes, Frau Ott, it is a trial, but if my Johann has the strength to bear his fate, I must have the strength to bear mine, No, Frau Werner, there is no official confirmation yet, we cannot expect one in the nature of things, I will not participate in the Heroes Remembrance Day ceremony this year, Certainly Frau Luschke, I will be most happy to contribute to the street winterhilfe *collections and to the one-pot meal organization." She keeps her head back and her chin up, and when she goes home she takes care to rub out the dents and cuts where her fingernails dig into the palm all the time.*

All the time, too, she knows there is a way out. There is a voice out there in the black that could tell her what she needs to know, but it is the enemy's voice, and even if it says what she wants to hear, to open to it is making a chink in the armor, letting in a line of communication that could send who knows what along it. It must not be. But the others know, too, the silly women in the shops with their foolish shapeless bearing and their civilians' faces, and one day someone sidles up to her in the bread-queue and starts to mutter, "Frau Edel, you don't know me, but I know about you and your predicament, now I know it wouldn't be right for you but surely it can be for me, after all we are neighbors. Anyway, what I have to say is he's all right, they send out these lists you know and I think you can trust them, well they got his name right and everything. Excuse me, I mustn't say any more, but just the same it's true, he's all right, and maybe he'll be able to come home, you know, afterward. . . ." Off she scuttles, like a little mouse that's laid down a crumb before the cat.

And the grief goes. It goes immediately, like a bubble that's pricked, and only as it goes can you feel the solid weight that's been there all the time. But as she walks back with the black heavy bread in her bag, she's thinking, and she's feeling something else, this time an anger, and it's high up in her chest not low down in the belly. Why should she have suffered all that time, and for nothing? How dare that other woman take her suffering away

*from her, and make it worth nothing, like a gesture, a few words of polite-
ness that nobody means? She does not go to her apartment with the shining
surfaces and the shut windows, no, she walks on to the Town Hall and the
office where the* Ortsleiter *sits.*

*Later the women in the bread-queue jostle her and look angrily as if they
would like to shout, and the bread ration is seventy grams short and
slammed down on the counter like a brick, but she faces them all down and
starts to walk away. Only when she gets to the door something breaks and
she turns round and starts to scream at them, Don't you understand, if you
let them through on one thing you'll let them through on all, we mustn't
take anything from them, not even a name . . .*

*They just bunch and stare at her silently and in the end she goes away,
trying to put her hat on straight again where the pin has got dislodged. But
as she goes, the boys in the street, not yet military age, not in the uniform of
the* Jugend *even, they look at her and hold out their left arms and chop
down on them with the blades of their right hands. There is no guillotine
here, they take them all to* Gau *headquarters now, according to the new
regulations.*

Places of execution are no longer to be mentioned on Rundfunk *transmissions, in case they should become adversely associated with necessary
measures of repression.*

Something funny happened after that last dream, because I can't remember anything about it at all. I think they must have given me another
dose of something, to knock me out properly. I woke up on the morning of
the 5th still in my *Traumtank* bed, but I couldn't even remember getting
into it. It must be a good sign. I thought straightaway that I must have got
through to something they didn't want me talking about to the others—or
maybe they didn't even want me speculating about to myself, in case it
affected my reactions another time.

Raven confirmed this by coming in as I was getting up. He was polite,
which is unusual, and sort of calm, as if he'd made a decision about
something. He told me I could go back to the compound, but I'd be
dreaming again tonight, and if events were successful I might well be
transferred the following morning to the IAA itself, the *Institut für
Anerkennung und Analyse* in Berlin. "You've got beyond me now," he
said in a jokey sort of way. "You can tell your friends they may not be
seeing you for a while.

"One more thing," he said on the way out. "I'm arranging a special
briefing for you late this afternoon, just time enough for the information

to be absorbed. Come over with your bag packed. You won't be able to talk to anyone after the briefing."

I went over to see Else, rather hoping she would feel obliged to give me a passionate farewell, but she had Kent with her. He didn't seem terribly pleased, or even impressed, by what I told him. He said nothing for a long time, and then all that came out was "Well, look after yourself, Richard." As if I could, even if I wanted to! They say round the messhall that he's been having bad dreams, and not only when he's on duty.

The briefing, when it came, was really remarkable. There were two people besides Raven. One said nothing at all, but just looked at me. Measured is more the word. He kept looking at me, and then dropping his eyes to a folder, and looking back again. After a bit he just started turning over the pages. But I lost interest in him as soon as the other one started talking.

He told me he was from the Advanced Weapons Research Laboratory at Munich, where nearly all the big breakthroughs have been made—not the Rolls-Royce ramscoop, it's true, but the ERWIN satellite system and the "free-fall" flying crowbar missiles and the MERMAID sub-detectors and all that sort of thing. His job, he said, was to brief Dreamers of real potential. I wondered for a moment how many of us there were floating around.

"What you have to understand," he said, "is that the Yanks have a President who is completely gaga. He thinks he's in the Wild West, for God's sake. If they want to attract his attention for any weapon system, they have to call it by some name out of the Billy the Kid comics.

"Well, there are some we know about. One is GHOST SHIRT, which is a system of point defense for ICBM launchers against any sort of missile attack. They reckon they can see the missiles coming, even from space, compute times and trajectories, and knock them down without atomics or even explosives, just ram into the missile and spill it all over America in bits, if it doesn't vaporize. We think that's a good system, very likely to work, but only against attacks of the sort now foreseeable.

"We are more worried about some of the others. We've heard, for instance, of SUNDANCE. This could easily be disguised as a peaceful project, not that anyone would be fooled. They would send up satellites to collect solar power and beam it down to special receiver banks in the form of microwaves. It could work, too, and they need it, especially as they're running out of oil and their nuclear-energy program is so bad, with all the accidents and meltdowns. But once they have this stuff up in the sky, what's to prevent them having a guidance malfunction, eh? They could

present it as an accident, but you could have a city cooked without any
prospect of interception."

"We would still retaliate," I said.

"Yes, we would. SUNDANCE would be best against civilian and unpro-
tected targets. But there are rumors also of BUCKSHOT. We think their
Mars landing program is a blind for this. If they have manned ships
working out in the solar system where we can't even see them—or not till
HEIMDALL is operational—they might be able to locate small asteroids
and alter their orbit enough to make Earth-impact."

"And what would happen then?"

"A strike by a major boulder, even, in the center of an ICBM 'dense
pack' would take it out for certain. If they could fire a shotgun-spread of
them . . . and at the same time operate SUNDANCE against our communications and GHOST SHIRT against what we managed to launch,
they could expect to get off with minor damage, while we, of course,
would be helpless. And then we'd get DOG SOLDIER."

"What's that?"

"Using the Russians." Nobody made any comment on that at all. The
Slavs who failed to qualify for Germanization have been held east of the
Urals for forty years, but we all know they'd like nothing better than to
come at our throats, if it's only with bows and arrows.

"And us?" I asked. "What do we have?"

Then he told me about MJOLLNIR and BIFROST and
SJALFVEGIR. These are all names from Norse Germanic mythology, the
hammer of Thor, the rainbow path to the home of the gods, and the
sword the dwarves made for Frey, lord of fertility. I don't think I ought to
put down anything about them in clear, even in a daybook, but I took it as
a great mark of confidence that they were prepared to discuss such things
with me. I'm not surprised they're kept secret from *Beobachter* leader-
writers!

"You see," Raven told me at the end, "we are letting you right in to the
center. We expect something big in return. Dream well, Richard. It is
more important than you know—even to you."

Dream Transcript, RAG 9
5th July 1985, Oxford

A face, looking at me. It could be quite a handsome face, if there was
something behind it, but as soon as you look at it you know the spirit is

missing. *The whole face is too round, and the mouth drops open a little, and while one eye stares straight at you with a kind of honest interest, the other is just a tiny bit off, as if the owner can't keep both at once from wandering. The hair is clipped all round the forehead and the temples as if to make the face look even rounder. But above all it's the skin. It looks loose, as if the tiny muscles underneath it have never worked. They say you use seventeen muscles to smile, and if you only use sixteen of them, people can tell at once you don't mean it. That's why acting is such a hard trade. This face smiles all the time, but it never means it. Its coordination has gone.*

Not just the face either, because the face's owner has an arm, too, and the arm is holding a short iron bar. Not at the right place, near the end, but too near the point of balance. Still, it's trying to strike with it, stiffly and clumsily, with no wrist movement, but pushing out from the shoulder, with a grunt, again and again, beginning to stamp with the right foot at the same time. White slaver is beginning to come from the face, and a look of wild excitement is coming into its eye.

In front of the face—here, I can tell what he is! He has the black uniform and the silver braid and the double runic S on his collar. This is a Rottenführer *of an SS* Einsatzkommando. *What is this dream trying. . . . Yes, yes, I'll go on before it fades.*

A crowd of people has come out into the square. They look nervous, and the men are wearing hats and have black beards. Look, doctor, they're Jews, I've seen pictures of them. [At this point the subject became extremely disturbed and required reassurance and encouragement.] *Well, the Jews are looking at the lunatics and the lunatics are edging toward the Jews, but they don't seem to know what to do.*

The Rottenführer's *lost patience now, he steps forward and*—this can't be a true dream, it must be some kind of enemy transmission—*he hits a Jewish child on the side of the head with an iron bar. His coordination is perfect, like a tennis-player, and the child goes down at once, she's dead. Now the lunatics have got the idea, they're trotting forward, but the Jews don't seem quite ready to run away. One is shouting something at the* Rottenführer, *a woman has gone down on her knees and is clutching at him, but the rest have started to scatter, only now it's too late. They're all mixed up. I can see one of the lunatics astride an old man, he's trying to hit him on the side of the head, he is hitting him, but there's no swing at all in his blows, it's more a kind of grinding, with the blood running from a dozen cuts at once, but the old man is still wriggling and trying to get his face out of the dirt.*

Everyone is running around the square now, except for those who have

been caught, they're dodging in and out of the vehicles and gun-limbers
that are parked here and there. Some of them have got up to the windows of
the one big house at one edge of the square, and there are two men looking
out. One is young, an aide-de-camp, a captain. The other is a general, a
lieutenant-general I think, looking down with contempt and disgust on his
face. The younger man is pointing, talking to him, begging him to order it
stopped. I can hear him shouting, "They are killing women and children in
the street outside Headquarters." The general turns away, he flicks his fingers to a private standing by the window.

Outside the lunatics hunt the Jews through the village square of Karno,
while the Einsatzkommando watches. Inside the Wehrmacht plan the next
stage of the drive on Moscow.

What did the general say? He said, "Draw the curtains."

But who would give iron bars to madmen?

Final report on subject Dreamer
Richard Adolf Grenville,
dictated by Edward Raven, Director of Analysis,
Institute for Dream Technology, Oxford

It is clear that the subject—as he diagnosed himself in dream RAG 8
(q.v.)—was a species of *Feindhörer*, that is to say, one who listens with
credulity to enemy transmissions, an offense punished with the greatest
severity on the Axis side during the Unification War.

The real questions are, where did the subject derive his dreams, and
why did he persist in following such a perverse line, in spite of apparent
surface loyalty and desire to cooperate?

As for the first question, it is not clear whether the subject was describing real events or not. To take dream RAG 9, it is known that there *is* a
village in Russia named Karno. However, German armies never reached it,
and there was of course no Wehrmacht drive on Moscow. It is impossible
to state whether an *Einsatzkommando* would or would not have carried
out such actions as those described, within the overall policy of *End-
lösung,* or "final solution." One has to remember that Grenville's other
dreams of the Unification War, involving the case of the *Feindhörer* (RAG
8), the staged border provocation incident (RAG 7), and the measures
taken to prevent racial contamination by foreign forced labor (RAG 1),
seem in line with historical facts, though not relatable to single incidents.
There is also the puzzling case of the "Falklands" dream (RAG i), which is
neither history nor plausible future. The evident conclusion is that

Grenville dreams neither of what was, nor what will be, but of what *might have been:* reality, as it were, but transposed a quarter tone in the direction of horror.

As for the reason behind this perversity, we have succeeded in identifying this beyond question. Scrutiny of Somerset House records by the Federation archivists has proved beyond doubt that "Grenville" in this case is an anglicized form of German "Grünfeld." Such anglicizations were, however, resorted to in the 1930s only by those anxious to disguise connection with Germany, namely, Semitic refugees. We are now certain that Grenville's father, though made a "conception helper" on grounds of his excellent record in the Oilfields war, was the son of a Jew who had concealed his origin from all. Grenville is accordingly a *Mischling* and, it seems, a throwback. His case provides damning evidence against the American "environmentalist" school of psychology; strong evidence for the Germanic theory of genetic determination.

Knowledge of this fact opened the possibility of a final "sacrifice briefing" in the (vain) hope of eliciting one successful Dream. At the close of this Grenville was terminated by lethal injection, under the provisions of the Racial Purification Act, 1949.

His loss is to be regretted. However, it is clear that at a deep level he was incapable of participating in the sunlit German dream. Instead he preferred to wander in the byways of history, leading only to the forests of nightmare.

Valhalla

Gregory Benford

Adolf Hitler worked the action of the pistol. He clacked a round into the chamber. He stared at it.

Eva Braun numbly picked up the cyanide capsule from the table in front of them. She opened her mouth slightly and stared glassily at the small pill.

They sat on a rich red couch that stood out from the bleak gray concrete of the bunker walls. Hitler's face was puffy and waxen.

"Bite down hard," he said in a flat, rough way that was barely like the famous harsh, powerful voice of the ancient films.

He raised the muzzle of the Lüger to his temple. Eva sighed softly and opened her mouth again. So there were to be no last, loving words.

That was when I chose to materialize.

Hitler caught the ultraviolet flicker as I came into being before them. *"Ich sagt—"* he said harshly, rasping, and my pickups translated, "I said we were to be left for ten minutes—" and then he saw me.

I was gratified at his shock. I looked exactly like him.

I wore the same clothes, the general's gray field uniform, with the high-peaked hat. All details were correct, even down to the pale, sickly face and the trembling hand, a reminder of the assassination attempt by his own Army officers.

He pressed it against his left side. Echoing him, I did the same. I stepped over a broken wine bottle, my boots crunching on the glass, and said, *"Führer!* I have come to you across a thousand years to this, your supreme moment."

It was perhaps a bit florid, but our analysts had calculated that it would strike the correct note. There had been much high-flown, desperate rhetoric in these final days in Berlin. In his state of depression and nervous collapse Hitler could respond only to the most exaggerated of statements. He had ignored Albert Speer when the man came to make his farewell some days ago. Speer was an exact, cool type. Such a manner would not work for my purposes.

"I . . . you look. . . ." He waved the Lüger vaguely, eyes watery.

I moved swiftly and took the pistol. The primary thing to avoid was any sound that would cause the staff officers outside to open the heavy door. If they came in and found us, history would be altered and our entire scheme would fail. I would be flung forward into the future. Hitler would still kill himself, most probably, but the perturbation of the time flow would prevent us from ever returning to this moment.

"Yes, I can explain that," I murmured. "Madame?"

I leaned over Eva and gently lowered the hand that held the cyanide. She would not disturb events if she was treated formally; that much was clear from the personality profile we had reconstructed from historical data. She glanced at Hitler and began wringing her hands. On her face conflicting emotions warred, but there was no resoluteness, no projection of focused intelligence. I could see the psychotheorists had been wrong about her. She was no canny power behind the throne.

Hitler said, "If this is a plan of Goebbels—"

"Führer, this is no futile attempt—"

"I will *not* leave Berlin. I will not allow a, a *dummy* to take my place." He raised a trembling finger and shouted. "I will *not* run and sneak and hide from my subhuman enemies who—"

"Of course not. The world will respect what you do here."

"This cheap joke! You dressed up!—I will not have it!"

Hitler leaped to his feet, full of raving bantam energy. His eyes bulged with a sudden fury, more like the old films. I had to cut him off before the staff outside heard. It would mean a change in the scenario we had worked out, but that could not be helped.

"Immortality, *Führer!* That is what I offer. I have come to you from the future!"

He paused. "What . . . ?"

I rushed ahead. "Think of the times ahead, *Führer.* There will be glorious days again—I know. I have come from there. More than a thousand years from now you will be the most famous of all men from this time."

He faltered and the rage in him burned away. Exhaustion returned to the ruined face. "I . . . a thousand . . ."

I had lied only slightly about his fame. There was a physicist whose name had greater weight in our time, but it would not be wise to mention it. It was an odd coincidence that they both lived in the same land at the same time.

And a larger lie: I was not merely from a future age. Physics was not so simple. But subtleties such as that could scarcely penetrate the swarming mad mind I addressed.

Still, my own code of honor demanded that I make only minor excursions from the truth. I would have to be careful.

"Your world goals, *Führer*—would you like to know how they fared?"

"I . . . goals . . . .?" He seemed in a daze. "Jewry . . ."

"Yes! To cleanse Europe of Jewry! And the destiny of Germany, sir?"

"Deutschland . . . it is finished . . . their own weakness . . . not my doing . . . I gave my all . . . but there were . . . cowards . . . traitors . . . spies . . ."

"You fought to make Germany the dominant power in Europe, yes? I am able to tell you, *Führer*, that fifty years after this dark day, it was done!"

"Deutschland . . . destroyed . . . Berlin . . ."

"Jewry never returned to the body of Europe, *Führer!* They never returned to your homeland in such numbers again, ever." This was true, but not for the reasons he would imagine. "And Germany shall rise from its ashes. Its economy shall excel the Bolsheviks, equal the American capitalists within four decades."

He brightened. He looked at me and then at Eva. "Is this . . . can you be . . . Eva . . ."

"That is how the future of Europe will be. You have done your great task." I smiled and clicked my bootheels together.

He would not catch the irony in the gesture, or in the word "great"— he was too embedded in his own fantasies. Yet I had quite strictly told the truth. He had broken down the whole structure of the world he was born into, and left behind a Germany and a Europe deeply divided. These events were great in the sense of their size and implications. He would, of course, interpret the word in a different sense. That was what I expected, but it did not alter the fact that I had told the truth. To achieve a noble end one must keep to the truth.

Eva Braun said in a strained, thin voice, "Adolf, it is as you said it would be. Your faith . . ."

Hitler brightened, his eyes rolling with sudden fresh excitement. The man still had some crazed inner reserves. "Yes! I knew it! I held to the dream of Deutschland when all those around me failed. Indomitable! And this, this—"

"*Führer,* there is little time," I said rapidly, soothingly. "I come from a society you cannot envision, but in my time you are understood better than now." This, too, was true. We could analyze the past with the tools of exact sociometric theory. "We are devoted to justice. We look backward to your time and we see errors, great unfairness. My people have sent me to you, to correct injustice."

He frowned, blinked. He wavered, almost reeled. What fresh fantasies did my words summon up for him? His hands jerked, clasping at empty air.

As we had suspected, though there would be bursts of the old energy, he was near collapse. Probably he was unable to understand much of what I said. My subtle phrasings surely eluded him.

"For you to die here by your own hand, *Führer,* after all that you have done—such an outcome is, to my society, unthinkable." I smiled again.

Hitler's gaze shifted. For a moment I thought he was going to faint and all our hopes would be dashed.

But no—he was staring at the room behind me. It was the sitting room of his personal suite, crowded with curious wooden furniture. The dregs of parties—pieces of discarded clothing, bottles, half-finished plates of animal-flesh food—were scattered through it. But Hitler was staring at the blue aura behind me. I saw suddenly that it framed me in a halo of fire.

Hitler's eyes widened as this registered. He took a step forward. "Valkyrie!" he cried.

I calculated swiftly. *Valkyrie.* My translating subsystem told me that this meant, literally, the chooser of the slain. They were maidens who conducted the souls of heroes slain in battle to Valhalla.

In some deranged way Hitler thought the future I was describing was a Nordic heaven.

I was tempted to let him think so. But then I saw that to do so would be unjust to him. He had to make as informed a choice as was possible. Honor demanded that.

"No, *Führer,*" I said quickly. "You are not destined for Valhalla yet. There is no need to die. I—"

"I am the greatest warrior the world has ever seen!" He stiffened. Spine straight, he thrust out his chest. The smoldering fury kindled again. "I destroyed the Poles, the simpering French, the—"

"Of course, in our time we know this," I said in soothing tones. "Have no doubts. Though I come from more than a millennium in the future, this war remains the largest the world has ever seen." I did not add that the explosions to come in a few months would end forever the possibility of a rational large-scale conflict, and this fact more than any other made the Second World War so important an event.

"Adolf," Eva said soothingly, "this man is not a god. He says he is from the—"

"I heard! I saw a vision once . . . on the Rhine . . . the blue . . ."

He moved unsteadily to touch the ultraviolet shimmer behind me. I stepped aside, but the glow followed me. The portal was still centered on me and Hitler could not reach it. He grasped at it a few times and then vaguely let his arms drop.

"She is correct, sir," I said. "My society has sent me back to this moment to rescue you. Your life should not end here. I will take you into the far future, *Führer*. Into a more just world, where—"

His head snapped up. Abruptly he was the man he had once been, vibrant, possessed. "Very well! I see a glowing blue Valhalla and you tell me it is the future. These are names! Only names! I saw it there on the Rhine and now I see it for what it truly *is*—" He raised a finger, wagging it dramatically, as in the old days. "—And the dreams, my dreams are not finished. I knew it! Goebbels told me never to submit, and I have not! I have held on, and now you come for me. It is as I—"

There was a hollow knock at the door.

Hitler blinked and then smiled. He turned toward the door. "They . . . outside . . . if they can see this it will put backbone into my generals . . . I will . . ."

This was crucial. I put out a restraining hand. "No, it is not possible."

"What? If they see you, see—"

"*Führer*, history—the history of this particular world—depends on your staff never seeing you again. In their eyes you will die in here."

"I . . . do not . . ."

"It is the natural order of things. I have come to save you for the future. There is nothing more you can do for this Germany, this land that did not deserve you."

I spoke passionately, for I believed these words. They had their effect. Hitler nodded wearily and said raggedly, "Deutschland . . . did not stand by me . . . deserves this . . ."

Eva Braun said clearly, "This is why you are dressed so."

I nodded. She was more clever than the historians had thought. Intellectuals, they always underestimate the natural shrewdness of those in the distant past.

But Hitler ignored her remark. Perhaps with his damaged ears he had not even heard it. He smiled, mouth twisted into an arrogant smirk.

"I rescued Mussolini, yes? It is only right that some higher power should in turn save me, eh?" He paused, lost in his dulled thoughts. I remembered that Mussolini had been captured by partisans only a few days before, and shot, and then hung upside down in a marketplace with his mistress, for all the crowd to see. That memory was, we thought, the reason why Hitler and Eva Braun were taking this way out. But Hitler chose now to remember only his troops' rescue. This was typical of the irreality that pervaded his bunker in these last days.

"I am the architect of National Socialism and without me it will die, die, and . . ."

He was rambling now. I stepped backward, knocking aside a broken chair, and checked the parameter matrices around the blue corona of the portal. It detached from me and filled with motes of orange and yellow.

"I built it . . . there was no one else who saw the vision. . . ." He was right, of course. The other great doomed movement of the era had Marx and Lenin and Stalin, but National Socialism was the work of a single figure.

And all that was still roughly true, in my own timeline. The truth—far too technical to convey to this addled tyrant—was that I was not from *his* future. The laws of causality and of mass-energy conservation prevented me from diving directly into my own past. I had to trans-slip sidewise to this similar world, to move both in time and in probability-space. Otherwise causality paradoxes would rend me, atom from atom, in one curt crimson flash.

I came from an alternate world, in which Hitler's legions had mastered the Soviets. The crucial difference lay in the 1942 Churchill Treaty, which resolved the sluggish war on the western front, giving the German General Staff a free hand in the vast steppes of the East.

Only the American entrance in 1943, prompted by the hugely stupid Japanese attack at Pearl Harbor, kept the war going. German submarine attacks on American shipping renewed the western war, leading to a final, crushing defeat for Germany in 1947.

By then the Final Solution had been carried out in full. The Gypsies, the Jews, millions of assorted Slavs . . .

Those years left a black stain on all civilization, one far worse than in this particular probability-world. Yet this Hitler before me was cut from the same cloth. In my world he had been victorious for longer, done darker deeds. And left even deeper hatreds that had simmered a century without diminishing.

In our world Hitler had grown fat in the stalemate of the middle 1940s, toasted by the occupied nations, honored as a demigod in vast torchlit rites in the thronged streets of Munich. His pudgy, satisfied face beamed down from posters, content, serenely presiding over the muffled cries of the continuing slaughter that spread through all of Europe. When German engineers began the first television broadcasts, Hitler used them with the intuitive genius he had displayed in his stadium speeches, manipulating his people with a dark, skillful fury.

Its job finished in Germany, the SS became more systematic and careful in the extermination of a new general category of hapless souls, the *Reichs*-criminals. Hitler victorious had not mellowed, but he directed the press to portray him that way. The propaganda campaign did much to undermine the Allied resolve, delaying the German defeat by years.

And in turn, carving the horror of that decade of catastrophe into the memory of the survivors.

This world had gotten off easy . . .

A pounding on the door. In another instant the generals might force it open.

"Führer! Go now."

"I. . . ." He turned slowly to the couch. "Eva . . ."

She did not rise. She knew.

I had to seize the moment, to deflect his thoughts toward his destiny. "There is a greater end awaiting you. Take it now!"

I laid a hand on his shoulder and urged him forward. I did not push. I merely helped.

Eva Braun did not rise. As I helped the old man forward, I saw her pick up the capsule from the table.

I felt the fields clutch at him, pull him away from me. There.

Quickly I sat on the couch.

The Lüger!—there it was, on the table.

He had been holding it in his right hand. I grasped it the way he had and checked the action. It was ready.

Eva Braun was holding the cyanide, looking at me.

I said to her, "You must understand. There are reasons why he must go alone. It is—" I had difficulty looking into her eyes. "It is for the best. The best for you."

She said nothing. I knew I should force her but that would be wrong. And I could not pull the trigger for myself until she had taken the poison. The texts were clear on that point—she had died of poison.

I spoke rapidly, fixing her watery eyes with mine to keep her from looking toward the murmuring blue aura.

"You see, we are a society devoted to justice. We have perfected it in our time to a degree you cannot imagine. It is the consuming passion of our age. We indulge ourselves, perhaps. This era was a great, warping trial, in my world. We must expunge its traces in our collective psyche."

"You make no sense . . ." she said wanly, clasping the pill.

"I cannot explain. Our ways are alien to you. We cannot alter the history of this era, and we are blocked from visiting our own past. Yet our people cry out for, for . . ."

I could not go on, could not summon up the words to name the emotions I—great-grandson of a man who had stayed in Europe then, despite his Gypsy origins—I felt sweep over me.

I gestured mutely at the blue corona. Hitler was partway through it now, moving in slow motion like a swimmer in deep water, as the tangled timelines warped around him, sucking him forward.

I looked at her beseechingly, and somehow she caught some flicker of my meaning. Eva Braun murmured, "I believe I understand."

She put the capsule in her mouth and bit down. I think she smiled at the last instant.

A sound from the door. I raised the muzzle to my temple. They would find the two bodies, as history said.

I looked up at Hitler swimming in the fluxlines and he rotated back toward me. He had seen ahead of him, into the room we had prepared for him.

He turned toward me and on his face I saw the surprise and the terror, witnessed the yawning scream begin. I would join him in an instant, when the bullet crashed into my brain and the life-essence that this ugly vat-grown body carried, the life-essence that was truly me, would return, drawn in through the closing portal and forward into my unforgetting future, where Hitler would be trapped.

No sound escaped from that pocket of folded space-time. Only cool blue, remorseless light poured through.

For a last abiding moment I savored the image of Hitler turning, spinning in the crackling blue aura, his mouth stretched wide, trying to flee from the sight of the devices and machines and animals ahead of him. Turning fruitlessly away from the things that would do justice at last, and could bring bubbling up in him an infinite pain, infinitely prolonged.

I pulled the trigger, eager to slip through the portal, eager to hear Hitler's scream.